Delores Fossen, a *USA Today* bestselling author, has written over 150 novels, with millions of copies of her books in print worldwide. She's received a Booksellers' Best Award and an *RT* Reviewers' Choice Best Book Award. She was also a finalist for a prestigious *RITA*® Award. You can contact the author through her website at deloresfossen.com

Nicole Helm grew up with her nose in a book and the dream of one day becoming a writer. Luckily, after a few failed career choices, she gets to follow that dream—writing down-to-earth contemporary romance and romantic suspense. From farmers to cowboys, Midwest to *the* West, Nicole writes stories about people finding themselves and finding love in the process. She lives in Missouri with her husband and two sons, and dreams of someday owning a barn.

Also by Delores Fossen

Saddle Ridge Justice
The Sheriff's Baby
Protecting the Newborn
Tracking Down the Lawman's Son

Silver Creek Lawman: Second Generation
Last Seen in Silver Creek
Marked for Revenge

The Law in Lubbock County
Lawman to the Core
Spurred to Justice

Also by Nicole Helm

Hudson Sibling Solutions
Cold Case Identity
Cold Case Investigation
Cold Case Scandal
Cold Case Protection

Covert Cowboy Soldiers
One Night Standoff
Shot in the Dark
Casing the Copycat
Clandestine Baby

Discover more at millsandboon.co.uk

CHILD IN JEOPARDY

DELORES FOSSEN

COLD CASE DISCOVERY

NICOLE HELM

MILLS & BOON

First Published in Great Britain 2024
by Mills & Boon, an imprint of HarperCollins*Publishers* Ltd
1 London Bridge Street, London, SE1 9GF

www.harpercollins.co.uk

HarperCollins*Publishers*
Macken House, 39/40 Mayor Street Upper,
Dublin 1, D01 C9W8, Ireland

Child in Jeopardy © 2025 Delores Fossen
Cold Case Discovery © 2025 Nicole Helm

ISBN: 978-0-263-39694-2

0125

MIX
Paper | Supporting
responsible forestry
FSC
www.fsc.org FSC™ C007454

This book contains FSC™ certified paper and other controlled sources to ensure responsible forest management.

For more information visit: www.harpercollins.co.uk/green

Printed and Bound in the UK using 100% Renewable Electricity at CPI Group (UK) Ltd, Croydon, CR0 4YY

CHILD IN JEOPARDY

DELORES FOSSEN

Chapter One

Deputy Slater McCullough saw the baby the moment he opened his front door. Still, he blinked a couple of times to make sure his eyes weren't deceiving him. They weren't. He was looking down at a tiny newborn wrapped in a white blanket that was nestled into an infant car seat on the welcome mat of his porch.

Once he shook off the shock, Slater's head whipped up, his gaze firing around the darkness. He spotted a flare of red taillights just as a vehicle sped out of sight on his driveway that led to the road.

What the hell was going on?

Moments earlier, someone had knocked at his door, and since his house wasn't exactly on the beaten path, he'd figured it was someone in his family who'd dropped by. He hadn't taken long to get from his bedroom to the door, but obviously during that short span of time someone had left the baby and driven off.

Since Slater had put on his holster on the way to the door, he slipped his hand over the butt of his service weapon and continued to glance around, looking for any signs of danger while he also checked the baby. Sleeping. And thank God, he or she didn't appear to be harmed. There wasn't a mark or a bruise on that tiny face.

He didn't have to give a lot of thought as to why someone would have left the child here. He was a cop, after all.
A deputy in the Saddle Ridge Sheriff's Office. Abandoned
babies were rare in the small ranching town, but it did occasionally happen, and the baby could have been brought
here by someone desperate enough to leave the infant on a
cop's doorstep.

Even though it was mid-October and the sun had already set, it wasn't cold. Another thing he could be thankful for. Still, he didn't want the baby out in the night air, so
he hoisted up the carrier, brought it inside and set it on his
coffee table while he took out his phone. He called Sheriff Duncan Holder, who was not only his boss but also his
brother-in-law, and even though Slater knew Duncan was
off shift, he answered right away.

"A problem?" Duncan immediately asked.

The question was edged with concern, probably because
Slater never called just to chat. Duncan and Slater's sister,
Joelle, and their infant daughter lived only a mile away, and
if there was a family matter to discuss, Slater paid them a
visit.

"Someone left a baby on my doorstep," Slater said. "I
didn't see who. The person sped off before I could catch any
details about the make of the vehicle or the license plate."

Duncan was silent for a couple of moments and then muttered some profanity. "Is the baby all right?"

"Fine as far as I can tell." But Slater did more than just
a visual check of the infant's face. Sandwiching the phone
between his ear and shoulder, he eased back the blanket
and saw the blue pj's with little birds and clouds. He lifted
the top that was no wider than his hand and saw what he'd
already suspected.

"It's a newborn," Slater relayed. "The umbilical cord is

still attached, and it doesn't appear to be a home job for clamping off the cord." Which meant the baby had likely been born in a hospital, or at least with someone with medical knowledge attending the birth.

Slater heard Duncan relay the info to Joelle, and since she was also a deputy, she would no doubt start the search for missing infants along with having the night deputies combing the area for the vehicle. The CSIs would have to be called in as well to examine the baby's clothes and the carrier. And finally, Child Protective Services would have to be alerted. Thankfully, they had a foster home nearby that took in infants.

While Duncan finished giving the info to Joelle, Slater did a check of the baby's lower body. Still no signs of any kind of injury except for a bruise on the heel of the baby's right foot. Since all three of his siblings had babies, he recalled that was the location where blood was drawn for tests. So, more proof that this newborn had been born in a hospital.

"The baby's a boy," Slater added to Duncan, doing a quick check in the diaper. They'd need that gender info to compare to any missing babies, but the diaper also told Slater something else. It was dry, and since the baby didn't appear to be dehydrated, it meant he'd recently been changed.

Slater was about to relay the heel bruise and the dry diaper to Duncan when he heard a sound that stopped him cold. Something or someone had stepped onto his porch. Only then did he remember that he hadn't locked the door.

He hadn't heard the sound of a car engine nor seen any headlights through the windows, but he doubted it was a coincidence that he'd get a visitor minutes after someone had left the baby. It was possible this was the child's parent who'd already had second thoughts about what'd hap-

pened and had parked at the end of the driveway and come
back for the baby.

"I might have a visitor," Slater whispered to Duncan.
"I'll call you back."

Slater ended the call so he could put his phone away and
free up his hands. It definitely wasn't something he wanted
to happen, but it was possible this might turn into some kind
of altercation. Because even if this was a remorseful parent,
there was no way Slater could just hand over the child, not
until he was certain the little boy would be safe.

Keeping an eye on the doorknob to see if it moved, Slater
eased himself in front of the baby and waited. He didn't
have to wait long.

The door opened a fraction. "Slater?" the woman asked.

She'd used his first name, not Deputy McCullough, but
Slater didn't recognize the voice.

"It's me, Lana Walsh," she added.

Slater frowned and his shoulders snapped back. No way
had he expected Lana to show up.

Or to have abandoned a baby on his porch.

For one thing, he hadn't seen Lana in nearly a year.
Eleven months and twelve days to be exact. He knew the
specific date because Lana had come to his dad's funeral.
A hellish day that even now spurred the equally hellish
memories of finding his father murdered.

Yeah, that wasn't going away anytime soon.

There'd been dozens of people at the funeral, but Slater
had spent a good half hour talking to the sisters even though
they weren't what he would call close. They once had been,
though. He'd dated Lana's sister, Stephanie, when they'd
been in high school, but when their parents had moved them
to San Antonio, he and Stephanie had only kept in touch
with the occasional text and lunch. His contact with Lana

had been less frequent than that because she'd gone into the military, but he was pretty sure she was out now and was working in personal security.

"Come in," Slater muttered.

Lana stepped inside, and she spared him a glance before her attention slashed to the baby. The breath she released seemed to be one of relief, but there was no relief on her face. She locked the door behind her and went to the window as if keeping watch.

She hadn't changed much in the past eleven months and looked more like Stephanie's twin than a younger sibling. Also, while Stephanie went for glamour, Lana clearly didn't. Her dark brown hair was short and with a choppy cut. No makeup. She wasn't wearing an actual uniform, but her outfit had a military vibe to it with her dark jeans, black T-shirt and boots. It didn't seem to Slater that she'd recently had a baby. That sort of thing, though, could be hard to tell.

"Start talking," Slater insisted.

She nodded, then swallowed hard. "Is the baby yours?" Lana asked.

This night had already had some huge surprises, but that question was another one. "No." But he did do a quick mental calculation to see if that was possible.

His last relationship had lasted for over a year and had ended six months ago when the woman had taken a new job in Dallas. It'd been an amicable breakup, so Slater was still in touch with her, and if she'd been pregnant, she would have told him.

"No," he repeated with much more conviction. "Is he yours?"

Lana took another of those deep breaths. "No. Stephanie gave birth to him."

Slater automatically glanced back to see if he recognized

any of Stephanie's or Lana's features. The baby had dark brown hair, but other than that, there wasn't a resemblance that stood out.

"Stephanie said she was your surrogate," Lana explained. "That she was carrying the baby for you. Did she?"

Well, hell. That was another surprise. And an out-and-out lie on Stephanie's part. Slater wanted kids someday, but he doubted he'd ever go the surrogate route.

"No," he said for the third time just as his phone rang.

The sound echoed through the room, causing the baby to stir and then whimper. Lana hurried to him, automatically rocking the carrier and murmured soothing sounds, something he'd seen his siblings do to quiet their babies. Still, Slater kept his gaze on Lana and the newborn while he looked at the phone screen.

"Duncan," he muttered.

"Don't tell anyone I'm here," Lana insisted.

Slater felt his frown deepen. "Duncan is the sheriff," he spelled out.

She nodded. "Please don't tell him or anyone else I'm here," Lana repeated. *"Please."*

Even though he didn't have nearly all the answers he wanted and didn't know why Lana had made such a request, Slater decided to take the call. "I'm chatting with my visitor now," Slater immediately relayed to the sheriff.

"Do you need backup?" Duncan asked.

"No." And he tried to figure out the best way to deal with this.

Stephanie had lied about being his surrogate. He'd need to know why. But if Stephanie had carried through with that lie for whatever reason, she might have also had Lana bring the baby to him. Of course, that prompted even more questions.

"Hold off on sending anyone out to my place for now,"

Slater settled for saying. He didn't want to have this talk with Lana while CPS or backup deputies were trying to arrest her or take the baby. "I'll call you back in a few minutes."

Slater hoped Lana heard the "few minutes" part because that was all the time he was giving her before he let Duncan know that she was his visitor.

"You're really not the baby's father?" she asked, and he could tell she was hoping the answer was yes.

"I'm not," Slater verified. "Now, why did your sister lie, and why do you have her baby?"

Lana pressed her lips together for a moment, but Slater still heard the sob that was threatening to tear from her throat. Tears shimmered in her eyes, but she blinked them back. After several long moments, she opened her mouth, then closed it as if rethinking what she'd been about to say.

"Seven months ago, Stephanie came to me and told me she was pregnant and that she was carrying the baby for you," she finally muttered. Lana made a visible attempt to steel herself up. "I'd just gotten out of the air force and had started working for a security company, and Stephanie wanted me to help her set up a fake identity and a secret place where she could stay while she was pregnant. A sort of safe house."

"A safe house?" he questioned. "Why? Was she in danger?"

Again, she took her time answering. "Our parents would have disowned her if they'd found out she was pregnant. At the time, they were pushing for her to marry someone within their social circle."

Ah, Slater could fill in some of the pieces now. Stephanie and Lana's parents, Leonard and Pamela Walsh, were old money, with old connections.

And the epitome of rich snobs.

Their estate near Saddle Ridge had been plenty impressive, but he'd heard the one they moved to in San Antonio was even grander. They'd "tolerated" Stephanie dating Slater in high school because his family came from money, too, but he'd known that neither Leonard nor Pamela would have even considered him worthy of anything serious with their daughter.

"If our parents disowned Stephanie, she would have lost her trust fund," Lana added. "I wrote mine off years ago, but Stephanie doesn't work, and she would have lost her income while she was pregnant."

Slater knew what "wrote mine off" meant. Lana had basically thumbed her nose at her snobby parents and had gone into the military. He had to admire her for making her own way, but that didn't give him answers to his immediate questions.

"So, Stephanie got pregnant, lied to you by saying she was my surrogate and then asked you to hide her away so she didn't have to face being penniless?" he summarized.

Lana nodded. "She didn't tell our parents about being pregnant. She insisted she was on the verge of a breakdown and told them she needed some peace and quiet for a while."

"They bought that?" Slater asked.

"No. I'm sure they didn't, but by the time Stephanie told them, I'd already set up the secret house for her outside Austin, and she went there within the hour. My parents looked for her. Hard," she emphasized. "But if they found her, neither Stephanie nor I was aware of it."

Slater took a moment to process that. It was possible the couple had found their daughter and just monitored her. They could have learned she was pregnant and decided to wait her out. But they probably hadn't heard about the surrogate part. Because if Leonard and Pamela had thought their daughter was carrying his child, they would have come after him. Not physically, but they would have no doubt tried to make his life a living hell.

"So, who's his father?" Slater asked, tipping his head to the baby.

"I'm not sure," Lana admitted. She went back to the window and looked out again. "Stephanie and I had grown apart over the past five years or so, and I don't know who she was seeing." She swallowed hard. "When I was setting up the secret house, I ran a background check on her. On my own sister," she muttered with some self-disgust. "If she was dating someone, she didn't post anything on social media."

That wasn't like Stephanie, who went with TMI when it came to sharing. Well, when it came to sharing details that wouldn't rile her folks. So that told him that her baby's father wouldn't have met with parental approval.

"Two questions," Slater said. Now that he had the background, he wanted to move this back to the present. "Where is Stephanie, and why do you have her baby?" After that, he'd want to know what she was looking for out the window.

Lana turned and her gaze locked with his. "I have her son because I believe he's in danger. And Stephanie can't protect him because she's dead." Her voice broke and a single tear slid down her face. "Someone murdered her."

Chapter Two

Lana had to fight hard to stop herself from breaking down. She couldn't do that. She had to stay strong. Once she figured out what was going on and the baby was safe, then she could grieve for her sister.

"Murdered?" Slater repeated, automatically taking out his phone. "When and where was Stephanie killed?"

She had to clear the tightness in her throat before she could answer that. "This morning at a hospital in Austin."

That was apparently enough info for him to fire off a text to someone. No doubt to get details of the investigation. "Before you tell me how the hell Stephanie was murdered in a hospital, explain why you keep looking out the window. Is someone after you?"

"I believe so. And I don't know why. Or who," Lana quickly added. "I don't know a lot of things right now, but I need to fix that. It's why I came here. I need answers. I have to know if the baby is in danger."

Slater leveled that intense gaze on her. She'd known him most of her life, but she'd never seen him in cop mode. Before tonight, he'd always been the hot cowboy that her sister had dated in high school. The hot cowboy she'd had a secret crush on. But now, Slater was simply the person she needed to keep her nephew safe.

If he was her nephew, that is.

Lana still didn't know if this was Stephanie's biological child or if she had indeed been carrying the baby for someone else.

"Tell me what happened leading up to Stephanie's death," Slater said when he finally broke the silence.

The explanation wasn't going to be easy, and Lana knew each word would give her a slam of memories. A slam of fear, too, and that's why she took another look out the window. Thankfully, she didn't see anyone or anything suspicious.

"Like I said, Stephanie was living at the safe house I set up for her, and she was using an alias, Melody Waters," Lana started. "She called two days ago to tell me she was in labor, so I drove straight to Austin and was with her when she gave birth. Everything went well with the delivery, and I could tell Stephanie loved the baby. Since she was calling him Cameron and didn't say a word about surrogacy, I figured she'd tell me the truth."

"You doubted her surrogate story?" he was quick to ask.

"I did, right from the start," Lana admitted, "and it didn't help when she refused to tell me who'd hired her to have the baby. She didn't give me your name until…" She stopped after realizing she needed to back up and tell him something else first. "This morning, Stephanie got a call. I don't know who it was from, but I could tell it terrified her."

Lana could still see how the color had drained from her sister's face. How her hands had trembled. And the fear had burned in her eyes.

"The phone she was using was a burner, one that I'd given her when she went into hiding," Lana explained. "And to the best of my knowledge, she only used it for making her

OB appointments. That's why I was surprised when someone called her on it."

"Did you hear any part of the conversation?" he wanted to know.

"No. Stephanie didn't say anything to the caller. She just listened. Then she told me to take Cameron to you, that he was your son and that she'd been your surrogate," Lana continued. She had to swallow hard before she continued. "She even gave me this."

Lana took the folded envelope from her jeans pocket, handed it to Slater and watched as he read it.

A muscle flickered in his jaw. "This first page is an Acknowledgment of Paternity, naming me as the baby's father. The second page is a surrogacy contract."

"Yes, I read them," she admitted. Her sister had used her real name and had signed both documents. Since Slater's signatures were there, too, Lana figured they had been forged. "I have to believe Stephanie had a good reason for doing that." She paused. "The last thing Stephanie said to me was for us to keep Cameron safe."

His attention whipped away from the document and to her. "Safe?" he questioned.

She nodded again. "Trust me, I grilled Stephanie about that, and she said she thought someone had found out about her having a baby. Someone who might not have his best interest at heart."

"Was she talking about your parents?" Slater asked.

"I'm not sure, but I have a hard time believing they'd hurt a baby. It's true they would be riled to the bone at Stephanie having a child, but I can't see them taking out their anger on Cameron."

Slater made a sound that could have meant anything. He certainly didn't jump to agree with her, and she recalled that years ago her parents had moved the family from Saddle Ridge because Slater's father, then Sheriff Cliff McCullough, had been investigating her parents for the disappearance of a teenage boy, Jason Denny. Lana had only been eleven at the time, but she knew Jason had been dating Stephanie and that her parents hadn't approved of the relationship.

No criminal charges had come out of the investigation, and later when Jason had resurfaced, he'd claimed someone had threatened him and that's why he'd run away. Jason refused to say who'd done the threatening, but maybe Slater's father believed her parents had been responsible.

And they might have been.

Lana didn't know the scope of her parents' dirty dealings, but she was well aware they were ruthless. It was the reason she'd cut them out of her life.

"I didn't push Stephanie nearly hard enough to tell me the truth about what was going on," Lana continued. "I thought there'd be time for that later, especially since Stephanie was insisting that I go ahead and take Cameron to you. I left the hospital and drove around for about an hour before I decided to return and talk to Stephanie. Just to make sure she was certain about handing the child over to you."

Now she had to pause again and remind herself to breathe. All the grief and fear were smothering her, and she had to look at the baby to try to steady herself. Lana had never needed an anchor to stave off panic, but she needed it now, and the baby was the ultimate reminder of what was at stake here.

"When I got back to her hospital room, there was chaos," she muttered. "I heard one of the nurses say that Stephanie had been smothered. I glanced in the room and...well, I saw her lifeless body before a nurse shooed me away and insisted I leave the area. She didn't seem to realize that I'd been with Stephanie earlier."

Lana figured she'd been in shock, because she had mindlessly walked away with Cameron cradled in her arms.

That's when she had spotted the man.

"I believe I saw Stephanie's killer," Lana spelled out. "He was peering out from one of the other rooms, and he set off every alarm in my body. I knew there was nothing I could do for Stephanie so I immediately turned around and hurried out another exit. He followed me, but once Cameron and I were in my car, I managed to lose him on the highway."

"And you came here and left the baby on my doorstep," Slater stated, clearly not approving of that.

Lana groaned. "I was worried about Cameron's safety, so I dropped him off and left only after I saw you open the door. Then I quickly drove away to make sure the man hadn't found me. If he had, I planned to lure him from the baby by having him follow me. I was never far away, and I had every intention of coming right back for him. I just didn't want him with me if I met up with that man."

"At any point did you consider calling the cops for help?" he asked, and there was a snarl in his voice now. Of course there was. The lawman in him probably didn't allow for gut feelings.

Lana needed yet another breath to finish this. "The man at the hospital was a cop."

Slater stared at her and looked ready to curse. Or to challenge that. "Name? Description?"

Lana had no trouble recalling these details since they were fixed in her mind. Just like that image of her dead sister. "About six-two. Brown hair, brown eyes, muscular build. The surname Johnson was on his uniform."

"Austin cops have their badge numbers next to their names," he pointed out.

"Yes, but I couldn't see his. He had his communication radio positioned in front of it." Probably intentional.

Well, maybe it was.

If he'd wanted to conceal his identity and murder a woman, he probably wouldn't have shown up in uniform. Not unless he was cocky or totally sure he could get away with murder.

Slater didn't get the chance to fire any more questions at her because his phone dinged, the sound shooting through the room. He silently read the text before his gaze slid back to her. She figured those intense blue eyes had unnerved plenty of suspects.

"Austin PD is investigating the suspicious death of a thirty-three year old woman, Melody Waters, aka Stephanie Walsh," he relayed to her.

So they knew who Stephanie really was. Lana wasn't sure how they would have come up with that info since Stephanie had insisted on using the alias for all of her medical appointments. It was possible, though, that Stephanie had had her real driver's license in the overnight bag she'd taken to the hospital.

"There's no officer named Johnson assigned to the case," Slater added while he continued to read. "The initial report is that next of kin has been notified."

So that's why her mom had called. A rarity for her. Lana took out her phone and showed him the two missed calls from her mother, Pamela. She hadn't left a voicemail, and Lana hadn't returned the calls yet since she'd been focused on keeping Cameron safe.

"There's no mention of you in the report," he continued, "only that Stephanie had informed the medical staff that she'd arranged for someone to take the baby to his father as per a surrogacy agreement." He lifted up the contract that had been in the envelope she'd given him. "Did you do this for her?"

"No. Not the other document, either. I didn't know she had them until she gave them to me at the hospital." Lana tipped her head to the contract. "That one might have come from an actual surrogate clinic. During that background check I mentioned that I did on Stephanie, I found out she'd visited a surrogacy clinic eight months ago. She would have been pregnant with Cameron by then, but it's possible she had a prior appointment there that I wasn't able to find."

"So Stephanie might have truly been a surrogate?" Slater muttered, glancing at the baby.

Lana had to shrug. "Maybe, but then why would Stephanie tell me you were the one who hired her?"

He didn't get a chance to speculate about that because her own phone rang, and she saw her mother's name on the screen. Slater must have seen it, too, because he said, "Are you going to answer it?"

She automatically shook her head. Her default response when it came to her parents, but she knew this had to be about Stephanie, so she stepped aside to take the call. While she did that, Slater stepped away as well, muttering something about updating the sheriff.

"Mother," Lana answered, trying to keep her voice low so she wouldn't wake the baby or disturb Slater's call.

"Your sister is dead," her mother blurted. "Murdered." A hoarse sob tore from her throat. "What do you know about it? Why didn't you stop it?"

Lana wasn't surprised by her mother's response. Even though Stephanie was the older sister, their parents had always blamed Lana for Stephanie's failures. It was yet another reason Lana had cut them from her life. But she wasn't immune to the accusation.

Why didn't you stop it?

That was a question Lana figured she'd be asking herself for the rest of her life. Over the years, she had been there for Stephanie countless times, but she hadn't been there when Stephanie needed her most. And worse, she was a cyber-security specialist at Sencor, a company that specialized in personal protection. She had bodyguard training. That hadn't been enough, though, to stop what had happened.

"Do the police know who killed her?" Lana asked.

"No," her mother snarled. "They're idiots, all of them. Your dad and I hired a team of private investigators. Not from that place where you work, either. We wanted the best."

Of course her mother had thrown in that dig, and Lana didn't even bother trying to convince her that Sencor was one of the highest-rated security companies in the state. Obviously, though, ratings didn't matter with Stephanie dead.

"The PIs will get to the bottom of it," her mother insisted, "and you're going to help them. I know you hid Stephanie from us all this time. There's no way she could have managed that on her own. I just didn't know why until the cops said Stephanie had been a surrogate. A surrogate!" her mother spat out as if it were the worst of felonies.

So her parents knew that as well.

"Did this so-called surrogate parent murder her?" her mother pressed.

"I don't think so," Lana said, but she had no idea if that was true. Slater hadn't murdered Stephanie. She was now certain of that. But that didn't mean her sister hadn't connected with her killer at the surrogacy clinic.

"You need to come home, Lana," her mother went on.

"You need to help the PIs sort all of this out so we can punish the person who killed Stephanie."

Lana waited for her mom to mention the baby. But she didn't. Certainly, if the hospital had learned Stephanie's true identity, they would have mentioned the baby as well. Maybe, though, the baby didn't mean anything to her mother, since she was dismissing Cameron as she'd dismissed the surrogacy itself.

"Did you hear me, Lana?" The venom in her mother's voice went up a notch. "Come home now. Your father is beside himself. So am I. And Marsh, too. He's ripped to pieces."

Lana knew that Marsh Bray was the man her parents had chosen for Stephanie to marry. A merger of two rich families who cared more about the business and social benefits of the union than they did their kids' happiness. That said, Marsh had always seemed on board with marrying Stephanie. The same couldn't be said for Stephanie, though. Lana didn't think her sister despised Marsh, but she definitely hadn't been eager to become his wife.

She heard Slater end the call with the sheriff, and since she wanted to know what Slater had told him, Lana quickly made her excuses to her mother. "I'll call you soon," she said, and hung up.

"Duncan will be speaking to the lead detective in charge of the investigation of Stephanie's murder, and he'll try to obtain footage from the hospital cameras," Slater said. "He'll also get us a list of all Austin cops named Johnson. It's possible, though, if this guy truly did kill Stephanie, then he was wearing a fake uniform."

Yes, that had already occurred to her, and part of Lana wished she'd confronted the man then and there. But she'd been too broken for that. Too worried about Cameron. Now that she was thinking more clearly, she realized she'd let him get away.

"My parents have hired PIs," she told him, only so he wouldn't be blindsided if one of them showed up in Saddle Ridge. "I have no idea who knows about that surrogacy contract or the Acknowledgment of Paternity, but if and when it comes to light, my parents will believe you're Cameron's father. In their eyes, that'll make you a top suspect for Stephanie's murder."

"I'm not going to keep the papers a secret," Slater was quick to say. "In fact, I'm taking you and the baby to the sheriff's office so we can both do statements that'll then be turned over to Austin PD."

She was shaking her head before he even finished. "But what about Johnson? If he knows where the baby is, he might try to come after him." If that's what the cop wanted, that is. Lana had no way of knowing if he did.

"You and the baby will be protected," Slater said with absolute confidence that Lana didn't feel, and she would have voiced plenty of disapproval about his plan if her phone hadn't dinged with a soft alarm.

Lana's heart dropped to her knees.

"It's not a text," she rattled off while she unlocked her phone screen. "It's an alert from my security system. Someone's broken into my house in San Antonio." She'd set up the security system more than a year ago, and this was the first alert she'd ever gotten.

"Will the system notify the security company or SAPD?" Slater asked, moving closer to her as she pulled up the feed from the cameras she had positioned both inside and outside the house.

"The company will be the one to notify me," she supplied just as she got a second ding from the automated monitor.

Lana ignored it and adjusted the camera angle until she saw the person, the man, who was now in her living room. His back was to the camera, but there was no mistaking the cop's uniform he was wearing. He had his gun gripped in his hand.

"Johnson?" Slater asked.

"Maybe," she muttered and kept watching. The breath stalled in her throat when he turned, and she saw his face and name tag. "It's him."

"I'll text Duncan to call the Austin PD detective in charge of your sister's murder," Slater said, though she heard the doubt in his voice. Like her, Slater probably figured Johnson would be long gone before a detective showed up.

But why was Johnson there?

The drawn gun was a sign that he probably hadn't come for a friendly chat. Had he gone there to kill her? To take the baby? What the heck did he want, and had he truly been the one to kill her sister?

Lana continued to watch as the man made a quick check of the other rooms, and then he took out his phone. Lana automatically thumbed up the audio so she could hear, and after, Slater finished his text and moved back closer, no doubt so he could listen as well.

"She's not here," Johnson snarled to the person he'd called. Lana tried to shift the camera so she could see his phone screen, but the glare made it impossible for her to decipher the number. "She probably went to the deputy in Saddle Ridge." He paused, listening, and Lana wished she could hear the other side of this conversation. "All right. I'll go to Saddle Ridge, to the deputy's place now, and take care of the kid and her."

Her heart had already been racing. Her breathing, too,

and that certainly didn't help. This man was coming for Cameron and her.

Lana watched as Johnson slipped back out her front door and disappeared from view before she looked up at Slater. "We have to leave. I'll take Cameron—"

"No," he interrupted, taking out his phone again.

Again, she was ready to argue, but then Slater spelled out exactly what he intended.

"I'll have someone take him and you to the sheriff's office where you'll both be safe, but I'm staying put. When Stephanie's killer comes here, he'll be walking straight into a trap."

Chapter Three

Slater kept watch out one of the windows that would give him a good view of the road that led to his house. He wasn't sure what the heck was going on, but he was hoping he could get some answers from "Officer Johnson" when he showed up to "take care of the kid and her."

To prepare for that, Duncan had immediately arranged for a backup deputy to be with Slater and for Duncan and Deputy Sonya Grover to take Lana and the baby to the sheriff's office in town. Lana had been plenty hesitant about leaving with Duncan and Sonya, maybe because she now had a distrust of cops or because the plan seemed too risky.

There was indeed a risk, but Slater wanted to face down Johnson when Lana and Cameron weren't around to be hurt. Judging from the tone Johnson had used in that short phone conversation, he didn't have good intentions.

Slater checked the time. It'd been nearly two hours since Lana had gotten that alert about the break-in, plenty enough time for Johnson to make the drive from San Antonio to Saddle Ridge. He glanced across the room at Deputy Luca Vanetti, who was keeping watch on the other side of the house.

"No sign of him," Luca relayed, obviously noticing the glance Slater had given him.

"None here, either." And the admission made Slater want to curse along with second-guessing himself.

He hadn't officially alerted San Antonio PD about the break-in at Lana's place because if Johnson was indeed a cop, Slater hadn't wanted him to know they were onto him. Leaks could and did happen, so Slater had figured better to be safe than sorry. However, Slater had called his brother Ruston, who was an undercover detective with SAPD, and had asked Ruston to quietly monitor what was going on.

Ruston hadn't even attempted to get to Lana's house and intercept the intruder because Johnson had stayed less than a minute after telling the caller he was going "to Saddle Ridge, to the deputy's place now." In case Johnson had meant another deputy, all the cops in the sheriff's office had been put on alert, and none were alone and without backup. Since everyone was texting Duncan every fifteen minutes, Slater knew Johnson hadn't shown up at those other places, either. None of his fellow cops had been attacked or killed.

Slater felt the tightness come in his chest as the memories prowled into his head. He'd been a deputy for ten years now, and for the first nine years, he had, of course, been concerned about losing a family member or friend since two of his three siblings and his dad had been cops. But then his father had been gunned down, murdered by an unknown assailant, and the concern was much, much stronger.

It was a dark tangle of emotions, including fear and anger that he hadn't given his father justice.

He wasn't sure he could lose anyone like that again. Hell, he wasn't sure he could get through this loss at all, ever, and as long as his father's killer was out there, then Slater had failed at one of the most important things in his life. All the cop training and experience meant nothing until someone had paid for shooting his father in the chest and leaving him to die.

"You can tell me to mind my own business," Luca said, snapping Slater out of his miserable thoughts, "but is the baby yours?" It was a reasonable question since Luca, too, had gone to school with Stephanie and Lana, and he knew that Slater and Stephanie had dated.

"No," Slater assured him.

That was one of the few things Slater was certain of. He'd never had sex with Stephanie and had never visited a sperm bank or a surrogate clinic. And that meant Stephanie had lied.

"I'm guessing Stephanie was scared," Slater added. "And she knew I'd protect Lana and the baby."

Of course, that led Slater to a big question—who or what was Stephanie scared of? Her parents were a good guess, because there was that threat of losing her trust fund. But he couldn't see her folks murdering their daughter. Still, it was possible, and it was why Pamela and Leonard Walsh were on his suspect list. Not at the very top, though. At the moment Officer Johnson held that position, and Slater needed to know how this man fit into the pieces of the puzzle.

His phone vibrated with a call, and Slater saw Ruston's name on the screen. "I don't think your guy is coming to your place tonight," his brother immediately said. "I've had a monitor on the traffic cams, looking for this Officer Johnson, and there was an accident about an hour ago. Someone ran a red light, plowed into a black SUV, disabling it. The driver of the SUV ran from the scene, and he matches Johnson's description."

Slater cursed. "Do you have the camera footage?"

"I got a couple of still images from the footage. Sending them to you now," Ruston said just as Slater's phone vibrated again.

Even though they were grainy images, Slater had no trouble seeing that it was indeed Officer Johnson. The first photo was of the collision itself, and the next was of the man exiting the vehicle. The final shot was of him running away, and that meant the guy likely wasn't a real cop. If he had been, there probably wouldn't have been a reason to hurry away like that. However, staying put would have meant having to explain why he was wearing the uniform.

"I just filled Duncan in on this," Ruston went on, "and he said for Luca and you to head on to the sheriff's office so you can figure out what to do about Lana and the baby."

Slater muttered more profanity. Not because he didn't want to return to the sheriff's office and deal with the situation of Lana and the baby. He did. But he'd also wanted to catch a possible killer.

"We'll be there in ten minutes," Slater said, ending the call so that he and Luca could head into the garage where he'd parked the cruiser.

Slater also reset his security system in case Johnson finally did show up, and then did something he rarely did. He activated the security camera that was part of his doorbell. It was something he normally reserved for when he was expecting a package and there was inclement weather in the forecast.

Even though Slater suspected Johnson wouldn't be making a trip to Saddle Ridge tonight, he and Luca still kept watch. And saw nothing out of the ordinary. This was ranching country, where traffic pretty much dried up after dark, and tonight was no exception. They made it all the way to the sheriff's office without encountering another vehicle.

When Slater stepped into the building, he immediately

saw Lana in Duncan's office. She was feeding the baby a bottle while she studied something on a computer screen that Duncan was showing her.

At the sound of Slater's footsteps, her head whipped up, her gaze slicing across the bullpen and reception to meet his. There was plenty of concern and wariness in her green eyes, and he so wished he could tell her the danger had passed. But it obviously hadn't. Not with Officer Johnson still out there.

Slater certainly wasn't untouched by the fear he saw on her face. He hated that she was going through this especially when there wasn't a surefire fix to the danger. Apparently, he also wasn't immune to something else.

The realization that the old attraction was still stirring between them.

Well, it was for him, anyway. The heat had been there for years, lying dormant and then igniting every time he saw her. Each time, he'd shoved the attraction firmly aside. Or rather had tried to do that, since any kind of romance between them could create more ire for her from her parents. Added to that, Slater had dated her sister, and Lana had been in the military, nowhere near Saddle Ridge.

But she was here now.

And his body obviously wanted to remind him of that.

Once again, Slater pushed aside the heat and joined them in Duncan's office while Luca went to his desk. Slater thankfully got the quick mental adjustment he needed. Because Lana was looking at images on the screen. It didn't take Slater long to realize these were photos of Austin cops with the surname of Johnson. In the top corner of the screen was the close up shot of the man running from the scene of the wrecked SUV.

"He's not a cop," Lana immediately said. "At least not one with Austin PD."

None of them seemed surprised about that, but Slater understood the sound of frustration that Duncan made. "We're running facial recognition now to try to get a match," he added.

That was a good step, but it might not be enough. "What about the hospital cameras? Maybe there's something on the footage to tell us who he is."

"Austin PD is still examining that." Duncan made another of those heavy sighs. "The cameras in the hallway had been tampered with, so there's no feed of the man going into or out of Stephanie's room. He didn't leave anything obvious behind, either, but the CSIs have gathered plenty of hairs and fibers and have sent them to the lab."

Slater figured getting anything from that was a long shot since dozens if not hundreds of people could have gone in and out of that room in the past week. Still, it was something that had to be checked.

The baby caught Slater's attention when he made a kitten-like sound after he finished the bottle. Lana set the bottle aside and moved him to her shoulder to burp him. The maneuver wasn't completely smooth, but Lana was obviously taking good care of the newborn. And under bad circumstances. Her sister was dead, and there appeared to be a killer after her.

"Why?" Slater said, voicing the question that was running through his head. Both Lana and Duncan looked at him. "Why would Stephanie's killer want to come after Lana? What's your theory?"

Both Lana and Duncan considered that for several moments, and it was Lana who spoke first. "Johnson said he would take care of me and the kid," she said. "So maybe that means someone is trying to cover up the fact that Stephanie had a child."

Slater and Duncan made quick sounds of agreement. "Who would want to do that?" Duncan asked her.

"My parents," she readily admitted. "And maybe the baby's father." Lana shifted her attention back to Slater. "Duncan's already taken a DNA sample from the baby. That might give us some answers. Fast answers," she emphasized, "since the lab will be using rapid analysis. We could have results in a matter of hours."

True, but there was no need for him to spell out that the only way they'd get a match was for the baby's father to already have his DNA in the system. That could happen if the guy had a criminal record or a job that required such info, but the vast majority of people weren't in law enforcement databases.

They all turned toward the doorway when Sonya stepped in. She was holding her laptop. "The facial recognition program came up with a hit," she said, turning the screen so they could see it. On the left was the image they'd gotten from the security camera, and on the right was the mug shot of a beefy bald man.

Lana made a soft gasp. "That's him." She repeated her words while she was making an obvious effort to rein in her emotions. Hard to do that while she was looking right at her sister's killer. "Who is he?"

"Buchanan, aka Buck, Holden," Sonya provided. Placing the laptop on the corner of Duncan's desk, she opened a file of notes that she likely planned on using to do a report. "He's thirty-nine and was arrested three years ago for stalking. He got probation."

"Stalking?" Slater questioned. "That's a huge escalation

to murder, impersonating a police officer, and breaking and entering."

Sonya nodded. "I'll do a thorough background check since there could be something else. Maybe something expunged from his record," she added. "A year ago, he and his younger brother inherited about thirty million when their parents were killed in a car accident, so unless he's blown through it, he's got plenty of money for legal fees."

"Since he's likely rich, maybe Stephanie and this Buck Holden ran in the same social circles?" Duncan suggested.

"Maybe," Lana said, but she didn't sound very convinced. "He doesn't look like Stephanie's usual type, though. She went more for the guys who were hot enough and good-looking enough to be on those calendars…" Her words trailed off when her attention slid to Slater, probably because she recalled that Stephanie had gone for him.

Slater refused to be flattered by what she'd just said. And he wanted to refuse to notice the slight flush that colored Lana's cheeks. It was better to focus on other things. No shortage of those, because he had plenty of questions flying through his head. How had he gotten involved with Stephanie? And why had he killed her if they hadn't been involved?

"I'll go through all of Stephanie's social media posts and see if there's any mention of Buck," Lana said after clearing her throat.

"I'll do the same for Buck's posts, if there are any," Sonya tacked onto that.

That would likely take some time, but there was something else that had to go at the top of their to-do list. "Lana will have to give a statement to Austin PD," Slater spelled out. "That won't be a fast in-and-out since this is a murder investigation. And they'll want her to give the statement in person. Added to that, Lana will have to get into the past eight months or so of Stephanie's life at the safe house." He looked at her. "Did you bend or break any laws to arrange that for her?"

"No," she insisted, but then she paused. "There might be some legal questions about Stephanie using an alias when she had the baby. Questions, too, about those documents I gave you."

Slater had to agree on that, but since Lana hadn't done those documents, the blame for it would be on Stephanie. And she wasn't alive to defend her actions or to be charged with any wrongdoing.

"I can take Lana to Austin," Slater went on, "but with Buck at large, it might not be the safest trip."

"You'll have backup," Duncan was quick to say, but then his attention went to the baby. He sighed. "Since we don't know who his bio-father is, Austin PD might take custody of him until it's all sorted out and then hand him over to the surviving parent."

Lana shook her head. "I don't believe Stephanie would have wanted that. She was hiding. And it's a good bet that she was doing that because she was terrified of the bio-father."

No one in the room could argue with her, and it was possible the baby's dad had been the one to murder Stephanie. Either that, or he'd hired someone like Buck to do it. No way did Slater want Cameron in clear view of a killer or his henchman.

Lana turned to him. "For now, can you just keep it to yourself that Stephanie wasn't your surrogate?" Slater groaned, but she talked right over that. "Yes, I know it's withholding evidence, but this way, we can control who has him. We won't have to hand him over."

His heart wanted to go along with that. Mercy, did it, but

he couldn't. Slater tapped his badge to remind her she was talking to a cop. "That's obstruction of justice."

She huffed, closed her eyes a moment and then pled her case to Duncan. "All right, then can someone keep Cameron safe here in Saddle Ridge while I'm in Austin? Safe," she emphasized. "Because it's not just Buck we have to worry about. That call he made at my house means he's working for someone or with a partner."

"Cameron can stay at the ranch with Joelle and me," Duncan readily agreed. "We have a baby and a full-time nanny, and I can bring in a reserve deputy to help keep watch."

Slater could tell that still wasn't ideal for Lana, but then there were no ideal scenarios as long as Buck was at large and free to kill. Still, Lana knew both Duncan and Joelle, and Lana and she had even been friends in school. Added to that, Joelle was a deputy as well and had the training to protect the newborn.

"All right," Lana finally said, brushing a kiss on the top of the baby's head before she eased him back into the carrier. "Do you need a statement from me, too?" she asked Duncan.

Duncan didn't get a chance to answer, though, because of the sounds of voices. One of which was loud and insistent, and even though it'd been years since he'd heard this particular voice, Slater instantly recognized it.

Lana's mother, Pamela Walsh, and she was calling out Lana's name.

And she wasn't alone. Her husband, Leonard, was with her and so was a tall, blond, thirtysomething-year-old man. Hell. They had enough to deal with tonight without adding visitors like this to the mix.

Deputy Brandon Rooney was working at the front desk, and he immediately got to his feet to direct the trio through the metal detectors. No alarms sounded, which meant none of them were armed.

"Lana," Pamela repeated when her attention landed on her daughter.

Lana immediately moved into the doorway of Duncan's office, and Slater thought she might be doing that so her mother didn't see the baby. Possibly because Pamela might try to take him. No way would he and Duncan let that happen, not until they had sorted out Cameron's paternity, but Pamela and her husband might try to cause a scene. Also, it was possible the blond guy with them was their lawyer.

Both Duncan and Slater moved into the doorway with Lana, positioning themselves on each side of her so they could face down what might turn out to be trouble. Luca and Brandon had moved behind the visitors while Sonya kept a watchful eye on them from her desk while she continued to work on her laptop.

Pamela and Leonard looked pretty much as they had years ago, and despite recently learning of their daughter's murder, they didn't look grief-stricken or disheveled. Just the opposite. Pamela was wearing expensive-looking brown pants and a cream sweater while Leonard was in a perfectly tailored suit. The blond guy had on khakis and a white shirt. He was the only one of the trio who appeared to be grieving or in shock.

So maybe not a lawyer, after all.

"How'd you know I was here?" Lana asked, taking the question right out of Slater's mouth.

Pamela and Leonard both froze for a moment, but then Pamela hiked up her chin. "Leonard has friends in Austin PD. They told us you were here."

This time Slater said the "hell" out loud, and he glanced at Duncan to see if they were on the same page with this.

Of course they were. There was no way a cop should have divulged that kind of information.

"I'll want the names of your friends in Austin PD," Duncan insisted, aiming a hard glare at Leonard and Pamela.

"I don't have to do that," Leonard snarled.

"All right," Duncan said, taking out his phone. "I'll make an official complaint through Austin PD Internal Affairs to open an investigation into divulging information regarding a murder investigation to a civilian. I'm sure they can get to the bottom of it and then discipline the officers involved."

Slater hadn't thought it possible, but Leonard's jaw tightened even more. "Detective David Sullivan," he said. "His father used to work for me."

Duncan put his phone away, but Slater had no doubts he'd be making a call to Austin PD to file a complaint against Detective Sullivan.

"David was doing me a favor," Leonard added, maybe hoping to minimize the trouble he'd just gotten the detective into. "He knew Pamela and I were crushed by Stephanie's murder, and we needed to find Lana, to make sure she was all right."

"I pressured them, too," the blond guy said, and then he came closer to extend his hand to Duncan and Slater. "I'm Marsh Bray. Stephanie and I were…close."

"My parents wanted Stephanie and Marsh to marry," Lana provided, earning her a sharp look from her mother.

"I'm in love with Stephanie," Marsh further explained as if not bothered by Lana's comment, "and it was my hope that Stephanie would someday agree to be my wife. That's why I gave her this time she'd asked for. That's why I waited." His voice wavered on the last word. "And now she's dead."

The grief seemed genuine. Seemed. But Slater had too much cop in him to take this at face value. Maybe Marsh hadn't been as patient as he was claiming. Maybe he'd gotten so enraged over Stephanie that he'd murdered her. But that left Slater with a huge question.

Was Marsh the baby's father?

"We need you to come home with us," Pamela said to Lana. "We need you to explain to Marsh and us exactly what happened to Stephanie." She paused. "A nurse at the hospital said Stephanie had had a baby. Is it true?"

Slater kept his attention on Marsh. The man certainly wasn't jumping to say the child was his. Just the opposite. There seemed to be some dread creeping into his expression.

"We know that Stephanie was a surrogate," her mother went on. "We hired PIs to try to find her, and we found out about her visit to a surrogacy clinic. There was a charge for it on her credit card. Why would she do that? Why would she go to a place like that to get pregnant and carry a child for someone else?"

Since the questions were aimed at Lana and not him, Slater had to figure that the surrogacy clinic hadn't given Pamela and Leonard that particular bit of info.

"I don't know," Lana muttered, and Slater knew it wasn't a lie.

Her mother groaned and squeezed her eyes shut a moment. "I'm not asking out of idle curiosity. I need to know what happened to my daughter."

"That's what we're trying to find out," Lana assured her, and she made a show of checking the time. "We need to leave so I can give a statement. That might help them find who killed Stephanie."

Slater so wished she hadn't just spelled that out to them, since he didn't want anyone other than the cops here in the sheriff's office to know that he and Lana would be on their way to Austin.

"I'll call you after I give the statement," Lana added.

Slater hadn't thought that would be enough to make them leave, but they turned and headed toward the exit. Neither Pamela nor Leonard made a move to give their surviving daughter a hug or offer any words of comfort. That confirmed what Lana had already told Slater about being written out of her parents' lives.

"We'll need to take an alternate route to Austin," Lana said the moment their visitors were gone. "I don't trust any of them not to spill that we'll soon be on the road."

Good. He and Lana were of a like mind on this. "We can use the old highway and not the interstate."

Duncan nodded. "I'll have Luca drive with me to take the baby to the ranch, and Sonya can follow behind the two of you as backup. Brandon can man the office until I can get another deputy in here with him."

Brandon and Luca both made sounds of agreement, but Sonya stepped forward with her laptop in hand. "I found something," Sonya said, turning the screen so they could see the photo. "This was posted on Stephanie's Facebook page fifteen months ago."

Slater, Lana and Duncan all moved in to take a closer look. It was a couple's shot of Stephanie at what appeared to be a party, but Slater didn't recognize the smiling dark-haired man who had his arm draped around Stephanie's shoulder. Lana must not have, either, because she shook her head.

"Who is he?" Lana came out and asked.

"Patrick Holden, Buck's brother," Sonya provided, and then she shifted to another open tab with a different photo of Patrick.

One for his obituary.

A quick glance at the date of death showed that he'd died only a week ago.

"Cause of death?" Duncan immediately wanted to know.

That grim look on Sonya's face told him they weren't going to like the answer. "He was murdered."

Chapter Four

Lana kept watch out the window as Slater drove on the back roads toward Austin, and she knew Slater was doing the same thing. Keeping watch. Looking for any signs of an attack.

Sonya was behind them, also in an unmarked Saddle Ridge cruiser, and she, too, was no doubt in vigilant mode. If there were any signs of trouble, she'd be able to respond.

Part of Lana wanted Buck to resurface, to come after them so they could stop him and toss him in jail. Cameron was safe, and if a showdown was coming, maybe it would be better now than later. After all, she couldn't keep Cameron in protective custody indefinitely. Even though the baby had had a horrific start to his life, he deserved a whole lot better. But better wasn't going to happen with Buck at large.

Her interview with Austin PD might help with the at-large status. Maybe there was something she could say that would pinpoint Buck's location. Then she and Slater could grab some sleep before returning to Saddle Ridge. A return that wouldn't happen tonight because of the already late hour, and it was the reason Lana had arranged for them to stay at a small house owned by Sencor, the company she worked for. She hadn't wanted to trust the security at a hotel or a short-term rental.

"Are you okay?" Slater asked.

She didn't need to know what had prompted the question. Lana had heard yet another sigh leave her mouth. She'd heard the deep, ragged breaths she'd been taking as well. She'd never had a panic attack, but, mercy, it felt as if everything was closing in on her.

"There's been no time to grieve," she settled for saying. Lana nearly left it at that, but she knew the grief was just the tip of the iceberg. "I'm worried about Cameron. Worried what else Buck will do."

Slater made a sound of agreement. Coming from most people, that would have seemed like a blasé response, but Lana could practically feel the emotions coming off him in hot waves.

"Stephanie and I weren't close," she admitted. "But she was my sister." She paused, debating if she should even voice her next comment about his father. A check of the time convinced her just to go for it. They still had thirty minutes before they arrived in Austin. "How did you deal with the grief of losing your father?"

Slater stayed quiet for so long that she was about to launch into a *forget I said that* apology. "I haven't," he muttered, and then winced as if he hadn't intended to spill that. "I'm still dealing," he amended a moment later. "Maybe I always will be. It's possible that's something that never goes away. Sorry," he tacked onto that. "I should have come up with something more, uh, supportive."

"No," she insisted. "I'd rather have the truth. I'd rather know what I'm up against."

Again, he paused. "If your experience is anything like mine, then what you're up against is what I call death plus. A natural or accidental death causes you to grieve in a thousand different ways. But murder, well, murder causes you to grieve, and hurt, and go through all the regrets and feelings that you should have done something to stop this from happening. That you should have done more."

Yes, she was already feeling some of that. Clearly, Slater was, too.

"Find someone to talk to if you can," he went on. "That might help. I did some grief therapy for a while. Just don't shut down."

The last part seemed as if it'd come from personal experience. "Is that what you did?"

"Yeah," he admitted while he continued to keep watch. "I ended a two-year relationship because it didn't feel right. Me, being happy, continuing with my life when my dad was dead. So I put everything aside but the job. Because it's the job that'll get my father justice."

"And give you some peace," she finished for him. Slater made another of those sounds of agreement.

Peace didn't seem anywhere on her radar right now, but Lana was positive that catching her sister's killer would be a start. "I keep going over every moment in the hospital," she said, hoping that saying it aloud would trigger some fresh memory that would give them that *start*. "I don't recall seeing Buck before then, but maybe he was around."

Lana stopped, muttered some profanity and then groaned. "I work for a security company, installing systems and setting up protocols to keep people safe. I couldn't do that for my own sister."

"Trust me, I get that," he said.

Of course he got it. He was a cop, and his father was dead. "I believe it was Buck who called Stephanie this morning." Heavens, had it really been less than twenty-four hours? In some ways, it seemed an eternity.

"Austin PD will have her phone," Slater reminded her. "They might be able to figure out if it was Buck."

She knew the odds of that were slim, but, yes, the cops would try. Still, she figured Buck wouldn't have been careless enough to use a phone that could be traced back to him.

"The hospital cameras were tampered with," she explained. "And it's no easy feat breaking into my house. I keep all the doors and windows double-locked. I have to assume that Buck or his accomplice has the skill set to do those sort of things."

"Yes, but he didn't disable your security system," Slater pointed out in a tone to let her know he was giving that some thought. "Why not? I mean, if he was able to tamper with the hospital cameras, why not do that at your place?"

Lana immediately thought of a possibility. "My system isn't easy to disable." But then she had to shake her head. "The same should have been true of the hospital cameras."

"True, and that could mean Buck didn't care if you knew he'd broken in. Maybe he thought if you were there, he could just overpower you before anyone could respond to the security alarm."

The thought of that sent a shiver down her spine. Because Buck could have possibly done just that.

Slater reached over and gave her hand a gentle squeeze. "We'll catch him. Something might turn up in his background check that'll tell us just what his skill sets are when it comes to tampering with equipment." He eased his hand back and gave her another quick glance. "Or it could be someone you know. Someone who would have known how to access your house."

He sounded very much like a cop right now, and she was thankful for it. Focusing on the investigation was the only thing taking the edge off her nerves.

"I don't have a boyfriend or anyone like that I'd trust with my security codes," she stated.

Slater glanced at her, maybe a reaction to the no-boy-friend admission, but despite everything going on, she felt the blasted attraction again. Lana blamed it on the emotional cocktails swirling around in her body. Slater was like a safe harbor right now, and that had likely amped up the heat.

Or at least that's what she was telling herself.

This wasn't the time or the place to get into the fact that she'd always wanted him. And that he'd always been off-limits because of Stephanie. Now he was off-limits because it was obvious Slater wasn't in the right frame of mind to deal with attraction and such.

"How about your parents?" he asked.

She opened her mouth to say they wouldn't have broken in, but Lana had no idea if that was true. "They might have hired someone to break in if they thought Stephanie was there. But I can't see them hiring, or even knowing, some-one like Buck."

"Maybe," Slater muttered, not sounding at all convinced of that. "Consider this. Your parents find out Stephanie's dead and they know she visited a surrogacy clinic. They must believe the baby was born from that surrogacy and isn't their grandchild because they didn't even ask to see him."

No, they hadn't. At the time, Lana had been thankful for that because she hadn't wanted the risk of them trying to take the baby. But they hadn't even asked if he was all right.

"I think I know what might be playing into this," she said. "Might," Lana emphasized. "My father's planning on running for the state senate next year. A murdered daughter will generate press, but it'll be the sympathetic kind. Some people, though, are opposed to surrogacy, and it could be my parents would rather keep that hush-hush."

"Your dad would be that worried about negative press?" Slater asked, but then quickly waved that off. "Yeah, he would be. So, how exactly would he handle things if he finds out there was no surrogacy and that Stephanie has perhaps been in hiding all this time?"

"He wouldn't handle it well," she was quick to admit. "Neither would my mother. Or Marsh, for that matter. The plan is for Stephanie to marry Marsh in that whole traditional wedding deal that'll flash across society pages all over the state. It would considerably sour the image if Stephanie had just given birth to another man's baby. Right now, the surrogacy story likely suits the three of them just fine."

But not Lana. Because she was certain the surrogacy was a lie. A lie that had led to her sister's murder.

Lana was still considering that when a sound cut through the cruiser. She instantly got a jolt of adrenaline before she realized it was her phone. Austin PD came up on the dash screen, and because she figured Slater would want to hear this conversation, she took the call on speaker.

"I'm Detective Lisa Thayer," the caller said after Lana had identified herself and informed the caller they were on speaker. "I'm sorry to have to do this, but I'll need to reschedule your interview. The ME is finished with an autopsy, and I need to get a briefing from him."

"My sister's body?" Lana asked.

The detective paused. "Yes," she finally said. "And I'm sorry, but I can't allow you there for that," she was quick to add.

Lana wasn't sure she could have handled that anyway, but she was hoping the autopsy could confirm how Stephanie had died and who had killed her. She thought the "who" was Buck, but unless he'd left some form of trace evidence or DNA, then it would be hard to pin the murder on him.

Just because Lana had seen him near Stephanie's hospital room, it didn't prove he'd been the one to kill her.

"Any chance you can come into the station tomorrow at ten?" Detective Thayer asked.

Lana glanced at Slater and got the nod. "Yes, ten is fine."

"Good. I'm guessing you're probably already on your way here to Austin," the detective commented. Neither Slater nor she answered. They didn't know this cop, and while she was likely trustworthy, there was no need to announce their location. "I just wanted to know if you needed an officer to accompany you to wherever you'll be spending the night."

"No," Lana assured her. "We have backup with us."

"Good," Thayer concluded. "FYI, I just sent the background check report on Buck Holden to the Saddle Ridge sheriff. I haven't had a chance to read it myself, but I will before the interview tomorrow morning. I'll see you then," she tacked onto that, and ended the call.

Since they weren't going to the police station, Slater headed toward the safe house. She didn't need to put in the address since she'd memorized the route. Best not to put that kind of info in the GPS in case someone managed to hack it.

"I'll let Sonya know what's going on," Slater said, taking out his phone to call the deputy. "How good is the security at this place where we're staying?"

"Good," Lana verified.

"Enough so that Sonya can peel off and go home once we're inside? She could come back tomorrow to escort us to the interview."

Lana thought of the security measures she'd personally put in place on this particular house. "Nothing is hack-proof," she admitted, "but it's as safe as it can possibly be. We should be fine with Sonya returning home." She hoped so, anyway. The sad truth, though, was if Buck was plan-

ning on attacking them, he would do that with or without
Sonya being present.

Slater nodded and made the call to Sonya while he continued the drive to the house. It wasn't a showy place, of
course. A simple two-story stucco tucked into a cookie-
cutter neighborhood. The lots were large, and the fences
were high. This wasn't a community where residents had
block parties or stopped by to chat. It was the reason the
house had been chosen. Most residents were couples who
were at work all day and not around to see the comings and
goings of others.

Slater finished talking with Sonya and then called Duncan to fill him in and request a copy of the report on Buck
the detective had sent him. He'd just gotten the assurance
from Duncan that it would be emailed to him as Slater
pulled into the driveway of the house.

She used her phone to open the garage and immediately
closed it behind them once they were inside. She also did
a sweep of the place to see if any cameras and sensors had
been triggered. They hadn't been, but that wouldn't stop her
from doing a room-to-room search.

Slater was obviously in agreement with her about that
because they went in together. And they both drew their
guns. They stopped for a moment, listening for any sounds
that someone was there. Nothing. Then he tipped his head
to the left to indicate he'd start the search there. Lana went
to the right and into the dining and kitchen area.

Since the house wasn't huge, it didn't take them long
to go through the rooms there, and they went up the stairs
together where she knew there were three bedrooms and
two baths. She didn't release the breath she'd been holding
until they cleared each one and saw no signs of a security
breach or break-in.

Slater texted Sonya to let her know all was well, and they made their way back to the bedroom that had been converted to an office and security command post. Once again, she used her phone to bring the monitors to life. Six of them mounted on the wall and each of them showing the feed from a different security camera.

"There are internal cameras and monitors," she explained, "and if they're triggered, then that'll show up on the screens." Lana motioned toward the door and windows. "This can become a panic room if necessary. The bathroom's through there." She tipped her head to the door. "And there's even a supply of food and water. Backup communications, too."

He made a sound of approval but then shook his head. "No way did you set all of this up since Stephanie's murder," he stated.

"No. It's been here for about six months. It's used to hide spouses of domestic abuse, victims of stalkers, that sort of thing. I set up something similar for Stephanie since I could tell she was scared." She stopped. Had to. And Lana took a moment just to level out her breathing. "I just wish I'd pushed her harder to find out what had terrified her. If I had—"

Slater cut off the rest of that by pulling her into his arms. "You can't do this to yourself, because I'm sure you did everything possible to keep her safe."

"I didn't arrange for a bodyguard at the hospital," she was quick to point out.

"Because you didn't know the threat was there. Stephanie probably didn't, either, or she would have asked for more protection. She certainly had no trouble asking you to hide her away while she was pregnant."

Lana knew that was true, but it still didn't ease this guilt that felt like a deadweight on her shoulders.

They stood there for several long moments, and Lana became aware of their body-to-body contact. Nothing sexual. Well, nothing meant to be sexual, anyway. Slater had given her a hug of comfort, that was all, but being pressed against him reminded her body of the attraction. Since that attraction could be a deadly distraction, she stepped away, ready to explain that nothing could happen between them. She didn't get a chance to do that, though, because his phone rang.

"It's Joelle," he relayed, giving her an instant jolt of panic. Lana prayed nothing had happened to the baby.

"Is Cameron all right?" Lana asked the moment Slater took the call on speaker.

"He's fine," Joelle was quick to assure her. "I know it's hard, but try not to worry about him. He's getting plenty of TLC."

"Thank you," Lana muttered, knowing that she would indeed still worry. However, she also owed Joelle and Duncan a huge thanks for taking care of the baby. No way had she wanted to bring him all the way to Austin.

"Are you settled in somewhere so we can talk?" Joelle asked a moment later. "I've just started reading through the report on Buck and something jumped out at me."

"We haven't had a chance to read it yet," Slater explained, booting up the laptop that was on the desk. "What jumped out at you?" he asked as he started to log in to his account.

"The cops are investigating Buck for his brother's and his parents' deaths. In fact, he's their prime suspect, but they don't have any evidence to charge him." Joelle paused, and it sounded as if she was muttering what she was reading. "Wow, listen to this. Their late parents' will was worded so that any grandchild would inherit a hefty share of the estate, and Buck might have been willing to eliminate not only his own brother but his brother's offspring."

Lana's stomach twisted, and her heart began to pound. This was why Buck had killed Stephanie. Well, maybe. Why had he waited until after she gave birth to get rid of any competition for family money? Maybe because he hadn't been able to find Stephanie?

"Any other motive for Buck to kill other than the money he inherited?" Slater asked. He accessed the report, the pages loading on the screen.

Joelle paused again, and Lana figured she was skimming the report. "There's a history of what I guess you could call sibling rivalry. Buck and Patrick were involved in a fistfight when Patrick was in college. It landed them both in jail. Temporarily, anyway, until their parents bailed them out."

"Please tell me DNA samples were collected," Slater said.

"They were, since the fight led to a serious injury of a bystander. Buck was initially charged with that, but the charges were pleaded way down. I'm guessing it was because of pressure or influence from the parents. Anyway, I just read a couple of witness statements that said Buck always seemed to have it in for his brother. I'm guessing because he didn't want to share the family estate with him."

That brought Lana back to a big concern. "Patrick's only been dead a week so if Stephanine and he were involved, he could be Cameron's father. If Buck sees Cameron as a threat to his family inheritance, then the baby will be a target."

"Yes," Joelle agreed. "That's why I'm hoping there'll be something in this report that'll help the Austin cops find him. His face is being plastered on the media as a person of interest so that might..." Her words trailed off. "Oh, God," she said on a gasp.

"What's wrong?" Slater demanded, but he seemed to stop skimming the report, too. He froze, and Lana hurried to the laptop to see what had caused the reaction. She saw it the moment Joelle spelled it out.

"Oh, God," Joelle repeated. "Austin PD thinks Buck might have been the one who killed our father."

Chapter Five

Slater kept watch of the security monitors, fought off the fatigue and rehashed everything he'd uncovered since Joelle's bombshell.

Buck might have been the one who killed our father.

Since Buck hadn't been on Slater's radar before tonight, Slater hadn't latched onto the theory. But that had changed after he and Lana had spent the last two hours going through any and all background on Buck.

They hadn't found any direct proof, but the connection was indeed there, and Slater could now see why Austin PD had flagged it as part of their investigation into Buck's involvement in the deaths of his brother and parents. It was yet another circumstantial piece that when put with the other pieces could point to murder.

"I should have seen this sooner," he muttered, scrubbing his hand over his face to keep himself alert and awake.

"How?" Lana questioned. "It wasn't even your father's case."

True, but after poring over every one of his dad's investigations, he should have widened the net to other cases. If so, he might have found the details about Alicia Monroe, a nineteen-year-old woman who'd disappeared from Weston, a small town near Saddle Ridge. There'd been enough blood at the scene of Alicia's small apartment to declare her dead, but they'd never found her body. Alicia's mother, Maryanne, had been old high school friends with Slater's parents and had asked his dad, then sheriff, to look into the matter.

And his father had.

Slater had managed to find notes about it in an old file that his dad had marked personal. In those notes, his dad had listed several scenarios and suspects for Alicia's death. It'd been a lengthy list since Alicia had apparently been considered a party girl and had a huge circle of friends.

Including Buck.

There'd been nothing concrete about Buck in his dad's notes or in the investigation that the Weston PD had conducted, but Buck had been a person of interest since he'd had a relationship with Alicia. And a volatile temper even back then. Several people had verified that the breakup with Buck hadn't been amicable, but there were no specifics about such things as stalking or violence. Buck had been just nineteen at the time, and with the lack of evidence, he'd been questioned and released. That wasn't the end of the story, though.

Slater stared at the notes now. Observations made by his father that had started nearly twenty years earlier and had continued until right before his death. Even though Alicia's death was considered a cold case, his dad had continued to dig into it, had continued to ask questions, had still considered it an active if unofficial investigation. That maybe meant he'd continued to ruffle some feathers as well.

Had Buck found out about the investigation and murdered Slater's dad to silence him once and for all?

Maybe.

There was one note in particular that troubled him. The month before his father's murder, he'd jotted down a comment that he wanted to reinterview the persons of interest, and he'd listed some of Alicia's friends, including Buck. If his father had actually talked with any of them, there was no indication of it in the file notes. Or maybe he'd died before he could add them.

The bottom line was his father could have spoken to Buck, spooked him, and that could have prompted Buck to murder him.

"Do you remember when Alicia disappeared?" Lana asked, drawing his attention back to her. Not that it'd strayed far since she was literally sitting shoulder to shoulder with him.

"I do." He'd been sixteen at the time, and even though it'd happened one town over, it'd caused some panic among the townsfolk who'd speculated there might be a killer on the loose. "You?"

She nodded. "Stephanie knew Alicia, and she talked a lot about the murder."

Slater turned toward her before he realized that shoulder to shoulder could quickly turn into mouth to mouth. He eased back his chair a little and waited for her to continue.

"After Alicia disappeared," Lana went on, "Stephanie confessed to me that she'd sneaked out of the house when she'd been grounded and had gone with a friend to a party at Alicia's. Apparently, Alicia's parents were out of town so there was no adult supervision."

That rang an instant bell with Slater. "Yeah, I remember Stephanie calling me and asking me to take her to a party. She didn't tell me where, only that it was at a friend of a friend's. I couldn't go, so I guess she went with someone else."

"Does that bother you?" Lana came out and asked. "That Stephanie saw other guys when you two were dating?"

"No." And he didn't have to think hard about that response. "Stephanie wasn't exactly the 'settle down with one guy' type. And we were teenagers. We had enough on-again, off-again times that I dated other girls during the offs."

He studied Lana's face and saw what he always saw simmering there. The heat. The old attraction they'd never acted on because of Stephanie. Lana looked as if she wanted to say something about that, but then she glanced away, visibly regrouping and getting them back on the subject of the investigation.

"From what I can recall, the party happened about a week before Alicia disappeared," Lana went on. "I remember because it was Stephanie's sixteenth birthday, and she was grounded. I think that's why she went. So she'd have a celebration of sorts. But then she got there and said there was a lot of drinking and some drugs, and when some fights broke out, she and her friend left."

Slater considered that. "Was Alicia involved in the fights?"

"Not that Stephanie said."

Still, it was something to consider, and Slater made a mental note to try to find out from anyone who'd attended. "Was Buck at the party?" he wanted to know.

He saw the regret in her eyes a split second before she shook her head. "I don't recall Stephanie mentioning him."

That would have been a long shot, and Slater was sorry he'd brought this up. It was no doubt a reminder that Stephanie was dead and couldn't be questioned about the party.

"I'm guessing Stephanie didn't mention the party to the Weston cops?" Slater asked.

Another shake of her head. "Not a chance. She'd sneaked out of the house when she was grounded and was probably with someone our parents wouldn't have approved of. She would have been in serious trouble."

He considered that a moment. "Serious trouble," he repeated. "Was there anything like physical abuse from your parents?"

It twisted at him that Lana didn't immediately deny it. Instead, she dragged in a long breath. "My mother slapped Stephanie and me a couple of times when we broke the rules. She didn't want a whisper of gossip about our behavior, so when the gossip happened, she often flew off the handle."

Slater wasn't surprised that this was the first time he was hearing of this. He'd always suspected that Lana's parents weren't the sort to air any dirty laundry and would make sure their daughters did the same.

And he wondered if that played into what had happened to Stephanie.

It was hard for him to believe one of them had murdered their own daughter, but it was something he had to consider. After all, Stephanie would have no doubt broken plenty of their rules by having the baby.

Lana tapped something on his father's notes. It was the date Alicia's disappearance had been categorized as a murder. "We moved to San Antonio shortly after this," she said.

He'd known that, but he hadn't connected the move to anything involving Alicia. And maybe it wasn't. It was yet another thread, though, that needed to be checked.

"Do you recall your parents ever talking about Alicia?" he asked.

She paused and then went with another headshake. "They rarely discussed anyone who wasn't in their social circles. You were the exception," she added. "You must know they didn't approve of you dating Stephanie."

"Yeah, I knew, and I think that was part of the appeal for your sister. Being with me was breaking the rules."

Lana didn't argue with that. But she did yawn, a reminder that it was already past midnight. She quickly tried to cover the yawn and look back at the notes, but he knew it was time to call it a night.

"Let's try to get some sleep," he suggested, glancing at the monitors and then at the sofa. "I can sleep in here and keep an eye on the security cameras. I'm guessing they'll make some kind of sound if someone comes near the place?"

Lana nodded and held up her phone. "It'll beep, and the system will alert me, too, on the app." She motioned toward the adjoining bath. "There are toiletries and even some clothes in there. Not sure any of them will fit you, but my boss tries to keep a wide range of sizes stocked in case he has to move someone here with just the clothes on their back."

Slater had showered and changed into clean clothes right before Lana had left the baby on his doorstep so he figured he'd be okay, especially since they'd be heading back to Saddle Ridge as soon as her interview was finished.

Lana's phone dinged with a text, and she frowned when she glanced at the screen.

"One of your parents?" Slater asked.

She shook her head. "It's Taylor Galway, someone who used to be friends with Stephanie, but I know they had some kind of falling-out. Taylor wants to know if it's true, if Stephanie is really dead. I suspect now that word of her death is out, I'll be getting more calls and texts," she added in a mutter.

"That might not be a bad thing," Slater said. "Did Stephanie have contact with these friends while she was hiding out?"

Lana's first instinct was to say no, that Stephanie had been too scared for that, but she simply didn't know. "Maybe."

That would have been his guess, too, and if Stephanie had spoken to anyone, she might have doled out some info that could help with the investigation. Lana clearly picked up on that, too, because she fired off a response to Taylor.

It's true, Lana texted as Slater looked over her shoulder. She waited a few moments but got no response back from the woman. "I really don't think Stephanie had contact with Taylor, though, because the couple of times the woman's name recently came up, Stephanie didn't have anything kind to say about her. Just the opposite."

"Do you know why?" he asked. It wasn't an idle question. Sometimes, bad blood led to bad stuff happening.

"I'm not sure. I recall Stephanie calling her a backstabber, and she added some choice words of profanity to that." She paused a moment. "It's possible their falling-out was over Marsh."

"Marsh?" Slater certainly hadn't expected that.

Lana nodded. "Our parents were pressuring Stephanie to marry Marsh, but I know that Marsh was once involved with Taylor, so maybe Taylor wasn't over him. Or maybe she just didn't want Stephanie hooking up with her ex."

Ironic since it appeared that Stephanie hadn't wanted Marsh. At least she hadn't wanted to marry him, anyway. It was possible, though, she would have changed her mind about that had she lived.

Even though Lana yawned for the third time, she went to the window and looked out. Despite this being a residential neighborhood, the city lights were right there, only a few blocks away, and there were even more lights beyond that. In the distance, there were the sounds of traffic and even the howl of a police siren. He wasn't sure how people slept with that kind of noise going on, but he'd have to give it a try. He needed at least a little sleep to stand a chance of having a clear head.

"A fish out of water," he muttered. That's what he felt like right now.

The corner of Lana's mouth lifted. "I felt that way after we moved from Saddle Ridge. Stephanie was in her element in the city, but I never was."

That was a reminder of the things he and Lana had in common, and if there hadn't been a two-year age difference between them, Slater figured he would have dated Lana in high school, not Stephanie.

Maybe sensing that the moment was turning too personal, Lana turned from the window. "I'll be in the room right across from here."

She started in that direction, only to stop when Slater's phone rang. "Is it Joelle?" she immediately asked, and he knew the concern in her voice was because she was afraid something had happened to the baby.

He shook his head. "It's Duncan."

Lana didn't relax one bit, so Slater quickly answered the call and put it on speaker. "Lana's in the room with me," he informed Duncan just in case he needed to soften any bad news he might have. "Is the baby all right?"

"He's fine," Duncan assured him. "And there's been no sign of any kind of trouble here. What about there?"

"Nothing," he said, and then waited for Duncan to get into why he'd called. Thankfully, he didn't have to wait long.

"Two things. I just got back two reports. The first is for Stephanie's cell phone records. The person who called her in the hospital used a blocked number. No way to trace it."

That surprised exactly no one. Of course a killer planning a murder wouldn't have left something that could be linked back to him. But it did make Slater wonder why the person had called Stephanie. Or maybe the call wasn't from the killer at all but from someone else.

"The other report I got back was from the Rapid DNA test," Duncan added a moment later. Slater heard him drag in a long breath. "Cameron's father isn't Patrick. It's Buck."

Chapter Six

With Slater right by her side and Detective Lisa Thayer across the table, Lana sat in the interview room of Austin PD and read through the now-typed statement she'd just given about her sister's murder. It was all there. All spelled out.

Details that twisted and ate away at her like acid.

In hindsight, she could see so much potential for an outcome like this. Stephanie's secrecy. The fear she'd seen in her sister's eyes. Lana hadn't gotten to the source of that fear, hadn't managed to fix it in time, and now Stephanie had paid the ultimate price.

"Buck," Lana muttered under her breath when her gaze landed on his name in the statement. She was well aware she'd spoken it like profanity, and it wasn't the first time. It was something she'd been doing most of the night and now into the morning.

She couldn't wrap her mind around Stephanie hooking up with a man like Buck, especially since according to those photos on social media, she had been involved with Buck's brother, Patrick. Knowing Cameron's bio-father didn't lessen Lana's love for her nephew, not one bit, but she knew it made their situation even more complicated.

If Patrick had been the dad, he could have petitioned for custody of Cameron. Had Patrick not been murdered, that is. But Buck was very much alive. And possibly a killer. Lana didn't want someone like that to try to stake a claim on the baby.

"There's still no sign of him," Detective Thayer remarked after checking her phone. "Buck," she added, though no clarification was needed.

Lana wondered where he was. Wondered if he was trying to figure out how to get to Cameron or her. She doubted the man would just run and hide, and part of her hoped he didn't. She didn't want to have to look over her shoulder for years, waiting for Buck to attack.

"You've got enough to arrest him if you find him," Slater said. Not a question. He was no doubt just looking for verification.

Thayer nodded. "We've got the security camera footage from the break-in at Lana's. The footage, too, of his hit-and-run. That'll be enough to hold him while we build a case for murder."

Murder.

There it was. Another word all spelled out, and even though it wasn't fresh info, just hearing it brought back the avalanche of emotions. Lana had spent half the night crying for a sister she wasn't even sure she loved. That had brought on yet another mother lode of guilt, not loving her only sibling. But there'd been so many times when Stephanie just hadn't been likable.

That lack of love didn't extend to Cameron, though. Just the opposite. Lana had loved him from the moment she'd laid eyes on him. And now she had a fierce instinct to protect him from the scum who was his biological father.

Did Buck know that he was Cameron's father?

Maybe.

That could be the reason he'd gone after Stephanie, but

it was just as likely he would want to eliminate Stephanie and Cameron regardless if he or his brother was the father. Because any baby born to either of them would be a threat to the inheritance.

Thayer's phone dinged with another text, and her face seemed to relax a little. "Your parents and Marsh Bray are coming in at one today for interviews. Their lawyers had been stonewalling that, but I guess they gave in." The detective looked at Slater. "If you're interested, I can let you observe the interviews."

"I'm very interested. Thanks," Slater added.

The detective sighed a little when she turned to Lana. "I'm afraid I can't extend that offer to you. Slater's a cop with a vested interest in the outcome of this investigation, but I can't let civilians observe."

"I understand," Lana said, and she did. She wanted this all done by the book so that Buck wouldn't be able to shake off some of the charges on a technicality. She wanted him to serve the maximum time possible.

Thayer checked her watch. "It'll be at least four hours before the interviews," she said. "You're welcome to wait in the lounge, or you can come back. I can have a police escort follow you to wherever you want to go."

"We have a deputy from Saddle Ridge waiting outside," Slater explained, standing when Thayer did.

As planned, Sonya had returned to Austin to escort them to police headquarters for the statement, and she'd be following them when they drove back to Saddle Ridge.

"Any chance during the interviews you can bring up Alicia Monroe and any possible connection to my father's murder?" Slater asked Thayer.

The detective certainly didn't jump to agree to that. Nor did she ask who Alicia was. That was because she'd already mentioned that she had gone through all the case notes on Buck and had seen that Buck had once been involved with the murdered teenager.

"You can't think that Leonard and Pamela Walsh know anything about that particular murder," Thayer finally said. "Do you?"

Slater shrugged. "Stephanie was at a party at Alicia's house, and Stephanie clearly knew Buck, so maybe her folks did, too." He stopped, shook his head. "Yeah, it's a long shot, but I'd like to know if they, well, have any details we don't already know about. It's possible when you bring up Alicia's name, they might recall Stephanie mentioning Buck or her."

Lana considered what he'd just said and had a theory. "When Stephanie and I were teenagers, our parents made a habit of hiring PIs to keep an eye on us. They didn't want us getting into any trouble that would cause bad publicity. So they might have known about Stephanie going to that party." She paused. "They might have known about Buck and Alicia, too."

"If they did, why wouldn't they have volunteered that sooner?" Thayer came out and asked.

Lana didn't have to think about this. "Again, bad publicity. They might have hoped to keep my sister's pregnancy under wraps, but when she was murdered, they would want to do any possible damage control."

"Not lying to the police, though, right?" Thayer questioned.

Lana had no choice but to just spell this out. "Lying is second nature to them. And right now, their focus isn't on losing a daughter but rather keeping a lid on unsavory details that might come out. They won't be happy to learn that a thug like Buck fathered Stephanie's child."

Thayer stayed quiet a moment. "So, maybe I can use that. They don't know he's the father, right?"

"They didn't learn it from us," Lana assured her.

"Good. Then I can mention it and see how they react. That'd be a good lead-in to bringing up Alicia and that party."

Lana wished she could see her parents' reaction to that. And Marsh's. She wondered if Marsh would see Stephanie's pregnancy as a betrayal. If so, that would give him motive for murder.

"I'll let you know everything that happens in the interview," Slater told Lana as they made their way out of the interview room.

Lana had had no doubts about that and murmured a thanks while she considered something else. "Once they know about Buck being Cameron's father, my parents might feel obligated to try to get custody of him. I mean, how would it look in the press if they didn't?"

It sickened her to think of handing over that precious baby to people like her parents. Thankfully, there'd be no way Buck could try to assert his parental rights. Not with his criminal record and the charges about to be leveled against him. Buck wouldn't be a threat to custody. However, her parents might put up a good fight if they thought it would benefit them.

After they made their way down to the bottom floor, Slater texted Sonya to let her know they would soon be coming out of the building. That would mean another uneasy walk through the large visitors' parking lot.

She and Slater retrieved their weapons from the security checkpoint at the front of the building and stepped outside, immediately glancing around for any signs of a threat. There were some uniformed cops going in and out of the sprawling headquarters complex. Some civilians, too. The place was a beehive of activity, which didn't settle Lana's nerves one bit.

As they threaded their way through the sea of parked cars, Lana's phone vibrated, a reminder that she'd silenced it during the interview, and she frowned when she saw her mother's name on the screen. She didn't answer, not wanting to deal with either of her parents right now, but her mother immediately texted her.

Did you see the headlines? her mother asked. Someone is spreading lies about Stephanie.

Groaning, she showed the message to Slater just as he got his own text from Detective Thayer. The media's picked up the story about Stephanie's murder.

Great. It had to be bad press for the cop to give them a heads-up. Lana figured she'd need to glance through the article on the way back to the safe house. Not now, though. She didn't want the distraction.

That thought had no sooner crossed her mind when Lana sensed the motion to her right. She snapped in that direction, her gaze automatically scanning for any sign of threat. She didn't see any, but every nerve in her body was yelling for her to take notice. That danger was near.

And every nerve in her body was right.

Before she could even see exactly what the threat was, the man jumped out from behind the back of a large SUV, and Lana caught just a glimpse of the weapon before he jammed it against her chest. She felt the jolt of the stun gun go through her. Felt it rob her of all of the sensations in her body except for the pain. She could feel the pain. Every bit of it. And it literally brought her to her knees.

The feeling in her legs vanished, and she was suddenly boneless. Unable to move. Lana had no choice but to drop down on the concrete. Hard. So hard that it seemed to send a jolt through her.

Beside her, she heard the frantic footsteps, the spewed profanity, all mixed with the sickening thud of flesh slamming into flesh. But she couldn't tell what was going on.

Oh, God. Was this Buck, and was he now going after Slater since he'd neutralized her? And she was neutralized. There was no question about that. Lana couldn't reach for her gun. She couldn't do anything to save Slater and herself.

It took every ounce of her energy, but Lana finally managed to roll onto her back so she could look up at the nightmare that was playing out in front of her. Slater hadn't managed to draw his weapon, and he was in a hand-to-hand fight with a hulking brute. It was Buck all right, and he was even bigger and bulkier then he had seemed in his photos. He towered over Slater and outweighed him by at least fifty pounds. She could only watch as Buck slammed one of his huge fists toward Slater's face.

Slater managed to turn just in time so the fist was a glancing blow rather than a full-on punch, but that deflection didn't stop Buck. He merely tried again, and when that one missed, he grabbed hold of Slater's shoulder to drag him closer.

Around them, Lana could hear the shouts, and she prayed help was coming. Buck's face was etched with rage, and she had no doubt if he got the chance, he would beat Slater to death.

Lana tried to kick out, hoping she could make contact with Buck's leg so she could off-balance him, but the impact only seemed to anger him further. He looked down at her, cursing her.

"You're a dead woman," he snarled.

The threat cost him, because Slater took advantage

of Buck's distraction and drew his gun. Buck acted fast, though, latching onto Lana's hair and dragging her up in front of him as a human shield. He pressed his back against the SUV.

"I'll snap her neck," Buck growled, the raging heat and anger in every word. "I'll kill her where she stands."

"No, you won't," Slater said. In contrast, his voice was all ice. As was his expression. "Because then you'll have no cover. Look around you, Buck. Look at what you're up against."

Lana couldn't fully turn her head, but from her peripheral vision, she could see several cops. All had their weapons drawn and aimed at Buck. She felt Buck's breath quicken and could feel his heart slamming against her back. Lana also felt something else. The movement of Buck's arm. When she felt the cold barrel of a gun jam against her head, she realized he, too, was armed.

"Yeah, but she'll still be dead," Buck taunted. "Tell your badge friends to back off, and she lives."

Lana figured there was little to no chance of that. She suspected Buck wanted to use her to get to Cameron, and once she'd served her purpose, he'd kill her just as easily as he had Stephanie.

But she wouldn't help him get to Cameron.

No way.

She'd die here before she let that happen.

"I think you badges call this a standoff," Buck grumbled. "None of you has a clean shot. Can't risk shooting me without putting bullets in her and any other unlucky person in the parking lot."

Lana knew all of that was true. But she also knew that Slater wouldn't just let Buck drag her away from here.

"So here's my suggestion," Buck went on. "Lana and

me get in this SUV, and I drive off. I dump her a couple of blocks over—"

"No," Slater said, his fierce gaze locked on Buck. "You'll let her go now and will surrender to Austin PD."

Buck made a snarky yeah-right. "And I guess you'll say I'll live happily ever after."

"No," Slater repeated. "You'll be arrested and tried. But the alternative is dying right here, right now. At least with a trial you stand a chance of walking away a free man."

He did. But Lana tried not to think of that as a possibility. She wanted this monster to pay for what he had done, for what he was continuing to do.

Lana tried to keep her breathing steady and tested some of her muscles. Slowly, the movement was starting to return. Not enough for her to have full control over her body, but she could maybe do something. Lana did more testing, trying to loosen the muscles in her neck while she tried not to panic over Buck's tightening grip around her throat.

She made direct eye contact with Slater, trying to let him know that she was about to attempt something. Something he likely wouldn't approve of, since it would be dangerous. But anything she did at this point could turn out to be fatal. It was the same if she did nothing at all.

Yelling to give herself a jolt of adrenaline, Lana rammed the back of her head into Buck's face. She put as much force behind it as she could manage, and when he howled in pain, she rammed her elbow into his gut. That wasn't nearly as effective as the headbutt, but it was enough to cause him to loosen his grip on her. The second he did, Lana dropped to the ground.

The sound of the shot immediately blasted through the air.

For a horrifying moment, she had no idea who'd been

shot, and she was terrified that Buck had managed to shoot Slater. She looked up, trying to pick through the blaring morning light, and she saw Slater. Standing and with his gun still aimed.

Buck collapsed next to her.

She saw the blood spreading on the front of his shirt, but that didn't stop Buck from reaching for her. He was going to try to pull her back into that human shield position. But Slater put a stop to that. He took hold of her arm and dragged her away from Buck, and in the same motion, he kicked away Buck's gun.

Three other cops, including Sonya, moved in, all of them continuing to keep their guns trained on Buck. He didn't move, though. Didn't try to grab her again or attempt to fight back. Not that he could have. Lana was pretty sure he was bleeding out.

Slater hoisted her up, moving her behind him and anchoring her between him and a car. Good thing, too, since Lana didn't have the feeling back in many parts of her body and she wasn't sure she could stand on her own.

"Ambulance is on the way," someone shouted. Several of the Austin cops moved in and one began to check the wound on Buck's chest. "Is this the guy wanted for murder?"

Slater muttered, "Yes," but continued to stare at Buck. "Did you kill Stephanie?" he asked.

Buck laughed. Or rather attempted one, anyway. It sounded more like a throaty gurgle. "No comment," he managed.

So, even now, he wasn't going to confess to relieve his conscience. Maybe because he thought he was going to live. Lana seriously doubted that, though, and obviously so did the cop tending to his wound. He was adding pressure to try to slow the bleeding, but it wasn't working.

"Did you kill Sheriff Cliff McCullough?" Slater tried again.

Buck didn't snarl out a verbal response, but he stared at Slater for a long time. In the distance, Lana could hear the wails of an ambulance.

"Did you kill him?" Slater repeated, speaking now through clenched teeth.

"I'm not gonna give you that," Buck muttered, his voice growing weaker while the rage still flared in his dying eyes. "Here's what I'll give Lana and you. The truth. I'm not working by my lonesome. I've got a helper. A cold-blooded one. And Lana and you are going to die."

Chapter Seven

Slater fought the adrenaline crash with another cup of strong black coffee. Even though it was his third cup, he could still feel the fatigue all the way to his bones. Judging from the exhausted look on Lana's face, she was dealing with the same thing.

That and the flashbacks.

Yeah, those had already started, and Slater figured they wouldn't be letting up anytime soon. Buck had come darn close to killing both of them, and that wasn't something they'd just be able to shut out.

Lana stood at the window of the break room in Austin PD headquarters, drinking her own cup of coffee and staring out at the crime scene that was now being processed in the parking lot below. Buck's body had already been moved, and there was a final canvass going on for any evidence Buck might have left behind.

Slater had had to surrender his gun, of course. That was standard procedure, though he was certain none of the cops here thought he'd overreacted. Deadly force had been necessary, period, and if Slater hadn't shot and killed Buck, then Lana might be dead. There were plenty of witnesses and even surveillance footage to back that up.

He and Lana had already given their statements of the

incident. Technically, they were free to go, but Lana hadn't jumped at the chance to go back to the safe house only to return so that Slater could observe Marsh and her parents' interviews.

And Slater couldn't blame her.

Buck's words were no doubt repeating like gunfire in her head. *Lana and you are going to die.* The thing was they just didn't know if the threat was real or if it'd been one last shot by a dying man. Buck had indeed spoken to someone on the phone when he'd broken into Lana's house, so he hadn't been working alone. However, that didn't mean the accomplice would continue to do his bidding now that he was dead.

It was somewhat of a miracle that Lana hadn't been seriously injured, but Slater had still insisted she be examined by the EMTs. Thankfully, they hadn't found any damage from her being hit with the stun gun.

"Are you okay?" Lana asked, turning from the window and fixing her gaze on him.

Slater knew it wasn't a simple question. Nor did he have a simple answer. Only three hours earlier, he'd killed a man. A man who'd seemed hell-bent on murdering Lana. But Buck had been more than their attacker. He'd been a suspect in the murders of Stephanie and Slater's father. Maybe Buck had ended both their lives.

And maybe he hadn't.

"Now I know how people feel who've had loved ones disappear," she muttered. "No real answers. Only speculation."

Yeah, he understood that. Of course, a disappearance wasn't necessarily a murder. Murder was final. But without the answers as to the who and the why, he and Lana wouldn't have that elusive closure. Mercy, he needed that, and he was certain Lana did, too. It was the only way they were going to be able to look past the now and move on to the future.

At the thought of "future," the baby came to mind, and he knew Cameron was weighing heavily on Lana right now. It was obvious she loved the baby and was worried about him. That's why it was critical for them to find out the identity of Buck's accomplice.

Slater had plenty of wheels in motion for that. Both his fellow cops and Austin PD were digging through Buck's phone records and financials, looking for anything that could give them a lead. Slater wanted to dive right in to that research, too, and he would just as soon as they got these interviews out of the way. Maybe Marsh or Lana's parents would spill something that would help.

The door to the break room opened, and both Slater and Lana automatically reached for guns that weren't there. Lana, too, had had to surrender her gun since personal firearms weren't allowed in the headquarters.

Their reaction, though, wasn't necessary since it wasn't a threat. It was Detective Thayer, and judging from her troubled expression, something else had gone wrong. Lana must have picked up on it as well.

"Is the baby all right?" Lana asked, the frantic edge in her voice.

"As far as I know," Thayer said. "I haven't gotten any alerts or anything."

That verbal assurance didn't appease Lana, and Slater saw her fire off a text to Joelle. Something Lana had already done several times since Buck's death. His sister's response was equally fast and told Lana that all was well.

"I'm not here about the baby," Thayer went on once Lana looked up from her phone. "I wanted to let you know that someone leaked to the press." She walked closer to them, bringing up some images on her phone.

Slater steeled himself up to see pictures of Buck's body. Or maybe even Slater shooting the man. It was so easy these days for people to post such things on social media. If the photos were "compelling" enough, then media would pick them up, too.

Both he and Lana leaned in to take a look, and he heard the soft sound of surprise that Lana made when she realized what she was looking at. Not Buck. But rather Stephanie. And these weren't death photos but rather of Stephanie clearly in party mode.

In the first shot, Stephanie was wearing just her underwear and was dancing. Since she had a cocktail glass in her hand, she had likely been drinking. The second one was of another party with Stephanie making out with some guy. Neither shot was flattering. Ditto for the third. It'd been taken from behind, and a grinning, inebriated Stephanie was looking over her shoulder just as she was about to dive into a pool.

"Who posted these?" Lana wanted to know.

"We're not sure, but they were on Stephanie's Facebook page," Thayer explained. "Stephanie obviously hadn't used the page in a while, but she had it set to public, which means anyone could have tagged her so they'd wind up there."

"You can trace the person who posted these?" Slater asked.

Thayer shrugged. "The photos were published from a new account, one without an actual profile name, only numbers, but we'll try to find who's responsible." She paused.

"And the pictures were also put on every one of Stephanie's friends' pages."

Lana dragged in a long breath. "Could Buck have done this?"

"No," Thayer was quick to say. "These showed up an hour ago, and they hadn't been scheduled in advance. Maybe it's some kind of smear campaign from his accomplice, but that doesn't feel right."

Slater made a sound of agreement. "An accomplice wouldn't want to draw this kind of attention." That got nods from both Lana and the detective.

"So why do it?" Lana asked. "Stephanie's dead. She…" She trailed off and muttered some profanity under her breath. "This could be meant to get back at my parents." Lana stopped again and groaned. "Or someone who wants to make people believe Stephanie was irresponsible and deserved to die."

That could be a large pool of people. Stephanie had likely made some enemies, and Slater had no doubts that her parents had, too.

"Anyway, I thought you should know about this before the interviews," Thayer said, checking the time. "The Walshes and Marsh Bray will be here soon, and any info about Stephanie's potential enemies might come out in their statements. If they haven't seen the photos already, I'm sure they soon will."

No doubt, and maybe that would set one of them off enough that they'd reveal something they'd rather keep secret.

"I'll come back and get you when the interviews are ready to start," Thayer told Slater right before she walked out.

Since Lana looked unsteady on her feet, Slater went to

her and took a huge risk. By pulling her into his arms. Hugs, even one of comfort, could still spur the heat between them. And it did this time, too, but they obviously had way too much on their plates to think about acting on it.

He hoped.

Sighing, Lana dropped her head on his shoulder. "I want to ask my boss to use some of the Sencor resources to help us. Traffic cam footage, deep background checks, informal interviews with anyone who was near the hospital when Stephanie was murdered. Anything that'll link to Stephanie, Buck or anyone he might have been working with."

Slater had already considered this angle. "I can't agree to anything illegal," he spelled out.

"It wouldn't be. But they've got the manpower to interview anyone who crossed paths with Stephanie and Buck. Somebody must know what happened and why Stephanie went into hiding when she realized she was pregnant with Buck's child. Unless the blowup between them was totally in private, then there might be something to find."

That was a long way to go back, eight months or so, but Slater could see the reasoning for that to be the starting point. With Stephanie in hiding, Buck might have been digging to find her location, and if so, there could be traces of that. Traces that then might link back to his partner.

"All right," Slater said.

The moment the agreement was out of his mouth, Lana eased away from him so she could compose a text, no doubt to get the ball rolling on the search. When he heard the swooshing sound of the text being sent, he expected Lana to move back to the window. Or anywhere else in the room that wasn't so close to him.

She didn't.

Lana came right back into his arms, and he heard the

whisper of a soft sob that she managed to choke down. She was grieving. Scared, too, and Slater wished he could do something to help. The only thing he could manage, though, was to stand there and hold her.

The moments slid by, and he wasn't sure exactly how much time passed before she moved again. This time, she looked at him. Their gazes locked. Held. Her breath met his. Slater saw the grief. But the heat was there as well, and it didn't seem to matter that neither of them wanted to feel like this. Not now, anyway. That didn't stop it. Didn't stop Lana from moving in and doing the unthinkable.

She pressed her mouth to his.

It wasn't a hard, hungry kiss born of need. Not solely, anyway. The need was there, but this seemed to be so much more. Slater tried to give her exactly that—more—without pushing this too far. He simply kissed her.

Of course, there was nothing *simply* about it since this was Lana. The heat rose as the pressure of her mouth went up a whole bunch of notches. That wasn't all, either. With the new level of the kiss came the maneuvering of their bodies, and that didn't stop until they were pressed against each other. Until this felt like a whole lot more than just a kiss.

Thankfully, they both seemed to regain their common sense at the same moment because they stepped away from each other. Slater was sure he looked as if someone had sucker punched him, because he was gulping in breaths as if this had been a making-out marathon. Lana wasn't faring much better. She looked shocked and maybe appalled that she had done such a thing.

"Don't say you're sorry," he insisted when she opened her mouth. "No need. You can blame it on the grief and the fact that we were nearly killed today. You can blame it on whatever you need it to be."

She stared at him a long time and shook her head. "I try not to lie to myself," she murmured. "So I'll blame it on this pull I've had to you for...too long," she added in a whisper.

Slater had known the heat was there, but he might have questioned that "too long" part if the door hadn't opened. Even though he and Lana were no longer standing close to each other, they still moved farther apart, and the guilt was probably flashing like a proverbial neon sign on their faces.

Detective Thayer stuck her head inside the partially opened door, and she seemed to hesitate for a second or two before her gaze went to Lana. "Your parents and Marsh are here. But they've asked to speak to you before the interviews. I told them I'd check. You can say no," Thayer tacked onto that.

Lana didn't just say no or anything else, but then she nodded. "I want to see how they react to Buck coming after me."

Slater wanted to see that reaction, too. Heck, he wanted to see them respond to a lot of things, including if they had any part in their daughter's murder. Of course, neither of them would likely just admit to that, but they might say something off the record.

Thayer waited as if checking to see if Lana was certain, and then she murmured, "I'll bring them here to the break room."

Lana pulled back her shoulders and ran her hand through her hair, obviously trying to make herself look as steady as possible. She was pulling it off, too. For the most part, anyway, but Slater dreaded that Lana was about to have to face the emotional wringer her parents would no doubt put her through.

It didn't take long before the door opened again, and the detective ushered in Leonard and Pamela. Marsh was right behind them. None of them rushed to Lana, but Leonard gave Thayer a dismissive glance before insisting, "We'll speak to our daughter alone."

"No, you won't," Lana said before Slater or Thayer got the chance. "Slater and the detective are staying put."

Oh, that did not please Leonard, and Slater saw the anger tighten every muscle in the man's face. "Fine," Leonard spat out. "We only wanted to make sure you were okay. I understand from news reports that you were attacked in the parking lot."

Lana nodded. And didn't add anything else.

Pamela huffed and aimed a glare at Thayer. "Obviously, you've failed at your job if a thug can go after my only surviving daughter right under your nose." Tears sprang to her eyes, and Slater wondered if they were genuine.

"Lana wasn't under police protection when she was attacked," Thayer said, the annoyance coating her voice. "And my team and I are not only investigating the attack but your other daughter's murder."

"But you let that thug get to her," Leonard said. His voice cracked. "A thug who must have raped Stephanie since he fathered her baby."

Thayer fired a quick glance at Lana and Slater to see if they'd spilled. Both shook their heads, indicating they hadn't.

"What makes you think Stephanie had Buck's baby?" Slater came out and asked.

Judging from the way his face went tight again, Leonard was sorry he'd admitted knowing that. Slater made a mental note to check and see if anyone in Austin PD was continuing to feed Leonard information.

"That horrible man was the father of Stephanie's baby?" Pamela asked, and the woman seemed genuinely shocked.

She turned her wide eyes toward Marsh as if checking to see if he knew.

Marsh shook his head. "Did he rape Stephanie?" he immediately wanted to know. But he didn't wait for an answer. He groaned and closed his eyes for a moment. "Did he?" he repeated, posing the question first to Leonard and then to Lana.

"I don't know," Lana admitted.

"It would explain so much," Marsh went on. "There was no reason for Stephanie to go into hiding the way she did unless she was scared of Buck."

Slater had to admit that rang true with him. But it might have only been a part of it. "And maybe she didn't want to face you and her parents."

Another flash of anger crossed Leonard's face, but Pamela and Marsh didn't have the same reaction. Marsh groaned, stepped away and pressed his forehead against the wall. Pamela went to him, patting his back.

"I don't know why Stephanie wouldn't have gone to the police," Pamela murmured. "Instead, she went to Lana, and now she's dead. Lana could have been killed, too," Pamela quickly tacked onto that, but the arrow had already found its mark. Some of the color had drained from Lana's face, and she was no doubt going through another round of guilt over her sister's murder.

"Did Buck confess to killing Stephanie?" Marsh asked when he turned back around to face them.

Slater had to shake his head. "He said no comment." Slater debated if he should say more and then decided to go for it. "He claimed he had an accomplice."

That got the expected reactions from the three visitors. Shock, followed by concern. Leonard's concern, though, quickly morphed into what seemed to be his default reaction. Anger.

"You should call in the Texas Rangers," Leonard snarled, snapping toward Lana. "And I can arrange for private security for you—"

"I can arrange my own security," Lana interrupted.

Leonard made a show of rolling his eyes. "Clearly, that's worked out well for you. How close did you come to dying today, Lana?"

"Close," Lana admitted, and she didn't wither under her father's intense glare. "But I'm not handing over my safety to you."

"What the hell does that mean?" Leonard demanded.

Again, Lana didn't verbally respond. She just stared at her father, waiting. It was a good ploy, and Leonard lost the waiting game because he muttered more profanity.

"I don't know what it is you think I've done, but you're wrong," Leonard grumbled.

"If you've got the resources to find out the identity of the man who fathered Stephanie's baby, then I figure you know a whole lot more," Lana spelled out. "Enough that you could have maybe stopped Buck from killing Stephanie."

"No." Leonard's denial was fast and loud. It took him a couple of seconds to rein in his temper. A temper so fierce that it made Slater believe this was a man who was capable of murder. Or at least capable of getting someone to commit murder for him.

But why would Leonard want Stephanie dead?

Was he so consumed with his image and reputation that he thought she was better off dead? If so, then he could have joined forces with Buck, who had his own strong motive for wanting Stephanie eliminated. But then, that left the baby. Slater didn't want to think Leonard or even Buck capable of harming a child. And maybe that hadn't been the plan. The baby could have simply been given to someone who had no idea of his paternity. That would mean, though, eliminating anyone who might spill the secret down the road.

Such as Lana.

Yes, the theory of Leonard and Buck teaming up might work, but the teaming could have been done with Marsh and Buck. Or Buck and Pamela. Slater silently groaned. Because the accomplice could be someone else, and maybe the trio in this room were indeed innocent.

"Did any of you know Buck?" Slater came out and asked.

Marsh was the first to respond. "I didn't know him, but after I saw a picture of him, I think he might have been at parties that Stephanie and I attended. He seemed familiar."

"But you never spoke to him or vice versa?" Slater pressed.

Marsh shook his head. "And I don't recall Stephanie showing any interest in him."

"Of course she wouldn't," Leonard snapped. "The man was scum. Stephanie wouldn't have given him the time of day."

Maybe. But there was that whole bad-boy, forbidden-attraction thing, and while Slater wasn't certain if that would have appealed to Stephanie, he couldn't rule out that the sex between them hadn't been consensual.

"What about the two of you?" Slater continued, glancing at both Pamela and Leonard. "Did either of you know Buck?"

"No," Pamela said, and Leonard repeated that, but it seemed to Slater there wasn't a whole lot of conviction in the man's answer.

"You're sure?" Lana challenged. "Because as we speak, there are people combing through old social media and articles. If there's any connection between Buck and the three of you, they'll find it."

"They won't find anything," Leonard snapped, and his glare had returned. But Slater thought he saw plenty of nerves beneath that steely stare.

"If I've crossed paths with Buck, I don't recall," Pamela muttered. "And I think I would have."

So, she'd given herself an out. Maybe a genuine one, but Slater didn't intend to trust any of them. His cop's instincts told him that they knew more than they were admitting.

"Like I said, I think I saw Buck at parties," Marsh spoke up. "It's possible, too, that he was an acquaintance of my ex. I seem to recall Taylor mentioning Patrick, and that means she likely knew Buck, too."

"Taylor?" Slater questioned, recalling the text Lana had gotten from a woman by that name.

Marsh nodded. "Taylor Galway," he provided.

Leonard muttered the woman's name like profanity. "She should be arrested for stalking and harassing both Stephanie and Marsh."

That got Slater's attention, and he also remembered Lana mentioning that Stephanie and Taylor had been friends but had a falling-out. "Stalking?" he prompted, aiming that at Marsh.

Marsh's sigh was long and heavy as if he was tired of rehashing this particular subject. "I ended my relationship with Taylor two years ago when I started seeing Stephanie. It was never serious between Taylor and me," he was quick to add. "Stephanie was always my one true love." His voice trailed off, and he blinked back tears.

"I assume Taylor didn't take the breakup well?" Slater asked.

"She didn't," Leonard snarled. "Like I said, she stalked

and harassed Stephanie and Marsh. Always trying to tear them apart. I wouldn't be surprised if Taylor was the reason Stephanie went into hiding."

Slater considered that a moment. Maybe it had played into it, but his money was still on the pregnancy and Buck. "Did you report any of Taylor's behavior to the police?" But he already knew the answer.

"No," Leonard said, confirming Slater's thoughts. The man wouldn't have wanted that publicity. "Marsh kept a file with dates and stuff in case…well, in case things escalated," Leonard explained.

"I'll want to see that file," Thayer was quick to interject.

Marsh nodded. "I'll send it to you." He swallowed hard. "I saw the photos of Stephanie that someone posted. I think Taylor might have done that."

"Any proof?" Thayer asked.

"No, but it's something Taylor would do. She hated Stephanie," he added in a murmur. "Taylor hired a PI to look for Stephanie when she disappeared."

"What?" Lana blurted. "Why would she do that?"

Slater had the same question. If Taylor hated Stephanie so much, she'd want her gone, not found.

Marsh gave another of those weary sighs. "Because Taylor said until I had a clean break with Stephanie that I could never move on. She wanted Stephanie to tell me to my face that it was over between us."

Slater decided they were painting a picture of a deeply troubled woman. One who might not be emotionally stable.

Marsh took out his phone. "Yesterday, shortly before I learned that Stephanie had died, I got a text from Taylor," he said, scrolling through his messages. "It was about Stephanie."

"A text about Stephanie?" Lana said. "And you're just now telling us?"

"I just now remembered," Marsh muttered. "Once I heard Stephanie was dead, I forgot all about it. All I could think of was the woman I loved had been murdered."

Marsh's hands were trembling now. So was his voice. The cynical cop in Slater wondered though if it was all an act. Marsh continued to scroll until he found the one he was clearly looking for, and he held up the screen so Slater and Lana could read it. According to the contact, it was indeed from Taylor.

I found Stephanie, Taylor had texted. Now, this can all finally be over.

Chapter Eight

Despite the sickening worry and dread, Lana smiled when she saw Cameron on the FaceTime call to Joelle. The baby was sleeping, and everything about his precious little face looked so peaceful. Lana was thankful for that. She didn't want him to sense any of the fear.

But the fear was there.

For Lana, it was bone deep. And it wouldn't be going away until they had answers about Buck's accomplice, who might or might not be Taylor. At the moment, they just didn't know, but Lana was hoping they could soon remedy that since Detective Thayer had already called the woman. Taylor hadn't answered, but Thayer had left a terse voicemail for Taylor to contact her right away.

Maybe Taylor would do that and admit to any part she'd played in Stephanie's death. While Lana was hoping, she added that maybe Thayer was getting yet more details in the interviews with Marsh and Lana's parents. Slater might pick up on something, too, since he was observing them.

Lana had elected to wait in the break room for those interviews to finish and had been trying to get some work done using her phone, but she'd finally admitted her focus was practically nil and had made the call to Joelle.

Thankfully, Joelle had understood how important it was

for Lana to see the baby and had quietly slipped into the makeshift nursery. The sight of Cameron had given Lana some peace of mind. So had seeing the nanny in the room with the baby. Ditto for Joelle wearing a shoulder holster and gun. Joelle was an experienced deputy and would protect not only her own baby but Cameron, too, if there was a threat.

"You haven't seen anyone suspicious?" Lana verified after Joelle had slipped out of the nursery and back into the hall.

"No." Joelle smiled, but there was a steely resolve in her cop's eyes. "And if I did, there are armed ranch hands here to back me up. Also, Luca's downstairs. He'll be here until Duncan gets home."

Lana already knew all the security precautions, but it was good to hear them repeated.

"How are things going there?" Joelle asked.

Lana's mind was whirling with everything they'd learned, and it was hard for her to sort out what Slater had already told Duncan in an update call right before he'd left to observe the interviews.

"I suspect my parents know a lot more than they're saying about Stephanie and Buck," Lana admitted.

Joelle's quick sound of agreement told Lana that the deputy had come to the same conclusion. "Your father won't make it easy for the cops to investigate any wrongdoing."

"He won't. He did speak to Slater and me without his lawyers, but he had two with him when he went in for the official interview with Detective Thayer. I suspect they'll keep him and my mother from saying something they'd rather keep to themselves."

And it riled Lana to the core that they would do that instead of leaving no stone unturned to get justice for their murdered daughter. Yes, Buck was dead, but there was no absolute proof that he'd actually killed Stephanie. It was possible his accomplice had done that.

Lana mentally stopped and shook her head.

She couldn't see Marsh or her parents sneaking into Stephanie's hospital room to kill her. But maybe one of them did. Or perhaps it'd been Taylor. That's why it was so important to speak to the woman, but Lana reminded herself that what Marsh had said about Taylor might not even be true. He could be throwing Taylor under a bus to cover up his own guilt. Still, she did recall Stephanie saying that she and Taylor were no longer friends.

The break room door opened, and thankfully this time Lana didn't reach for her gun. A sign that hopefully her nerves were settling just a little. Her nerves settled even more when she saw Slater.

"Joelle, call me if anything…well, if there's anything," Lana told the woman before they ended the call.

"Is everything okay at the ranch?" Slater asked, tipping his head to her phone.

Lana nodded. "I just wanted to see Cameron, so I Face-Timed with your sister." She went closer, studying his face to see if there were signs that he was about to deliver some devastating news.

But Slater shook his head. "Nothing new came out in the interviews. Your dad admitted on the record that he knew Buck had fathered Stephanie's child, but he said he got the info from an anonymous call made to one of the PIs he keeps on retainer."

Lana wanted to roll her eyes. "The PI could have hacked into police records to get it, or my father could have another mole here in Austin PD." Either, or both, was possible, and it was a reminder for Lana not to trust someone just because they were a cop.

Slater took hold of her hand and gave it a gentle squeeze. "Your mother broke down during her interview. The tears seemed real enough."

That didn't surprise Lana. "Stephanie was my mother's golden child. Well, more golden than me, anyway. She knew she stood no chance of pushing me into an arranged marriage, but I believe she thought she could pressure Stephanie into it."

"Pressure?" Slater questioned.

"Stephanie's been arrested twice. Once for DUI and another for possession of a small amount of narcotics. Both times, our parents got her out of it. No parole, no community service. The charges just went away. Stephanie never came out and said it, but I think she was worried they'd hold that over her and use it to keep her in line." She paused. "Obviously, that didn't work."

Slater stayed quiet a moment. "Maybe it did. Have you considered that Stephanie being in hiding was exactly what your parents wanted? No, that doesn't mean they wanted her dead," he was quick to add. "It could mean that they'd hoped to sweep the pregnancy under the rug and have her return to marry Marsh."

Lana thought back through her conversations with Stephanie, and while her sister had never admitted to something like that, it could definitely be true. And that meant she had possibly been used as a dupe in all of this.

Slater's grip tightened on her hand, and he eased her to him. No kiss this time. He just held her while she tried to process another disturbing possibility in this investigation.

"Do you want me to go ahead and call Sonya so we can start the drive back to Saddle Ridge?" he asked.

Her first instinct was to say yes because she desperately wanted to see the baby. But Lana held back on that response and spelled out her concern. "Be honest. If I'm near Cameron, will that put him in more danger?"

Slater pulled back from her and met her gaze. "I don't know. If we go with the theory of Buck wanting to eliminate any competition for his family estate, then there shouldn't be a threat to Cameron and you since Buck's dead."

True. But the threat still felt very real. "No other relatives who might take up claim to the money?"

"No. I checked on that while I was in observation for the interviews. With Patrick and Buck both deceased, the inheritance would go to their heirs. Right now, that's only Cameron, and there isn't anyone on record who could challenge that claim."

Lana didn't want a penny of that estate for Cameron, but she also knew it might not be her decision to make. "What about heirs who might come forward? A secret baby maybe?"

"It's possible," he admitted, "but I can't see Buck working with someone who could inherit something he wanted to keep all for himself."

"No," she agreed. "So, maybe not a threat for the money but possibly Buck left orders with his accomplice. Orders to kill me because I helped hide Stephanie from him."

"Maybe." He paused, repeated that and then groaned softly. "But this feels bigger than that. Buck could have killed you on the spot, but he didn't. He stunned you instead and was obviously going to try to escape with you."

"He could have just wanted a human shield," Lana muttered, blinking back the flashbacks. "The plan could have been to kill me as soon as he was out of harm's way."

If so, that bolstered her revenge theory, that Buck wanted her to pay for helping Stephanie. But would he have been so obsessed with payback that he wanted to strike out at her from beyond the grave?

Or was this about something else?

Something that involved her parents and maybe Marsh, too? If so, she and Slater could dig into that in Saddle Ridge.

"Call Sonya," Lana said just as her phone rang, and the moment she saw the caller, she answered it on speaker. "Taylor," she greeted, but she didn't manage to say more because Taylor spoke right over her.

"Why does an Austin cop want to talk to me?" Taylor demanded. "She left a voicemail telling me to contact her. What does she want?"

Lana ignored the woman and went with a question of her own. "Where are you, Taylor?"

Taylor's huff was plenty loud. "Why does an Austin cop want to talk to me?" she repeated, enunciating each word as if talking to a child.

Lana debated how to go with this, but then Slater gave her a nod. "The cops want to talk to you about Stephanie's death."

"Of course," she said in the same tone as an annoyance but not anything big. "Well, they'll waste my time and theirs because I don't know anything about it. She's dead, period." Taylor paused. "She is dead, right? That wasn't all some kind of stupid hoax, was it?"

"Stephanie's dead," Lana verified, speaking around the sudden lump in her throat. Even though she and Stephanie weren't best pals, it still hurt to hear Taylor's callous attitude toward her sister.

"Good," Taylor declared, but then she must have realized who she was talking to. "I'm sorry for your loss and all, but you know I'd be lying if I said I wish Stephanie was alive."

"Yes," Lana softly agreed, and then went with another question. "Why did you hate Stephanie so much?"

A burst of air left Taylor's mouth, not quite laughter but close. "Oh, let me count the ways. I was seeing Marsh when Stephanie horned in on our relationship. She got your parents and Marsh's to persuade him to dump me so Stephanie and he could go through with what would have basically been a business merger marriage."

Lana thought back to something Marsh had said. "Marsh called Stephanie the love of his life."

That brought on a string of raw profanity from Taylor, and she ended it with, "No way in hell. He just said that to keep your precious daddy on his side. Marsh has political aspirations, too, and Leonard Walsh is his ticket. That's all."

Lana wasn't sure she'd ever heard Marsh mention anything about politics, but it was possible he was brownnosing her father to keep in his good graces. But Marsh's feelings for Stephanie had seemed genuine. *Seemed.*

"Now that Stephanie's out of the way, Marsh will come back to me," Taylor went on. "And I can play nice with your father, too, because that's how much I want Marsh."

"Did you want Marsh enough to kill Stephanie?" Lana blurted before she could stop herself.

Taylor made an outraged gasp. "No. Of course not. That man on the news killed her. The same man who tried to murder you."

It didn't surprise Lana that the attack had already hit the media, and she wondered just how much detail was already out there. "So you didn't have any part in Stephanie's murder? Because that's what the cops want to question you about."

"No part whatsoever," Taylor insisted. "And I'll tell the detective that, too. There's no crime in hating a man-stealing ex-friend." She paused. "I've heard some rumors. Did Stephanie have Marsh's baby?"

Slater pressed his finger to his mouth in a *keep quiet about that* gesture. Lana hadn't planned on spilling it, anyway. "Why would you care if the child is Marsh's?" Lana argued.

"Because a baby would give him a tie to Stephanie. I don't want any ties." Her tone was now one of a pouty child. "I want him to see her for what she was. A cheater who didn't care one bit about him. If Stephanie gave birth to his baby, then he might never get over her."

Lana couldn't be sure, but it sounded as if Taylor choked back a sob. She doubted the sadness, or whatever emotion she'd heard, had anything to do with Stephanie, though.

"You should talk to Detective Thayer about this," Lana finally said. Not that Thayer would answer the question of the baby's paternity, but the conversation might end up being productive for the investigation.

"I don't want to talk to her," Taylor whined. "In fact, I'm not going to talk to any cops. They'll have to arrest me first, and then I'll use my lawyers to bury them."

That was a threat with no teeth because Thayer had cause to interview Taylor. The woman's hatred for Stephanie was plenty motive to work with Buck to commit murder.

Taylor ended the call, but before Lana could even put her phone away, it rang again, and she saw yet another familiar name.

"It's Julia Munson," Lana told Slater. "Someone I work with at Sencor." She answered it and said, "Julia, I'm putting you on speaker. Deputy Slater McCullough is here with me."

"Hello, Deputy McCullough," Julia greeted, and she launched right into the reason for the call. "We found something that probably won't be a news flash to you, but it con-

firms something. We interviewed visitors at the hospital
where Stephanie died, and a new father, Asa Burkhart, was
recording the maternity ward where his daughter had just
been born. I'm sending you the footage now."

Moments later, Lana's phone dinged again, and she automatically held her breath. Julia had said this wouldn't be
a surprise, so Lana already had an idea of what Slater and
she were about to see. Still, it felt as if someone had clamped
a vise around her lungs.

The recording loaded, and there were a couple of seconds
of the new father panning his phone around while providing
a few verbal details like the name of the hospital, the room
number and the obstetrician. When the camera shifted toward the other end of the hall, Lana saw the man.

Buck.

He was in a small alcove with the vending machines, and
he peered out. Just seeing him gave Lana another slam of the
flashbacks of him stunning and grabbing her in the parking lot. But those slams were a drop in the bucket compared
to what she felt as she watched him move out of vending
and across the hall. He disappeared into Stephanie's room.

Lana nearly shouted to alert someone to stop him. But
the avalanche of dread came when she realized it was too
late for that. Buck had already murdered her sister and now
he, too, was dead.

That was all of the footage, the blur of motion as Buck
went into Stephanie's room. The new father had obviously
finished recording since there was no footage of Buck coming out.

"The hospital security cameras were tampered with,"
Julia explained, "but they were working again by the time
you came back to the hospital with the baby. There's about

a half-hour lapse between Buck entering the room and your arrival."

A half hour when Lana hadn't known that her sister had been murdered. "Yes," Lana said. "I was driving around, deciding what to do. Stephanie had wanted me to take the baby to Slater, but I decided to go back and talk to her, to make sure she was certain this was the right thing to do. I didn't see Buck when I left the first time, but I believe I saw him after I came back."

"You probably did," Julia provided. "We got footage from a dash camera of a taxi that shows Buck outside the hospital thirty-two minutes after he went into Stephanie's room. That would have given you time to drive around and return."

So he had lingered around. Maybe because he'd been trying to find Stephanie's baby. It sickened Lana to think about what could have happened when she saw Buck outside her sister's room, how close he had been to Cameron.

"Was anyone with Buck?" Slater asked.

"No," Julia answered, "but we're checking for other dash-cams and private security equipment to try to track his movements. There are traffic cams around there, but it's my guess he avoided those since Austin PD hasn't been able to find any footage of him."

That was Lana's guess, too. Clearly, Buck had been concerned about being recorded, and that's why he, or maybe his accomplice, had tampered with the hospital security cameras.

"There's more," Julia added a moment later, and Lana could tell from her coworker's tone that this was not going to be good news. "I'm guessing you're both familiar with a woman named Taylor Galway?"

Lana certainly hadn't expected Julia to bring her up. "Yes. In fact, she called me right before you did."

"Did she admit to hiring a computer hacker?" Julia asked.

"No," Slater and Lana answered in unison.

"I thought not. It's not something you'd admit to a cop," Julia added. "Anyway, last night Taylor hired BoBo."

Lana groaned and looked up at Slater to provide an explanation. "BoBo is a well-known hacker with no loyalty whatsoever. His favorite scam is to have a client pay him well for info and then to turn around and find out how he can get even more money by informing someone of the hacking."

"Bingo," Julia agreed. "And about an hour ago, BoBo, aka Robbie Jansky, called here asking to speak to you. He said you'd be very interested in some information he came by. I told him you were tied up with some personal stuff and agreed to the thousand bucks he was asking for."

"I'll pay you back," Lana was quick to say.

"I knew you would, and I also figured it'd be worth the price. BoBo usually has something good. And, Deputy McCullough, I know all of this must be setting your cop's teeth on edge, but please understand, we don't use any of the hacked info in court cases. We use it as more of a jumping-off point to find our own data and sources to corroborate what he gave us."

Julia had been right about Slater's teeth being on edge. There was definitely some disapproval on his face, but that didn't stop him from pressing Julia for what she'd learned. "And did this hacker give you something good this time?"

"He did." Julia stopped, sighed. "Well, you might consider it more of a hornet's nest, but here goes. BoBo hacked into Leonard's emails and learned that Lana's father not only knew Stephanie was pregnant, but he also knew her location at least for the last three months she was alive. There's a flurry of emails about it between him and one of his PIs."

Lana wanted to curse, and it meant her father had out-

and-out lied to her. Of course, she suspected that wasn't the first time he'd done something like that.

"The PI had Stephanie and Lana under surveillance," Julia went on. "And Buck, too."

"Buck?" Slater repeated.

"Buck," Julia verified. "The emails don't come out and say that Leonard knew Buck had gotten Stephanie pregnant, but Leonard instructed his PI to keep close tabs on the man to make sure he didn't go sniffing around Stephanie again."

"And did he keep close tabs on Buck?" Lana wanted to know. Because if he had, her father might have known that Buck planned to kill Stephanie.

"He did. There's another flurry of reports about that and even some surveillance-type photos of Buck shopping and eating out."

"Please tell me Buck was with someone in those photos," Lana said. "Someone who could have been his accomplice."

"Nothing, but again, this is a jumping-off point. Using the hacked PI reports, we now have some locations where we know Buck was. You know how this works, Lana. We'll go to those locations and talk to people. Look for more security footage. We'll create a digital map of where he was and who he might have encountered."

Yes, Lana did know this was how it worked. The info from BoBo was essentially tips from a criminal informant, and none of it could be used to make an arrest. However, if the accomplice did turn up on camera or through eyewitness accounts, then the cops could get the pieces to put the person behind bars.

Lana hoped.

She had to believe there'd be justice for her sister and a

safe future for Cameron. That she wouldn't have to spend the rest of her life looking over her shoulder for a killer.

"Now, to the hornet's nest," Julia added a moment later.

Lana shook her head. "I thought that was my father knowing about Stephanie and Buck."

"No, there's more. I just don't know if it's related to Stephanie or if it means anything at all, but the way it's worded makes me think there's something your dad's trying to cover up."

"What?" Lana managed to say.

Julia cleared her throat. "Does the name Alicia mean anything to either of you?"

Lana felt as if someone had punched her, and she figured from the way Slater's jaw tightened, he felt the same way. "Alicia Monroe," he provided. "My father was investigating her murder when he was killed. And we recently learned that Buck was a person of interest in Alicia's death."

"Yes, I pieced that together when I did a search for the name. The email didn't mention her surname, by the way," Julia tacked onto that. She stopped, muttered an apology. "Let me start from the beginning. In one of Leonard's emails to his PI, the PI expressed some concern about Stephanie being a loose cannon. His exact words," she emphasized.

"Did my father say why?" Lana asked.

"The timing fits for him finding out she was pregnant so maybe that's it. But it was also around the time your dad first mentioned Buck and that he needed to be monitored. Again, Leonard's exact word. And now here's the hornet's nest. Leonard adds, and I quote, *I don't want another Alicia on my hands.*"

"Oh, God," Lana heard herself mutter.

She looked up at Slater to see his reaction. Every muscle

in his face had turned to iron. And Lana knew this was indeed a hornet's nest.

Lana cursed. Had her own dad played some part in murdering Slater's father?

Chapter Nine

Slater sat in the living room of the safe house and continued to scour the reports that were pouring in. Reports from Duncan, Luca, Julia and Detective Thayer. Nothing was as nerve-rattling as Julia's earlier news.

I don't want another Alicia on my hands.

Still, Slater was hoping he'd find something to either link Leonard to Alicia's and his dad's murders or be able to clear him as a suspect. After all, everything was circumstantial. Even that remark about Alicia. Leonard could have possibly just been worried about Buck murdering someone else, and in this case, that someone else would be Stephanie.

But there was a problem with that theory.

How had Leonard even known about Buck's connection to Alicia? Slater had only recently learned of it himself. And if Leonard had indeed suspected that Buck murdered Alicia, why hadn't he given that info to the cops?

That was one of at least a dozen questions for which Slater didn't have an answer, and it was the reason he was glad Lana and he had decided to delay the trip back to Saddle Ridge so they could immerse themselves here in the investigation. Exactly what they'd been doing for the past three hours.

Getting to the safe house, though, hadn't exactly been

a piece of cake. Within minutes of leaving the police station with Sonya as backup, they realized they were being
followed. Slater had called in the plates to Thayer, who'd
quickly informed him that the vehicle belonged to a PI
agency that Leonard frequently employed.

Since Slater hadn't wanted the PI or Leonard to know
the location of the safe house, that'd meant trying to lose
it. Not easy in Austin traffic. So Slater had called in the big
guns. He'd had Thayer send out a patrol cop to pull over
the vehicle. The moment that'd happened, Slater and Sonya
had sped away.

Thankfully, that'd been the only drama of the afternoon,
and now Lana sat across from him, working on her laptop
and probably digging through the same reports he was. He
was hoping a second pair of eyes would catch something he
might miss. Hoping, too, that they'd get that one vital piece
of info that would blow this case wide open.

Slater hated that the hornet's nest revelations had come
from a hacker. As a cop, he wanted to find this BoBo and
arrest him. But as the son of a murdered man, he was grateful for what they might be able to use to build a case against
Leonard. So far, though, they didn't have nearly enough
for that.

Because he was a cop, Slater had had a fierce debate with
himself when it came to telling Detective Thayer about the
hacked emails. No way could she use any part of them in
her investigation, but it hadn't felt right to keep them from
her. And Lana had agreed. Even though it might ultimately
cast a negative light on Sencor for dealing with hackers like
BoBo, Thayer needed to have the big picture.

Thayer, of course, hadn't exactly thanked him for spilling details that would essentially muddy the investigative
waters and might lead to nothing. Still, Slater figured it

wouldn't hurt to have a third person, Thayer, looking at this new information with the hopes of verifying it. So far, though, verification simply hadn't happened.

"Ted Bennington," Slater said, hoping that by saying it aloud, it would jog something. Lana immediately looked up from her laptop, her attention zooming straight to him. "He's worked for your father for over twenty-five years." And he was the PI in the hacked emails. "Do you know him?"

"I've met him a couple of times when he came to visit my dad. He seemed all business, and he certainly never said anything about his actual job."

That made sense. Leonard wouldn't keep a blabbermouth on the payroll. "Bennington would have worked for him when Alicia was murdered, and we know that Stephanie went to a party at Alicia's. So, if it weren't for those three last words in the email, I would dismiss what Leonard said as some cautionary tale of him not wanting Stephanie to end up dead like Alicia."

Lana nodded. Then sighed. "But those three last words are there. *On my hands*," she recited. "That sounds a lot more personal than a cautionary tale."

It did, and that's why Slater was piecing together other theories. "Bennington or another PI could have seen or heard something that would ID Buck as Alicia's killer. I'm having a hard time figuring out why they wouldn't have taken that info to the cops, but maybe what they saw or overheard involved Stephanie. Not as a killer," he was quick to add.

She nodded again, and her forehead bunched up as she gave that some thought. "But maybe the PI heard or saw something that would in turn incriminate Stephanie. My dad would have definitely tried to cover that up, and in doing so, he might have covered up Buck's guilt. That could work." She paused. "But then why would Buck go after your father?"

Slater shrugged. "Maybe my dad was asking the wrong questions, and Buck got spooked."

"And maybe my father got spooked, too," Lana added. She set her laptop aside and leaned forward. "Just speculation here, but whatever the PI or my father learned about Alicia could make him some kind of accessory after the fact. That's some serious jail time."

"Yeah, it would be." And that led Slater to another point. "Alicia's body was never found, so maybe that's where Leonard comes in. Maybe he or his PI helped Buck dispose of the body in some way." He stopped and scrubbed his hand over his face. "But again, his reason for doing that would be to protect Stephanie."

Lana made a sound of agreement. "Stephanie never once mentioned anything about Alicia's murder, and I think she would have let something slip if she had witnessed it."

Slater made his own sound of agreement. "But what if Buck convinced Leonard that Stephanie had been involved in some way? That would spur Leonard to do a cover-up."

"It would, and it would also explain why my father wanted to monitor Buck. Maybe he wanted to make sure Buck didn't get too close to Stephanie." She stopped. "Of course, all the monitoring didn't stop Buck from killing her."

Slater heard the pain in Lana's voice. Saw it on her face, too, and he set his own laptop aside to go to her. Yes, it wasn't exactly a safe move, not with them being alone, but he hated to see her suffer like this. However, Slater had barely reached Lana before his phone rang, and when he saw Detective Thayer's name on the screen, he knew it was a call he needed to take.

"You're on speaker," Slater said when he answered. And he hoped she was calling with good news.

"I just interviewed Taylor Galway," the detective said.

Surprised, Slater shook his head. "I guess she changed her mind about coming in."

"Well, she brought three lawyers with her and spent most of the interview saying no comment, but she came in without any additional prodding."

"Did Taylor admit to posting those pictures of Stephanie?" Lana asked.

Thayer groaned softly. "That was one of the no comments. Ditto for hiring a hacker. About the only thing she did admit to was that she hated Stephanie and that she had an alibi for the time of Stephanie's murder. It's an airtight alibi, by the way. She was front and center at some charity fashion show."

"As an accomplice, she wouldn't need an alibi," Slater muttered.

"No, she wouldn't, but she might have thought it best if she wasn't anywhere near the hospital at the time of the murder. And she wasn't. The fashion show was on the other side of the city." Thayer paused a moment. "I didn't get Buck's phone records until after Taylor left so I'll have to get the woman back in here to question her about it."

Slater latched right onto that. So did Lana. They both moved closer to the phone. "Buck called Taylor?"

"Twice," Thayer verified. "But don't get your hopes up. It wasn't recent. The techs had to go back six years to find it. Hardly a smoking gun unless they'd been planning murder all this time."

No. Those calls were likely about something else. Probably a party or something.

"Any calls about a murder would have likely been done

on burner phones," Slater muttered. "What about the phone Buck had on him when he died?"

"A burner, but he hadn't used it to call anyone yet. There weren't any in his house, either, but there were two crushed ones in his garbage. The techs will see if they can recover anything from those. Other than the phones, there was no evidence in his house as to what he'd been planning."

So Buck had been thorough. Slater had hoped he wouldn't be. "Have the techs been able to access any of Buck's emails?"

"Not a one," Thayer said. "Everything on his laptop was encrypted, and so far, they haven't been able to get past it. They'll keep trying," she tacked onto that, maybe just trying to give them a glimmer of hope. "What about the two of you?" Thayer asked. "Have you found anything?"

"No," Slater said, and Lana echoed the same. It was Lana, though, who continued.

"If the hacked emails do point to my father as being Buck's accomplice, my father will never admit to it. In fact, we won't even get to ask the question because his lawyers will block it," Lana spelled out. "So I'm thinking of calling my mother to see if she knows anything."

"You think she'll admit it if she does know something?" Thayer asked. "Because I didn't get the impression she'd go against your father."

"She won't," Lana was quick to say. "But I think she's grieving for Stephanie, and that makes her vulnerable." Lana stopped, cringed. "I know that sounds callous—"

"It doesn't," Slater interrupted. "You need answers about your sister's death, and your mother might be able to provide them. And, no, I'm not saying Pamela had anything to do with killing her own daughter, but she's got eyes and ears, and she might have heard or seen something that'll help us ID Buck's accomplice."

"Yes," Thayer quickly added. "All of that. I have no idea if this accomplice is dangerous and will come after the two of you. Or heaven forbid, the baby. But I know I'll feel a whole lot better once we have this person. Call your mother," she insisted. "And let me know what she says."

Lana assured Thayer that she would, and Slater ended the call just as Lana took out her own phone. However, she didn't press her mother's number. She sat there a moment as if trying to gather her thoughts. He didn't blame her. This could turn out to be a critical conversation.

"If I tell her you're listening, then my mother will almost certainly be more careful about what she says," Lana said. "But I want you to hear every word. You might pick up on something I miss."

He nodded, though he knew what this meant. If the call was on speaker and Pamela spilled something incriminating, then her lawyers could argue that the admission had been obtained illegally. But she could only do that if she knew Slater was listening.

Slater cursed because he knew what he was about to do. He was going to bend the hell out of the law with the goal of finding a killer's accomplice. No way would he have done it if the threat to life had been over, but it wasn't. Lana and possibly the baby could still be in the line of fire.

He nodded. "Put the call on speaker," he instructed. "I won't say anything to let her know I'm listening."

She nodded as well, and she finally pressed her mother's number. Thankfully, they didn't have to wait long because Pamela answered on the first ring.

"Lana," her mother said, the word rushing out with her heavy breath. "Are you all right?"

Since this was more concern than the woman had previously shown, Slater was surprised. Clearly, so was Lana.

"I'm safe," Lana replied, her response obviously cautious.

"Good." Her mother let out another heavy breath and repeated it. "I was worried because you refused the bodyguards your father wanted you to have."

"Yes, and we got rid of the PI he had following us," Lana was quick to point out.

"Your father and I are both worried about you," her mother said as if that excused everything. "We don't want you involved in something that could be dangerous. Deputy McCullough can't protect you the way we can."

Lana looked at him and managed a weary smile. Despite everything that was going on, Slater latched right onto that smile, savoring it and committing it to memory. He and Lana hadn't had many quiet, warm moments, but that was one of them.

It didn't last.

"Are you there?" Pamela demanded. "Did you hear what I said?"

"I heard," Lana assured her. "Where is Dad now?"

"In his office. He's so upset," she added in a mutter, and she lowered her voice to a whisper. "Some man called him and said he'd been hired to hack into his emails. He tried to blackmail your father."

BoBo had obviously struck again. The hacker was attempting to get paid three times for his crime.

"Blackmail," Lana repeated. "What is he going to do about it?"

"I'm not sure," Pamela was quick to say. "He's with some of the lawyers and the PIs now."

But not the cops. Nope. Slater was betting Leonard wouldn't be reporting this to the police, and he made a mental note to tell Julia that she should warn BoBo that he could be in danger for poking a rattlesnake like Leonard.

"What emails did this man hack?" Lana pressed.

"I have no idea, but they must have been important because your father hit the roof. I'm sure he'll find the hacker and make him pay."

Yeah. Slater definitely needed to give Julia a heads-up.

"Mom, I'm calling to let you know that a video has surfaced," Lana continued. "It proves Buck murdered Stephanie."

Pamela gasped. "Oh, God. So it's true. He really did kill her."

"It's true," Lana verified, and then paused. "There's been a lot of security camera footage collected of Buck, and one of Dad's PIs was following him. Did you know that?"

"No." Pamela sounded adamant about that, too. "Why..." But that trailed off. "Because he was worried about Stephanie. Rightfully so." She cried out a hoarse sob. "I wish the PI would have been able to stop Buck. I wish someone could have, and then Stephanie would still be alive."

"Yes," Lana muttered, and it seemed to Slater that she was affected by her mother's grief.

"Alive," Pamela repeated a moment later, "and she would have done the right thing."

Lana pulled back her shoulders. "The right thing?"

"Stephanie would have married Marsh." Again, Pamela was adamant. "I'm sure of it."

That caused Lana's sympathy for her mother to vanish. "I think Stephanie's priority would have been her son." She looked as if she wanted to add a *maybe* to that, and he understood why. After all, Stephanie had had Lana bring the baby to him, so maybe she'd never had any intention of raising the child.

"I think you're wrong," Pamela argued. "Stephanie showed no interest in being a mother."

"That might be, but she had a baby," Lana argued right back. "Your grandson."

"That child is not my grandson," Pamela spat out.

Lana's eyes went cold and flat. "So you won't be challenging me for custody of him?"

"Of course not…" She stopped again. "Wait, are you saying you intend to raise that baby?"

"My nephew," Lana said. "Yes. I love him and I'll raise him. I think that's what Stephanie would want me to do."

"Stephanie would have wanted to put her past behind her and marry Marsh. Marsh is a very forgiving man, practically a saint, but I don't believe even he would want to raise Stephanie's mistake. Unless…has Marsh said something to you about that? Is he willing to raise the child with you?"

Lana cursed, and it wasn't under her breath. It was plenty loud enough for her mother to hear. Pamela scolded her, but Lana talked right over her. "Stephanie did the paperwork to declare Slater as the baby's father, so if I raise Cameron with anyone, it'll be him."

"With that cop?" Pamela said like the profanity Lana had just used. The woman geared up for what would no doubt be a tirade, but Lana ended the call.

"Sorry for bringing you into that," Lana muttered. "I don't expect you to be a father to Cameron."

She was giving him an out, but Slater didn't jump on it. At the moment, he wasn't sure what his future would be with Lana and the baby, but he sure as hell didn't want to be excluded.

Sighing, he moved onto the sofa with her, but before he doled out any TLC to repair the damage her mother had just done, he tapped her phone. "Let Julia know to warn BoBo."

She nodded so fast that calling Julia must have already been on her to-do list. Lana sent the text, and then every last drop of energy seemed to drain right out of her. Or so he thought. But then Lana did something that he was certain shocked both of them.

She kissed him.

Her mouth landed on his, not particularly hard, but this wasn't just a peck of reassurance, either. It was a full-blown kiss that she quickly deepened.

The taste of her roared through him and fired up everything inside him. Much too hot, much too fast. This was the kind of kiss that lovers shared. A foreplay moment right before landing in bed. And while his body was suddenly all up for that, Slater figured it wasn't a good idea. Not at the moment, anyway.

Lana only took her mouth from his when she was forced to breathe, and she gulped in some air. "I'm not going to say I'm sorry," she insisted. "I'm not going to regret this." She stopped, though, and squeezed her eyes shut a moment. "All right, maybe I regret it some. It feels as if I'm using you to help me get through the grief."

Slater wanted to nip this in the bud. "Were you attracted to me before Stephanie died?" he asked.

She blinked, nodded. "Yes."

"Then the heat is real, period, and there's no rule against kissing someone you're attracted to because it feels good. Or because it makes you feel as if you're not in this alone. Because you're not."

Lana stared at him a long time, and the corner of her mouth lifted as if she might manage a smile. The sound of her phone ringing put an automatic stop to that, though. She muttered something about it probably being her mother and looked at the screen, only to shake her head.

"It's Taylor," she said, and Lana's sigh told Slater that she really didn't have the desire to deal with the woman, but that didn't stop her from answering the call on speaker.

"I want you to meet me, and I don't want you to bring a lot of cops with you." Taylor said in lieu of a greeting. "Just Deputy McCullough and you. Hear that? Just the two of you. I can't make it today, but I'll be at True Blue Coffeeshop tomorrow morning at nine."

"And why would I want to go there?" she asked. "Why do you want to see me?"

Taylor huffed. "You'll want to do it because it's important." She added a duh.

"If it's that important, why not just tell me over the phone?" Lana demanded.

"Because I know something you don't, that's why." The woman's tone was beyond mere snark. "Be there tomorrow if you want to know the name of the person who teamed up with Buck to murder your sister."

Chapter Ten

Lana made the mistake of taking in a deep breath just as Slater walked into the living room after finishing his shower. He smelled amazing, not just of soap, but his own unique scent that lingered just beneath.

His hair was damp, and he ran a hand through it, all that was needed to make it look as if it'd been tousled and fallen in the perfect way to frame his face. A face that apparently had the ability to arouse her with a mere glance.

If they hadn't been neck-deep in an investigation, she might have gone the reckless route and kissed him again. But she instinctively knew that a kiss wouldn't just stay a kiss. The heat had escalated too much for that. The next time their mouths met, they'd likely end up in bed. That's why she'd kept her distance from him the night before and now this morning. And she'd been faring fairly well until she'd seen this hot, damp cowboy version of the man who seemed to have nailed down more than his share of hotness.

Lana cleared her throat and drank some coffee while she glanced out at the Austin skyline. She certainly hadn't expected to spend another night at the safe house, but that's what she and Slater had ended up doing. All to accommodate Taylor, who wouldn't budge on giving them the info unless it was in person. Of course, it had occurred to them that this could all be a ruse to draw her and Slater out, but after a long debate, they had decided to go for it.

With serious precautions.

Even though Taylor had insisted they not bring any cops, that wasn't going to happen. Detective Thayer and some of her fellow officers had already scoped out the coffee shop, and while they would be keeping watch in a building across the street, one of the cops would be undercover as a waitress. After all, if Taylor truly did know something about an accomplice and had withheld that, the woman could be charged with obstruction of justice.

Taylor would no doubt curse and protest if an arrest happened, but Lana didn't care. The only thing she wanted was the name of the person responsible so he or she could be arrested. Then, she and Slater could return to Saddle Ridge, and…well, she didn't know what would happen next, but "next" couldn't even begin until she was certain Cameron would be safe.

"How's the baby this morning?" he asked, tipping his head to her phone she was still holding. Slater also knew that while he was showering, she'd phoned his sister.

"He was awake and so alert," Lana said, well aware that she sounded like a gushing new mother. But Cameron had indeed been alert, and even though she'd read that a newborn's eyes couldn't focus well, it had seemed the baby was looking right at her.

"You'll be back with him soon," Slater assured her.

"Yes, hopefully soon and with no killer after us." She waved that off, though, when he started toward her, no doubt to dole out some TLC. "It's okay. I don't have much faith that Taylor can actually give us a name, but I'm hoping whatever she tells us will lead to something."

Slater made a sound of agreement and sank down on

the sofa next to her, bringing his scent and that amazing face even closer to her. "If Taylor is the accomplice, then the danger could be over even if there isn't enough to arrest her. Everything in her background points to her being an obsessed ex-girlfriend. She has no history of any kind of violence and no criminal record."

That was all true. Marsh hadn't even gotten a restraining order against Taylor when she'd basically stalked him. And not once had she attacked Marsh. Well, nothing official anyway, and Marsh certainly hadn't mentioned it.

"You're saying that without Buck to do her bidding Taylor won't try to kill us," she stated.

Slater nodded. "I can't say the same, though, about what she might do to Marsh, and I hope he's taking precautions. Taylor won't be happy if he doesn't reunite with her now that Stephanie is out of the picture."

Again, that was true, and while it would be awful if Taylor hurt or killed him, Lana had her own concerns without taking him on.

Slater's phone dinged with a text, and Lana immediately guessed who it was. And she was right.

"Sonya's waiting for us out front," Slater said as he read the message.

That meant it was time for them to leave for the True Blue Coffeeshop. Time to step out the door and pray that all their security measures were enough to keep them alive.

Since the plan was for Slater and her to return to Saddle Ridge right after the meeting, they grabbed their things, and Lana locked up on their way out. They got in the cruiser in the garage, checking their surroundings as Slater backed out.

Lana glanced at Sonya, who was also making some glances around, but she thankfully didn't see any alarm on the deputy's face. Didn't see anything or anyone suspicious, either.

Both she and Slater had already mapped out the safest route to the coffee shop, so they didn't go the most direct way since it would have meant long stops at traffic lights. Stops where someone could have taken shots at them. Instead, they went the side streets that were not only less busy but also meant fewer stops.

When they arrived at the True Blue, Slater went past the shop and as planned parked in a lot just around the corner. Of course, anyone looking for them would easily spot the cruiser, but they hadn't wanted to use a lot where someone would have had time to plant explosives or such.

They parked, and after getting the green light from Thayer, she and Slater went inside while Sonya waited in her cruiser. The deputy would be able to swoop in quickly if something went wrong and get Slater and Lana out of there fast.

Still keeping watch, they stepped in to the expected strong scents of coffee and sugary pastries. True to its name, the decor was of varying shades of blue, and despite it being crowded, Lana noticed Taylor right away. She was at one of the back booths, away from the storefront windows. That was by design as well, since it was where the undercover cop had seated her.

Taylor was drinking something white and foamy from a cobalt mug while reading something on her phone and didn't seem to immediately spot them. When Slater and Lana slid into the seat across from her, she finally looked up.

"I thought you might chicken out and not come," Taylor grumbled. "You'll be glad you didn't."

Lana hoped she was right, and she wondered if Taylor knew what kind of risk she was taking. Especially if she was about to spill anything about the hacker she'd hired. Thayer wouldn't arrest Taylor on the spot for that, but Lana had no doubts that the woman would eventually be charged. For now, though, the plan was to see if Taylor actually had any info helpful to the investigation.

Slater waved off a waitress who came over to ask if they wanted anything, and he pinned his stare to Taylor. "Tell us why we'll be glad about deciding to come here."

Taylor had a long sip of her drink first, and when she lifted her gaze, Lana saw the red in her eyes. Maybe from crying. But Lana figured she'd shed no tears for Stephanie. This had to be about something or someone else.

"Who's Buck's accomplice?" Slater came out and asked.

Annoyance flashed through Taylor's eyes. "I'll get to that, but there are some other things you need to know. Marsh and I are over. Yesterday, when I went to his place to try to comfort him, he basically told me to get lost. The SOB didn't even want to see me." She clamped her teeth over her bottom lip for a moment. "After all the waiting around I did for him, he wanted nothing to do with me."

That didn't surprise Lana, and judging from the sound Slater made, it didn't surprise him, either. Marsh was all about Stephanie. Well, he seemingly was anyway, and if he'd planned on getting back with Taylor, he likely would have done it after Stephanie disappeared. Did that mean that Taylor was about to try to get some revenge by naming Marsh as the accomplice?

"So, this means I don't care what happens to the SOB," Taylor went on. "And I'm done protecting him."

That got Lana's and Slater's attention. "You protected Marsh?" Slater questioned. "How?"

"By not telling the cops that Marsh knew where Stephanie was hiding out. He knew," Taylor insisted, shifting her gaze to Lana. "Marsh found out just a week before Stephanie was killed. And I think your father knew that Marsh had found out. He might have even been the one to tell Marsh."

Again, Lana wasn't surprised since she now knew that her father had indeed learned Stephanie's location. It was something he probably would have passed along to Marsh in the hopes that it would spur Stephanie and Marsh to reconcile.

"Did Marsh go see Stephanie when she was here in Austin?" Lana asked.

"Probably," Taylor spat out. "Of course, he never admitted that to me, and I don't have any actual proof that he saw her. But Marsh was a sad, sick puppy when it came to Stephanie, and he was too blind to see that Stephanie didn't even want him. I blame your father for that, too. He made Marsh believe the only woman for him was your precious sister."

Lana blamed her father for that as well. But then, he'd done a lot of things that she disapproved of.

"How did you learn that Marsh knew where Stephanie was?" Slater pressed when the woman fell silent.

Taylor's attention went back to her drink. "I had a PI keep track of him. I did it for his own good," she was quick to add. "Because I needed to know if he was about to make a huge mistake by trying to see Stephanie. Like I said, I was protecting him."

"Yet Stephanie is the one who ended up dead," Slater threw out there.

Taylor's gaze slashed back to him again. "Marsh didn't kill her. He's not Buck's accomplice."

"Do you believe that because you're still in love with Marsh?" Lana wanted to know.

"I believe it because it's true," Taylor snarled. "I didn't ask you to come here so I could get you to arrest my ex-lover. I want your father arrested."

Lana waited, but Taylor didn't add more. She certainly didn't add any proof, and then it occurred to Lana what might be going on here. Taylor clearly blamed Leonard for orchestrating the relationship between Marsh and Stephanie, and Taylor wanted him to pay for that.

"Are you saying that Leonard is Buck's accomplice?" Slater demanded.

Taylor gave a firm nod. And that was it. Nothing more.

Slater huffed. "If you have proof that Leonard is the accomplice, then you should have told Detective Thayer."

"I'm not telling her anything," Taylor snapped. "She questioned me like I was a common criminal, and I won't be treated like that."

"So instead you're telling us, knowing we'll report it to Thayer," Slater summarized. On a heavy sigh, he leaned back in his seat. "There's just one problem with that. No cop will arrest Leonard Walsh just because of what you've said. They need proof."

Taylor gave him an indignant look. "I have proof," she said, picking up her phone from the table. "I remembered this picture I took, but it took me a while to find it because I've put my photos in several different online storages over the years. It's all the proof you'll need that Leonard and Buck are best buds."

Lana held her breath and waited while Taylor tapped her screen and showed them the photo. It appeared to have been taken at a party, not a recent one, either, and it was of her father and Buck. Her father was smiling and had his arm slung around a very youthful, fresh-faced Buck. There were no traces of the thug that Buck had become in recent years. In this shot, he looked like the other preppy-dressed partiers milling in the background.

One of those preppy partiers was Marsh. Lana had no

trouble recognizing him, either. He was standing back from Buck and Leonard, but he didn't seem to have his attention on them.

"When was this taken?" Slater asked.

"According to the date in the storage cloud, it was nearly twenty years ago," Taylor answered. "That would have been my first year of college. I think Leonard was there because Marsh's family hosted it."

So that's why Marsh was there. Perhaps Lana's mother had been, too.

Slater made an odd sound, a sort of grunt that came deep from within his chest, and Lana turned to see what'd caused it. She doubted his reaction was because of this old picture of her father and Buck, which in no way proved they were best buds or had ever conspired to commit murder.

Slater took the phone, causing Taylor to snarl out a protest, but he ignored it and enlarged the photo. Not the portion with her father and Buck. But of the person next to them. And that's when Lana saw it.

Or rather Lana saw *her.*

Alicia Monroe.

Sweet heaven. It was the young woman who'd been murdered nearly twenty years ago. The woman whose murder Slater's father had been investigating. Slater clearly saw her, too, and he muttered some profanity under his breath.

"Buck was a person of interest in Alicia's murder," Slater said. "And here they are."

Yes, they were in the same photo, which was proof that Buck did indeed know her. But in this picture, there was an odd sort of dynamic going on. Marsh was looking at Alicia. Lana could see that now. And Alicia wasn't looking at either Buck or Marsh. No. Alicia and Leonard were staring at each other, and in that frozen snapshot of time, Lana could practically see the attraction sizzling between them.

Lana gasped. Oh, mercy. Had her father and Alicia been lovers?

Chapter Eleven

While Slater read through the latest report from Detective Thayer, he kept an eye on Lana. The worry was still etched on her face, but she was definitely more relaxed as she sat in the rocking chair and fed Cameron his bottle. Slater thought he was more relaxed as well now that they were back in Saddle Ridge.

But being home didn't mean they were safe.

He'd hoped Taylor would be able to give them proof of Buck's accomplice so the person could be arrested and any potential threat neutralized. That hadn't happened, though. The woman hadn't provided them with any proof that Leonard and Buck were coconspirators. Heck, she hadn't even given them proof that Leonard had been involved with Alicia.

It had certainly looked that way, though, to Slater.

And that created a boatload of questions and concerns. Had Leonard and Alicia had an affair? Maybe. Julia at Sencor was digging into that. But even if the pair had been lovers, it didn't mean Leonard or even Buck for that matter had been responsible for Alicia's death.

Still, the photo was pretty damning since Leonard was a married man, and at the time of that lustful look, he'd been nearly forty, and Alicia had been just eighteen. Any relationship between them would have been a scandal, but it wasn't anything Leonard could be arrested for.

Or even questioned about.

He and Lana had discussed that on the entire drive back to Saddle Ridge, and they'd agreed that if they confronted her father about it, he'd dismiss it as a simple party photo. Which it very well might be. That's why Julia and Lana were looking for more, and Slater was certain Lana would get back to the search when she'd finished feeding the baby.

He was thankful Cameron had needed a bottle. Thankful, too, that Lana had been the one to give it to him, and to burp him. Even with all the uncertainty surrounding this investigation, Lana needed this moment or two of downtime.

The other thing they needed was a long-term plan. For now, staying at his family's ranch was a good temporary solution. Here, in this makeshift nursery where Cameron had plenty of protection. Here, in the two guest rooms he and Lana were using where none of their suspects could come just waltzing up and try to finish what Buck had started.

But *here* wasn't home for Lana.

Soon, she'd want to find somewhere more permanent to live with Cameron. Slater was just hoping she'd hold off on that until Buck's accomplice had been arrested.

Lana was still holding Cameron against her shoulder when her phone dinged with a text. "It's Julia," she relayed to him, keeping her voice at a whisper. She glanced through whatever Julia had sent, sighed and got up to ease Cameron back into his crib. The baby didn't even stir and stayed fast asleep. "She just emailed me a report with some pictures."

Slater went to her, and they moved to the other side of the room where they'd set up a small office area, and she opened her laptop to access the email and two attached photos. Not of her father and Alicia but rather of Buck and

Stephanie at a party. These weren't from twenty years ago, either, and looked fairly recent.

"This was taken last year," Lana provided, reading through the report in the email. "Julia found them on social media." She paused to read some more. "Julia also interviewed four people who were at that party, and two of them verified that Stephanie and Buck had come together. Another, Cassandra Milburn, has agreed to talk to me about Stephanie."

Julia had provided the woman's number with instructions for Lana to call Cassandra first chance she got. Lana immediately did that, putting the call on speaker when it was answered.

"Lana?" the woman greeted. "Julia said you'd be calling me, and that Deputy Slater McCullough would be with you and that he'd want to talk to me, too."

"Yes," Lana verified. "You're on speaker, and Deputy McCullough is listening." She paused. "I don't believe we've met."

"We haven't. Stephanie told me about you, though, so when Julia brought up your name, I knew who you were."

"You were friends with Stephanie?" Lana asked.

"Friendly," Cassandra corrected. "We traveled in the same social circles and have similar backgrounds. My mother was an assistant attorney general for the state. Old money and a mile-wide snobbery streak," she added in a tone to indicate that had been a thorn in her side.

Yes, that was a similar background, and Slater was hoping that meant Stephanie had confided in this woman.

"How honest do you want me to be about your sister?" Cassandra came out and asked.

"Honest," Lana insisted.

"Good. Because I didn't want to paint a rosy picture when Stephanie was going through a tough time."

Lana sighed again. "A tough time with Buck?"

"No. With your parents. They were pressuring her to marry Marsh, and she was rebelling in her own way, and one of those ways was to hook up with Buck. I don't need to tell you that he was a bad boy to the core. Not the redeemable kind, either. I always thought Buck was dangerous, and when Stephanie got involved with him, I tried to warn her that she was playing with fire."

"Why did you think Buck was dangerous?" Slater asked, hoping this would dovetail with Alicia's murder as well.

"Because I dated him when I was sixteen," she admitted without hesitation. "He was an exciting adrenaline junkie who knew how to have fun. His mood could also change in a heartbeat." Cassandra's voice wavered on that last word.

"Was he ever violent with you?" Slater pressed.

"No, but after we had an argument, I thought the potential was there for violence. He scared me, Deputy McCullough, and that's why I ended things with him. He didn't take that well, and I didn't know how to handle him because I was a teenager, and he'd been my first boyfriend," Cassandra added. "After the breakup, he stalked me for a while until my mother intervened and put a stop to it. She never told me what she said to him, but Buck quit bothering me."

So, Buck didn't handle rejection well. At least he hadn't back then. Maybe that's what had happened with Alicia? Maybe he'd lost his temper and killed her, and Alicia hadn't had Cassandra's powerful mother to intercede.

"Was Buck ever violent with my sister?" Lana asked.

"I don't think so. They had a hot and fast affair, and like I said, I believe Stephanie was rebelling against your parents. And then she got pregnant," Cassandra tacked onto that.

Lana jumped right in with another question. "You knew she was pregnant?"

"Yes, I'm a doctor, and Stephanie came to me after she'd done a home pregnancy test. I can't get into the specifics of what we discussed since doctor-patient confidentiality continues even after death, but I will say that Stephanie was worried about how your parents would react."

Lana and he both stayed quiet a moment, processing that. "But she wasn't worried about Buck?"

Cassandra wasn't so quick to answer. "I thought you might ask that, and I've been trying to figure out what to say. Judging from the stories on the news, Buck murdered her? Is that right?"

"Yes," Lana confirmed.

Again, Cassandra took her time to respond. "I will say that whenever I met with Stephanie, she didn't claim to be scared of any person in particular. She was just adamant that I not tell anyone she was pregnant."

Slater considered that a moment. Since Cassandra had already warned Stephanie about Buck being dangerous, it seemed reasonable that Stephanie would have voiced any concerns she had about the father of her baby. Maybe, though, those concerns had surfaced later.

"I'm really sorry about Stephanie," Cassandra added a moment later. "Could you please tell me what will happen to her child?"

"He'll be taken care of," Lana was quick to say. "I have an online appointment with a lawyer tomorrow and will be petitioning for custody."

"Good, I'm glad," Cassandra said. "I have to go, but if you have any questions you think I might be able to answer, feel free to call me."

"I will," Lana assured her, and ended the call.

They sat there in silence for several moments, and Slater

decided to spell out what they'd just learned. "Buck probably didn't sexually assault Stephanie."

Lana made a sound of agreement. "And she likely went into hiding, initially anyway, because of our parents and not because of Buck. That doesn't mean, though, that Buck didn't threaten her afterward."

Slater was fast to agree with that as well. "If Stephanie had trusted Buck, she wouldn't have done the Acknowledgment of Paternity, naming me as the baby's father."

Lana's gaze came to his and held. "You could challenge me for custody because of that. Stephanie obviously wanted you to raise her son."

"Because she knew I'd protect Cameron from Buck. Or from your parents. Or from anyone else for that matter who might be a threat to him," Slater reminded her. "And, no, I still have no intentions of challenging you for custody."

Lana didn't seem surprised by that, only reassured. Good. She had enough to deal with without worrying about Cameron's future.

"Thank you," she muttered, and she glanced at her laptop as if ready to go back to work.

But she didn't.

She stood, went to him, leaned down and kissed him. Slater hadn't seen it coming so he hadn't had time to steel himself for the heat. It hit him full blast and dissolved the reins he had on this need for her. With no reins, he moved right into the kiss as well, letting her taste and the feel of her mouth take him to another time, another place. Where there was no investigation, no threat. Where anything was possible.

He started to stand so he could pull her to him, but Lana placed her palm on his chest, indicating he should remain seated. Instead, she was the one who initiated the body-to-body contact by moving onto his lap. Her breasts landed against his chest, and her hip pressed against the zipper of his jeans.

Slater immediately felt the heat skyrocket. So did the need. Then again, the need was always there when it came to Lana, but with her mouth on his, it drilled the point home.

Everything inside him pointed to her. To this edgy heat that she had created inside him. To all these intense feelings he had for her. And there were so many feelings. Too many to sort out, and even if he had wanted to do that right now, he couldn't. No way could he think straight when she was kissing him like this.

She slid her hand around the back of his neck, bringing him even closer to her. Deepening the kiss. And giving the heat another jolt that it in no way needed. This wasn't just a kiss. This wasn't just foreplay. This was many steps beyond that, and it was those steps that could lead them straight to bed if they weren't careful.

Slater's body was all for them landing in bed, but his brain knew there would be consequences. Consequences that he did not want for Lana. When the timing was better, when it was right, he wanted only pleasure for her. Now, though, there would be guilt and doubt, and so many other things that he didn't want her to feel.

Even after mapping out all the reasons why he should stop, Slater didn't do that. He took more of the kiss. Took more of Lana. Until the need had turned into a fiery ache that was demanding to be sated.

"Just a little more," she murmured when he started to ease back from her.

The more was, well, a lot, but Slater just sank right into the kiss and let her take what she needed. Somewhere along the way, he lost sight of why they should even stop, and he found himself taking hold of her and pulling her closer. And closer. Until he'd turned Lana so she was now straddling him.

This definitely wasn't going to cool them down, but it gave him a good glimpse of what it would be like for them to have full-blown sex. It'd be amazing, that was for certain.

Amazing, with really bad timing.

He latched onto that thought again, but it wasn't helping him fight this battle he was having with himself. Slater couldn't figure out how to make himself stop. Thankfully, though, Lana seemed to figure it out. He eased back, gulping in air, and she looked at him.

"I'm not sorry," she said just as Slater said, "Don't you dare apologize."

The corner of her mouth quivered, and she smiled. It was an incredible thing to see, and it eased some of the ache in his body. Not the need, though. Nope. It was there to stay. But it felt so good to see her smile.

"You've been a fantasy of mine for a long time now," she admitted.

He was flattered. And aroused all over again. Slater hoped, though, that she wasn't about to qualify that with something he didn't want to hear. Something along the lines that it would never work between them. Thankfully, she didn't go that route. She just kept it at that, which kept the door open to them fulfilling a fantasy or two when things weren't so uncertain.

"Work," she said as if trying to convince herself to move.

But she didn't move one inch. Lana stayed on his lap and continued to stare at him until that need took on a whole new urgency. Slater was a hundred percent certain he would have acted on that urgency had Lana's phone not started ringing. Both of them muttered some profanity at the interruption and then checked the crib to make sure the sound hadn't woken up the baby. It hadn't. Cameron stayed asleep.

Lana took out her phone and muttered more profanity when she saw the name on the screen. So did Slater, because it was Pamela. While Lana's mother wasn't the last person he wanted to speak to, she was close to it. Apparently, Lana felt the same way because she groaned softly when she moved off his lap and onto the chair next to him.

"Lana," her mother said the moment she answered, and Slater immediately heard the distress in the woman's voice. It seemed as if she'd spoken her daughter's name on a sob.

"What's wrong?" Lana asked, clearly picking up on her mother's tone.

"That man who tried to blackmail your father just called me," Pamela blurted, her words running together.

"BoBo," Slater muttered on a groan, but he kept his voice low enough so that Pamela wouldn't hear him. He figured Pamela might hang up if she knew he was listening.

"What did he want?" Lana pressed.

"He wanted money." Pamela made another of those sobbing sounds. "He claimed to have emails from your father and one of his private investigators. Emails that prove your father knew where Stephanie was the whole time she was pregnant."

So, Austin PD hadn't managed to arrest BoBo yet if he was calling Pamela. Or maybe the guy was already out on bail and looking for yet another way to cash in on the hacking job that Taylor had paid him to do. It was also possible that BoBo hadn't managed to get a cent from Leonard so he'd then gone after Pamela.

"Is it true?" Pamela pleaded. "Did your father know where Stephanie was when she was pregnant?"

Lana groaned again. "What did Dad have to say about it?"

"He's not here, and he's not answering his phone. Marsh doesn't know where he is, either. I'm sure your father's avoiding me because he doesn't want to answer my questions."

"Is he aware you know about the emails?" Lana asked.

"I think so. When he didn't answer his phone, I sent him a text to let him know the blackmailer had called me, and I asked him how I should handle it. Then the blackmailer told me about those emails so I tried to call your father again. I left him a scathing voicemail," she added, and broke down into what sounded like a full-fledged crying jag.

Slater figured the woman had to be plenty upset, but considering she'd been married to Leonard for nearly four decades, she must have known he was capable of keeping a secret like this. Yet she seemed stunned and heartbroken. Either it was an act or Leonard had truly done a stellar job at hiding the truth.

And maybe not just this truth, either.

He thought of that photo, of the way Alicia had been looking at Leonard. Then he recalled Cassandra's warning about Buck being dangerous. It was possible that Leonard had known about Buck's dangerous streak, too, and that the streak had gone all the way back to Alicia. That left Slater with a huge question.

Had Leonard known that Buck murdered Alicia?

If so, Leonard might have been hell-bent on keeping Buck away from Stephanie. It could have been why he'd had both Buck and Stephanie under surveillance of his PIs.

"Your father knew where Stephanie was," Pamela went on, "and he didn't tell me. He let me worry all that time. And I was worried sick," she ranted. "I needed to see my daughter. He knew that, and still he didn't tell me."

"I'm not trying to excuse what Dad did," Lana tried to

explain, "but Stephanie wouldn't have wanted to see you or Dad. She didn't want to see anyone, including me. Maybe because she was scared of Buck or maybe because she didn't want to face you while she was pregnant."

Her mother didn't answer right away, but she continued to cry. "There's more," she said. "Lana, there's more."

Lana's gaze fired to his, and Slater saw plenty of fresh concern there. Slater was sure he was showing some concern, too, because he didn't like the sound of that.

"What?" Lana asked when her mother didn't add anything to that.

"After that horrible blackmailer called me, I phoned Taylor."

"Why?" Lana was quick to demand.

"Because I heard your father mention her. Something about her being the reason this man was trying to blackmail him. I didn't know what Taylor had done, but I figured she'd be able to give me answers."

"And did she?" Lana prompted after her mother broke into a fresh sob. This one was even louder than the other one.

"Taylor gave me…something. Something I don't want to believe," Pamela wailed. "Lana, I think I need to leave. I think I should go to a safe house, a place like the one you set up for Stephanie."

Now there was alarm on Lana's face. "Did Taylor threaten you? Are you scared of her?"

"No." And that was all Pamela said for several long moments. "I'm not scared of Taylor. I'm scared of your father."

Lana groaned and scrubbed her hand over her face. "Why? What happened? What did Taylor tell you to make you afraid of him?"

"She said…" Another sob stopped Pamela. "Taylor said

that it was your father who killed Stephanie and that it wasn't the first time he'd killed someone." Both her voice and her breath broke. "Taylor said he killed Slater's father, too."

Chapter Twelve

Part of Lana just wanted to stay shut inside the ranch house with Cameron and Slater. She wanted to hold on to this peace that settled over her whenever she was with the two of them. But the peace was merely a facade, and she didn't stand a chance of it being real until she had all the answers about her sister's murder.

And Slater's father's.

One look at Slater, and Lana could see there'd be no peace for him, either. For nearly a year he'd been driven to find the person who'd ended his father's life, and now he might finally know.

Might.

"My mother could be wrong," Lana spelled out. Not for the first time, either. She'd been saying variations of that for the past hour since her mother's bombshell call.

Slater finished reading through the latest text he'd gotten from Duncan and nodded. Yes, he was well aware that anything to do with her mother could end up being a wild-goose chase, but now that the allegation had been made, it needed to be investigated. They had to know if Leonard was truly the person behind Sheriff McCullough's, Stephanie's and maybe even Alicia's murders.

Of course, they couldn't just go charging in and demanding answers from her father. Nor could they simply send in the cops, because Leonard would just stonewall with his lawyers. No, this had to be done with some finesse, and Lana had known from the moment she'd ended the call with her mother that as Leonard's daughter, she was their best bet at learning the truth.

Slater hadn't immediately agreed to that, of course. He wanted her safe, but safe wasn't going to get them those answers.

"Your mother just arrived at the secure location," Slater relayed after firing off a text response to Duncan. "It's Ruston's apartment in San Antonio, and he's the one who escorted Pamela there. He doesn't actually live there anymore now that he's married and has a baby. He commutes from Saddle Ridge, but he kept the place in case he had to pull some all-nighters on an investigation."

"Good," Lana said. "Thank you for arranging that."

The accommodations probably wouldn't be up to her mother's usual high standards, but Ruston was a cop at SAPD, and that meant his apartment would have decent security. Not that Lana expected her mother to be in actual danger and in need of such measures, but still, precautions needed to be taken in case everything Pamela had said was true. If her husband was indeed a killer, then he might also go after a wife who'd revealed what could be his deadly secrets.

"The next step is for us to decide, well, the next step," Slater continued a moment later.

Yes, they'd discussed this, too, but Slater hadn't yet approved the plan that Lana had suggested.

"There's no proof of my father doing anything, nothing to arrest him on," she reminded him. "And there's the part about him stonewalling any and all cops who could question him about what my mother claims. But I believe he will talk to me, especially if I frame it as a visit to tell him about some concerns about my conversation with Mom. He'll want to know what I have to say."

She hoped. But her father could be unpredictable, and he might very well try to shut down any and all conversations.

"I could just call him and ask for a meeting," Lana went on, knowing she hadn't yet convinced Slater this was the way to approach this. "Of course, you'd go with me. Maybe Sonya, too, though it'd probably be best if she waited outside as backup."

Backup that Lana prayed wouldn't be needed. She didn't believe she and Slater would be walking into an actual ambush. She couldn't imagine her father arranging something like that at his home.

The muscles in Slater's jaw seemed to be at war with each other. "You really think your father is a killer?" he came out and asked.

It was something she'd been rolling around in her mind, and Lana still didn't know. "I'm not sure. I think he could be capable of murder," she admitted.

Slater's sound of agreement let her know that he felt the same way.

"As you know, he's ruthless, and I could maybe see him killing to cover up a crime." She had to try to ease the lump in her throat to get out the rest. "But for Stephanie, that feels different. It would have been premeditated. And for what? Because she'd defied him by getting pregnant with Buck's baby? That just doesn't make sense."

He made another sound of agreement. "Maybe your father had another motive for wanting her dead. For instance, maybe Stephanie was planning on blackmailing him about something. Or she could have been planning some bad publicity campaign to smear him."

Slater stopped, shook his head. "That doesn't seem like a strong enough motive, either," he amended. "Your father seems the sort to fight fire with fire. If Stephanie had threatened him in some way, he could have run his own smear campaign against her. He certainly would have had plenty of ammunition for that."

"True," Lana muttered. "And that brings us back to Buck. He had motive to kill Stephanie, and maybe my father isn't his accomplice. Taylor could be. Now, she's someone with motive to want Stephanie dead."

Of course, if Taylor was the accomplice, then that meant Leonard could be innocent. Well, of this particular crime, anyway. That didn't mean he hadn't had some part in killing Slater's father.

She took out her phone, lifting it for Slater to see. "Should I call him and arrange a meeting?" she asked.

Slater sighed. Then nodded.

Lana didn't waste any time in case Slater changed his mind. She pressed her father's number and was somewhat surprised when he answered on the first ring.

"Where's your mother?" her father demanded.

"I'm not sure," Lana lied. No way did she want to spill over the phone anything her mother had said. She wanted to see her father's face, to try to gauge if he was lying or withholding something. "What happened?"

Her father cursed. "I have no idea, but she's not here at the estate. I came home because one of the housekeepers called me and said your mother left with a packed bag about an hour ago."

That would have been when her mother had driven to meet Ruston, and it didn't surprise Lana that one of the "housekeepers" had alerted her father. Leonard no doubt had many employees to keep an eye on things.

"Mom called me," Lana informed him, "and I want to talk to you about some of the things she said."

"What did she say?" he demanded.

"I'll tell you when I see you," Lana insisted right back. "You said you were at the estate?"

"I am, but I want to know what your mother told you," he snapped.

"Slater and I'll be there in about thirty minutes," Lana said, and she ended the call, but not before hearing her father snarl out Slater's name.

Of course, Leonard tried to call her right back, but Lana declined the call as she went to the crib to kiss Cameron. The baby was asleep, and the moment she and Slater stepped out of the room, the nanny came out from the nursery across the hall and took the baby monitor that Lana handed her. They'd already talked to Joelle, Duncan and the nanny about this possible plan so everything was in place for them to leave immediately for the estate.

Including Sonya.

The deputy saw them coming down the stairs and stood to go with them outside to the cruiser. Slater, Sonya and Lana were already armed, all three wearing shoulder holsters. Lana had put a jacket over hers, but Sonya and Slater had kept theirs visible. She also knew the deputies were carrying backup weapons.

Slater had a quick word with Joelle and Luca, who'd be doing guard duty while they were gone. Which hopefully wouldn't be long. In an ideal scenario, her father would confess to, well, everything, and Slater could have him arrested. The threat to Cameron could be over and done within an hour.

Lana doubted, though, this would be an ideal scenario.

Her father likely wouldn't admit to anything, but in his shock over hearing what his wife had said, he might spill something they could use to build a case against him. And if he was innocent, then it would be time to take a harder look at Taylor. Or even Marsh for that matter, since it was possible that he'd been so jealous and outraged about Stephanie being pregnant that he'd snapped and had her killed.

As they'd done on previous trips both here in Saddle Ridge and in Austin, they kept watch, looking for any threats. Unlike those other trips, Sonya was driving in the cruiser with them so she could provide immediate backup if they were attacked along the route. But there were no signs of anyone suspicious, just the usual late-afternoon rancher and farmer type of traffic that would normally be on the road that led to the interstate.

Lana couldn't shut off her thoughts, and as each mile took them closer to the estate, she realized it'd been over five years since she'd been to her parents' home. For a good reason. They'd both made it obvious they hadn't approved of her lifestyle despite her military service giving her father some good press for a daughter "serving her country." Maybe that had been the difference between Stephanie and her. They'd both rebelled, but her rebellion had been tolerable compared to her sister's.

"You can still change your mind about this," Slater said, reaching across the seat to give her hand a gentle squeeze.

She looked at him, and for some reason the skin-to-skin contact made her think of that scalding kiss they'd shared. A kiss that probably would have led to a big *where is this going?* discussion if her mother hadn't called. At the time, Lana hadn't been happy about the interruption, but in hindsight, it was a good thing. The personal discussions would have to wait. As would more kisses.

And she hoped her body understood that.

At the moment, it only seemed to want to spur her to dole out another kiss.

"I won't change my mind," Lana answered. "We need to do this."

Slater didn't dispute that, but she figured he'd rather be doing this chat alone with her father. Or maybe with Sonya as backup and with Lana tucked away safely at his family's ranch. It was tempting for her to want the same thing, but there was no way she would let Slater face down her father without her.

As expected, the drive took only a half hour since it was on the outskirts of San Antonio and not directly in the city. Sonya followed the GPS to the massive wrought iron gates that fronted the twenty-acre estate. Every acre and every building on the grounds had been designed to impress. That included the sprawling three-story house that sat at the end of a tree-lined private road.

The gates were already open, letting Lana know that despite her not returning her father's call, he wasn't going to deny them entry. Then again, it was possible he kept them open these days since this wasn't a high-crime area.

Sonya pulled to a stop behind a shiny silver Jag that was already parked in the circular drive, and after taking a couple of deep breaths, Lana looked at Slater, and when he gave her a go-ahead nod, they got out. Like the rest of the house, the porch was massive and spanned all the way across the front of the house. Again, it was meant to impress with the nearly dozen steps leading up to it.

They went to the double doors to ring the bell. The doors opened, though, before she could do that, and she met her father's steely, narrowed gaze head-on. Yeah, he was not happy.

Her father was dressed in one of his pricey suits, a pale gray one that was nearly the same color as the expertly placed threads of "salt" in his salt-and-pepper hair. She doubted he'd groomed himself for their visit, either. This was his norm.

"This visit wasn't necessary," he grumbled. "You could have told me this over the phone."

Lana opened her mouth to argue that, but then she spotted the woman standing in the foyer behind her father. Taylor.

"What's she doing here?" Lana asked.

"I came to warn him about Marsh," Taylor spoke up before Leonard could answer.

Her father huffed, and while he didn't roll his eyes, it was a close enough gesture to let Lana know he wasn't happy about Taylor's visit. Or maybe he was objecting to her accusations. As far as Lana knew, Marsh was still the golden boy.

"Marsh is up to something," Taylor went on. "I just know it."

They stepped into the foyer, and Taylor came closer, moving to her father's side. Really close to his side. So that their arms were touching. It was a little thing, but it seemed…big. And Lana immediately wondered if something was going on with these two.

Were they having an affair?

But she rethought that. Until Marsh had ended things with Taylor only the day before, Taylor had seemed completely obsessed with the man. Still, that didn't mean Taylor hadn't had a relationship on the side.

Her father turned to Taylor, and again, it seemed to Lana that something passed between them. Something too intimate for this to be a visit for Taylor to gripe about Marsh.

"Taylor, I need to speak to Lana and Slater," Leonard said, clearly not inviting Taylor to be part of that conversation. No surprise there, since it would be a chat about things his wife had claimed.

"But I haven't finished telling you my suspicions about Marsh," Taylor protested, sounding like a pouty brat. "You need to hear them, Leonard. You need to understand that Marsh could be a dangerous man."

"I want to hear what you have to say," he assured her, "but I have to talk to Lana and Slater first."

Her father's words didn't match his expression. Leonard seemed to be ready to get rid of Taylor. However, he didn't spew out one of his usual tirades that he likely would have to most people. That could be yet more proof they were having an affair.

"I'll wait for you then," Taylor insisted, not heading for the door but into the formal living room that was just to their right. The moment the woman flounced in, a housekeeper came in to offer her a drink.

Sighing, her father gave Taylor one last glance and then motioned for Lana and Slater to follow him. He headed in the direction of his office, and along the way, Lana saw a man in a suit who was no doubt one of Leonard's assistants or lawyers. Maybe even a PI. She didn't know his name and was thankful when her father didn't invite him into the massive office with them.

"Where's your mother?" Leonard demanded the moment they were behind closed doors.

"Someplace safe," Lana settled for saying.

Her father cursed. "Did you convince her that she wouldn't be safe here, right here in her own home?"

"No," Slater and Lana said in unison. It was Lana who

continued. "Mom said she was afraid and she wanted to go where she wouldn't be at risk."

Leonard stared at her as if she'd just told him the most unbelievable lie he'd ever heard. "What exactly did she say?" he demanded, and now he wasn't just glaring, he'd also clenched his teeth so tight that Lana was surprised he could even speak.

Lana glanced at Slater, and while they'd already discussed what to say, she wanted to make sure he hadn't changed his mind about being so direct. His nod indicated he hadn't.

"Mom believes you might have had some part in Stephanie's murder—"

"What?" her father howled before Lana got a chance to finish.

"Were you Buck's accomplice?" Slater came out and asked.

If looks could kill, her father would have ended Slater's life right then, right there. "No," he said, his voice a low, dangerous growl. "Of course not. I wouldn't kill my own daughter."

"Not even if she was about to cause you a publicity nightmare?" Lana pushed.

Leonard turned that icy look on her. "No," he repeated. "Not even then, and I sure as hell wouldn't have worked with a hothead like Buck. I think the only reason Stephanie got involved with him was because she was trying to get back at me for pushing her to marry Marsh."

That was exactly what Lana had thought he would say. She certainly hadn't expected him to accept any blame. So that's why she went ahead and hit him with the next accusation.

"Mom also thought you might have had something to do with Alicia Monroe's death," Lana said. "And before you deny knowing who that is, I personally saw a photo of Alicia and you at a party."

Her father had already opened his mouth, no doubt to interrupt her again with verbal fire, but that caused him to go silent for a couple of moments. "What the hell are you talking about?" But he didn't give her a chance to respond. "You think because I was at a party with some woman who ended up dead, that I could have killed her?"

Lana shrugged. "Mom seems to think that's possible."

He tried to speak, but apparently the muscles in his throat didn't immediately cooperate. He gutted out some profanity, groaned and went to his desk to drop down in his chair.

"Your mother actually believes that?" he questioned with his face now buried in his hands. "She truly thinks I could have murdered Stephanie and that woman."

"My father, too," Slater added.

Lana expected that to ignite a fresh flash of temper in her father. It didn't. He groaned again and kept his hand on his face for what seemed an eternity. When he finally looked at them again, it wasn't anger she saw. But rather hurt.

Hurt that he could be faking, she reminded herself.

"Well, it's obvious someone has brainwashed your mother," he finally muttered. "I'm guessing you're not going to own up to it being you? Or you?" he asked, shifting his gaze to Slater.

"It was neither Lana nor me," Slater said, and now he was the one who paused. Maybe because he didn't intend to point the finger at Taylor. "Pamela called Lana out of the blue and asked for protection because she was afraid of your involvement in these murders." Slater stopped again. "Did you kill them?"

"No." He squeezed his eyes shut a moment and repeated

it. "I had nothing to do with murdering my daughter, Alicia or your father."

"Then why would your wife think that?" Slater pressed.

"I have no idea," Leonard was quick to say. "Maybe she's trying to get back at me for something she thinks I did."

"It must be a pretty bad *something* for her to accuse you of murder," Lana pointed out. "An affair, maybe? Or maybe lying to her about knowing exactly where Stephanie was when she was so worried about her?"

Her father didn't deny either of those things, and judging from the way his jaw set again, Lana thought he might order her and Slater out of his office. He didn't get a chance to do that, though, because two other things happened.

Slater's phone dinged with a text. When he showed Lana the screen, she saw that the message was from Sonya, and the deputy was giving them a heads-up that Marsh had just arrived and gone into the house. Moments later, she heard Taylor shout something.

Leonard gave a weary sigh when Taylor's shouting got even louder, and he stood and went to the door. He'd barely had time to open it when Taylor barged in.

"You aren't going to believe why Marsh is here," Taylor blurted.

"I asked her if she was responsible for Stephanie being murdered," Marsh quickly volunteered. "Because someone left this on my car."

Marsh held up a grainy picture of what appeared to be Taylor and Buck. If Lana wasn't mistaken, they seemed to be at the same coffee shop where Taylor had met with her and Slater.

"It's a fake," Taylor insisted. "I wouldn't kill your precious Stephanie," she snarled with Oh, so much venom in her voice.

Marsh looked at her, and it didn't take long for his stare to become a glare. "I don't believe you," he stated. "You disgust me."

Taylor whirled toward Leonard as if she expected him to defend her. He didn't. That only fueled the woman's anger, and she aimed all of it at Marsh.

"You disgust me," Taylor fired right back at him. "And I'll make you pay, Marsh. Just wait and see. You'll pay for what you just said."

And with that, the woman stormed out.

Chapter Thirteen

Slater listened to Taylor shouting profanities and threats all the way out of the house. Moments later, Sonya texted him to let him know that Taylor had gotten in her Jag and driven off. Slater was betting, though, that she wouldn't stay gone. There was something going on between her and Leonard, and Taylor would no doubt return once she'd burned off some of her anger.

"I'm sorry," Marsh muttered, directing the apology to Leonard. "I didn't know Taylor would be here, but when I saw her car, I thought she might be...well, I didn't know if she was trying to make you believe I was the one who killed Stephanie. I didn't," he emphasized, glancing at all three of them.

"But you believe Taylor did team up with Buck," Slater said, taking the photo from Marsh to get a better look.

Slater studied the image, but it was hard to tell if it had indeed been photoshopped. Even if it was the real deal, though, it didn't prove Taylor's guilt. After all, the woman had already admitted that she knew Buck.

"I don't know for certain," Marsh said. "But something's going on with her." He groaned, shook his head. "She wanted us to get back together, and when I told her no, that it was never going to happen, she just seemed to lose it."

Slater glanced at Leonard to see how he was reacting to that. Not well. He was scowling and looked to be on the verge of muttering something. He didn't. When he noticed Slater staring at him, he shut down and on went his poker face. If the man was having an affair with Taylor, though, he probably wasn't pleased about Taylor trying to reconcile with Marsh.

Well, maybe he wasn't.

It was possible that if an affair was truly going on between him and Taylor, it was only about sex.

"You can keep the photo," Marsh told Slater. "In case you want to send it to the crime lab. I took a picture of it," he added, lifting his phone.

Slater nodded, but while it probably wouldn't give them any new information, he would indeed send it to the lab since it possibly contained fingerprints of the person who'd left it. If those prints belonged to Leonard, then it could add to the circumstantial evidence against him.

Marsh said his goodbyes to Leonard and headed out, but when he opened the office door, Slater didn't see the guy in the suit who'd been there earlier, and he wondered if this "assistant" had stepped out to make sure Taylor had truly left.

"Where's your mother?" Leonard asked Lana the moment Marsh was gone.

Lana sighed. "I'm not going to tell you that."

And just like that, Leonard's fierce anger returned. "She won't answer my calls, and I have to talk to her. I need to find out why she's telling these lies about me before the lies get out of hand."

In other words, before the press picked up on them. But Slater had no intention of helping the man defuse that kind of bad press. Apparently, neither did Lana.

"No," she said, and there was no indication in her tone that she would change her mind.

Her father must have realized that, too, because he cursed again. "Get out," Leonard told them. "Both of you. Now."

Slater looked at her and nodded. They weren't going to get a confession or anything else from her father. The man had dug in his heels and had already taken out his phone, no doubt to get started on finding his wife. Slater had to make sure that didn't happen. At the moment, Pamela didn't have a guard with her, but that could be arranged.

He and Lana threaded their way through the massive house to the front door and out onto the porch. Still no sign of the guy in the suit, but Slater immediately noticed the black Mercedes that hadn't been there when they'd arrived.

Sonya stepped out of the cruiser and looked at them from over the top of the vehicle. "It's Marsh's," she said, tipping her head toward the thick gardens on the right side of the house. "He muttered something about going for a walk."

Slater immediately got an uneasy feeling about that. If Marsh had needed to cool off, why do it here? Why not just go back to his own place?

Some movement from the corner of his eye caught his attention, and Slater saw something else he didn't like. Taylor's car. It was parked up by the gate—which was also on the right side of the property. He couldn't tell, though, if she was still inside.

"She drove off but then came back," Sonya explained as Slater and Lana started down the steps.

Maybe waiting for all of them to leave so she could go in and try to mend fences with Leonard. But again, that made Slater uneasy.

"Did she get out?" Slater wanted to know. If she'd seen

Marsh walking, Taylor might have wanted to continue her argument with the man.

"It's possible," Sonya admitted. "The passenger side of her car is hidden by the gate post."

It was, and Taylor could have slipped out that way if she hadn't wanted Sonya or anyone else to see her.

"Get in the cruiser," he told Lana.

But he was already too late.

The shot blasted through the air, tearing into the wood column right next to where Lana was standing. She dropped onto the limestone steps. So did Slater, and he immediately tried to pinpoint where the shot had come from. If he wasn't mistaken, it had come from the area where Marsh had gone for his "walk."

Slater drew his gun and lifted his head. No sign of the shooter, but thankfully Sonya had taken cover back in the cruiser. That was where Slater wanted Lana to be right now, but there were eight porch steps between them and the driveway and another ten feet of space after that. Not especially far, but they'd be easy targets if they stood still.

Another shot came right at them, and the shooter had obviously adjusted his aim because this one smacked into the step just above Lana's head. Lana was clearly the target here, and the shooter had too good an aim. He had to get her out of the line of fire and fast.

Cursing, Slater caught on to Lana and rolled with her to the side. More shots came. One right behind the other, each tearing up the stone and sending shards flying. Slater prayed none of them hit Lana.

They finally reached the side of the steps, and they dropped down into the shrubs. The bushes definitely wouldn't stop any bullets, but at least this way, the shooter might not be able to see them.

"Stay down and let's move," Slater instructed. He wanted them away from the spot near the porch where the shooter had last seen them.

Lana had drawn her gun, too, and she kept it gripped in her hand as she maneuvered onto her belly. Her breath was gusting now, and she was probably getting hit with the mother lode of adrenaline. She had to be terrified, but she got moving, crawling away from the porch.

The shooting didn't stop, and even though Slater hadn't actually counted the number of bullets fired, he figured the shooter either had more than one weapon or had reloaded. In other words, he or she had come prepared for this.

But who was it?

Who was trying to kill Lana?

It was possibly Marsh, who hadn't actually gone for that walk after all but rather had positioned himself for this attack. But it could also be the guy in the suit who worked for Leonard. If so, Leonard would have been the one to order Lana's murder. Maybe just as he'd ordered Stephanie's.

However, Slater's money was on Taylor.

He had no idea if she'd had firearms training, but that wouldn't be hard to get. And with her temper, she could want to get back at Lana—especially if Taylor was Buck's accomplice.

I'm not working by my lonesome. I've got a helper. A cold-blooded one. And Lana and you are going to die.

Those had been Buck's dying words, and while Slater had hoped it was all a lie, it was possible this was the plan Buck had set in motion before Slater's bullet had killed him.

There was a flurry of more shots, and Slater moved so he could send his own bullet in the direction of the shooter. He double-tapped the trigger, hoping he'd get lucky and take out this person. There was no yelp of pain, though, no thud to indicate a bullet hitting flesh.

And the gunfire continued.

But Slater heard something else. The sound of a car engine, and it was moving closer to him and Lana. Hell, he hoped the shooter hadn't managed to get into a vehicle and was now planning on ramming into them. The alarm he saw in Lana's eyes let him know she was thinking the same thing.

His phone dinged with a text, and when Slater managed to get it out of his pocket, he saw Sonya's name on the screen. And her message eased some of the knotted muscles in Slater's gut.

"Sonya's moving the cruiser between us and the shots," he relayed.

It was a welcome ploy, but it wasn't without risk to Sonya. The cruiser was bullet-resistant, but that didn't mean gunshots couldn't get through. If the shooter was determined enough, he or she could now try to kill Sonya.

More shots came, and Slater could hear them now slamming into the cruiser. He could see the cruiser, too, through the tiny gaps in the row of thick shrubs. Sonya wasn't just maneuvering so the cruiser would be a shield. Slater thought Sonya was trying to get into position so he and Lana could be able to crawl into the cruiser through the passenger-side door.

In the distance, Slater heard a welcome sound. Sirens. Maybe Leonard had called the cops, but he was betting Sonya had been the one to do that. Even if Leonard's assistant wasn't the one firing those shots, Lana's father probably would have preferred to handle this himself and not deal with the publicity that was certain to follow.

At the thought of Leonard, Slater glanced back at the

porch steps. He couldn't actually see the front door from his position, but he didn't think it was open. He hadn't expected it to be, but where was Lana's father right now? Was he cowering inside, or was he waiting for his assistant to finish the job he'd started?

Sonya continued to draw fire as she backed the cruiser into place, and the moment she was dead even with him and Lana, she must have leaned across the seat because the back door of the cruiser opened.

There wasn't an easy way to get inside it since it meant them squeezing through the shrubs that scratched and tore at them. Still, it was better than staying put where they could be shot and killed if the shooter changed positions.

The wail of the sirens got even closer, and Slater gave Lana a final push through the shrubs so she could scramble into the back seat. He was right after her, and he slammed the door shut behind them.

"Get down," Slater told Sonya. "It's too dangerous to try to drive out of here."

Sonya made a quick sound of agreement and dropped down. Good thing, too, because the next shot finally weakened the side window and put a fist-sized hole through it.

Slater climbed on top of Lana, his front against her back so he could try to protect her. He knew she wouldn't thank him for the move. She wouldn't want him risking his life for hers, but Slater stayed put.

And waited.

He also lifted his head enough to try to see if the shooter was coming for them. One last-ditch effort to kill them before the cops arrived. But he didn't see anyone. Nor did he hear anything other than the sirens.

The shots had stopped.

Slater cursed, because that probably meant the shooter

was trying to get away, but he intended to have Leonard, Taylor, Marsh and the assistant all tested for gunshot residue. If one of them had fired all these shots, then the test might prove it.

"Two SAPD cruisers," Slater relayed to Sonya and Lana.

"I called them," Sonya said, and he heard her make a call, no doubt to fill the responding officers in on the situation.

The cops in the cruisers didn't drive toward the house. They stayed at the gate, maybe waiting until Sonya had given them a picture of what had happened. And what could possibly happen if the shooter started firing again.

"Unknown number of people inside the house," Sonya said, responding to a question she'd been asked. "But, yes, the owner, Leonard Walsh, is here. Or rather he was. And, no, I don't have eyes on him." Sonya paused. "What?" she blurted. "You're sure?"

That got Slater's attention, and the alarm shot through him when Sonya looked at him. He could tell from her expression that something was wrong.

"It's Taylor," Sonya said. "She's in her car. And she's dead."

LANA SAT IN the interview room at SAPD headquarters and read through the statement she'd just given Detective Josh O'Malley about the shooting. Slater's brother, Ruston, was there, standing with his back against the wall, but he hadn't participated in the interview because it could have been construed as a conflict of interest.

Because of where the shooting had taken place, everything was being done by the book. Her father had a lot of political pull, and it was obvious no one here wanted that pull used against them. But even her father couldn't stop himself from being interviewed.

And interrogated.

From what Slater and Ruston had said, Leonard had been treated just as anyone else in his position would have been. As a possible suspect or at least someone who might have key information. A woman had been murdered; the shooter had attempted to kill Lana and two cops.

That wasn't going to be swept under the rug.

"This is accurate," Lana said after reading the statement that she then signed. She figured Slater was doing something similar in the interview room across the hall. Now that they'd gotten the formality of the interview out of the way, she needed to see him. She needed to make sure he was truly okay.

They'd both been examined by EMTs, and their cuts and scrapes from the shrubs had been treated. Ditto for Sonya, who'd gotten nicked by some of the glass when it'd been shot out in the cruiser. But Lana knew none of their injuries were serious, which meant they'd gotten lucky.

Unlike Taylor.

As Lana, Slater and Sonya had been driven away from the estate in one of a patrol cars, she had gotten a glimpse of Taylor. The woman had been slumped against the steering wheel of her Jag, and she had a gunshot wound to the head. It hadn't looked self-inflicted to Lana, and she would be surprised if it had been, because Taylor didn't seem the type to take her own life.

"Can I get you some water or something to eat?" Detective O'Malley asked Lana as they stood.

She shook her head. Lana figured she should be hungry since she hadn't eaten since lunch, but there was no way she wanted to try to eat. Not with her stomach still churning.

When O'Malley walked out, Ruston went to her, and maybe because she looked ready to collapse, he put his arm around her and led her out of the room. Thankfully, Slater was right there, waiting, and Lana went to him, slipping right into his welcoming embrace. He brushed a kiss on her forehead, and while it was such a simple gesture, it took away some of the ice that had seemingly seeped all the way to her bones.

Mercy, it was wrong to need Slater like this, but Lana couldn't seem to stop herself. Maybe it was a combination of the intense attraction, the memories of that kiss, grief over her sister's murder and the spent adrenaline from coming so close to dying. If that was it, then it was a potent blend that made her want to hold on to him and never let go.

"Did everything go okay in there?" Slater asked his brother.

Ruston nodded but didn't get a chance to add anything before his phone rang. "I need to take this," he said, stepping away from them.

Lana eased back enough so she could look up at Slater. "What updates do you have?" Because she knew he'd been communicating with both Duncan and Detective Thayer in Austin. Communicating with the cops here, too, since so many of them knew him through his brother.

"Taylor was murdered," Slater said after he drew in a long breath. "The shot that killed her came from the window on the passenger side of her car."

Lana considered that for a moment, thinking of the placement of trees and shrubs by the gate. It was possible her killer had been able to make that shot without Taylor even seeing him.

But who had killed her?

"They tested my gun," Slater went on, "and the shot didn't come from me."

She hadn't thought for a second that it had. Slater had fired into the trees, not in the direction of the gate.

"Did Taylor have a gun with her?" Lana wanted to know. "Could she have been the one who fired shots at us?" Though the logistics of that would be hard unless Taylor had shot at them and hurried back to her car, only to be killed there.

He shook his head. "No gun and no GSR on her. The CSIs will compare the bullet that killed her to any others the shooter might have left behind."

"So, the theory is one gunman," she concluded. "And Taylor could have been killed either at the beginning of the attack on us or at the end."

"Either," he confirmed. "And since the attack only lasted a couple of minutes, the ME probably won't be able to pinpoint the exact time of the kill shot."

A couple of minutes. It had felt like a lifetime or two with them pinned down and bullets flying.

"Marsh is up the hall giving his statement," Slater went on. "But I heard him tell the detective that he heard the shots and hid so he wouldn't be hit. He thought Taylor was shooting at him."

That seemed reasonable since Taylor had threatened him. Well, it was reasonable unless Marsh was lying and had been the shooter.

"There wasn't any GSR on Marsh," Slater let her know before she had to ask. "Of course, he could have worn gloves and disposed of them somewhere on the grounds. The CSIs will look for that," he added.

Good. But twenty acres was a lot to search, and Marsh could have hidden them in plenty of places. Places he was well aware of, since he was a frequent visitor to the estate.

"Your father is still in interview, too," Slater went on.

"He waited until his lawyers were here before he agreed to give his statement."

"Did they test him for GSR?" Lana immediately wanted to know.

Slater's mouth tightened. "Not yet. His lawyers are fighting it, claiming that Leonard is a victim, not the perpetrator."

Lana huffed. "That could mean he's guilty." But she had to mentally wave that off. Her father was arrogant enough to believe he was above such measures of the law, and even if he was innocent, he likely would have refused any test.

"I'm hoping his lawyers won't be able to stall forever," Slater muttered, but there was enough doubt in his eyes to let her know that it could indeed be the outcome.

"What about my father's assistant and the housekeepers?" Lana asked. "Is it possible one of them was the shooter?"

"They're all being questioned, all being tested for GSR," he assured her. "The estate does have security cameras, but your father said they weren't on at the time, that he normally only has them on at night. Is that true?"

Lana had to shrug. "I know there are cameras, but he never gave anyone access to the control panel for the security system." She paused. "You think it's a coincidence that the cameras weren't on during the shooting."

"Maybe." Slater groaned softly. "I don't like coincidences, but maybe this is one."

"True," she admitted. "It doesn't feel right that my father would orchestrate an attack at the estate. If he wanted to send someone after us, he could have done that on our drive back to Saddle Ridge."

That wasn't exactly a comforting thought, but it's how she would have done it had she been a killer.

"Has my father said who he believes fired those shots?" Lana asked.

"He thinks it was Taylor and that she then killed herself." Slater took another of those long breaths. "I suppose it's possible if there was a second gunman who shot her and then took her weapon. He or she would have also had to wipe the GSR from her hands." He shook his head. "I'm not sure there was enough time for a gunman to do that in between the shots being fired at us. Unless…"

"Unless there were two people involved in this." She stopped, groaned. It was too much to think of having multiple killers after them.

"The CSIs are going through Taylor's house as we speak," Slater went on. "Ruston's been getting regular updates and texting them to me. They're already found two burners that were used to call Buck, and they're focusing on finding other communications she might have had with him."

"Burners," Lana muttered, and she let the meaning of that sink in. The phones could be proof that Taylor was Buck's accomplice. After all, if she simply wanted to talk to the man, she could have used her regular phone. "It was stupid of Taylor to leave those lying around."

"Stupid or she was set up," Slater said, spelling out exactly what Lana was thinking.

"It would tie up everything in a neat little bow if Taylor was the accomplice. She's dead and can't say otherwise." And that led Lana to another thought. "If Buck's real accomplice thinks he's out of potential hot water, maybe he won't come after us again. Maybe the attacks will stop."

"Yes," he murmured as if considering that. "No more attacks, but also maybe no answers about Alicia's and my father's murders. You might not ever be sure, too, of who worked with Buck to kill Stephanie."

Again, that was all true, and while Lana desperately wanted the attacks to be over and done, she needed the truth, too. And she was certain Slater felt the same. Neither of them would just let this drop, and soon, Buck's real accomplice would understand that and would no doubt once again try to kill them.

"We can go back to Saddle Ridge and regroup," Slater said, once again answering her unspoken question. "We can look for proof of someone entering Taylor's house to set her up."

Yes, that would be a good place to start, especially since she figured they wouldn't be getting any immediate answers from her father.

She turned to the sound of the approaching footsteps and saw Ruston making his way back toward them. He was still sporting the scowl that'd appeared on his face when he'd left to take a phone call.

"What's wrong?" Slater immediately wanted to know.

"This," Ruston said, holding up his phone so they could see the screen.

The image was clear enough, but Lana had to shake her head. "That's my mother."

"It is," Ruston verified. "I gave your mother the codes to my security system in case she had to step out for some reason and told her to keep the system on when she was there so that I'd get an alert if someone tried to break in."

That was a good precaution, one that Lana herself had suggested. That would prevent Ruston from having to personally check on her mother while he was at work.

"Your mother apparently did step out," Ruston went on, "and I just got a call from my security company because she didn't get the code punched back in time to prevent it from being triggered."

Lana shook her head. "Why would my mother leave your apartment?"

"That's something I think you'll want to ask her." Ruston motioned toward the time stamp of his mother's return, and she saw that it was about fifteen minutes ago. Then Ruston shifted to another photo of her mother. "I had the security company go back through the feed, and this is a photo of Pamela leaving."

Once again, he tapped the time stamp.

And Lana immediately realized why he was scowling. Because her mother had left the apartment over an hour before the shooting at the estate. That wasn't all. The security camera had caught Pamela's purse at just the right angle for Lana to see something else.

The gun that her mother was carrying.

Chapter Fourteen

Slater knew this had already been a hellishly long day, but it apparently wasn't over yet. After finishing with the San Antonio cops about the shooting, they'd returned to the ranch in Saddle Ridge, and even though Lana looked ready to drop after getting Cameron down for the night, she still had one more thing on her to-do list.

She had to call her mother.

Lana needed answers as to where the woman had been during the shooting. Answers that she'd then pass along to Duncan, Ruston, Thayer and any other cop involved in the investigation. Well, if there was anything new to pass along. For Duncan, that would be easy since he and Joelle were just down the hall in the main suite. Slater could update the others with short texts.

Sighing, Lana sat on the foot of the guest bed, the baby monitor right next to her, when she made the call to Pamela. It wasn't the first attempt since they'd seen that photo of her mother leaving the apartment with a gun in her purse. Lana had tried to call her immediately afterward, but the woman hadn't answered. Definitely not something Slater and Lana had wanted.

However, Pamela had texted back within the hour to check and make sure Lana was all right and to let her know that the San Antonio police had asked her to come in for an interview about the shooting. Pamela didn't offer any details of that interview and had messaged that she would be able to speak to Lana later.

Well, it was later, and Slater sincerely hoped the woman responded. If not, he was going to have to call Ruston again and see what he could find out. Slater wasn't surprised that the cops would want to speak to Pamela, since the shooting had happened on the estate where she lived.

And because of the recent rift she'd had with her husband.

Yeah, the cops would definitely want to question her about that, since it could play into motive. If she was the shooter, that is. Slater had no idea if Pamela was actually capable of that, but it was possible, especially if there had been an affair going on between Taylor and Leonard.

Since Lana put the call on speaker, Slater heard the three rings and silently cursed, figuring this was about to go to voicemail. It didn't, though. Pamela finally answered.

"Lana, are you sure you're all right?" Pamela immediately asked.

"Slater and I are fine. He's here with me, and I have the call on speaker so he can listen." Lana's tone stayed cool. "I'm sure you've heard, though, that Taylor is dead."

"Yes. It's all such a mess. The detective who questioned me wouldn't say what had happened so I called Marsh, and he filled me in."

Marsh, not Leonard, and that meant there was still a rift between husband and wife.

"Did you see the person who shot at you?" Pamela added.

Lana paused, maybe to see how her mother would respond to the silence, but Pamela kept quiet as well. "No," Lana finally said.

"I'm so sorry." Pamela sounded genuine about that, and it

made Slater wish he could see the woman's face so he could try to detect a lie. "Do you think it was Taylor?"

Lana sighed again, and instead of answering her mother's question, she went with one of her own. "Why'd you leave the apartment earlier today?"

"I told you. I went to the interview with the detective at SAPD."

"Not then, Mother. Before that. Before the shooting. You left the safe place you had us arrange for you, and you had a gun with you."

Again, Pamela went silent for several moments. "I didn't want to tell you about that, but I met with a private investigator." Another pause, even longer than the others. "I asked the person to dig up any dirt on your father. And I'm sure there's plenty of that to find."

Slater couldn't argue with that, but the timing seemed way off. "You were worried about your safety," Slater pointed out. "So why not just talk with the PI over the phone?"

"I did speak to her briefly, but I wanted to meet with her in person to make sure our conversation wouldn't be recorded. Leonard has a lot of important people in his pocket, and I didn't know if this particular PI was one of them. It's Julia Munson from Sensor. She works with Lana."

He and Lana exchanged glances, and Lana immediately fired off a text to Julia. No doubt to confirm there had indeed been a meeting.

"What do you expect Julia to find on Leonard?" Slater asked Pamela.

"Anything I can use. I plan on divorcing him," Pamela added, and her voice wavered. "And I'll need any and all ammunition. Before I left the estate, I copied some files from Leonard's computer, and I wanted Julia to see if there was something in them."

Slater huffed. "If you copied the files without permission, then you probably won't be able to use anything incriminating."

"That's what Julia told me, but I asked her to look, anyway." Another pause. "I want proof that he was having sex with Taylor. Taylor!" she repeated, and there was a jab of fury in her tone. "I've turned a blind eye to that sort of thing for years, but I'm fed up with it. Taylor flaunted the affair by telling her friends all about it. Leonard should have known the gossip would get back to me."

Slater wondered if Pamela had just spelled out her motive for the shooting. She could have fired the shots at him and Lana as a diversion with the actual target being Taylor.

"Did the detective who questioned you take your gun?" Slater asked.

"No. I didn't have it with me when I went to the police station. I took it to the PI's office because, well, as you said, I was scared. I didn't know if Leonard was going to use one of his goons to try to silence me."

And there was Leonard's motive all spelled out. Again, Taylor could have been the target to stop her from gossiping about their affair. It sickened Slater to think Lana could have been killed in what would have been just collateral damage to Leonard. Or to Pamela. Then again, the same could apply to Marsh.

As far as Slater was concerned, all three were still suspects, and that's why he sent his own text. This one to Ruston to remind him they needed to get Pamela's gun.

"Anyway, since I decided I could trust Julia," Pamela went on, "I asked her to put an entire team together to go through those files and find anything they could. Not just about his affair with Taylor but with others. I know there were others," she added in a mutter.

Slater thought of the photo Taylor had shown Lana and him. "Did he have an affair with Alicia?" Slater came out and asked.

"I honestly don't know," Pamela said, and all the anger seemed to have seeped from her. There was a weariness in her voice now. "I didn't suspect it at the time, but I asked Julia to go back as far as she could. If he carried on with Alicia, there might be some proof of it."

Maybe, and Slater figured it was practically impossible to keep something like that a total secret. Maybe Julia would be able to find something, and if so, there'd be the link from Alicia to the murder of Slater's father.

"I'd like to stay here at the apartment awhile longer," Pamela continued. "Maybe just a day or two, but I plan on getting my own place. Julia said she could set that up for me, too. Where will you go that's safe, Lana?" she tacked onto that.

"Cameron and I will be fine where we are," Lana assured her.

Lana obviously didn't give her mother her location, and Pamela didn't ask. The woman probably suspected, though, that Lana, the baby and he were somewhere in Saddle Ridge.

"Have a good night," Pamela said, ending the call.

Before Lana could even put her phone away, she got a text. "It's Julia," she relayed. "She confirmed my mother came in to see her today."

"Does the timing work to give her an alibi for not being near the estate during the shooting?" he asked.

She shook her head. "Not really. According to Julia, she had a long conversation with my mother over the phone, but their visit only lasted a couple of minutes, long enough for my mother to give Julia the files and to pay the retainer."

Pamela definitely hadn't mentioned that, and if she'd told

the detective the truth during the questioning, the San Antonio cops would be looking for any proof that Pamela was in the vicinity of the shooting.

As if Ruston had read his mind, Slater got a text as well, and he was glad to see his brother's response. He figured it'd please Lana, too, so he read it aloud. "'Detective O'Malley and I are going to the apartment now to take Pamela's gun. It'll be sent for immediate testing.'"

Good. That way, they'd know not only if it'd been recently fired but if it was the weapon that'd been used to kill Taylor.

Lana sat there, staring at her phone as if trying to process, well, everything. They'd gotten so much information over the past two days and had been attacked twice. And even after all that, they still didn't know if Taylor had actually been Buck's accomplice or if she'd been set up. Heck, they didn't even know if the accomplice had anything to do with the attacks. They weren't exactly at square one in the investigation, but it felt like it.

The sound Lana made was of pure frustration, and Slater went to her. It wasn't a smart move, but he sat down next to her and put his arm around her.

"You believe what your mother said?" Slater asked.

"I don't know. I want to believe her, but that's not the same thing."

No, it wasn't, and he was glad she understood that. Glad that she could try to look at all of this with some objectivity. He rethought that, though, when she looked at him, and he saw no trace of that objectivity in her eyes. It was a mix of weariness, fatigue and…resignation.

Slater understood all three of those emotions. Because he was feeling them himself. The first two, the weariness and fatigue, were because of the attacks and the investigation. But the third, that was all about this intensity between them on a personal level. The attraction.

The need.

Yeah, it was all that and more, and even though it would have been easy to blame it on the sense of urgency and immediacy caused by the danger, it was more than that. Maybe it always had been but they'd managed to keep a leash on it.

The leash was gone now.

Slater could see that, too, in Lana's eyes as she stood, dropped both the baby monitor and her phone onto the bed and went to him. Before she even made it to him, they were reaching for each other.

Their mouths immediately met, and this was no gentle, soothing kiss. This was all about the need. All about that urgency. And there was no leash in sight that could contain this. Even more, Slater didn't want to contain it, and it was obvious that Lana felt the same way.

He couldn't say which of them deepened the kiss. It seemed to happen at the exact second, and with that same intensity, that was swirling around them. Her taste roared through him, but there was no time to savor it. No. The need was too strong for that. The savoring would have to happen later. This was all about sating that need that just wouldn't stop.

Her arms went around him, and he slid his around her waist, pulling them body to body. Until they were pressed against each other. Of course, that only amplified everything, especially since the hungry kiss continued.

Somehow with Lana still in his arms, Slater made it to the door to close it and lock it so they would have some privacy to finish this. With the baby just next door, there was always the possibility of an interruption if Cameron woke up, and if he did, they would hear him on the baby monitor. For now, though, they just focused on this, on being together.

The kissing somehow managed to become even more fierce, and that urged on some touching. He slid his hand over her bottom, cupping her, and pressing her against his erection. Lana did her share of touching, too, and ran her hands over his back, her fingers digging into him.

It didn't take long for them to start grappling to get out of their clothes. This had to happen much faster than either of them wanted, but they went with the breakneck pace. Slater caught on to her top, pulling it off over her head and tossing it aside so he could kiss her breasts. In the back of his mind, he knew he would like to savor this part of her even more, but this was going to be a situation where fore-play happened afterward.

Lana rid him of his shirt, too, but first she had to remove his shoulder holster. No easy feat, and Slater had to stop the kissing and touching for a couple of seconds while he helped her with that. Finally, though, they both had their shirts off, and to complete the skin-to-skin contact, he eased off her bra.

Despite the need demanding release, Slater took a moment to kiss her neck. And then her stomach. Of course, that only fueled the heat even more until Lana was pulling him toward the bed. Her back landed on the soft mattress, and he landed on top of her. He hadn't thought it possible, but the heat went up even more, and the battle began to get out of the rest of their clothes.

He wanted her naked, now, and obviously Lana had the same idea. Slater had to move off her so she could undo his belt. Again, not easy since their hands were frantic now, so he helped her with that as well and was thankful that get-ting her out of her jeans was a much simpler process. He slid them off her. Her panties, too. And soon he had his hands and mouth on a naked Lana.

She was beautiful, of course. Everything he'd expected and more. More because she moved with him as if they'd been born to be in sync with each other.

"Condom," he managed to mutter, and Slater took the one from his wallet before Lana tossed his jeans and boxers onto the floor. He was pretty sure they landed somewhere near Lana's jeans and panties.

"Now," she insisted.

And that's exactly what he gave her once he had on the condom. Slater pushed into her, feeling the slam of intense pleasure that nearly robbed him of his breath. He apparently didn't need breath to finish this, though, because Lana lifted her hips, starting the thrusts inside her.

The pleasure built. And built. Until Slater could feel the freight train of pressure roaring through him. He silently cursed that he couldn't hang on to the pleasure, but Lana couldn't hold on, either. Her climax rippled through her, clamping on to him and forcing him to let go.

Slater gathered her into his arms and gave in to the heat. He gave in to Lana.

LANA LAY ON the guest bed and waited for Slater to come out of the adjoining bathroom. Thankfully, her body was still buzzing from pleasure so she hadn't delved into any thoughts or regrets. She simply let herself stay slack while she kept her gaze pinned to the baby monitor.

Cameron was still asleep. For how long, Lana didn't know. Apparently, some newborns defied the cliché of sleeping like a baby, and Lana had learned in her very short time with him that sleep could last as little as an hour or stretch to three or four. That meant she had to be ready to get up and give him a bottle, which was the reason she'd put back on her clothes after Slater had gone in for the pit stop in the bathroom.

The nanny and Joelle had both offered to take the night shift for her so she could get some sleep, but Lana had declined. She needed to get used to Cameron's unpredictable routine, which was her new normal. Or rather it would be her normal once the investigation was finished.

Whenever that would be.

Lana shoved that aside, too, and concentrated on hanging on to her buzz. Slater helped with that by coming out of the bathroom. Unlike her, he was naked, and he certainly made an amazing picture walking toward her. His lanky body had just the right amount of muscles. His face, the right amount of character to prevent him from being an outright pretty boy.

He was smiling a little when he came to her, leaned down and kissed her. That helped rebuild the buzz, too, and the kiss turned so hot she nearly asked if he had a second condom.

"I don't want either of us to overthink this," she said instead.

That widened his smile. "Good." He ran his gaze over her body. "I seem a little underdressed."

She sat up, took his hand and looked him over as well. "It suits me." And she sighed. "You're...hot," she settled for saying.

Now he chuckled and moved in to give her one of his scorcher kisses when her phone rang. Both of them groaned, but they knew they couldn't just ignore it. Lana especially knew that was true when she saw the name on the screen.

"It's Julia," she relayed, automatically checking the time. It was just after 9:00 p.m., past the usual time for a friendly chat, so Lana answered it right away in case there was an emergency of some kind. "Is something wrong?" she asked, putting the call on speaker.

Julia certainly didn't jump to reassure her that all was well. "Yes. I'm obviously working late, and I found something in one of the files your mother wanted me to look at."

Since there were plenty of things a thorough PI like Julia could have found, Lana didn't speculate. She just waited for Julia to continue. Slater must have realized the potential for truly bad news because he started getting dressed.

"In one of the files, there were some copies of email conversations between your father and Buck. I intend to send them to a tech to make sure they're real and that the file is actually as old as it seems to be." Julia paused. "The emails appear to go back nearly twenty years."

Twenty years. Lana immediately made a connection with that since it'd been when Alicia was murdered. Judging from the intense look Slater got in his eyes, he'd made the connection, too.

"The emails by themselves aren't confessions," Julia went on. "The wording seems to be intentionally vague. Here, I'll just read you one, and you can see what I mean. This is from Buck. 'I moved her to where you said, and nobody saw me. There was too much mess to clean up so I left it.'"

Everything inside Lana went still. Yes, she could see why the email would have alarmed Julia. "And the date on them?"

Julia sighed. "The night of Alicia Monroe's murder."

Of course it was. "What was my father's response?"

"'Make sure no one finds her. Ever. If they do, you'll go down for this.'" Again, she paused. "It sounds as if Buck and Leonard were in on this together. Sounds," Julia emphasized. "That's why I want to have the techs look at it. It's possible someone planted this on your father's computer. Someone like BoBo."

That was true, but it was equally possible the emails were real.

"Why would Buck and Leonard have a conversation like this via email rather than texts or calls?" Slater asked.

Lana silently cursed herself for not having already considered that. It might be an indication these were indeed faked.

"I have no idea, unless they didn't want there to be any phone records. Burners were around then, but maybe one of them didn't have a burner. Still, if it's secrecy you're going for, then why keep the emails?"

Unfortunately, Lana could think of a reason. "Insurance," Slater and she said together. So obviously he'd considered this as well.

"This way, if Buck rats him out, Leonard has proof that Buck was involved. Maybe even the actual killer."

That was true, but Lana's stomach twisted. Because maybe Buck was just the cleanup man and her father had been the one to kill Alicia. Lana was still considering that when her phone dinged with an incoming call.

"My mother is calling," Lana relayed to Julia. "Does she know about what you've found?"

"No, I wanted to tell you first, but your mom copied the files before she gave them to me, and she said she planned to go through them. So maybe she found the emails as well."

Yes, and if she did, her mother would be frantic.

"Go ahead and take her call," Julia encouraged, "and if you have any questions, you can phone me back. In the meantime, I'll send these emails to one of our techs."

She ended the call with Julia so she could talk with her mother. The moment she heard her mom's voice, Lana knew that something was indeed wrong.

"Lana," her mother blurted. "Oh, God, Lana. Something horrible happened."

"What?" Lana asked through the muscles that had tightened in her throat.

"It's all there in the files from your father's computer." She broke into a loud sob. "It's all there."

"What's there?" Lana insisted.

Her mother didn't answer for a long time. "God, Lana. Your father murdered Alicia, and I believe I know where her body is buried."

Chapter Fifteen

Slater felt as if all the air had been sucked out of the room. Out of his body. And he had no doubts Lana was battling the same thing right now.

The shock and sickening dread of what Pamela had just said.

Your father murdered Alicia, and I believe I know where her body is buried.

Slater had to shove aside the emotion of that accusation and remind himself to think like a cop. And that meant questioning things well beyond the surface level.

"Pamela, what did you find to make you think that?" Slater demanded once he was able to speak.

"Some old emails from the files I took from Leonard's computer." Pamela was still crying, but her words were rushed, as if she couldn't say them fast enough. "I saw the date on them. It was when Alicia was murdered, and then I remembered something else. One of our vehicles had to be towed then. I don't know why I recalled it, but it just flashed in my head when I read those emails."

"Slow down, Mother," Lana instructed. "What does a possible car malfunction have to do with Alicia's murder and the emails?"

"Everything," Pamela insisted, and she repeated the word

several times before she finally continued. "I got a call from a tow truck company that night, and the person told me they had pulled the car out of a bog but there was some damage to the front end, and they wanted to know if they should go ahead and take it to the garage where the estate vehicles were normally taken for servicing and such."

Slater mentally worked his way through that. This was obviously a towing service that Leonard was accustomed to using if they knew where to take the damaged vehicle.

"A bog?" Lana questioned.

"Yes, I think they said it'd gotten stuck in the mud."

"Was Leonard driving the car?" Slater pressed, and again, he reminded himself that this could all mean nothing.

"I'm not sure. I don't think so. He was supposed to be at a fundraiser that night. I didn't go because I had one of my migraines, but normally, Leonard would have a driver take us to and from such things."

"Do you recall the name of the fundraiser or where it was held?" Slater wanted to know.

"I'm sorry, I don't, but you could probably check the date since it was the night Alicia was killed. I'm not sure, though, if people would actually remember Leonard being there or not. It's been so long."

Yes, it had been. Twenty years was a long time to try to confirm an alibi, but it was possible that someone had taken or posted photos of the event.

"I'm not sure why they called me instead of your father," Pamela went on several moments later, "and I didn't think of asking them. I just wrote down the info, including the location of the pickup and the time." She sobbed again. "It was at that old abandoned rodeo arena. The one out on Carston Road."

Slater knew the one. It'd been an active site for small rodeos when he was a kid, but it had shut down about twenty-five years ago. Which meant it would have indeed been abandoned and empty when Alicia had died. As far as Slater knew, the owners had just left the place to rot away. It was a good place to bury a body.

"I think Buck or Leonard took Alicia there," Pamela spelled out. "And I think a clue to where she's buried is in one of the emails. Buck told Leonard that he'd 'moved her to where you said,' and Leonard answered, 'Make sure no one finds her. Ever.'"

That was exactly what Julia had already relayed to them. "That doesn't give you a specific location for a grave," Slater pointed out. "Leonard or Buck probably wouldn't have allowed the tow truck to come that close if a body had been buried there."

"I agree, and that's why I kept digging through the files." Pamela paused a heartbeat. "I found another email. This one came the following day, and in it, Buck said, and I quote, 'I put her with the horses.'"

Slater glanced at Lana to see if she had a clue as to what that meant, but she shook her head. "Did he mean one of the stalls inside the old arena?"

"I don't think so," Pamela was quick to say. "I found an article on the internet about some horses being buried on the west side of the arena. Apparently, the owner created a sort of cemetery there."

That jogged his memory, and Slater recalled hearing about the burials. He quickly used his phone to do a search, and while there weren't many articles on the old arena that had once been called Rodeo Park, he did find one that mentioned the graves. Apparently, the owner had used the boggy area to bury some of the horses that had been champions.

"At the time of Alicia's death," Pamela went on, "the

rodeo arena would have been closed for five years. No visitors to find a fresh grave. And there's this other thing I found. Buck's grandparents had a ranch less than five miles from the arena. I'm betting he visited there when he was a kid."

Slater was betting the same thing, and while there was still no concrete proof that's where Alicia was buried, or that Buck and Leonard had been the ones to kill her, the circumstantial evidence was starting to come together.

Alicia and Leonard had been having an affair, and something could have happened between them. An argument that'd turned violent. Or maybe some kind of jealous altercation involving Buck, Leonard and Alicia that had led to her death. Unless Leonard confessed about that, they might never know exactly what'd happened, but if there was indeed a body at Rodeo Park, then that added some physical proof to the circumstantial.

Slater's attention went back to Pamela when she made another of those raw sobbing sounds. "And this means Buck and Leonard could have murdered Slater's father," she ground out. "They could have done it to silence him. Maybe Sheriff McCullough was getting too close to uncovering the truth."

Hearing that said aloud felt like another punch to Slater's gut, though his mind had already gone in that direction. And it was a direction he had to take.

"I'll start arranging for a CSI team to go out to Rodeo Park and check for any signs of Alicia's grave," he said, somehow managing to keep his voice level. Inside, though, was a whole different story. He was battling an emotional hurricane that was ripping right through him.

"You'll let me know if they find anything," Pamela muttered, and then she quickly added, "I have to go." And she broke down crying.

"Mom?" Lana tried, but the woman had already ended the call.

Lana turned to him, and even though he wanted to get started with that call to Duncan and the CSIs, Slater took a moment to try to settle some of the panic and dread he saw on Lana's face.

He pulled her into his arms and brushed a kiss on her forehead. "One step at a time," he murmured. "It could take hours or even days for Duncan to get a warrant to search the grounds. It's in his jurisdiction," Slater added. "So we won't have to deal with the San Antonio cops."

At least they wouldn't unless there was a body buried there. Then it would mean Leonard's arrest. Or at least the man being brought in for questioning. After that, a body would have to be sent to the medical examiner and maybe even a forensic scientist for evaluation. This was going to be a long, grueling ordeal, and at the tail end of it would be yet another new level of investigation into his father's murder.

After a couple of moments, Lana finally eased back and looked up at him. "Slater, I'm so sorry."

It took him a moment to realize why she was apologizing. Hell. No way did he want her to take a drop of blame for anything her father might have done. So he kissed her again. This time on the mouth. He hoped it settled some of her nerves because that's what it did for him, and then he stepped away from her to go up the hall to talk to Duncan. It would no doubt be a long conversation, followed by getting all the cogs moving for the warrant and the CSIs. In other words, it was going to be a very long night.

"I'll have Duncan come in here so we can talk," Slater

suggested. Of course, Joelle would likely want to be involved with that, too.

He left Lana while he went down the hall and lightly tapped on the door of the main bedroom. Slater immediately heard the footsteps, and a moment later both his sister and Duncan answered the door.

"What happened?" his sister wanted to know. Like Duncan, she wasn't dressed for bed, but Slater spotted two laptops and a baby monitor in the small seating area of the room.

"We need to talk," Slater said, motioning for them to follow him. "There have been some developments."

That was all he got a chance to say before Lana rushed out into the hall. She, too, had the baby monitor in one hand and her phone in the other.

"There's a problem," Lana blurted. "My mom just called and said she was going to Rodeo Park."

Hell. Not this.

"I tried to talk her out of it," Lana quickly added. "But she won't listen. Slater, she's already on her way there to look for Alicia's grave."

LANA CURSED UNDER her breath when she tried again to call her mother, and like the other four times, her mother didn't answer. The calls went straight to voicemail. Lana had left three other messages for her mother not to go anywhere near the Rodeo Park, but she didn't even bother to leave a fourth.

Her mother was no doubt on her way to what could be a burial site.

If Pamela did find something, then the evidence could be destroyed. But that wasn't even her biggest concern at the moment. It was Leonard. What would he do if he found out where his wife was going? As much as Lana hated to consider it, she had to.

Her father might try to murder her mother.

It didn't matter that Lana wasn't close to either of them. Heck, she didn't even like them. But she didn't want another person to die.

Obviously, Duncan and Slater felt the same way because they were hurriedly assembling a plan. A plan that was being amended as they spoke. At the first suggestion, Duncan and Slater said they'd be going alone, but Lana had nixed that. If anyone could convince her mother to back off, it'd be her. It had taken Lana some time to convince Slater of that, but he'd finally relented.

"Luca, Sonya and Joelle will stay here with the babies," Slater spelled out while he, Duncan and Lana strapped on their weapons.

Lana was thankful for the extra security since she didn't want Buck's accomplice to take advantage of their absence to try to kidnap Cameron.

"And, Duncan, you and I will take precautions in case this turns out to be something different from what it seems," Slater added to her.

She was quick to agree. Because she, too, had already considered several disturbing possibilities. Maybe her mother was the accomplice and this was to draw them out. Or the accomplice could be using her mother to set all of this up. The emails could be fake, designed to draw them all out to a secluded location where they could be attacked.

And that led right back to her father.

Or Marsh.

No way was Lana going to cross him off the list of suspects. After all, Marsh had been around when Alicia was murdered, too, and he could have murdered her alone or teamed up with Buck.

"Stay safe," Joelle muttered when they started for the door and the cruiser that was waiting for them outside. She kissed her husband and gave her brother and Lana hugs. "Stay safe," she repeated.

"We will," Duncan promised, and they stepped out of the house and into the night.

There was a chill in the air, and the drop in temps had caused a wispy gray fog to hover just over the yard and driveway. Lana hadn't needed anything else to rev up the tension inside her, but the spookiness only added to it.

"Try your mother again," Duncan instructed once they were on the road with Duncan behind the wheel and her and Slater in the back.

Lana did, but like the other times, it went straight to voicemail. This time, though, Lana did leave another message.

"Don't look for the grave, Mother. Sheriff Holder, Slater and I are on the way. Stay put."

Whether her mother would obey was anyone's guess, but Lana was hoping this spooky atmosphere and the night would at least give Pamela cause to stop and rethink what she was doing.

"Have you been to Rodeo Park before?" Slater asked her.

Lana shook her head. "I've only driven past it."

But she knew it wasn't far. Only about five miles away. Still, it would be a very long drive since they had to stay vigilant for any attacks along the way.

"My dad used to take me and my siblings there," Slater muttered, keeping watch out the window. "It used to be a fairly open field, but last time I saw it a couple of years ago, the nearby woods had practically taken it over. Unless your mother's dressed for a hike, she probably won't have gotten far."

Good. Better yet, maybe Pamela had already changed her mind and already turned back toward the apartment.

Duncan threaded the cruiser around the deep curves of the country road, and when they reached the turnoff, the road narrowed even more. Obviously, there wasn't a beaten track because what was left of the asphalt was pocked with potholes and even some weeds sticking up through massive cracks.

Thankfully, it didn't take long for a building to come into sight. Well, what was left of the building, anyway. Lana could see glimpses of what had once been a rodeo arena, but portions of the massive roof had collapsed. Slater had been right, too, about the woods reclaiming the place. The wild shrubs now littered what was once a parking lot, and the massive tree limbs were like a canopy that was doing an effective job of shutting out the sliver of moonlight.

Lana sighed when she saw something else. Her mother's car. It was parked in one of the few spots on the concrete where the weeds and shrubs hadn't spread. The headlights were on, and the driver's-side door was open.

But there was no sign of her mother.

"Keep watch," Slater reminded her when Lana automatically hurried to get out and find her mom.

He was right. This could still be some kind of trap, but if her father and Marsh had come here, they'd parked out of sight. Unfortunately, that would be plenty doable because of the trees. It was possible her father had even sent a henchman to silence her mother, and if so, it could already be too...

Lana cut off that thought. She couldn't think of another murder right now. She had to focus on getting her mother safely out of there so she didn't contaminate a scene that needed to be examined.

Duncan stepped from the cruiser and put his hand over his gun. "Mrs. Walsh?" he called out.

Her mother didn't answer, and the grounds were almost totally silence. There wasn't even any buzzing of mosquitoes. Worse, the fog seemed to be getting even thicker and was swirling around their legs.

Duncan called out to her mother again, and when there was no response this second time, Lana got out of the cruiser as well. She stayed behind the cover of the door, knowing it wouldn't do much good if someone tried to shoot her in the head. Still, she looked around and saw no one ready to gun them down.

"Mom?" Lana tried.

And there was an instant reaction. Sort of a muffled sound of relief, and several seconds later, her mother came out from behind one of the trees. Lana felt both relief and anger that her mother had come here.

Pamela wasn't near the crumbling arena building but rather on what Lana thought was the west side of the property where the horse cemetery would be. Her mother was holding a flashlight that she had pointed toward the ground.

"I didn't know who drove up," her mother said, not coming closer. She stayed put, her body partially hidden behind the massive oak. "I wanted to make sure it wasn't your father or Marsh."

Lana could understand that, but it didn't ease her anger. "You shouldn't be here," she warned her.

"I have to find out the truth," Pamela insisted.

"No, you don't," Duncan said, sounding very much like

the lawman in charge. "We'll have a warrant soon, and then a CSI team."

Her mother frantically shook her head. "It might be too late. If Leonard knows we're onto him, he could do something to destroy the scene. He could set a fire or something."

A fire would definitely do some damage, but it likely wouldn't obliterate a body in the ground.

"Come back to your car, Mrs. Walsh," Duncan ordered.

Again, her mother didn't respond. Not with words, anyway. But Pamela turned and started running.

Both Slater and Duncan cursed, and the three of them went after her. Thankfully, her mother wasn't hard to follow because she kept on her flashlight, and Lana could see it bobbling through the dark and fog as her mother ran. Not for long, though. Her mother stopped.

Then screamed.

The sound ripped through the night and caused her, Slater and Duncan to speed up. Lana tried to tamp down any worst-case scenarios. And failed. There were just too many dangerous possibilities, ranging from a killer to wildlife about to attack.

By the time they made it to Pamela, she turned. Her eyes were wide, and her mouth was open as if preparing for another scream.

"There," her mother said, and she aimed a trembling hand at something on the ground in front of her.

Steeling herself for what she might see, Lana moved closer. And closer. Until the fog cleared for a second or two so she could see the headstones for what she presumed were the horses' graves. Then she saw something else.

Something that sent her heart to her knees.

Because there was another grave, an unmarked one, and it wasn't covered, either. It was now a gaping hole.

Duncan fanned his flashlight into the hole and groaned. Lana soon saw why. At the bottom of the hole were the bleached white bones of what had once been a body.

Chapter Sixteen

Slater cursed when he caught glimpses of the body through the breaks in the fog. Or rather what was left of the body, anyway. Not all the bones seemed to be there, but there were enough of them for him to know it was human remains.

The skull was evidence of that.

The cop part of him warned him not to jump to any conclusions. That this might not be Alicia Monroe. But with the emails and the tow truck that'd picked up a vehicle here, it was hard for him not to look at those bones and see the young woman that Alicia had once been.

Duncan was muttering some profanity, too, and he fanned his flashlight around the grave, no doubt looking for any footprints that didn't belong to any of them. Slater didn't immediately see any, but the weeds and grass likely would have prevented deep impressions into the ground.

"It's true," Pamela sobbed. "It's all true." She buried her face against Lana's shoulder when Lana pulled the woman into her arms. "Leonard killed Alicia and buried her here."

Maybe, but no matter who this was, the scene had to be preserved. Of course, it had already been compromised. And recently. Slater looked at the mounds of dirt around the sides of the grave, and he was pretty sure someone had attempted to dig it up.

But why?

To remove the body?

If so, the person had failed because the body was still there. Maybe the digging had been step one, and the person was coming back to finish the exhumation. Again, though, he had to ask himself why. The immediate answer that came to mind was that Buck had realized the location was about to be compromised and had dug it up, only to die before he could finish the job.

Was that it?

Slater continued to mull that over and was about to escort Lana and Pamela back to the cruiser so that he and Duncan could start the necessary phone calls needed in a situation like this. But Slater stopped when the glint of something caught his eye. Duncan stopped, too, fixing the flashlight onto the upper torso of the skeleton.

And Slater saw it then.

A silver heart pendant on a thick chain.

"What is it?" Pamela asked, trying to get a look at what had caught their attention.

Lana must have thought they'd seen something ghoulish, because she gathered her mother into her arms and started leading her away from the grave. Slater was all for that. In fact, he wanted Lana back in the cruiser where she'd be safer, but first he used his phone to take some photos of the skeleton and that necklace.

A necklace he thought he remembered seeing before.

But where?

"Let's go with them," Duncan instructed, taking out his phone. "We still need that warrant, because anything we find here might not be admissible without it."

True, and it could mean a killer could walk. No way did

they want that to happen. Not when they had perhaps finally found Alicia's body.

While they kept watch around them and started back toward the parking lot, Duncan made a phone call to the county district attorney so he could give a push on that warrant. The fog had gotten even thicker now. Even if they managed that warrant in the next couple of hours, the CSI team might not be able to start right away because of visibility. Still, they had to try, and they might be able to set up enough fans and blowers to keep away the fog while they at least set up something to secure the grave and remains.

"Will you arrest Leonard for murder?" Pamela asked. It took Slater a moment to realize she was directing the question at him.

"I'm not sure what will happen," he answered honestly as Lana helped her mother into the back seat of the cruiser. Duncan got behind the wheel, and Slater took shotgun.

"He'll be arrested," Pamela concluded, breaking into another sob. "He must have killed Taylor. And Stephanie. I know it was Buck who smothered her, but Leonard would have been part of that, too."

Yeah, he would have been if Leonard was actually Buck's accomplice. It meant Leonard had also been responsible for the attacks on him and Lana.

Hell.

If Leonard had truly done all of this, then Slater would make sure the man paid and paid hard.

Lana kept her arm around her mother, but she pinned her gaze to Slater. "What did you see in the grave?" she mouthed.

Slater went through the photos he'd taken and enlarged the one that showed the heart pendant. Lana studied it, frowned and shook her head. "It looks familiar," she said, again mouthing the words.

He nodded an agreement and tried to force himself to think. And then Slater recalled the party photo of Alicia, Leonard, Buck and Marsh that Taylor had shown them. After Taylor's murder, the phone she'd had with her had been taken into evidence, and Slater was hoping that photo was still on the phone and that Taylor hadn't moved it back to the storage cloud the woman had mentioned.

Slater called the lab and said a quick thanks when someone actually answered. Better yet, it was a tech, Mark Gonzales, who Slater knew well.

"I need a favor," Slater said to Mark after they'd exchanged greetings. "I need you to check the photos on Taylor Galway's phone. I'm looking for a picture taken twenty years ago at a party. Leonard Walsh is in the shot. So is Buck Holden," he added, knowing that Mark would likely recognize those two faces.

Slater was hoping that Pamela wouldn't be listening to the conversation, but when he glanced back at Lana and her, he realized Pamela was now staring at him.

"Taylor sent me a picture of Leonard and Buck at a party," Pamela muttered, and she began to fish her phone from her pocket.

"Got it," Mark said just as Pamela started scrolling through her own photos. "I'm texting it to you now."

Slater's phone dinged, and the picture loaded. Yeah, it was the one all right, and he immediately saw what he'd been pretty sure he remembered.

The heart pendant.

Alicia was wearing it.

Hell. Slater doubted that was a coincidence, and it was

yet another piece of evidence pointing to it being Alicia's body in the grave.

"Thanks," Slater told Mark, and he ended the call. Since Duncan had finished talking to the DA, Slater passed him his phone so he, too, could take a look.

"Here it is," Pamela said, lifting up her own phone for them to see.

It was the same photo all right. The one that had convinced Slater that Alicia and Leonard had been having an affair. It was also the one where Marsh had seemed to be mooning over Alicia. And where Buck and Leonard had appeared to be very friendly.

"Why did you want to see it?" Pamela asked, but she didn't wait for an answer. She turned the photo back toward her, and her gaze combed over it. Anger flashed in her eyes. Raw, vicious anger that she quickly shut down. "Leonard was sleeping with her, and then he killed her."

"Why would he have done that?" Duncan came out and asked.

Pamela lifted her shoulder in a shrug and kept her attention on the photo. "Maybe because Alicia tried to blackmail him or something. He opened himself up to blackmail when he got in bed with her." She stopped and gasped. "The necklace," she muttered.

Slater and Duncan exchanged surprised glances. "What necklace?" Lana asked, taking the phone from her mother so she could see.

"That one. The heart," Pamela blurted, but then she made another of those sobbing sounds. "It's the same one. I'm sure of it."

Lana took hold of Pamela's arms and turned her mother to face her. "What do you mean?"

"I mean, your father bought that necklace. Or one just

like it. I found it in a little gift bag in his car—" Pamela stopped when her voice broke. "He said it was a birthday gift for someone who worked in his office. I thought he was lying, but I never thought…" She stopped again and began to cry while sucking in loud, jerky breaths.

Slater looked at Lana. There was no anger in her eyes. Just a deep sadness that seemed to go all the way to her heart. She had to be thinking that she'd lived under the roof of a killer. One who'd killed his lover and had her buried here.

"Oh, God. I'm going to be sick," Pamela blurted, and before Lana could even reach for her, she bolted from the cruiser.

Pamela ran toward the arena, catching on to a thick log post that had once framed the entry. She lowered her head, and Slater heard the retching.

On a sigh, Lana got out, no doubt so she could go to her mother and try to offer her some comfort. Slater and Duncan got out as well, and even though Pamela's life seemed to be falling apart right now, they kept watch around them.

Lana took slow steps toward Pamela and was still a good twenty feet away when Pamela's body lurched. It was as if she'd either dived forward or had been yanked by someone.

Pamela screamed. A blood-curdling sound that echoed through the arena. And then the woman disappeared into the darkness.

FOR A MOMENT, Lana stood there frozen in shock over what she'd just seen and heard, but she quickly shook it off and bolted toward the arena. Or rather that's what she tried to do when Slater darted in front of her.

"You could be gunned down if you go in there," Slater

said, using the warning as they continued to move with Duncan right next to them.

Slater was right, of course. It looked as if someone had grabbed hold of her mother, and if so, that person could be Buck's accomplice. And this could be a setup to draw them out of the relative safety of the cruiser and into a building where they'd be easier prey.

Lana considered calling out to her mother, but she decided against it. She'd heard her mother's scream well enough, and if Pamela was capable of doing that again, she likely would have.

Which meant she could be gagged. Or hurt.

Or worse.

Lana didn't want to consider the worst. Couldn't. She had to stay focused on whatever danger they were about to face inside.

Duncan and Slater were clearly ready for the danger. In the sprint toward the arena, they had both stayed low while drawing their guns. Lana did the same, and when they reached the building, none of them rushed in. They stood there for a moment and just listened.

Lana thought she heard some footsteps, but the sound that stood out the most was the creaking of the roof. She prayed it wasn't about to collapse on them.

Slater stepped into the darkness first, and he moved even lower, practically to a squatting position, no doubt so he wouldn't be an easy target. Duncan moved in behind Lana, shielding her, she realized. She didn't want or expect him to take that kind of risk, but Duncan would likely consider it his duty to the badge.

A few seconds passed before Slater moved even deeper into the arena. Lana and Duncan were right behind him, and now that her eyes had had time to adjust to the darkness, she was able to better see the place. It wasn't a closed-in space but rather had walls that went up about six feet, allowing for the night breeze to rush through. It felt cold and damp, and the entire place smelled of mold and things she'd rather not smell. There was a sense of death here.

The dirt-filled center area, where once the performances and competitions had taken place, was huge. The weeds had made it into this part of the arena, too, but they weren't nearly as thick as they were in the parking lot and on the grounds.

The roof had indeed collapsed on one side, but a good portion of it was still intact. As were the bleachers that stretched out most of the length of the competition area. To the right were the stalls. Again, a large space where the horses and bulls would have been contained.

Lana didn't see her mother in any of those spots.

So where had the person taken her? There had to be exits, and it occurred to Lana that might be the plan. To drag her mother in here, only to hurry out to a waiting vehicle so she could be taken elsewhere.

But why?

Was it because the accomplice wanted to silence her? Maybe. If so, then her father or Marsh could be here.

Or it could be *something else.*

As much as Lana hated to consider that something else, she knew she had to. If Pamela had been the one to work with Buck, then it was possible the only threat she, Slater and Duncan were about to face would come from her mother.

Following Slater's direction and pace and while keeping their footsteps soft, they moved even deeper into the building. Lana focused on keeping watch on the stalls and

the bleachers where there were plenty of spots for someone to hide.

Slater stopped, motioned toward the floor, and Lana saw
the scuff marks in the dust and dirt on the ground. And there
were more of them in the direction of the stalls. They started
toward them, but the sound stopped them cold.

It was a moan.

Lana couldn't tell if her mother had made it or if the
sound was one of pain, and again, she had to fight her instincts to bolt toward it. A good thing, too.

Because there was another sound.

A gunshot.

It rang out. A loud blast that tore through the air and sent
them to the ground. A second one quickly followed. Then
another. Lana couldn't tell where the bullets were landing,
but she prayed they hadn't hit any of them. Or her mother.
Of course, it could be her mother firing those shots.

Lana knew that her mother had firearms training and
had even competed in target shooting competitions when
she was younger. But that moan had come from the stalls,
and the gunfire seemed to be coming from the bleachers.

Oh, God. Did they have two attackers?

Any of their suspects could have hired a henchman. However, there was another sickening possibility that the two of
them had teamed up.

But why?

Was this about covering up Alicia's murder? Taylor's?
Lana didn't know, but she hoped she soon had the answer
so the danger could finally end.

There was another shot, and this time Lana had no trouble
figuring out where it had hit. It slammed into the log post
right next to Slater. Once again, they had to drop down and
wait out the next flurry of gunfire.

Slater looked back at her, their gazes locking for a couple of seconds, and Lana saw the storm of emotions and worry in his eyes that was no doubt in hers as well. She didn't want any of them to die, but it could happen. It was obvious the shooter wanted them dead.

After what seemed an eternity, the gunshots stopped, and the silence that followed allowed Lana to hear another moan. Again, it'd come from the stalls, and Slater began to inch his way there. He stayed close to the partial wall, and with Duncan and Lana right behind them, they were only a few feet away from the stalls and those moans when another shot rang out.

This one smacked into the ground, so close to Slater that Lana saw the dust that the bullet had kicked up land on his arm. Cursing, Slater moved back, but Lana reached for him, pulling him away from the stall. Just as another shot came. And another.

"The shots are coming from there," Duncan said, tipping his head to the top of the bleachers on the far side of the arena.

Lana pivoted in that direction, automatically taking aim, but she didn't see anyone. The shooter had likely dropped down into the footwell space below the seats.

The anger roared through her, and she cursed this person who wanted them dead. And why? Because the shooter didn't want to have to pay for crimes that he or she had committed? Well, she wanted this snake to pay, and somehow she would figure out a way to make that happen.

"I'll shoot into the bleachers," Duncan said, keeping his voice at a whisper since any and every sound seemed to echo in the arena. "The two of you go to the stall and find out who's moaning. Be careful," he added. "It could be a trap."

Yes, it could be, because the person in the stall might be lying in wait for them and possibly didn't even need help.

Slater stayed in front of her as they began to move, and behind them, Duncan started shooting. Lana could hear the bullets slamming into the metal seats of the bleachers, and she prayed his gunfire was pinning down the shooter so he or she couldn't get off more shots.

It seemed to work.

No bullets came at her and Slater as they hurried toward the stalls. There were at least a dozen of them, and it was hard to pinpoint exactly where they'd heard those moans.

Slater kicked open the first stall gate and then immediately moved back in case there was an attacker inside. But it was empty.

Behind them, Duncan continued to fire, pausing only long enough to reload, and she and Slater went to the next stall. The gate to this one had already fallen off so they had no trouble seeing that no one was inside it.

They moved on to the next stall with the same results. Empty. And Lana began to wonder if the person who'd moaned was no longer there. Was this part of the ruse to kill them? Maybe. But she and Slater kept moving. Kept checking, and they made it to another stall. Slater kicked in the gate, darted to the side.

And Lana heard the moan.

Neither she nor Slater rushed in. They stayed put a couple of seconds before Slater peered into the stall, and because Lana was pressed right against his back, she felt his muscles tighten even more than they already were.

She looked over his shoulder to see what had caused that reaction. And Lana saw the person lying on the ground. Not Pamela.

But her father.

Chapter Seventeen

Slater definitely hadn't expected to find Leonard in the stall, and a whole bunch of questions immediately began to fly through his head.

Why the hell was Lana's father here? What did he want? And where was Pamela? She certainly wasn't in the stall with her husband, so had she been taken?

Or was she the person firing those shots?

Slater figured any and all of those possibilities could be true, but for now he focused on Leonard.

And the gun that the man had gripped in his hand.

Leonard didn't aim the gun at them. In fact, he stayed against the wall, his body sort of slumped to the side. Slater didn't want to take a chance, though, that Leonard might turn that gun on them, so he reached in and snatched it away. All without Leonard putting up a fight.

The man moaned again and shook his head. "Who's shooting?" he asked, his words slurred.

There was indeed some gunfire going on, and it was all coming from Duncan. Either he'd managed to pin down the shooter, or else the shooter had given up the fight and was escaping.

"Leonard's in here," Slater relayed to Duncan, figuring that wouldn't be info that Duncan was expecting.

"I'll check him for more weapons," Lana insisted, moving into the stall so she could frisk her father.

Again, her father put up no resistance whatsoever, and when Slater used the flashlight on his phone to aim it at the man, he saw Leonard's slack face and unfocused gaze. It was possible he'd been injured, but there wasn't any blood. However, the sleeve of his shirt had been shoved up, and there appeared to be a puncture mark on his arm. Not from a weapon but possibly from a needle.

"How did you get here, Leonard?" Slater asked while he continued to keep watch around them. He didn't want someone hiding in another stall to attack him and Lana while they were occupied with her father.

Leonard shook his head and ran his tongue over his bottom lip. "Here?" he questioned.

Yeah, he'd been drugged all right, but Slater figured that didn't mean the man hadn't committed murder. He could have done this to himself so he'd look innocent. After all, they'd just found the body of a woman he'd likely had some part in murdering.

Outside the stall, Duncan's shots trailed off some, and he was probably testing to see if the shooter would start up again. Hopefully not. Even though he and Lana were in the stall, it wouldn't give them much protection from bullets coming at them. And Duncan was practically out in the open where he, too, could be gunned down.

"Lana," Leonard murmured, clearly trying to focus his eyes on his daughter. "What happened?"

"You tell me," she countered. "You can explain how you got here and why your former lover, Alicia Monroe, is buried in a grave just a stone's throw away."

There was rage in her voice, and Slater couldn't blame her

one bit. He was feeling plenty of that himself. Not just for Alicia but for the danger that had nearly cost Lana her life.

"Buried?" Leonard repeated, shaking his head, but then he stopped. Just stopped. And any trace of color drained from his face. "Alicia." He said the name as a low moan that ended in a groan.

"Yes, Alicia," Lana snapped. "You murdered her and—"

"No," her father argued, and while that response was still slurred, he seemed adamant about it. "I didn't kill her."

"Then who did?" Lana snapped.

Leonard shook his head again. "Buck, I think. I think he did it. Because he was jealous. He was seeing her, too."

Lana grounded out some raw profanity. "And why didn't you report that to the cops?"

"No proof." Leonard repeated that a couple of times, and while he sounded somewhat convincing, Slater wasn't ready to buy it.

Not with so many unanswered questions.

There were those emails in the files that Pamela had taken from Leonard's computer. Or rather had supposedly taken. Slater had to concede it was possible that was a setup to frame Leonard for a murder he'd had no part in committing.

"It's me," Slater heard Duncan say, and a few seconds later, he slipped into the stall behind him and Lana. "There's no movement in the bleachers, no sign of the shooter. Or Pamela. I've called for backup."

Good. Because Slater wanted all the help they could get, and he knew this was far from over. They had to find Pamela. And the person who'd fired those shots. They could be one and the same, but they had to know.

"What the hell happened to him?" Duncan asked, tipping his head to Leonard while he continued to keep watch on the bleachers and the arena.

"To be determined. But I think he was drugged." Slater motioned to the puncture mark on his arm.

"Self-inflicted?" Duncan immediately wanted to know.

"Again, to be determined," Slater repeated.

"Drugged," Leonard muttered, and he, too, looked down at his arm. "Yes. Someone drugged me."

"Who did that?" Lana demanded, and she clearly wasn't ready to dole out any TLC. If it turned out her father was innocent, there'd be time for that later. For now, they had to take every precaution.

And that included treating Leonard like the killer he very well could be.

"I, uh, don't know," Leonard said, his eyelids fluttering down.

Lana huffed. "How did you get here? What's the last thing you remember?"

Leonard didn't give her the fast responses that she clearly wanted. "Don't know," he said, but then his eyes popped open again. "I was at the estate. I had a drink. Then I woke up here." He stopped, groaned. "Alicia's dead?"

Duncan huffed, too, and took out his phone. "I'll request an ambulance." He hadn't managed to press in the number, though, when there was a shout.

"Help," someone yelled, and it was a voice that Slater instantly recognized.

Pamela.

"It came from the bleachers," Duncan said, and both Lana and Slater pivoted in that direction.

Slater couldn't see Pamela, but he had no trouble hearing a second shout for help. Either the woman was in trouble or else this was part of the ploy to kill them.

"I'll go look for her," Duncan said.

"You're not going out there without backup," Slater insisted.

Then he had a fierce mental debate with himself. No way would he leave Lana here alone in case her father's drugging was all an act. Leonard didn't have any other weapons on him, but he could have a henchman waiting nearby to kill Lana.

Slater took out the pair of plastic cuffs he always carried with him, and he slapped them on Leonard. "If he's got a phone on him, take it," he instructed Lana.

"He didn't have one," she answered.

Good. Slater didn't want Leonard to have a way to contact anyone. "If he's not the killer," Slater spelled out, "then the real killer put him here. He or she could have just murdered Leonard but didn't so maybe he's a patsy, meant to be set up for whatever else is supposed to happen here. But in case Leonard's faking being drugged, I don't want him to be able to communicate with any thug who's helping him."

That's why Slater tore off the sleeve of his shirt and used it as a gag on Leonard's mouth. Again, if the man was innocent he could dole out an apology later, but the restraints and the gag just might stop Leonard from issuing an order to kill.

"Help me," Pamela shouted again, and it seemed to Slater as if the woman was on the move. Maybe running.

Slater didn't intend to take anything happening at face value, and when he, Duncan and Lana moved out of the stall, he did so with one thought. When they got to Pamela, she, too, would be treated as a killer until proven otherwise.

He glanced at Lana, and there were so many things Slater wanted to say to her. But now wasn't the time. Later, though, he needed to tell her just how much she meant to him. For now, he settled for a warning that he hoped she would obey.

"Stay behind me and keep your head down," he insisted.

A fierce look went through her eyes. "You stay alive. Hear me? Stay alive," she repeated.

"You do the same," Slater fired back before brushing a quick kiss on her mouth. Very quick. Since this wasn't the time for that, either.

With Slater going first, then Lana and Duncan, they scurried out of the stall and toward the bleachers. Not directly toward them, though. They raced toward the wall. Slater wanted a look beneath the bleachers to see if he could spot Pamela and anyone else. He only hoped the seats were stable enough and didn't come crashing down on top of them.

The three of them stopped when they reached the bleachers and listened. Slater cursed the silence and the darkness. He couldn't see anything, but he especially listened for any footsteps behind them. He didn't want anyone sneaking up on them or trying to get into the stall with Leonard.

"Keep an eye on the stall with your father," Slater whispered to her.

Lana nodded and shifted her position so she could do that as they inched farther beneath the bleachers. That's when he spotted the flashlight lying on the ground. He couldn't be certain, but it appeared to be the one that Pamela had been using.

Slater turned it on, and the powerful light illuminated a good portion of the space under the seats. Still no sounds or signs of anyone, though, and just when Slater had started to believe that maybe someone had escaped with Pamela, he heard something.

Movement out in the arena.

They all pivoted in that direction, and in the darkness, Slater shifted the flashlight toward the woman. Pamela. She was running across the massive stretch of dirt that made up the arena floor.

And her hands were tied in front of her.

"Help," she shouted.

Slater moved so he could get a better look at her and check to see if she was armed. After all, her hands might not be tied at all. Pamela shouted out a call for help again and kept running.

He, Duncan and Lana moved out from the bleachers, and Pamela must have seen them because she started running toward them. She didn't get far, though, because the gunshot stopped her.

It slammed into the ground right in front of her, causing her to skitter to a stop.

And the shot hadn't come from Pamela, either. It'd come from the bleachers. Slater turned the flashlight in the direction of the shooter and cursed.

Marsh was standing there.

LANA HAD KNOWN Marsh most of her life, but she'd never seen him with a gun. Nor had she ever seen that expression on his face.

The expression of a killer.

She caught just a glimpse of him before he ducked down out of sight. Marsh hadn't been smiling or gloating as Buck had done. No, Marsh's stare had been pure ice, and the shadows created by the flashlight had made him look like the monster that he was. In that moment, Lana realized Marsh was a cold-blooded murderer.

Slater must have realized that, too, because he pulled Lana back, and while he kept both his gun and flashlight aimed at Marsh, he and Duncan kept cover of the bleachers.

"Stay put, Pamela," Marsh ordered when her mother started to struggle to get to her feet.

Marsh was peeking over one of the bleacher seats, his head barely visible. He didn't fire another shot. So, what was he waiting for? Maybe he had hired thugs on the way to help him. But she, Duncan and Slater had their own help in the form of backup that she hoped would be there soon.

"Marsh grabbed me and dragged me in here," Pamela sobbed. "He punched me, but I got away."

Despite the troubles that she and her mother had had, Lana was sorry that had happened to her. But Pamela was alive, and that was more than she could say for Alicia, Stephanie and Taylor.

But had Marsh been responsible for their murders? Lana wanted to shout that question, but she knew it could turn out to be a distraction that Duncan and Slater didn't need. Their goal right now was probably to get her mother out of harm's way and to make sure they weren't attacked.

At the thought of that, Lana turned to make sure her father was still in the stall. He was. They hadn't shut the door, and she could see him cuffed, gagged and sitting on the floor. She couldn't be sure, but she thought maybe he had slipped back into unconsciousness.

In the distance, Lana heard a welcome sound. Sirens. And she hoped it would prompt Marsh to surrender.

It didn't.

She heard the footsteps on the bleachers and braced herself for an attack. It didn't come. There was a thud as if someone had dropped to the ground. Several seconds later, the footsteps resumed and got a whole lot faster.

Marsh was running away.

Lana saw the split-second debate Duncan and Slater had about what to do. No way could they just leave her parents here, since Marsh could circle back and kill them. And they couldn't wait for backup, either, because Marsh could be long gone by then.

"Slater and I can go after him," Lana said.

She hoped it sounded much stronger than a mere suggestion. Because it was the best option. Duncan and Slater wouldn't want to leave her there while they went in pursuit, and whoever did go after Marsh would need backup. Duncan must have decided the same thing because he nodded.

"Go," Duncan ordered.

She and Slater took off running with Slater automatically moving in front of her again. Thankfully, they could still hear the sound of running footsteps, but they were on the other side of the arena so that's where they headed.

The fog was still slithering around the ground, so Lana couldn't actually see where their feet were landing, and she hoped they didn't trip over something. Hoped, too, that this wasn't a trap, but she had to accept that's exactly what it was.

They stayed low and kept moving, keeping watch around them in case Marsh had planted thugs out here to attack them. They ran, following the sound of those footsteps, and just ahead, Lana spotted Marsh. Thankfully, the trees weren't so thick here so there was light from the moon they could use to track his movements.

He was heading for the road.

And the car that was parked there.

They wouldn't have been able to see the vehicle when they arrived since Marsh had parked it in a bend just away from the arena. He'd no doubt done that on purpose. But why?

Why was he even here?

Marsh hadn't killed her parents even though he'd had plenty of chances, especially if he'd been the one who'd drugged her father and put him in that stall. And, yes, Marsh had fired shots at them, but most hadn't come close to hitting them. He could have just gunned them down, or rather tried to do that, when they'd arrived or when they'd been at the grave.

Lana didn't have the answer to any of those things, but she hoped she got the chance to catch and question Marsh.

Ahead of them, Marsh made a beeline for his car, but Lana kicked up the speed to close the distance between them. When they were only a few feet away, Slater bolted forward, diving at Marsh and tackling him. They landed hard on the asphalt.

Lana moved into a position so she could take aim at Marsh, but the man surprised her when he didn't fight. He looked up at her. Still no smile or gloating, but there was… something. She wasn't sure what, but that look chilled her to the bone.

Behind them, an explosion ripped through the arena.

The noise wasn't exactly deafening, but it had definitely been some kind of blast, and Lana's first thought was a horrible one. Had Duncan and her parents been killed? Oh, my God. Were they dead?

She gasped, instinctively pivoting toward the arena. So did Slater. And that's when Marsh made his move. Marsh rammed his elbow into Slater's jaw, knocking Slater off him. In the same motion, Marsh got to his feet and pointed his gun at them.

Lana could barely think, but she relied on her training. She brought up her own gun so she could fire. But Marsh managed to do that first. He pulled the trigger just as Slater caught hold of the man's legs and yanked him down. Marsh's shot went wild, slamming into a nearby tree.

The sounds of sirens got closer. So did the thuds of flesh punching flesh with the blows that Slater and Marsh were landing on each other. Both men still had their guns, and she knew it would be too easy for Marsh to try to put a bullet in Slater.

Still keeping watch for any help Marsh might have brought with him, Lana maneuvered around the fight, looking for any way she could put an end to it. She couldn't shoot. She couldn't risk hitting Slater. So she went old-school, and when Marsh pulled back his left hand to deliver another punch to Slater, Lana kicked Marsh in the head.

Marsh howled in pain and twisted his body to look back at her. It was the only opening Slater needed because he latched onto Marsh and put him in a choke hold. Marsh continued to fight, but Lana helped with that, too. She stomped down as hard as she could on his foot and then kicked the gun from his hand. It went flying and landed behind her.

But Marsh still wasn't finished with the fight. He clamped on to Slater's arm with his teeth and was flinging his head back and forth like a rabid dog. Lana delivered more kicks, this time to Marsh's kneecaps, and yelling in pain, the man dropped to the ground with Slater keeping his arm around Marsh's neck.

"I don't have any cuffs," Slater said, his breath gusting. The adrenaline was no doubt firing on all cylinders inside him, and he shot a glance in the direction of the arena.

The building was still in one piece, but Lana had no idea how much damage had been done. Or if Duncan and her parents had made it out alive.

"Backup will be here soon," she muttered to Slater and to herself for the reassurance they'd soon have help.

She was volleying glances at Slater, Marsh and their surroundings when there was another blast, the one much louder than the first. Lana could only watch in horror as she heard the sharp groan of the roof before it collapsed onto the arena.

Chapter Eighteen

Slater's heart slammed against his chest, and he had to fight his instincts to let go of Marsh and run toward the arena. Duncan and Lana's parents could be trying to claw their way out of the wreckage.

But he couldn't leave Lana alone with a killer.

And he had no doubts, none, that Marsh was exactly that.

Lana's hands were shaking and she'd gone ashen when she reached for Marsh's belt. It took Slater a couple of seconds to figure out what she was doing. She yanked the leather belt from the man's khakis and used it to make cuffs to restrain Marsh's hands behind his back. She didn't stop there. Lana took Slater's belt and did the same to Marsh's feet, hooking one belt through the other to essentially truss him up.

Slater snatched up Marsh's gun so the man wouldn't be able to somehow crawl his way to it, and he and Lana took off running toward the collapsed building. He was sure they were praying along the way. Slater certainly was, and he hoped that Duncan had somehow managed to get Pamela and Leonard out before the second blast.

The blue lights from the two approaching cruisers slashed through the darkness, and the moment the they stopped, Deputies David Morales and Ronnie Bishop bolted out of one of them. Luca and Deputy Brandon Rooney came out of the other.

"Arrest him and read him his rights," Slater instructed Luca, motioning toward Marsh, and he and Lana kept running with David and Ronnie right behind them.

Some of the muscles in Slater's chest unclenched when he saw that one of his prayers had been answered. Duncan was making his way toward them. His face and clothes were covered with dirt and dust, but he didn't seem injured.

Also thankfully, Duncan wasn't alone. Pamela's hands were no longer tied, and she was hobbling alongside her husband, who no longer seemed as drugged as he had earlier. Pamela bolted ahead of them and practically fell into Lana's arms.

"You made it out," Slater said, and there was a whole lot of relief in his voice and his entire body.

Duncan nodded. "We were by the stalls with Leonard for the first blast and were already outside for the second one." He looked in Marsh's direction. "Did he confess to setting the explosions?"

"Not yet, but he tried to escape. Then he tried to kill Lana and me."

Hearing his own words drilled home just how close they'd come to dying, and when Pamela let go of Lana, Slater pulled Lana into his arms. He didn't care who was watching. He just needed to hold her for a moment.

Like him, she was still plenty unsteady, and this would no doubt give them both hellish memories for the rest of their lives, but like Duncan, Leonard and Pamela, they were alive. They could deal with the rest later. He let go of Lana and turned back to her mother.

"Marsh was going to kill us," Pamela muttered. "He was going to kill us all."

Slater thought she might start crying, but she didn't. A fiery streak of temper crossed the woman's face, and Pamela bolted toward Marsh when she saw him. She hurled a string of vicious profanity at the man and tried to kick him before Luca held her back.

"You should be dead," Marsh snarled, aiming his own profanity at the woman. "You should have died in the blast. Hell, I wish I'd killed you a long time ago. You and your despicable SOB of a husband."

Judging from the way Lana, Pamela and Leonard stared at Marsh, they hadn't known his true feelings. Marsh had obviously kept his venom for them close to the chest.

Or maybe those feelings were a recent development.

Slater decided to test that theory.

"Did you want to punish Leonard for keeping Stephanie's whereabouts from you?" Slater asked.

"Yes," Marsh snapped while two of the other deputies began to untruss Marsh so they could cuff him. "I was worried sick about Stephanie. I couldn't think of anything but her and what she might be going through. And Leonard knew where she was and didn't tell me. So did she." He aimed a stone cold glare at Pamela.

Pamela frantically shook her head. "How? I didn't know."

"You should have known," Marsh yelled. "You should have been a better mother to Stephanie and she wouldn't have run off like that and hidden. And Lana was the one to hide her," he added in a snarl. "You kept the woman I love from me." Now he was the one who broke down and cried.

And Slater thought he knew how this had all played out, but he needed to hear it from Marsh. "Tell me what happened," Slater ordered. "Start with your part in Alicia's death. Because you wouldn't have known to come here had you not had some part in it."

It took a while for Marsh to gain enough composure to speak. "Buck is to blame for that."

"Buck?" Slater questioned. "He's the one who killed Alicia?"

"No," Marsh muttered, repeating that denial several times. He made a heavy sigh. "Alicia and I had just started seeing each other, and I went to her place and Buck was there." He swallowed hard. "Things got out of hand, and Alicia shoved me, told me to get out. I shoved her back, and she fell. She hit her head." His voice trailed off to a whisper, and Slater thought Marsh might be caught up in those memories of that horrible night. "There was blood. So much blood."

"What happened then?" Slater asked.

"Alicia was dead. And I didn't know what to do. I was in shock and couldn't even make myself move. Buck said he could take care of things but that I would owe him. I agreed. I would have agreed to anything just to make it all go away."

"You're a killer," Pamela blurted. "All this time I was pushing Stephanie to marry you, and you were a killer."

Marsh didn't deny it and didn't try to add any sugarcoating. Good. Slater didn't want to hear any lame excuses for the hell he'd caused.

"You and Buck emailed after he'd disposed of Alicia's body," Slater threw out there. "And after you learned Leonard had known where Stephanie was, you planted the emails on his computer."

Marsh didn't deny that, either. Couldn't. Because the truth was there, all over his face.

"And you made sure I found them," Pamela murmured. She turned to Leonard. "I'm so sorry. I thought you were the one who murdered Alicia."

Leonard was still obviously dazed, but he pulled his wife

into his arms, and he surprised Slater by murmuring, "It's all going to be okay."

No, it wasn't. Not for Marsh, anyway, and since the man was clearly in a confessing mood, Slater pressed harder. He wanted the truth all out there, and then Marsh could be hauled away to jail.

"Alicia's murder might not have been premeditated, but you knew Buck was going to murder Stephanie and that you were going to kill Taylor," Slater pointed out.

"I didn't know Buck was going to kill Stephanie," Marsh yelled just as the deputies got him out of the belts and cuffed his hands. They pulled him to his feet so he was now eye level with Slater. "If I'd known, I would have stopped him. I would have killed him."

"You knew Stephanie was pregnant with his baby?" Lana asked.

"He told me, but I didn't believe him. I thought the baby was mine." Marsh shook his head. "But then I realized if it had been, Stephanie wouldn't be in hiding. She was scared of Buck, and Buck was a monster."

"He was your partner," Slater reminded him. "You were his accomplice."

"Not because I wanted to be." Marsh groaned. "It all got so messed up. He killed Stephanie and then said if I didn't help him cover it up, he'd give the cops a recording he made of the night Alicia died. Buck blackmailed me while I was sick with grief over losing Stephanie. This is all his fault."

The wimp was trying to deflect the blame, but Slater knew there was enough blame for both Buck and Marsh. "It wasn't Buck's fault that you killed Taylor. Buck was already dead by then. Why did you kill her? Because she was getting too close to the truth?"

"She got to the truth," Marsh clarified. "Taylor had

worked it all out. She didn't have proof yet, but she would have kept digging until she found it. She wanted to hurt me for telling her to get lost." He paused. "In hindsight, I should have led her on and let her think she stood a chance of being with me, but I couldn't stand the sight of her. Not after all those things she said about Stephanie."

Yeah, hindsight might have saved Taylor long enough for them to figure out Marsh was the accomplice, but Taylor might not have been willing to play along with that.

"You were willing to kill Sheriff Holder, Lana and me to get back at Leonard," Slater stated. "Why didn't you just kill Leonard when you drugged him and brought him here?"

More anger fired through Marsh. "Because I wanted you all to pay for Stephanie dying. You should have figured everything out sooner, and then you would have come gunning for me. You were all supposed to get trapped in the first explosion, and the second one should have killed you all."

"How did you even know how to build explosives?" That question came from Duncan, who was motioning for the EMTs to move in to examine Leonard.

"Buck did them. All of this was his backup plan to cover his own butt if the cops pinned Stephanie's murder on him. He thought he was going to get away with that since he'd jammed the security cameras."

It sickened Slater to think Buck might have indeed gotten away with it if Lana hadn't seen him. Then again, if she hadn't, then Buck might not have come after her.

Marsh likely would have, though.

The rage was too strong for Marsh just to have dropped this. He wanted revenge for all those who'd kept Stephanie from him. And it didn't matter that Stephanie had been the one who'd initiated the hiding.

"I must have messed up the timing of the explosives,"

Marsh snarled. "Buck didn't leave good enough instructions. The first wasn't supposed to do much damage but give me time to get away once I had all of you in the arena. Then, the second one was supposed to go off within seconds so you'd all be punished for what you did."

Marsh stopped his tirade to launch into another one. All aimed at Leonard when the EMTs started taking the man toward the ambulance. Pamela was trailing along right behind them, and while she might never forgive her husband for his affairs, she certainly didn't appear to be ready to leave him, either.

"Who dug up Alicia's body?" Slater asked, trying to get Marsh back on track so he could get as much information from him as possible.

Especially since Slater had a huge question he needed answering.

"Buck did," Marsh muttered as if weren't important. "That was part of his backup plan, too. To use Alicia's body to blackmail Leonard so he'd help him. I figured I'd piggyback on that and use it to lure Pamela and Lana here. And you," he added, and now there was the tone of importance.

Marsh smiled at him. A sickening smile that slammed Slater with anger. Because Slater knew what was coming next.

"I shot your father because he wouldn't butt his nose out of the investigation into Alicia's death." Marsh said the words slowly, punctuating them with that smile that was straight from hell.

There it was. The answer Slater had needed. And it cut him to the bone. His father had been gunned down for doing his job.

Slater felt a hand on his arm and realized it was Lana.

He hadn't even noticed her moving closer to him. Hadn't noticed anything. Except the smiling monster standing in front of him. He'd always heard the expression "seeing red," but Slater hadn't known it was real. But the red came. Wave after wave of rage that was closing in on him.

"Kill me, Deputy McCullough," Marsh taunted. "You know you want to. That way, you get your so-called justice, and I don't have to spend the rest of my life in a cage."

Slater wanted that justice. Wanted it more than his next breath.

Or so he thought.

Then he felt Lana's grip tighten on his arm, and she gently turned Slater to face her. "Marsh will be punished every day he's in jail," she said. "No trust fund. No pampered lifestyle. He'll be with other killers who'll make him sorry he was ever born. He'll have to spend every moment looking over his shoulder, waiting to be attacked by monsters worse than he can ever imagine. Every moment will be his own personal hell that he can't escape."

The cockiness and taunting drained from Marsh's face. Slater could thank Lana for painting that vivid picture of what the man's future would be. Yes, Slater would get plenty satisfaction from killing Marsh right here, right now. But this way, Marsh would pay for the rest of his miserable life.

Slater gave Marsh one last look, and while the grief didn't vanish, some of the tightness did in his chest. Tightness he'd been carrying for a year since his father's murder.

"Thank you," Slater managed to say, and he leaned in and kissed her. Again, it wasn't the best timing, but he needed it.

He needed her.

"I'm in love with you," Slater heard himself say.

Even though he'd surprised himself with the words, it

didn't seem to surprise anyone else around them. Duncan muttered, "About time," and the other deputies voiced agreement.

Marsh cursed them, but Slater tuned him out as Duncan and the deputies led him away to one of the cruisers. He and Lana stayed put, and she smiled when she stared up at him.

"About time," she repeated, leaning in to brush a kiss on his mouth. "I've been half in love with you for a long time. Now it's the real deal, fully in love. Are you okay with that?"

"Better than okay," he assured her.

It wasn't exactly a prime spot for the kind of deep kiss they gave each other. After all, this was a crime scene, and the blasted fog was getting thicker. Along with the stench of the explosion, there was nothing romantic about it.

But it was still perfect.

Because of Lana. Because of the man he was when he was with her.

"Let's tie up any loose ends with Marsh," he suggested. "Then let's go to the ranch, give Cameron some cuddles and then find a bed so I can get you naked."

"The perfect plan," she quickly agreed, glancing at her parents. "And I'll say a quick word to them, too. All is not well there, but I don't want anything I feel for them interfering with what I feel for you."

Good. Slater wanted the same thing.

"You make me a better man," he told her. "You soothe me. You fire me up. You give me exactly what I need. I'm in love with you," Slater repeated, and thought he'd be saying that a whole lot more, not just tonight but for a long time. "And I want Cameron and you in my life forever."

Lana smiled. "Good, because I love you, too, and forever works for me."

She kissed him with that amazing smile. Kissed him and helped heal all those dark places that'd been inside him.

Yeah, forever would work just fine.

* * * * *

COLD CASE
DISCOVERY

NICOLE HELM

For anyone who has made something good
in the midst of tragedy.

Chapter One

Her phone trilled in the dark.

Chloe Brink rolled over to find the other side of the bed empty, which was good. *Best.* Considering the screen on her phone read *Do Not Answer*.

In other words, it wasn't work or something important. It was her brother calling her. At two in the morning.

She loved her baby brother and wished she could save him, but he was an addict. And until he accepted that, until *he* decided he wanted to change, her relationship with him had to be distant.

She was a sheriff's deputy. She couldn't rush in to save him from every problem. It would only get them both in trouble.

So she didn't answer.

The first time.

After the ringing paused, only to immediately begin ringing again, she sighed and did the inevitable. Maybe one of these days all the steps she'd taken to try to insulate herself from this need to be his—or anyone's—savior would actually work.

But not tonight.

She closed her eyes, let her head flop back onto the pillow and took a deep breath. "Ry, what is it?"

"I need your help."

She counted to three, inhaled deeply. Let it out. He didn't *sound* high, but that didn't mean anything. "We've been over this."

"Chloe, you don't understand. This is serious. It wasn't me. I don't know what to do. There's bones. It wasn't me. It's too old. Too deep. Chlo, I don't know what to *do*."

Panicked, clearly. But *bones* didn't make sense. She pushed up into a sitting position on the bed, tried to clear her mind. "What do you mean, Ry? I don't understand."

"By the barn. I've been digging for that new addition, right?"

She didn't say what she wanted to: *At two in the morning?* She let him blabber on only half making sense. At least it was just some jumbled talk about bones, not actual trouble with the law.

"You have to come. What am I supposed to do? I didn't do this. This isn't mine. It's *bones*."

Chloe went over everything her therapist had told her. It wasn't her job to clean up Ry's messes. He had to be responsible for his own choices.

But this wasn't the *exact* same thing. He wasn't in a fight with someone. He wasn't asking her to get him out of a ticket or an arrest. He'd just stumbled upon some bones—animal, probably—and convinced himself, perhaps with the aid of an illegal substance, it was a bigger deal than it was.

If she went over there, told him everything was fine, he'd stop bothering her for a few days. "Fine. Listen. I'll come over. But just to look at these bones, okay? But you have to stay put. And sober."

There was a pause on the other end of the line.

"I mean it, Ry. Not even a sip of beer. If I can't trust you to—"

"Okay. I promise. Nothing. Nothing else. If you just come over. Quick. I don't know what to do."

"Just don't move, and don't touch anything. Or *take* anything," she muttered, before hitting End and tossing her phone onto the empty side of the bed.

This was what her therapist didn't understand. Sometimes going over to help was the better course of action. She'd nip it in the bud and then be free of him for a few days. Best all around.

Best or easiest?

She groaned.

"Bad news?"

She didn't jolt, didn't open her eyes right away. She'd woken to an empty bed, so she figured he'd gone, because that was how this worked. Usually, that caused an ache around her heart, one she was determined to stop and never did—but tonight, him still being here was the last thing she wanted.

Just another one of her very own choices she had to face. She opened her eyes.

Jack Hudson stood, leaning his shoulder against the doorframe of her bedroom. He was dressed now, in the clothes they'd left work in: Khakis that weren't so perfectly pressed like they had been all through his workday. A Sunrise Sheriff's Department polo—untucked now.

But she knew what he looked like without all those clothes. *Hot.*

Maybe his hair was a little rumpled, but no one would think or even believe that it was *sex*-rumpled hair. Jack Hudson, the upstanding sheriff and uptight head of the Hudson clan, engaging in a clandestine affair with one of his deputies? *Impossible.*

She still hadn't spoken, and now she watched as Tiger

wound her way between Jack's long legs like she always did. Because that animal was just as foolish and weak as she was when it came to Jack.

"Chloe," he said in that half-empathetic, half-scolding tone.

He only ever used her first name *here*, what they were—and weren't—perfectly compartmentalized. Her fault as much as his, she knew, though she wished she could blame him and his rigid personality. But she'd put up walls to save herself too.

Because she was self-aware enough to know he could emotionally crush her if she didn't. She didn't think *he* knew that, and that was all that mattered.

"Just my brother. Needs me to come check something out. Typical." She slid out of bed, pulled on some sweats and put her smartwatch on her wrist. But Jack didn't leave.

She shoved her phone in her pocket. Keys and shoes were out in her living room. So she moved for the door, but Jack still stood there. Blocking her exit.

"You should head home," she told him. "A bit late for you."

He didn't say anything for a few moments as he studied her in nothing more than the glow of her smoke detector. They were shadows to each other, and yet it felt like—per usual—Jack Hudson could see *everything*.

"I'm coming with," he finally said.

Not *Would you like me to? Can I? Should I?* Not for Jack Hudson. "Not necessary, Sheriff." She threw that one at him when she wanted him to back off. Usually, it worked.

He didn't budge.

"It's two in the morning."

"Yeah."

"It's your brother."

"Yeah."

"I'm going with. We can either drive together or I can follow you, but I'm going."

"And be seen together at this hour?"

He didn't say anything. But he didn't move. Because no, Jack Hudson didn't relent. He was who he was.

Sometimes she thought she was as bad as her brother. Jack was her drug, and she couldn't give him up. Because he wasn't good for her—the secrecy; the way she couldn't get past that impenetrable, taciturn wall. But the way he made her feel when he put his hands on her was worth it.

She sighed, and she didn't relent, but Jack seemed to read the surrender in that sigh.

"I'll drive," he said, turning toward her front door.

"Of course you will," she muttered, and didn't bother to argue. She just made sure Tiger didn't bolt out the door with them in a shameless effort to follow Jack.

Chloe might be a mess, but she knew better than to throw herself against a brick wall that wasn't budging.

JACK HUDSON WAS well aware of his reputation. He knew what just about everyone thought of him. It varied a bit. To some people—particularly the law-abiding citizens of Sunrise, Wyoming—he was a saint. That was how he'd won the election for sheriff time and time again. To others—usually criminals and people related to him—he was an uptight ass.

Jack knew he was no saint, but he didn't quite agree with his siblings. Maybe he was a little strict, a little more controlled than *completely* necessary. But hey, they'd all somehow made it into adulthood in one piece and were mostly successful, and that was because of *him*.

He'd held the family together after his parents' disappearance when he was eighteen. He'd created Hudson Sibling Solutions to ensure his siblings always had jobs and to help other people with unsolved cold cases—solving quite a few, thank you.

Though never his own.

His parents—good, upstanding ranchers not involved in anything shady, that anyone had ever found—had disappeared on a camping "date weekend" one night seventeen years ago. Just vanished.

All these years later, hours and hours of police work, private investigator work, research from every single member of his family, no one had ever discovered even a shred of evidence of what had happened to Dean and Laura Hudson.

He told himself, day in and day out, that it was over. There would never be answers, and sometimes a man just had to accept the hard facts of life.

He was also an expert in denial.

The woman in his passenger seat, case in point. Chloe Brink hadn't *always* been a problem. Or maybe she had been and he'd just been younger and delusional. Hard to say now.

They'd been engaging in this whole *thing* for a year now, and he didn't relish the secrecy. It was an irritating necessity. But one of the short list of positives was that this was something his siblings had no idea about and, therefore, no say in, no opinions.

Everything that happened with Chloe was *all* his.

"Don't worry," Chloe said in the dark cab of his truck as he slowed down to take the turn into the Brink Ranch entrance. "Even if Ry said something about us arriving together in the middle of the night, no one would believe him. Or at least, not believe the real reasons."

Jack didn't respond, though it required him to grind his teeth together.

He knew she didn't understand his determination to keep

this a secret. He'd never tried to explain it to her because she wouldn't believe it. In her mind, he was embarrassed, and he knew her well enough—whether *she* wanted to admit it or not—that it stemmed from her own issues. It took a lot to be a cop in the same place where your last name was pretty much synonymous with *criminal*.

Hell, wasn't that part of why he liked her so much? He wouldn't say they were too alike outside their profession. Chloe was fun and friendly. No one had ever accused him of being either. Not since he was a teenager anyway.

But they both shared a dogged determination to see through whatever they thought was right.

What she would never understand—partly because of that dogged determination and a thick skull—was that people knowing about their...relationship...would cause problems for both of them.

He'd been around enough to know she'd bear the brunt of any negative reaction to their...relationship. It wasn't fair, it wasn't right, but it wouldn't matter what she did. Or what *he* did to try to protect her.

She was a woman, and she'd get the short end of the stick when it came to their work reputations. Right or not, police work—especially police work out here in rural Wyoming—was still male dominated. Jack dealt with the public enough to know a lot of people were still stuck in the Dark Ages.

He wouldn't let Chloe get a bad rap all because he... He was weak when it came to her, and that was *his* fault. He'd be damned if he let her take the fall for that.

So it had to be a secret, but that didn't mean he didn't care or was *embarrassed* of her.

It also didn't mean he had to like it.

Jack Hudson was well-versed in all the things he didn't like but dealt with anyway.

He pulled through the open gate to the old Brink place. It was open at a crooked angle and clearly had been that way for a while, as grass and vines had grown up and twined around it.

He didn't say anything about that either. Chloe's family was her business, and *maybe* he'd on *occasion* mentioned something about her brother, this ranch and so on, but she always put him in his place.

When he pulled up to the house, Ry was standing out in front of it, pacing back and forth. Jack could see the look on his face in the harsh light of the porch—just a light bulb screwed into the wall, no cover.

Ry was all nerves. Worry. Concern. But something was missing, and he'd dealt with Ry enough in a professional capacity to find it interesting. Chloe's little brother, for once, didn't look guilty.

Yeah, interesting.

"Why'd you bring him?" Ry asked on a whisper when they got out of the truck. Not quiet enough for Jack to miss it, but he pretended he had.

"What's the emergency, Ry?" Chloe asked, sounding less like a sister and more like a cop—but if she was thinking with her cop brain, she wouldn't be here.

"It wasn't anything to do with me. I just found it," Ry said, louder this time, making sure Jack heard it.

Jack studied Ry Brink. No doubt he'd been high at some point today, but whatever he'd been on was wearing off. He was jittery, gray faced. Scared.

Chloe's expression was blank. "Show us," she said. She switched on a flashlight Jack hadn't realized she'd grabbed on their way out, so he figured he could turn on the one he'd gotten out of his truck as well.

Ry leaned close; this time whatever he whispered to

Chloe was lost in the sound of insects buzzing and breezes sliding through the dilapidated buildings.

"Show us," she repeated, whatever Ry had said clearly not winning her over.

Ry led them away from the house, which had seen better decades. They quietly moved toward a caved-in barn. Ry. Chloe. Jack.

It was his desire to take over, to lead the way, but he tamped it down. Because this was Chloe's deal, no matter how little he liked it, and he'd only come along to ensure her brother wasn't laying some kind of trap.

Chloe might not think Ry capable, but Jack had spent his entire adult life seeing what drugs did to seemingly reasonable people. Part and parcel with a life in law enforcement.

They walked for a while in silence, and Jack noticed as they came around the side of the barn that there was a battery-powered lantern sitting in the dirt, tipped over, like it had been dropped there.

"I had this idea that I'd dig out a new entrance to the cellar," Ry said. And if he was telling the truth, it was clear he'd been high when he'd had that idea, because that wasn't going to work.

"The first one I hit, I figured it was animal. Dad used to bury the dogs out here. You remember, Chloe?"

She didn't say anything. She pointed her flashlight beam on the unearthed dirt. A shovel lay haphazardly next to the pile.

"Then I got a few more and… It's not animal bones. I know animals. It ain't animals."

Jack didn't believe that. Lots of people mistook bigger bones for human. He approached the hole with Chloe, shined his light at the ground as well.

He sucked in a breath. Heard Chloe do the same.

Human. Definitely. A full skeleton, almost. Jack swept his flashlight beam down the bones, his mind already turning with next steps. They'd have to notify Bent County. The Brink Ranch was a little outside Sunrise's jurisdiction—and besides that, they didn't have the labs or professional capacity to deal with dead bodies.

It might not be nefarious. Ranchers back in the day buried their kin on property. There were laws against such things now, but it didn't mean people always abided by them. This could be anything. It didn't have to be criminal.

Still, Jack studied the skeletal remains with an eye toward foul play. Hard not to. He swept his beam back up and noticed that something glittered. He didn't want to touch anything, destroy the scene any more than Ry already had, but he trained his light on that glitter and crouched so he could study it closer.

And it felt like the earth turned upside down, like every atom of oxygen in his body evaporated. He saw dark spots for a moment.

Chloe crouched next to him, put her hand on his back. "Jack? Are you okay? What is it?"

He had to breathe, but it was hard to suck in air. When he spoke, he heard how strangled he sounded. But he said what needed saying: "I recognize that ring."

Chloe peered closer. "How?"

"It was my mother's."

Chapter Two

Chloe figured she'd heard him wrong. She had to have heard him wrong. But he stood abruptly and took hard strides away from the remains. She was frozen, looking down at the skeleton in the beam of her flashlight. She tried to process what he was saying.

Because it couldn't be. Of all the crazy, impossible, terrible things this *might* be, it couldn't be that.

But she saw the ring, and Jack Hudson was not a jump-to-conclusions guy. He didn't say any random thought he had. The man plotted out his life to the millisecond. Even in crisis.

If he said that the little glitter of gold and diamond there in the dirt was his mother's, she believed him.

Oh God.

She stood up about as abruptly as he had. Crossed to him. There were so many…so many horrible revolving pieces to this. And she somehow had to find a path through.

For him. "Jack."

"I'll call it in," he said roughly.

"Jack—"

But he shook her off and lifted his cell to his ear. He'd have to call in Bent County. To get a dig team, the coroner.

Who'd likely have to call in a forensics team from somewhere farther afield.

Chloe's mind was whirling. Too many things at once. She had to focus. Tap into cop brain. She'd been through a million crises in the past six years of being a cop. She knew how to compartmentalize.

A seventeen-year-old cold case's first huge lead being your boss slash hookup buddy's mother's bones on your family's property?

Okay, the situation was new.

"They'll send out the detectives, a few deputies to zone it off. Get in touch with the coroner," Jack said.

"Gracie Cooper. We know her. She's good." Which, it wouldn't matter if she wasn't. She was the Bent County coroner. But it seemed a tangible thing to hold on to.

"There'll be a lot of questions for Ry."

"He'll hold up," Chloe said, with far more confidence than she felt when it came to her brother. But she'd make sure she kept him in her sight, and as long as she did that, she could make certain he held up.

Right now he was pacing from Jack's truck to some point just beyond, then back again. He raked his hands through his hair. He muttered to himself.

But he didn't run. She'd give him that in this moment. While keeping an eye on him to make sure it stayed that way.

Chloe didn't let her mind go to all the things this could mean. She didn't ask herself why—why now, why here, why anything. She focused on the next steps.

Jack would need to go tell his family. He could wait for some clearer confirmation. After all, that ring—even if it had been his mother's—wasn't irrefutable proof the skeleton belonged to Laura Hudson.

Chloe had to suck in a careful breath. She could still picture the woman all these years later. Because Mrs. Hudson had been the kindergarten-room mom since Chloe had been in class with Mary, Jack's little sister. Laura had embodied everything a mother *should* be, and nothing Chloe had ever seen a mother be, so she'd been fascinated.

But worse than that memory was the fact that this discovery affected not just Jack but also Mary, one of her closest friends. Anna, their other sister. All those Hudsons.

They'd worked so hard, but the answers had always eluded them. And Chloe had never considered what it might mean—good and horrendously awful—if they finally got them.

She looked at Jack in the shadowy dark. No matter what it meant, he shouldn't be here. He needed to be with his family.

"I'll oversee this, then have Ry drive me back to my place. You go home."

"We both know your brother's license is suspended. You're not having him drive you anywhere."

"Fine. I'll have someone appropriately licensed drive me home."

Jack shook his head. Stubborn no matter what. "I don't like that."

"You've got bigger things to deal with." He'd want to tell his family before anyone got word of this. He *needed* to.

He swallowed, looked hard into the dark—the opposite direction from where that set of bones lay in the ground.

The ground of *her* family's ranch.

Would he be okay driving home on his own? Even if it wasn't confirmed, it was *possible* that this was his mother. He probably shouldn't be driving anywhere by himself.

This is Jack Hudson you're talking about. Still, the idea of him driving by himself back to the Hudson Ranch after this... It didn't settle right.

"Maybe one of your brothers—"

"I can handle a two-mile drive." He snapped it out like an order. Boss to subordinate. But that wasn't really him, even when they *were* working, so she just nodded.

He needed to feel in control. She wasn't going to take that away from him in this moment. This horrible, awful, impossible moment.

"Then go," she told him. Because he didn't need to see the whole production once Bent County got out here. He didn't need to *see* any of this.

Still, he hesitated. She couldn't begin to imagine all the reasons he might have, but she reached out and put her hand on his shoulder. Friend to friend. Coworker to coworker. And, okay, whatever else they were when no one was around.

"Go. I've got this. You trust Deputy Brink to do her job. That's who I am right now."

His gaze finally met hers, dark. She couldn't read whatever lurked there—because he knew how to hide. Right in plain sight. Wasn't that the crux of so many of her problems with this man?

"I trust *you*, Chloe. Period," he muttered. Then he sighed, big and deep. "Promise me."

She could have pretended to misunderstand, but she knew him all too well. "I promise I won't let Ry drive me anywhere. Go. Be with your family. I'll get you an update once I have one."

She thought he might argue some more, but there was one indisputable fact about Jack Hudson. No matter how uptight, no matter how controlling, no matter how *everything*, his family came first.

So he walked back to his truck and went to them.

JACK WELCOMED THE numb feeling that settled over him. Numbness was better than pain, and pain was pointless until he had real answers. Even then...

If he thought he could hide this situation from his siblings until he had confirmation, he would have. But with Bent County involved, there were just too many ways the whispers would start.

And come knocking on the door of the Hudson Ranch.

So he drove home in the middle of the night, not sure how everything had just flipped on him. His entire adult life, suddenly different.

If that skeleton was his mother...

It wasn't a shock in that she was dead. He'd known both his parents had to be. There was no way they had disappeared on purpose. They'd been good parents, good people. They never would have left their six kids alone and defenseless.

Not on purpose.

So Jack and his siblings had known for a very long time that even if they ever found answers, there was no happy ending to this story.

But Jack had never fully realized, in all these years, how there had still been this awful bubble of hope inside him. A stray thought that they might be alive. That there might be a reason that wasn't terrible.

This strange little dream he might see them again someday.

And now that hope was gone.

It would take time to match the bones to his mother. It would take more time to filter through all the evidence. So they were dealing in unknowns for a while yet, and Jack was no fan of dealing with those.

But in a place the size of Sunrise, with a cold case that still lingered in the town's entire identity—in the Hudson family's entire identity—he couldn't hold off going to his siblings with the facts.

He had to tell them the possibilities.

He didn't drive his truck to the outbuilding where they parked their vehicles. He parked right out front of the main house and was greeted by a couple of Cash's dogs. He didn't crouch to pet them like he usually did. He went straight for the front door, punched in the security code and then stepped inside.

The house was dark and quiet, but only for a moment. He heard a stair creak, and then the hall light came on, illuminating Mary. She was the oldest of his two younger sisters but still eight years younger than him. He'd been an adult when their parents disappeared. Well, eighteen. She'd been ten.

And still she'd stepped up. She'd helped with meals, with keeping school paperwork organized. As she'd gotten older, she'd taken on most of the administrative tasks of running Hudson Sibling Solutions *and* the Hudson Ranch.

"What are you doing up?" he asked.

She put a hand over her ever-growing stomach. Pretty soon there'd be another baby around here. Such a strange twist and turn of fate these past few years. Marriages and babies and *adulthood* for his younger siblings, far beyond what Jack had ever found for himself.

He'd been keeping as busy as possible lately to keep from thinking too much about that.

"I was up using the bathroom for the hundredth time and heard the alarm disengage and the door open. It's four in the morning. Did something come up?"

It would be easy to lie to Mary. Being sheriff gave him the perfect alibi for everything, but Mary tended to see right through him. And really, there was no point in putting her off. This had to be done.

"Yes, something came up that we all need to discuss."

He watched her hand tighten on the banister, but no

sense of foreboding showed on her face. "What is it?" she asked calmly.

He couldn't tell her it wasn't serious like he wanted to. This was incredibly serious. "No one's in danger. But this is important. For all of us. Once everyone wakes up—"

"It seems like this is something that requires waking everyone up."

"It won't change anything. To wait."

Mary studied him for a few seconds. "Then it won't change anything to wake everyone up." She turned then, not waiting for him to agree or disagree.

Jack didn't follow, but slowly and quietly—no doubt for the sake of the still-sleeping kids, since his family usually didn't do anything quietly—his siblings began to arrange themselves in the living room.

Once everyone had settled, Mary nodded at him. She stood leaning against her husband, and Anna stood next to hers as well. Grant and Dahlia sat on the couch next to Cash. Carlyle stood behind Cash, clasping his hand at his shoulder. Palmer and Louisa settled themselves on an armchair.

Jack had gotten used to being a solitary figure long before his siblings had all coupled up. He'd been the man of the house. In charge. He'd needed that separation. To not be their brother anymore but to be the adult. To be in charge so he could keep everyone together until they were old enough to go on their own.

No one had. Oh, Grant had gone off to war; Mary to college; Palmer and Anna, the rodeo for a bit—but they'd all come back home. They'd all come back.

And now, in this moment, he was the only one who knew this terrible thing, and it killed him because he wanted to keep it that way. So his siblings would never have to feel this.

But it just wasn't possible. So he jumped right in. "There

was a body uncovered on the Brink Ranch. It had been there for some time. Bent County will take on the investigation and attempt to identify the body, determine a cause of death."

"Why'd you wake us all up to tell us this, Jack?" Anna asked. With the kind of gravity like she knew exactly why.

"There was a ring with the remains. I recognized it right away. Mom's wedding ring."

There was a moment of complete and utter silence, everyone absorbing those words. Then Jack watched as every single member of his family turned to each other. Mary buried her head in her husband Walker's chest. Anna turned away, but Hawk pulled her back into an embrace. Louisa wound her arms around Palmer's waist, Cash's grip on Carlyle's hand tightened, and Dahlia rested her head on Grant's shoulder.

Jack tried to swallow the obstruction in his throat to ensure his voice was calm and clear. It came out rusty. "This is not incontrovertible proof, but it's—"

"What about Dad?" Anna demanded. Her voice was harsh, but there were tears in her eyes.

"I don't have any answers, Anna. All I have is a ring." He thought that admission might break him in two, but when his heart kept beating and his breath kept filling his lungs, he figured he'd survive. "Deputy Brink is handling it. We all know we can trust her to handle it."

"Except this was found on her family's ranch?" Palmer said, no doubt echoing some people's thoughts on the matter.

But Jack didn't need to defend Chloe. Mary did it first.

"That doesn't mean anything," she said, standing up for her friend. "I trust Chloe. No matter what."

"The Brinks—"

Carlyle cut off whatever Palmer was going to say. No

doubt something about the Brinks and their connection to crime, drugs and a hell of a lot of trouble.

"The Bent County detectives will be the ones handling it, right?" Carlyle asked. "Hart and Laurel? They'll be doing the investigation, and we all know they're damn good at their jobs."

Thomas Hart and Laurel Delaney-Carson had worked with Cash and Carlyle a few months back, and their hard work had helped keep Cash from being blamed for his ex-wife's murder. Hart had also been involved in helping to solve a case last year when someone had tried to kill Anna.

They were both good detectives, and Jack trusted them. He had to.

"We'll be investigating too," Anna said.

"No," Jack said firmly, looking at his baby sister and the stubborn set of her chin. "We're staying out of this."

All eyes turned to him, surprise slackening every single person's features.

"Jack. You can't be serious," Grant said in his quiet way.

But Jack was very serious. He'd made this decision the minute he'd driven off the Brink Ranch. "This is a Bent County investigation. We will stay out of their way and let them investigate. There's nothing for us to do here."

"Do you have a head injury?" Anna demanded. "This is our parents we're talking about. *Our* seventeen-year-old cold case. Why the hell would we stay out of the way now that we actually have a lead?"

"Maybe once we have all the facts, we can decide to pursue it. But for now, we wait. Because none of us need to be involved in the details of our parents' remains." No one in this room needed to see what he'd seen tonight, needed to have that haunting them for the rest of their days.

For years, they'd tried to come up with clues to follow

when it came to their parents' disappearance. For years, they'd gone over the campsite. Their parents' pasts. Anything and everything. That had seemed innocent enough. Important enough that they could all be in on the investigating.

But nothing had involved bodies. Nothing had involved the reality of their parents being dead. Not just dead—*bones*.

No. None of them needed to see it. "We'll give Bent County the space to handle the investigation. There's going to be talk around town. People will want to know what we think. I want us to be as quiet about it as we can until we know for sure what we're dealing with. Because we don't know yet. All we know is, we've uncovered a ring that used to be our mother's."

For a moment, that old hope tried to grow back, but he ruthlessly plucked that weed of a thought.

His parents were dead, and it was someone else's job to figure out how. And why.

Chapter Three

Chloe was bone tired, but a text or a phone call wasn't going to cut it. Not for this.

She hadn't been back home. When the police had arrived at the ranch, she'd stayed through everything. Even when it became clear what they were dealing with, and someone pointed out that Chloe was one of the landowners.

The detectives hadn't liked that, but she knew enough to avoid anyone hauling her off the property. Just like she knew enough to keep Ry from being hauled off too. Once she'd gotten as much out of Bent County officers as she knew she was going to get, she'd driven Ry back to her cabin and insisted he stay put.

She didn't know if he'd listen, but it didn't matter. She had to drive back out to the Hudson Ranch and update the family.

Eventually, Bent County would get around to filling them in, but they were likely still organizing information. Chloe had to get in and tell the Hudsons some things before Bent County did so the Hudsons could organize.

Jack probably had a plan in place already, but he didn't know…

Chloe pulled up to the main house on the Hudson Ranch with nothing but dread in her stomach. She was used to delivering bad news. It went hand in hand with the job. And in a town like Sunrise, she was often delivering bad news to people she knew and liked.

But this was different. On so many levels. Complicated levels. And she just didn't know how to arrange it all behind her usual cop facade.

She got out of her car and trudged toward the porch. She'd been to the Hudson house for a variety of reasons over the years, but never for the reason Jack came to her place. Set lines. Set boundaries. Ones she'd helped enact because she'd thought it would somehow keep her safe from all her soft feelings.

It hadn't, and she didn't like to be reminded of that. She straightened her shoulders, knocked on the door. She'd changed into her Sunrise SD polo and put on her badge in an attempt to *feel* official on the outside since she didn't feel it on the inside.

Mary answered. She was dressed for the day, prim and proper as usual, even with her big pregnant belly. She was clearly tired, though, but Chloe wasn't about to tell her that.

"Aren't you pretty."

Mary's smile was faint, and she rolled her eyes. "I'm puffy and exhausted and ready to be done. I'm guessing this isn't a social call," she said, nodding at Chloe's badge.

Chloe tried to keep her smile in place as she shook her head. "No, I thought I'd update you all before Bent County swoops in."

Mary nodded. "Come on. We're all in the dining room." Mary led her deep into the house. Normally, there would have been lots of conversation, arguing, shouts and dogs barking echoing through the house before Chloe even got close to the dining room.

This morning it was silent. When she entered the room,

the only sound was the scraping of forks on plates, though she wasn't sure anyone was eating a lot.

The table was full, everyone—and there was a *lot* of *everyone* at this house—taking a seat. Paired up with their significant others. Cash's twelve-year-old flanked between him and Carlyle. Anna's baby tucked into her husband's arm.

And Jack, sitting at the head of the table. Surrounded by his family, and yet he looked so alone.

There was a chorus of unsure greetings from the table when Mary announced her arrival. Chloe refused a seat and a plate. "I just came to give you all a few updates. I'll be out of your hair in a few minutes."

It wasn't pure cowardice. She wanted to get out before Bent County showed up and asked why she was here. Besides, she had a shift to work.

"Izzy and I are going to go handle the dog chores," Carlyle said, her hand on Cash's twelve-year-old daughter's shoulder.

Chloe half expected the girl to argue. Even she knew Izzy didn't like to be shuffled off, but it seemed there'd already been discussion and agreement since she disappeared with Carlyle to take care of Cash's dogs without argument.

"Go on, then," Jack said, not unkindly but with that stoic detachment of his firmly in place.

"Another set of remains was found next to the first." Chloe had to resist the urge to clear her throat, but she couldn't resist the urge to look at Jack, to try to see what he was really feeling under that mask of stoicism.

Mostly, she figured no one would see that lost look to his dark eyes. They'd see the grim expression, the hard line of his mouth, and think he had it under control.

He didn't. Chloe knew he didn't, and she knew he'd die before admitting it to anyone. Even himself.

"Any identifying information?" he asked.

"They wouldn't tell me anything, but I took a slightly illegal and unauthorized picture of some evidence they gathered. I can show whoever is willing to bend the rules a little bit what I've got."

Immediately, most of the Hudsons crowded around her as she took out her phone. She pulled the picture up on the screen and tried not to betray her surprise when Jack stepped close enough in front of her to see it as well.

"You already saw one ring, Jack, but there was a ring with the other remains as well. They're both in this evidence bag." She zoomed in on the picture so they could see the rings.

Then she looked up at Jack. He didn't have to say anything. Chloe could see it in his eyes.

He nodded.

Chloe knew it would be Dean Hudson's wedding band, but maybe she'd hoped… Oh, she didn't know. There was very little possibility the two skeletal remains weren't the missing Hudson parents.

She had to remind herself to look away from Jack, to focus on her job. "The detectives will be by to fill you guys in. To ask questions, I'm sure. I…tried to convince them to let me, but it was a no go."

"It's best if it's a third party," Jack said. "We're all staying out of it, letting Bent County do their job."

Chloe opened her mouth to say something, but she forgot what because that didn't make *any* sense. "I'm sorry. What?"

"See?" Anna muttered. "Staying out of it doesn't make any sense."

But Jack's expression remained firm, and he didn't look at Anna. "Thanks for the update, Deputy Brink, but we think—"

"*You* think," Palmer interjected.

"—it's best if we let police handle this."

"Oh. Well, sure." She had just been resoundingly dismissed. She was so shocked by it, so confused by Jack's unusual response, she just stood there for a moment, not quite sure what to do.

"Are you sure you don't want any breakfast, Chloe?" Mary asked.

Chloe shook her head. No. She needed to leave. She needed… She glanced at Jack. He was calmly sipping from his coffee mug. But she recognized those careful, mild movements.

They were very deliberate. Very *careful*, like he was holding himself braced for a blow. He'd looked like that when Louisa had been kidnapped last year, when Anna had been in the hospital—basically any time a member of his family was in trouble, it was like there was a ticking time bomb inside he was doing everything he could not to detonate.

And it was *none* of her business. "Well, I'm heading into my shift. I'll…" She didn't know what to say if they didn't want insider updates on the whole thing. Well, not *they*. Jack.

But Jack ran the show. This time she had to clear her throat in order to speak. "I'll see you all later."

She turned on a heel, and she had no idea why she felt *emotional*. And just so very, very alone. But she walked out of the house having to work way too hard to fight back tears.

She just needed rest. After she worked her shift, she'd sleep. Of course, first she'd have to deal with what she was going to do with her brother. Which was a whole other headache she didn't have any answers for.

Before she could reach the bottom of the porch stairs, she heard Jack say her name.

She closed her eyes and sucked in a breath. Repeated her *Be strong* mantra a few times before she turned to face him.

"Thank you for coming out," he said, a little stiffly. "We appreciate the update."

She couldn't help but be amused despite everything churning inside her. She knew them all a little too well. "Mary made you come say that."

One side of his mouth *almost* curved. "My siblings can't *make* me do anything."

"But she did. Because she's Mary, and *she* can make you do things. Especially when she's that pregnant."

He shrugged, not refuting it. He squinted out at the mountains, the pretty Hudson Ranch, and didn't say anything. But he didn't leave either.

And she knew he *shouldn't* since he had all that family under his very own roof, but she could see the loneliness on him. Because like recognized like.

"They'll run tests," she said reassuringly. Maybe she didn't understand the hands-off stance he was taking, but she wanted him to know it was handled. "They'll do what they can to determine when. How."

"I know how it works, Chloe."

It was ridiculous the little thrill she got out of this man calling her by her first name when he damn well *should*. It wasn't like they were at work. "Sometimes it's good to hear someone else say what you already know."

He didn't say anything to that, and she knew she should go. *Had* to get out of here soon. But she just couldn't step away from him when he seemed so alone.

"They're not going to let me within a hundred feet of this case since my name is on the deed of the land. They've already questioned Ry. I'll be next."

"What about your parents?"

She shrugged, trying not to go on the defensive. He had every right to ask that question. Hell, *she'd* asked that question. "I imagine they'll do that too. But they'll have to get down to Texas to visit Dad in prison—and if they have better luck tracking down my mother than I ever have, more power to them. I'll be first because I'm here. Because I was there."

"I was there with you."

"I didn't mention it."

"Chloe. I called it in."

She shrugged. "You can always say I called you first and then you called it in."

"Why would I lie about that?"

"You know why, Jack."

"I know why *you* think I should lie, but I don't think you have any clue what *I* think."

She had no business getting pissed at him over relationship stuff. Mostly because she was just as much to blame for *everything* involved in this, but also because now so clearly wasn't the time.

But she was tired, and she was feeling all emotional over too many things to count, and *he* was the one who'd brought it up. So she snapped. "Oh, really? Then enlighten me. What does the almighty Jack Hudson think?"

"You think it's because I'm embarrassed. Because of your family or because I'm your boss."

"That's not embarrassing, Jack. It's unethical. Something you are historically very opposed to." She looked up at him to give him a kind of *so there* smirk, but his expression was serious, his gaze steady, and when he spoke, he spoke with all the gravity of the truth.

"I'm not embarrassed of you, Chloe. Not in the least."

Her foolish heart felt as though it actually skipped a beat. Was she really this pathetic?

Yes, yes you are. When it comes to him, you always have been.

She swallowed, trying to find some retort that would settle all this terrible longing inside her, but she heard the sound of a car approaching and turned toward it.

Not just any car. A Bent County cruiser was driving up the gravel road when Chloe had been planning to get out of here before they showed up. Because no doubt the detectives were inside.

"Damn," she muttered.

"Don't worry. I'm going to protect you, Chloe," Jack said, like that made any sense. But before she could ask him what on earth he was talking about, he was striding forward to meet the detectives.

JACK DEALT WITH the detectives. He didn't lie to them about being with Chloe when her brother called, but he didn't explain either. Since the detectives were more concerned with identifying the remains, keeping Sunrise SD out of the proceedings and the Brink family connection to the Hudson family, they didn't prod for answers. It wasn't relevant to the case.

He wouldn't let it be. He'd protect her reputation. No matter what.

The detectives didn't share any breaking new information. Next steps were with the forensic anthropologist and the assurance that all the Brinks would be questioned.

He might have balked at that, but at the end of the day, it was clear the remains had been in the ground for some time. Long enough that Chloe and Ry would have been kids when it happened. Maybe the detectives thought they'd seen something, heard something, would remember something from back then, but Jack doubted it.

First, Chloe would have said long ago. And even Ry didn't seem like the type who could keep his mouth shut about much. That's half of why he got in so much trouble. No criminal mastermind, there. Just a kid with no direction who'd gotten mixed up with drugs.

It amazed him, regularly, that Chloe had somehow come out of all that to be the good cop and good person she was.

She'd left pretty quickly after the detectives had arrived, having to get to her shift, and Jack had taken the detectives inside, working with Mary to gather all the information they had on their parents' case. He handed over years' worth of files.

"You don't want to make copies?" Laurel asked with a raised eyebrow.

"We have most of this stuff digitized, but we're happy to hand over anything that might help you get to the bottom of this." He ignored the disapproving look on Mary's face.

Hart looked from Mary to Jack, a handful of files now in his grasp. "It's going to be best if you guys stay out of it for now."

Jack nodded. "We plan to."

"You forget I've had to deal with your family before, Sheriff," Laurel offered with a smile, as if to put some kind of friendly spin on things. Jack didn't particularly feel like being friendly.

"I've made it clear to my family our best course of action is to step back and let you all do your job. I can't promise they'll listen, but I'll do my best to control the situation." That was what he'd done for the past seventeen years. No reason to stop now.

Hart and Laurel shared a look, clearly not believing him. But they didn't press the matter.

"We'll keep you as informed as we can. We're going to be looking into the disappearance again, but no real answers can come until the forensic anthropologist gives us a report. We don't have a timetable on that."

Jack nodded. He'd never dealt with a case like this, so he wasn't fully abreast of the procedure, but he knew the general proceedings when anyone had to call in outside agencies for help. No doubt it would be a long, drawn-out process. Even more reason for his family to stay out of it. Focus on the lives they were building, cases that needed their attention, the ranch.

Mary showed the detectives back out, and Jack tried not to think about how long this was going to drag out. How much he was going to have to deal with the speculation at work. How difficult it was going to be to keep his family reined in.

But difficult was the name of the game, wasn't it? It wasn't like things had been particularly easy lately. Sure, his siblings had paired off, some of them starting families, but there had been danger and threat at every turn.

No rest for the wicked.

And still, he just stood in the office where they kept their paper files and stared blankly at the now-empty drawer. Sixteen years of work. Research. Investigation. And he was just handing it over to two people who'd never met his parents.

Who'd never been hugged by his mother or listened to one of his father's corny jokes. People who'd never been surrounded by the love that Laura and Dean Hudson had imbued every last interaction with.

They hadn't been perfect people. He knew that. But they'd been good.

And he thought he'd grieved over it a long, long time ago.

He knew, mired in all this old grief, he was absolutely doing the right thing for his family. Maybe he couldn't save them from going through this all over again, but if he could make a buffer, a wall between them and all this old hurt, he would consider it a success.

"For the record, I may not agree fully, but I understand what you're doing."

Jack turned toward Mary, who was standing in the doorway, arms across her chest and resting on her pregnant belly. Expression disapproving even if her words were about understanding.

"What's that?"

"Trying to protect us from the harsh reality that our parents were murdered, put in a shallow grave some seventeen years ago, and we never would have found the answers if not for Ry Brink's random and likely drug-fueled decision to dig a hole."

Jack felt something inside him constrict at the tidy, emotionless way Mary laid out the truth.

"You saw something you don't want us to have to see," she continued.

He tried to block the image of that ring and bones from his mind, but he couldn't quite manage it.

"I think if you were honest about that, you'd have more of us supporting you. Even Anna might relent a little if she knew—"

"Hawk will keep her in line."

"I can't believe you just said that. Out loud. And no bolt of lightning came to strike you down like it very well should."

"I didn't mean it like that. I just mean he loves her. He'll protect her, and that means keeping her from diving head-first into all this." Not that Jack was sure he'd succeed, but

Hawk was the only chance of Anna actually listening. So Jack would depend on it.

Mary was silent for a long while. "Sometimes love isn't about protecting people, Jack. Sometimes it's just about loving them." She didn't wait for him to have any answer to that. She just left.

Jack refused to engage with that sentiment. It was his normal weekend off from the sheriff's department anyway, so he went out and did some ranch chores. He went through his *normal* day, trying to shut everything off.

But it only seemed to settle deeper, tying tight, heavy knots in his gut, in his chest. Every step, every breath became harder. Every minute that ticked by seemed to be leading somewhere terrible.

Only nothing out of the ordinary happened. He had a normal dinner with his family. Well, not *normal*. There was a heavy quiet that had taken over the house today. Even baby Caroline appeared to have gotten the memo and wasn't overly fussy or energetic. No one could seem to muster a conversation that didn't immediately lull into silence.

People excused themselves earlier than usual. No one ate dessert. Jack had cleanup duty with Carlyle, whose nervous energy seemed to suck all his own energy away. Or maybe it was the fact that he hadn't really slept.

Once she'd brought all the dishes into the kitchen, she paused, staring at him. Since he'd never known her to hesitate over just about anything, he raised an eyebrow. "Something you wanted to say?"

"Cash wanted me to run it by you first, but I figure I'd tell Zeke," she said, referring to her brother *not* mixed up in the Hudson household. "He's got all those crazy connections to underground spy people. I know you want Bent County handling it, but Zeke might have a line on a good... What did they call it? Forensic person or whatever? He knows some people who could poke around, and they wouldn't get in Bent County's way."

Jack wanted to dismiss it out of hand. He wanted to dismiss everything out of hand, but the more people looking into this who weren't his family, the quicker this could move. "That'd be fine, Carlyle. Thank you for asking."

They worked in silence for a while; then, just about when they were finished and he thought he could escape to the isolation of his bedroom, Carlyle said something that stopped him in his tracks.

"Chloe's a good listener."

Jack turned his head slowly to stare at her. Her blue-gray eyes held his, but she didn't look accusatory or like she was holding some secret over his head.

She shrugged. "I just know, from experience, sometimes you don't want to, like…be a burden to your family. And I could sit here and lecture you for a million days how you're not, but it doesn't change the feeling you don't want to unload on the people also going through what you're going through."

"What does that have to do with Deputy Brink?"

Carlyle rolled her eyes. "*Chloe's* a good listener. That's all I'm saying." Then she shrugged and left the kitchen.

Leaving Jack standing there, breathing a little too hard. It wasn't concern that Carlyle knew he had a more-than-working relationship with Chloe. He'd had a bad feeling for a while that Carlyle had some inkling of what was going on between them. But she'd never come out and said anything, and Carlyle wasn't exactly *subtle*.

It was Mary's words about love. Carlyle's words about unloading on people. It was the oppressive silence in the house, like grief had tightened its ugly chains around the whole ranch once again.

He didn't want it to. That first year after losing his parents had been the hardest damn year of his life—all their lives—and he didn't want it touching any of his siblings again. Ever again.

But here it was, and he couldn't seem to breathe. Couldn't seem to find a solution. No amount of keeping them separate from the realities seemed to change what they were all feeling internally.

Sad and shaken and quiet.

Except there was something else inside him. A tightening in his chest, a struggle to breathe. The pressure of seventeen years beating down on him, like someone pounding a stake into the ground, and he was the stake.

He was half-afraid he was having some kind of cardiac event, but there was no shooting pain in his arm. No losing consciousness. Just this overwhelming *pressure*—worse but not all that different from when things went off-plan.

Panic attack.

To hell with that. Just to hell with it. He strode out of the kitchen, out the back door and toward his truck. Normally, he'd make sure someone knew where he was, but he couldn't. He just couldn't.

He had to get out, and even though he wouldn't admit to himself where he was going, it didn't surprise him to pull off onto the shoulder of the road that led up to Chloe's cabin fifteen minutes later.

He didn't turn into the driveway. He idled on the shoulder, staring at the front door. She likely had Ry in there. She wouldn't want her brother staying out at the ranch when he was unpredictable, and likely there was some police presence still. So this was a pointless endeavor. He wasn't going inside. He wasn't going to use her like some kind of crutch.

He did just fine on his own. Had for sixteen years. He'd finished raising a family. He'd built a business, been a cop, become sheriff. There wasn't anything he couldn't control. All on his own.

And still he fished his phone out of his pocket. Still he brought up a text message to Chloe.

He shouldn't do this. He knew he shouldn't. That was the wildest part of everything that had happened with Chloe since he'd let his guard down at that ridiculous party last year. She had touched him, wearing that excuse for a dress, and it had upended something inside.

Every finely tuned, rule-following, controlled, upstanding rule he'd set for himself, killed himself to follow…

He'd break, every time, when it came to her. Just like he was doing right now, typing out the text.

You want to go for a drive?

She didn't respond, but not two minutes later the door to the cabin opened, and she stepped outside. Her hair was wet, and she was wearing sweatpants and a sweatshirt, but she smiled at him and walked toward his truck, her cat in her arms.

And weirdly, he could breathe again.

Chapter Four

Chloe hopped into the passenger side of Jack's truck, Tiger in her grasp. The minute she was settled, the cat immediately escaped and made a beeline for Jack's lap.

He looked rough. Oh, he hid it well. The stoic expression. The way, somehow, even though he likely hadn't slept at all, he looked as alert and in control as he always did.

But she saw the little things. The way his hand gripped the steering wheel. The impossibly tense clench of his jaw.

She wanted to reach across and rub her palm against it until he relaxed. But she didn't. Not yet. She wasn't quite sure what this was yet. Truth be told, she was always waiting for him to drop the hammer. End this. Just because he hadn't yet didn't mean he never would.

But he had a lot more than *her* on his mind right now, and she doubted he had the mental capacity to finally come to his senses when it came to whatever they were doing.

"So, where we driving to?" She didn't explain Ry was staying at her cabin. If he hadn't already known it, he would have come up to her door.

"I... I'm not sure," he said.

Worry slithered through her. She wondered if she'd ever once heard Jack say those three words. She tried to sound cheerful and unbothered, though. An anchor to how lost he seemed. "How about up around the scenic viewpoint?"

He nodded. "Yeah, that sounds good." He started driving, never once looking over at her. He drove with one hand on the wheel and one hand on Tiger, down the highway toward the turnoff that would lead up and around one of the smaller peaks, with pretty views out over the larger mountain range as a whole.

But not long after they'd passed the main entrance to the Hudson Ranch, he took a sharp and unexpected turn off the highway. Chloe had to grab on to the dash to keep from slamming into the door.

"Uh, where are we going?"

"Just a different place I know." His expression was grim, and even though he was making her a little nervous, she didn't say anything or ask any more questions. She just sat back and tried to figure it out herself.

It was a side road, but she was pretty sure they were on Hudson property. Confirmed when they drove past Palmer's new house that he and Louisa had finished about the time they'd gotten married.

Then the road changed from gravel to dirt and started going…up. Chloe's grip on whatever she could find tightened. She looked over at Tiger, whose eyes were half-closed as if it was naptime.

Meanwhile, Chloe's throat constricted, and her entire body tensed as it began to feel like they were driving straight up. Up the mountain. Chloe didn't consider herself squeamish about much, but narrow mountain roads weren't her favorite. That was why she'd suggested the overlook—the road up to it was paved and well maintained.

When he came to a stop and shoved his truck into Park, at such an angle gravity had her practically pressed to her door, she realized she'd been holding her breath. She let it out shakily, and Jack looked over at her.

For the first time today, she saw that grave, expression in his eyes turn to humor, which made her entire being *flutter*.

"Sorry. Forgot you get panicky about heights."

"Not panicky. Just not keen on tumbling to my death in a truck."

"Yeah, that's not panicky at all. Come on." He got out of the truck, Tiger in his arms like it was normal to carry a cat around. But for some reason, that cat looked content as could be wrapped up in Jack's arms.

Yeah, you know the feeling, don't you?

He grabbed a blanket from the back of his truck, tucked it under his free arm and then began marching toward some unknown point. He never said a word. She scurried after his long strides. She didn't mind heights when she was on her own two feet—or at least, that's what she tried to tell herself. Especially when Jack kept walking right up to the edge of what looked a hell of a lot like a cliff.

Chloe stepped very carefully behind him, but once she looked up from her feet, she stopped short.

"Jack," she breathed.

She'd seen a lot of pretty views. Sunrise and Bent County were full of them. She'd spent summers enjoying everything the Tetons and Yellowstone had to offer. She'd even gone up to Glacier with a friend from the police academy one summer. All those places had been awe-inspiring, gorgeous. It was amazing what the natural world could be.

But this was… She couldn't explain it. Not just the natural beauty of mountain and sky and land stretched out as far as the eye could see. There was something like a peaceful settling inside her. Like all her life, she'd been looking for this exact view, and now she'd finally found it.

The sun was sinking in the sky, but it wasn't sunset just yet. The world had taken on a softer, pinker hue, though. And Jack Hudson stood there, at the edge of this little out-cropping, holding her *cat*, and she knew she'd just...never get over him. Not in a million years.

One-handed, he spread out the blanket until she crouched to help him. Then they both sat down on it. The cat stayed curled in Jack's lap, definitely not about to give up comfort for the wild world around them.

This time she didn't resist the urge. She smoothed her hand down his jaw. He didn't relax, but he did turn to her. And when she wrapped her arms around him, all comfort, he accepted.

And finally, *some* of that tension left him.

Maybe when all was said and done, it wasn't the fantastic sex; it wasn't that he was so handsome or so good. It was this.

She seemed to be the only one who could comfort Jack Hudson. To ease that tension, to release some of those burdens he'd been perfecting carrying for so long. *She* had that power, and for all the ways this relationship was messed up and messy, she couldn't walk away from that.

When she pulled away, she didn't pull far. She leaned her head against his shoulder, and he rested his head atop hers while they both looked out at the sun's slow descent.

JACK DIDN'T REALLY know what he was doing. In so many different ways. He couldn't keep getting more and more mixed up with Chloe when he couldn't offer her anything except complications He didn't have time to just be *sitting* here, enjoying the feel of her head on his shoulder. There were things to do—ranch things, sheriff things, family things.

And still he sat, soaking in this moment in one of his favorite places on the ranch. The terms of his parents' will had been that he inherited the main house. The other kids had their pick of equal parcels of land once they reached eighteen, and Palmer had already staked out his. Grant was looking at one closer to the main road since Dahlia worked in town as the librarian. Mary and Anna seemed content to stay put in the main house and have their portions of land dedicated to the ranch, and Jack hoped they would always. Cash was still deciding what to do next after his cabin had been destroyed.

Jack had been in the main-floor bedroom since his parents had disappeared, and part of him figured he'd stay there till he croaked.

But he'd always secretly wanted to build a little house right here and wake up to that view every morning.

He shouldn't have brought Chloe here. She'd be part of that fantasy now too. And it was a fantasy neither of them could really afford.

Speaking of fantasies. "They're not going to listen to me, are they?"

She was quiet for a long while, and he wondered if he'd have to explain. He didn't want to. He already wished he hadn't said anything.

"I think you'd be surprised how much they'd listen to you if you were honest with them."

It made him think of Mary's little speech about love and protection. He didn't fully agree with her, but he understood a certain level of detachment in trying to hold everyone together, in trying to raise his siblings, had led to them thinking he was something of a benevolent dictator.

He didn't mind that. Maybe he even relished it a little bit since it made things easier. But it meant he'd lost the ability to know how to explain to them this was important. That his *protection* did come from love, no matter what Mary said.

"Then again, once they think about it, they'll probably figure out what you're actually doing."

"What's that?"

"Protecting them. It's what you're always doing. Everyone knows it. Sometimes you just irritate them enough with it, they can't see the forest through the trees."

"And what's the forest?"

"Love, Jack."

The word landed hard, right there at the center of his chest. He even tensed against it, and wished he hadn't because she'd no doubt feel it. But she didn't lift her head or scoot away. They sat there together. That silence wrapping around him like a cocoon, like a soft place to land.

Like the one place he could let his guard down enough to speak the truth. "I didn't realize that I still had this ridiculous hope they were still alive."

She rubbed a hand up and down his back, and he thought maybe he'd survive all this crushing weight if she kept doing that.

"Hope is the human condition," she said, a little too philosophically for his taste. But she shrugged and kept going. "No matter how many times he proves me wrong, I hope *this* time will be the time Ry gets clean, gets his life together. Sometimes I have this awful daydream that my mother comes back and wants to bake Christmas cookies together."

"Ouch."

"Yeah. Life's kind of an ouch."

"That's why I keep trying to turn into a robot."

Which made her laugh. A rare thing. Oh, she laughed with Mary, with Anna, with just about everyone. But not as much with him as he would've liked.

She lifted her head from his shoulder, stretched forward and squinted out at the sunset. Then she turned back and met his gaze.

"You're not much of an avoider, Jack. So why'd you come out here?" She didn't ask the other question that hung in the air: *Why'd you come get me?*

Which he didn't have an answer for. Not one that did them any good anyway. So he answered the one she'd voiced. "It's like all those years I did my best to clean the ghosts out of that house, and now they're all back."

"Maybe they aren't so much ghosts as…legacy."

"Is that different?"

"Sort of. You loved your parents. They loved you. You guys had—*have*—a great family because they built it on a legacy of love. That was always going to hurt when a piece of it was lost, but it's also like this…really cool thing. Because you've got Izzy and Caroline—and whatever Mary's going to name the baby, which she *refuses* to tell me even though I know they've decided. They're all getting raised in that same legacy even though they'll never get to meet the people who started it. Not everyone gets that, Jack. Which doesn't mean it's not sad or doesn't hurt, especially losing them the way you did, especially having to relive it now. It just means…sad isn't all bad. Sometimes ghosts can be a comfort instead of something to run from."

He knew a lot of people saw him as brave, strong. That whole saint thing again. No one seemed to understand he always felt like he was running from something.

Except Chloe.

He wanted her. To come home with him, to share his bed. Not just because of sexual chemistry but also because of this. The moments where it felt like she was the only one he could lean on when he'd spent so many years refusing to lean on anyone.

She managed to find just the right access point to crack him open. He'd never understand how or why; he just knew that she did. And when he leaned on her, he didn't feel guilty or ashamed. She never let him.

Somehow it figured it'd be one of the few women in his life who was completely off-limits.

"We should get back."

She nodded, and that was that. She collected Tiger, against the cat's protests. Jack shook out the blanket, and then they walked back to his truck and drove all the way to Chloe's cabin without saying a single word.

He pulled into the drive this time, idling. She let Tiger out of the vehicle and then got out herself, but she leaned in.

"You don't have to wait for me to get in the door, Jack. I'm a big girl."

He nodded.

But he waited all the same.

Chapter Five

Chloe knew he wouldn't drive away just because she'd told him to. He'd wait until she got inside. She supposed it should irritate or frustrate her, but considering her parents hadn't cared that much about her when she'd been a *child*, she couldn't muster up taking offense to Jack's tendency to overprotect.

Hell, she didn't just not take offense—she downright loved it. She'd been taking care of herself and everyone else for as long as she could remember. She'd even dedicated her life to a job that protected other people, best she could.

Yeah, she didn't mind someone out there caring enough to protect *her* for once.

And that is why you find yourself in a dysfunctional, secret relationship.

So lost in her own thoughts, she nearly stepped on something on her porch, but she pulled her foot back in the nick of time.

A snake. Maybe two. Except not *full* snakes. Chunks. Mutilated. Chopped into pieces strewn about her pretty porch. She might have been able to convince herself it was the work of an animal except for the fact that the head of one was sticking out from one of her planters of cheerful pansies. *That* was pointed, and it made her stomach turn over a little bit.

"Call it in."

She nearly jumped a foot. She'd been caught so off guard by the snake, she hadn't heard Jack come up to see what had made her stop.

"Jack, it's a sick prank."

"Fine. I'll call it in."

She looked away from the gruesome sight and scowled at him. "Jack Hudson, you will not waste Sunrise's resources on something so pointless."

"Okay. You've called it in to me. I'll take the report. And the pictures." He patted his pockets, pulled out his phone and started taking pictures of the splattered remains.

"You're not on duty."

"I'm the sheriff. I'm always on duty."

Chloe rolled her eyes, but there was, per usual, no arguing with him. He took the pictures. He noted the time, looked around the house for footprints or tire prints that didn't belong to him or her cruiser.

Chloe went to the garage to figure out what she could use to clean it all up. Part of her wanted to make Ry do it, because God knew this probably had to do with him, but then he'd be out here with Jack, and she tried to keep them from being in the same orbit as much as she could.

Embarrassed of your own brother. What a great sister you are.

She strode into her garage, pushing away those old thoughts. Because Ry *was* embarrassing. He made bad choices she didn't approve of, and while that might not reflect on who *she* was as a person, while she might not be able to take over and stop him from those bad decisions, they *did* still affect her, and she got to have feelings about that.

She was a *damn* good sister, considering what her baby brother had put her through.

She blew out a long breath, attempting to get her rioting

feelings under control. How ridiculous that they were more about Jack and her brother than chunks of mutilated snake all over her porch.

Maybe Jack was right, and this was connected to last night. If she removed all feeling from the situation, it was plausible. But there were a *lot* of plausible explanations. Especially since her brother was staying with her right now and he was a beacon for trouble.

She got a shovel, then trudged back to the front porch. For all the ways she was used to Jack taking over, it still surprised her when he tried to grab the shovel out of her hand.

"I've got it."

"I'll do it," he replied. "You just want it buried out back, right?"

There was that forever internal fight. Let someone else handle it versus handle it herself. Jack was the only one in her acquaintance whose stubbornness ever matched her own, and it had made her complacent. She didn't want to be that.

Except she didn't want to fight him. She let him take the shovel, scoop up the snake remains—he'd even gotten some gloves from his truck and picked out the one in her flowerpot. Then he buried it all while she stood there...internally arguing with herself.

And still, per usual, she came to no answers. Because Jack was...

A problem.

Once he was finished, he put the shovel away himself, not even asking her where it went. Still, she knew he'd put it in the exact right place. And there was something about the current situation—the potential that his parents had been murdered and buried on her family's ranch—that made her fully realize just what had made him this way.

She liked to think *Oh, that's just Jack Hudson*, but it was more, wasn't it? Trauma. Through and through. He'd been forced to take care of five siblings and a ranch at *eighteen*. And instead of faltering, instead of losing himself in drugs or bad behavior as her brother had with all their trauma, Jack Hudson had built himself into *this*.

It was amazing. But more than that, for the first time, she really just felt sorry for him. The pressure he must have put on himself. The sheer weight he carried on those broad shoulders and probably didn't even realize it. Probably didn't even think to share it.

Because he'd always had to do it on his own.

It made a lump form in her throat because she knew all too well what that felt like, and still she knew he'd taken on more.

When he returned to her on the porch, his expression was grim. "I want you to come stay at the ranch."

Okay, *that* was a step too far, even with all this emotion swirling around inside her. "Honestly, Jack, what do you think this is besides some bad joke? Either by one of Ry's friends or some kids whose beer I poured out last week or maybe the guy I arrested for domestic assault last month or—"

"Two skeletal remains were found on property you partially own last night, then it just so happens you get a threatening prank at your cabin today? That's enough cause. Go on inside and get Ry."

She blinked, so taken aback by all this that she felt like she'd forgotten how to fight when her whole life had been about the fight. "For what?"

"He's coming too. I'll call Mary. We'll have two rooms ready."

For a long time she could only stare at him. Ry at the Hudson Ranch? Ry with *all* the Hudsons. And her. No. "Jack, Ry isn't…"

"I know what Ry is and what he isn't," Jack returned. "You're both going to be looked after until we get to the bottom of this."

Chloe felt like she couldn't breathe. *Looked after.* It was one thing in secret. It was another thing if he was *looking after* things in front of his family. Another thing if Ry was involved.

"Jack, we can't…"

"I understand your reticence, Chloe, I do," he said, his voice low and less cop-Jack and more the Jack he only ever was when they were alone together. "But this is concerning. I can't just ignore it, and I can't just let you handle it on your own when you've got Ry and a job to contend with and this could be… We don't have the first clue what happened here or with my parents. Until we do, we have to act with all the caution in the world so no one else gets hurt."

He tried to hide it, but she could easily see all that grief he'd talked about up at the overlook there in his dark eyes, and she didn't know how to argue with that. So she went inside to tell her brother they were going to stay at the Hudson Ranch.

JACK LET CHLOE drive Ry and Tiger over to the ranch in her personal car, though it pained him. They both had a shift tomorrow, so he could drive her to her cabin on the way into Sunrise headquarters and pick up her patrol car.

Maybe this whole thing was an overreaction. He could admit that he did that sometimes when it came to people's safety. But the saying *Better safe than sorry* was his own personal mantra. Maybe it *was* someone who was ticked off Chloe had arrested them, and she was as trained and capable of handling it as anyone, but it could just as easily be a threat that pertained to last night's discovery. And that made everything more tenuous.

Either way, someone had laid a threat at her door. The real shock was, she hadn't really fought him on it. She'd gone inside, collected her things and her brother—maintaining a clear barrier between him and Ry.

Jack wasn't sure which one of them she didn't trust, truth be told. He was pretty sure she had a clear head when it came to her brother, but Jack also understood—even though his siblings tended to stay on the right side of the law—how easily someone you felt responsible for could blind you to the reality of a situation.

Jack pulled up to the main house, Chloe parking her car next to his truck. It was dark now, but the external house lights were on, along with a few internal.

Ry looked up at the house with wide eyes as he got out of Chloe's car. Jack understood the mind of an addict a little too well. He was likely adding up how many hits he could get for the different things he saw. Jack hoped for Chloe's sake that Ry could keep it together for this.

Ry didn't say anything. Chloe seemed pretty determined to keep him and Jack from speaking at all, and Jack had no problem with that. He led them inside to where Mary was pacing the living room, Walker looking on disapprovingly from one of the armchairs.

"What happened?" Mary demanded. Not of Jack but of Chloe.

"Your brother overreacting?" She crouched and let Tiger go. The cat went all of three steps to lean against his leg.

"A mutilated snake was very purposefully strewn all over Chloe's porch sometime this evening," Jack said, trying to keep any and all inflection out of his voice.

Mary's expression pinched. "Then I have to agree with

Jack about you guys coming here. That timing... When you've never had anything like that happen—and then all of the sudden, bones and snakes. I don't like it."

"Well, you've got us in your clutches now. The magical Hudson Ranch, where nothing bad happens," Chloe said, irreverently, of course.

Jack's scowl deepened, but he didn't have to defend his position. Mary did it for him, and Jack was well aware Mary's very pregnant belly helped soften the message, and Chloe's belligerence.

"We have an extensive security system. You won't even get one of those doorbell cameras at your cabin."

Chloe wrinkled her nose. "Those can't protect you. All they can do is potentially identify whoever might be engaging in criminal behavior in their view."

Jack narrowly resisted rolling his eyes.

"Well, we've got some rooms made up. Follow me and I'll show you where to put your things. Are you hungry? We'll get you all set up." Mary was ushering them out of the room and up the stairs before anyone had a chance to answer any of her questions.

Walker was standing now, frowning at the stairs after his wife. "I tried to tell her to relax and let someone else handle it."

"Yeah, how'd that work out for you?"

Walker grinned. "Yeah, well, I know she's exhausted, because she let me help make the beds."

"Are you sure you shouldn't take her to a hospital right now?"

"That's not funny. I tried."

Jack chuckled. If there was anything that gave him *some* level of comfort, it was the fact that his siblings had all ended up with people who tried to take care of them and ran into the same roadblocks he always did.

"This whole snake thing seems pretty personal. Meant to make her scared," Walker said, growing serious.

Jack nodded because he agreed with the assessment, but he didn't say anything else because he could also tell Walker was fishing.

"The thing is, stuff like that only scares you if you know why you're being threatened."

Jack tried not to tense. Failed. "First of all, she wasn't scared. Not nearly scared enough for the situation. Second, I've known Chloe a long time. She's one of my best deputies. She doesn't know anything, or she would have said."

"What about the brother?"

Jack's mouth firmed. He wasn't any fan of defending Ry Brink. The guy had given Chloe a lot of grief over the years, and Jack figured he'd earned all the negative talk aimed his way. But... "I'm not saying Ry couldn't be involved in *something*, but those bones were buried on the Brink property a long, long time ago. Chloe *and* Ry would have been kids when it happened."

"Kids know things, too, Jack."

Unfortunately, Jack couldn't argue with that.

Chapter Six

Chloe didn't sleep well. When she caught snatches, she had dreams of skeletons and snakes. Her subconscious was *real* subtle.

The sun was only a faint glow in her window when she gave up and got out of bed. She'd check on Ry, go for a run and then figure out a way to sneak some coffee without having to sit down to a whole Hudson breakfast.

She considered tracking down her traitorous cat, but she had a feeling she knew exactly where Tiger would be this morning, and it was best if Chloe stayed away.

Satisfied with her plan, she got dressed in her running clothes, then quietly left the bedroom Mary had put her in last night. She knocked on the door next to hers—no answer. She eased the door open, but the room was empty. Dread curled in her stomach.

She thought she'd scared Ry enough into staying put, into not causing trouble, but when had that ever been the case?

She berated herself as she did her best to *silently* hurry down the stairs. She needed to make sure he'd left and wasn't wreaking havoc somewhere on Hudson property. Or sneaking around this house trying to sniff out some booze.

But when she reached the bottom of the stairs, she breathed a small sigh of relief. Ry was there, creeping toward the front door. Maybe he'd slept and was only now considering his escape. She certainly hoped so.

"What the hell are you doing?" she hissed at him.

He jumped and whirled. Then his shoulders slumped in relief when his eyes landed on her. "I wasn't doing nothing," he whispered right back.

She didn't bother to correct his grammar like she might have ten years ago. Back then she'd been so sure she could change him, mold him, at least get him to graduate high school so he'd stop hanging out with their father and *his* no-good crew.

No such luck there. Now she just hoped she could keep him sober for however long she put up with the Hudsons trying to protect them from whatever was being threatened. Then go back to the hands-off life her therapist had suggested was best.

How on earth had she gotten twisted up in this very complicated situation? She should have known all those years ago, when her father had been adamant about transferring his assets to them before he'd been arrested, that having her name on the ownership of Brink land was only ever going to bring her trouble.

So much trouble.

She got close to Ry and waved her finger at him. "You promise me, *promise me*, you don't know what that snake thing was about?" She'd already had this conversation with him in the car last night, but he'd been a little drunk after finding her secret stash while she'd been out watching the sunset with Jack.

Because that was what a girl got for doing something she wanted to do.

But anyway, she wanted to make sure he'd still promise when he was sober.

"Nobody knew I was staying at your place, Chlo. Even if they did, they're gonna steer clear of a cop's house. Why would my friends want to mess with you?"

She believed him, mostly because for all the trouble she'd had with Ry before, it was nothing like this. Nothing that targeted her directly. He'd only ever asked her to get him *out* of trouble. Or for money. No petty dead-animal games with her brother's equally useless addict friends.

It really bugged her that the most reasonable explanation for the snakes was connecting it to the skeletal remains on the ranch. Bugged her because it meant she agreed with Jack, and it meant it would make sense for them to keep staying here.

But boy, was her brother the biggest liability.

"Morning."

Ry let out a little yelp of surprise, and Chloe reached for the gun she was not wearing, thank goodness. But when she turned to face the source of the voice—Jack, of course— she noted his raised eyebrow like he knew exactly what she'd been doing.

"Going somewhere?" he asked casually.

But there was nothing casual about the way he looked at Ry. Cop to criminal. Looking for signs that he'd done some-thing wrong. Just like Chloe herself had done.

But when Jack did it, she had to fight the urge to stand between them. To defend her brother.

"A run," Chloe said, offering him her best sunny smile. "I was trying to convince Ry to go with me, but he's not much into exercise."

Jack nodded as if he believed her story. She knew he didn't.

"Chloe tells me you're good with animals," Jack said. Directly to Ry.

Ry stared at Jack, unblinking for a full minute. "Er, yes, sir."

Chloe wanted to laugh, even with her insides all twisted up. She wasn't sure she'd ever heard her brother call anyone *sir*, but Jack was the kind of guy who brought it out in people, she supposed.

"I've got a job for you, if you're wanting to avoid running."

"Uh." Ry looked at Chloe, clearly hoping for her to make an excuse for him.

"He'll take it," Chloe supplied instead. She didn't relish the idea of Jack and Ry hanging out, but she'd seen that look on her brother's face when she'd caught him trying to creep out of here. He'd been ready to go stir up some trouble, and the only thing that ever kept him out of trouble was work. Work with animals was even better. He *was* good with them. Much better than he was with people, that was for sure.

"Cash could always use a set of hands. I'll take you over." Jack tilted his head away from the front door and toward the back of the house. "Follow me."

"Uh. Okay," Ry said, clearly uncomfortable, but it was hard to argue with Jack when he was in Mr. Ruler of the World mode. Which was most of the time, she supposed.

Ry took a few hesitant steps forward before Jack began to lead him out of the room.

"You wait right here, Chloe," Jack said firmly, his back to her as he led Ry away. "We'll take that run together."

She scowled after his retreating form. She *hated* when he bossed her around. Well, in this kind of context, anyway. But since she was a guest in this house, she felt like she had to listen to him.

Which was really, really annoying.

JACK LED RY toward Cash's dog barns without saying anything. It was a bit early yet, even for the ranch, but Jack hadn't been able to sleep. He'd laid in his bed, staring at the ceiling, knowing Chloe was right above him. Talking himself out of going up there over and over again.

He felt terrible from lack of sleep, but he was damn proud of himself for having *some* restraint when it came to Chloe.

The morning was cool—a little overcast, so the dawn seemed to hang on longer than usual. Cash and Carlyle wouldn't be out at the barns just yet since it was so early, but it gave Jack a chance to have a one-on-one conversation with Ry Brink.

He studied the man. Slight and fidgety, but not angry. Uncertain and nervous, sure, but he didn't look like he was going to bolt or be defiant.

Jack didn't know what Chloe and Ry had been discussing this morning at the front door, but it definitely wasn't a *run*. A lecture about behavior, maybe, but Jack doubted Ry was up at the crack of dawn for *good* reasons.

Jack pointed to the dog barn in the distance. "You know about my brother Cash, right?"

"Sorta. He's got lots of dogs or something?" Ry looked around the barn like he was expecting them all to come running. "I do like dogs."

"He trains them, for all sorts of things. Carlyle Daniels works for him helping train them, but they can always use another body. It's a lot of work, training them and making sure they're in good shape. If you like dogs, it's a good way to spend a day. And you can spend as many days as you like doing it, as long as you follow instructions."

Ry pulled a face at that. Jack sighed inwardly. He dealt with people all the time who didn't like to be told what to do—his family, people he pulled over, flat-out criminals—

so he knew he had to lay this out in the simplest terms lest Ry be rebellious just for the sake of not following someone else's rules.

So he stopped, leaned on the fence and studied Ry with his most detached cop look. No emotion, no reaction. Just reason and sense. "I know you don't like cops—or me. And that's fine, I don't need you to."

Ry fidgeted, not meeting Jack's gaze.

"I know a lot of things about you, Ry. But first and foremost, I know this—your sister feels responsible for you. You mess this up, you mess her up."

Ry chewed on his bottom lip, looked around at the dusky dawn of morning across the ranch. "I know." Then he shrugged. "I don't do it on purpose. I don't like messing her up, but I can't seem to help it."

"Try. For as long as it takes to figure this out, give it your best shot. We can keep you busy. We can help in whatever ways you might need that don't include substance abuse. But I need to know you want to try."

Ry's frown was frustrated but not belligerent exactly. "I just like to have a little fun and get carried away sometimes."

"You're an addict, Ry. First step in helping your sister would be admitting that to yourself."

The frown turned into a scowl, with some pointed anger thrown in. "I didn't have anything to do with those bones, man."

"I don't think you did."

Ry looked up at him suspiciously. "Really?"

"It takes time for bodies to decompose, Ry. I can't imagine you were more than seven when those bodies were put in the ground. Even if they were newer, you don't strike me as mean enough to kill anybody."

"I'm not."

He did not say those words proudly. He said them almost as if he was ashamed of it. Jack couldn't say he liked that take on the matter. It gave him a different kind of worry—that Ry might *want* to be capable of murder.

But he could only handle one problem at a time. "Your dad, on the other hand..."

"It does sound like something my dad would do," Ry agreed. "I mean, I never heard about him killing anybody, but he sure liked to beat people up."

Jack knew this. He'd arrested Mark Brink for a domestic assault his first year working as a county deputy. But the girlfriend he'd beaten up had refused to press charges. And Jack never liked to think about what that might have meant for the childhood Chloe endured, even if her parents had divorced early on. But she'd bounced between the two—neither one upstanding, reliable or good parents, clearly.

"You ever see him get close?"

Ry sighed, not nervous or fidgety so much now. Bored. Craving a hit. Who knew. "The cops already asked me all about Dad. I don't have like some secret memory of him killing someone and burying them at the ranch, man. And there isn't anything in it for me if I protect him, so I ain't lying."

Jack nodded. Fair enough. And he'd told himself he'd stay out of it. He could hardly ask his siblings to do what he told them if he was investigating.

He had to let Bent County take care of it.

He squinted across the yard, saw Cash and Carlyle making their way from the main house. When they reached the fence where Jack and Ry were, Jack made introductions, even though Ry and Cash knew of each other.

Jack knew Cash and Carlyle could handle this, but still he hesitated leaving them with Ry. It felt a little bit too much like foisting his responsibilities off on someone else.

But he and Chloe had work, and this was the best-case scenario in keeping Ry out of trouble.

"You do as you're told, or I kick your ass. Got it?" Carlyle was saying to Ry after she'd explained their opening procedures with letting the dogs out.

Ry's eyes were wide, but he nodded. Carlyle flashed Jack a grin.

It did a lot to assuage his worries about leaving Ry here with them. Enough so that he headed back to the main house and Chloe. He wouldn't be surprised if she didn't wait for him, but he stopped by his bedroom and changed into clothes he could run in.

If it was a bluff, he'd call it. But when he returned to the living room, she was there—bending over, touching her toes, stretching out before her run, he assumed. And she was wearing skin-tight running gear, which did support her previous story. Yet he was having trouble thinking about anything but getting his hands on her.

He didn't know what it was about her that tested all that hard-won control he'd always been so proud of. He'd been attracted to other women before, had *liked* other women before, but something about the package of Chloe Brink made him feel like an entirely different person than the one he'd so ruthlessly crafted over the years.

She stopped stretching, looked over her shoulder at him. She didn't say anything, didn't voice her concerns, but he saw them in her eyes.

"Carlyle's in charge of keeping him in line," he said. "I think he's afraid of her."

Her mouth quirked. "Well, that does ease my concerns about going to work later. Carlyle *can* handle him. For a while, anyway."

"He'll be okay."

Chloe shrugged. "Maybe. Maybe not. But I can't twist my life around him. Learned that one the hard way." She blew out a breath. "Thought my cat would be trailing after you, per usual."

"Tiger found someone he likes better than even me." When she raised an eyebrow, he couldn't stop himself from smiling. "Izzy."

Chloe smiled at that too, as he'd been hoping she would. "Well, he's in good hands, then."

"So, run?"

Her smile died and she sighed. "You hate running, Jack."

"I don't hate it."

"You *hate* it, and I think your family would find it a little weird you're doing something you hate with me at the butt crack of dawn. I don't need a bodyguard."

Which was probably true, and maybe he should just let this go. But he didn't. "I didn't realize you were an expert on the layout of the Hudson Ranch."

She rolled her eyes. "Jack."

"Chloe."

Something in her expression hardened. "I think you're supposed to call me Deputy Brink here."

He didn't know what this was about, but he could admit that something about being *here* made him a whole lot less interested in ignoring any tension there was between them. "Do you want to have a fight about it?"

She huffed out a breath. "No."

"Then let's go run."

"Fine," she muttered.

He led her outside, pointed to the fence line. "We can follow this out toward the highway, then turn back. Should be about two and a half miles."

"I usually do five."

Jack tried not to pull a face. "We can do it twice, then." What a waste of time.

But then she laughed and slapped him gently in the chest. "Messing with you. One round is fine. Think you can beat me?"

"My legs are longer."

"Is that a yes?" she returned, eyebrows raised.

But he only shrugged. She shook her head. "All right, buddy. Ready, set, go." Then she took off. Too fast to start a two-and-a-half-mile run. Or so he thought in the beginning. He assumed he'd catch up to her, but she always maintained a distance. It got slimmer the longer they ran, but even when he began to pour it on, she kept ahead of him.

When the house came back into view, he ran as hard as he could manage. He made it close, but she still beat him. And they both ended in the front yard, bent over hands on their knees, panting.

And laughing. He didn't know why she was laughing. Maybe because she'd won. He was laughing because it was ridiculous, when he very rarely got prodded into the ridiculous. He was laughing because it didn't seem to matter what they did or why—just being around her lifted all those weights on his shoulders he'd thought were permanent.

The way she laughed, smiled, enjoyed the smallest things.

"You're going to have to run with me all the time now," she said, wiping her forehead with her forearm. "Beating you is my best time in a while."

All the time. He tried not to think about it, because their jobs made it impossible, but he wondered if she knew how little he'd mind *all the time.* Forever.

When she looked over at him, gave him a little chest pat he figured was supposed to be a friendly, *good game*–type gesture, he couldn't help himself. He held her by the wrist, pulled her in.

She didn't resist, but she did look up at him warily. "Anyone could see us, Jack."

"Yeah." But he didn't move, and neither did she.

Chapter Seven

Chloe did not understand what was happening between them. For an entire *year*, the lines had been very clear, and both of them had been dedicated to keeping it that way.

But the past few days were getting all muddled, blurry, when it was the last thing that should be happening, what with skeletal remains and mutilated snakes and her own damn family. It was turning her soft.

Because she should have pushed him away, but she let him kiss her here. In broad daylight. In front of the Hudson house, which housed like a hundred people. People who would have questions, who would tell other people, who would erase all the lines they'd carefully drawn.

And still she drowned in the kiss. They weren't supposed to *do* this, but she couldn't stop herself because he kissed her with a gentleness that undid all her paltry walls. These were the ones that really got to her. He didn't pull this out often. Usually, there wasn't time for soft, leisurely. But his hands were on her face, his grip gentle as the kiss spun out into something that reached deeper than anything else ever had, until she felt like gravity simply ceased to exist.

He eased back, his dark eyes studying her face, his mouth still just a breath from hers. She wasn't quite sure how, after a year of sneaking around, something could change, but something had.

Maybe this place was magic. *Or a curse.*

She had to shake her head to get both ridiculous thoughts out. Step away from him to find some anchor in this storm. "We have to get to work." Her voice shook.

"Yeah." His voice didn't, but his exhale did.

Well, at least there was that.

She should break it off. Stop this right now. Before it got more complicated.

It was already way too complicated.

But she walked back into his home, shoulder to shoulder to him, and didn't say a word. They went their separate ways in the house, and she ran through the shower upstairs, got dressed for work and then ignored Mary's insisting she eat something. She knew Jack expected to drive her over to her cabin and drop her off at her cruiser, but she needed some space.

She didn't even get halfway to her car before she heard him call her name. She turned. He'd also showered, changed into work clothes. He looked put together as always, in his perfectly pressed khakis and Sunrise Sheriff's Department polo.

His expression was very grim, which wasn't all that unusual for work, but there was something about him that had her tensing.

"We have to get to the hospital," he said, striding toward his cruiser.

"The hospital. Why?"

"Suzanne just called me," he said, referring to the Sunrise administrative assistant. "Kinsey was at your place when—"

"You had someone watch my cabin overnight?" she demanded, surprised by this brand-new information, which he had neither shared with her nor asked permission to *do*.

"No, I had someone drive by a few times overnight and—"

"Without telling me?"

"Yeah, without telling you. Now, would you let me finish?" He jerked open the driver's-side door. "Kinsey was shot at. Suzanne says it was just a graze, but he's at the hospital getting it looked at, and we need to go down there and get his story."

Chloe's heart slammed against her chest, enough to get over the frustration with Jack doing all that without telling her. She hopped into the passenger seat. "You sure he's okay? Should I call Julie?" Steve's wife would no doubt be worried sick.

Steve Kinsey had been with Sunrise since its inception, moving with Jack over from Bent County. He was in his late forties and had three teenagers at home, who he liked to bemoan even though he did everything he could to take time off to make all their many birthdays, holidays and sporting events.

"He called Julie himself. He's fine," Jack said, pulling out of the Hudson Ranch and onto the main highway, which would take them into Hardy and to the hospital.

But his hands were so tight on the wheel that his knuckles were white. Back to a perfectly capable outer shell and nothing inside but ticking time bombs.

Chloe blew out a slow breath, trying to focus on the important things. Steve had been shot. At her cabin? "Was someone trying to break in?"

"Suzanne didn't have the details. We'll get them from him ourselves."

They drove for a while in silence. Sometimes she wished

she couldn't read him so easily. She tried—so hard—to keep her mouth shut. To let him deal with his stuff without trying to offer some kind of comfort.

This was work. This was that line they had *both* agreed on. And it was a line that had worked for a *year*.

But as they approached the hospital, she couldn't keep it in any longer. "It could have been anything, Jack. Not just the thing you asked him to do. That's the job."

"But it wasn't anything, was it?" Jack pulled the cruiser in front of the hospital, and they got out at the same time.

Jack took the lead, a sheriff down to the bone as he talked to the front desk and a nurse, before they were finally led into a room.

Steve sat on an exam table and even smiled at them—if ruefully—when they entered.

"I'm fine, boss. Just grazed me." He wiggled his bandaged arm. "Not even keeping me." He nodded at Chloe, then looked back at Jack. "I didn't see anything, though, that's the kicker."

"As long as you're okay, that doesn't matter."

Steve clearly didn't agree, but he didn't argue with the sheriff. He launched into an explanation. "I was driving by Brink's house on my way back to the station. Thought *maybe* I saw a light. Figured she'd just left one on, but since there'd been some trouble, I got out to check it out."

"You radioed that in?"

Steve nodded. "I parked in the driveway, turned the flashlight on and started to walk toward the side of the house. Told myself I was overreacting—but then, out of nowhere, I just heard *pop*. And felt it." He gestured at the bandage. "That was it, though. Must have run off. If they'd wanted real trouble, they would have *really* shot me. Would have been easy pickings," he said disgustedly.

Chloe felt sick at the thought.

"I called it in to Suzanne. I was ready to go check out the backyard, but Suzanne's fussing about ambulances and blah, blah, blah. I think Bent County is out there looking at it now."

"Bent County? But it's our jurisdiction," Chloe said.

Steve's expression was unreadable. "Sort of."

"What does 'sort of' mean?" Chloe demanded as Steve's gaze moved to Jack. "Jack, what does that mean?"

If Steve thought it was weird that she'd used his first name instead of *Sheriff*, he didn't act like it.

"I reported the snake to Bent County."

She didn't know exactly why that made her so angry except that he was...taking over while keeping her out of it. Something that involved *her* ranch, *her* brother, *her* house, her *life*. "I live in Sunrise."

"Yes, and I happen to think all of this connects to what was found on the ranch. And that's Bent County's case. Besides, it's a conflict of interest for Sunrise to investigate."

"That's *if* it has something to do with *me*. And I wasn't home. Either time. Maybe they thought I would be, should be, but it seems strange that if this was about *me*, they wouldn't make sure they knew exactly where I was."

"Unless they didn't want you there," Steve suggested. "Seems to me, creeping around your cabin is looking for something. Maybe they were looking for your brother."

Chloe didn't glare at Steve. She didn't even look at him. She kept her ire focused on Jack. Even if none of this was his fault, either, he was an easier target.

But his eyebrows were drawn together as though he was thinking. "Maybe it's not *you*. Not Ry. Maybe they *wanted* you out of the way. Maybe there's something *in* the cabin they want."

"What could I have in the ca…" She trailed off, a horrible thought occurring to her. "Some of my father's things. I have them in my garage."

JACK DROVE TO Chloe's cabin. She said nothing, and he didn't know what to say either, so the ride was in absolute silence. Seeing Steve had eased some of the tension about the situation—he really was fine and thinking clearly, but Jack still didn't like any of his deputies being hurt on the job.

But it *was* the job. And he had to focus on the next step of it: trying to figure out why someone suddenly had Chloe—or Ry, or her cabin—in their sights.

He pulled his truck into the driveway. Jack frowned at the fact that there wasn't anyone here. "I should call someone at County."

Chloe shook her head, already getting out of the truck. "If there was something to say, they'd be here or they'd have called me."

Jack sighed and followed her. She went right for the garage, that determined focus stamped into the expression on her face.

"He did all this stuff before he got arrested," she was saying, opening the garage, striding toward a bunch of boxes. "Wanted us to spend time on the ranch with him. Told us it was our *legacy*."

She started moving boxes, and Jack wanted to help, but he didn't know what she was looking for, and it seemed like maybe she just had to do this herself.

"He tells me he wants us on the deed. I've done all right for myself, if being a government patsy is all right. But he's worried about Ry. Wants Ry to run it, even though it's not profitable—but hey, it's a house. It's *something*, I figured." She tossed a tub out of the way. "Used all my guilt, all my worry about Ry to get my name on there too." She shook her head, clearly disgusted with herself.

"My first year at Sunrise. I know I was green, but I also knew *him*. I should have seen it for what it was. A criminal who knew his time was up. He tells me he's getting rid of stuff so he can be 'free' and all this other nonsense. Asks me if I want some family heirlooms. I should have said no. I *know* I should have said no, but I—"

"Nothing wrong with wanting family heirlooms, Chloe."

"Oh, come on, Jack. I know who my family is. Criminals begetting criminals. Sure, maybe I hoped somewhere along the line, the Brinks had this ranch because *someone* wasn't totally worthless. Maybe there was some immature fantasy about inheriting a sense of right and wrong from *someone*, but I know better. I should have known better."

She finally stopped moving things, her breath coming in pants from the physical exertion. There was an old antique-looking chest pressed back in the corner of the garage.

She glared at it. "I never looked through it. He used to do this thing. I couldn't quite believe it *wasn't* heirlooms, but I knew. I knew it was just the usual way he liked to mess with me."

"And how was that?"

She shrugged jerkily. "Once my parents really split, he was in and out of our lives. Sometimes he'd come around and Mom was tired of us, and we'd have to go spend a week or two at the ranch with him. He'd always have presents. For me. But they were just…joke gifts."

Jack doubted he'd agree with the word *joke*, but he didn't press. He had to bite the inside of his cheek to keep his mouth shut, but he did it.

"I should have looked through it and gotten rid of it." She swallowed, clearly emotional about the whole thing. "I was a coward."

"You're human, Chloe."

She didn't look at him, just kept staring at the chest.

And this was work. They weren't Chloe and Jack here. He was the sheriff. She was a deputy. There was a case to untangle. One they were both way too close to. He should call in Bent County for this, but...

She needed to handle this first step herself. She undid the latch, but paused before she lifted the lid and took a deep breath. She looked up at him.

"Whatever this is, Jack, I need you to keep in mind that if those remains are your parents, the chances my family had *nothing* to do with it are slim to none."

He knew she was right. That all the ways this was twisting was likely leading to a very clear place. Maybe that should matter to him, but with her staring at him like that, all emotionally wounded, it just didn't.

"Maybe."

She shook her head, and her eyes were a little shiny, enough to make his heart twist. When she spoke, though, she was firm.

"Not maybe. Basic reason."

"You're not your family, Chloe." He wished he could make her believe that. Wished there were some magical words he could find to erase all that pain for her.

"But they're mine all the same," she muttered, then lifted the lid.

She jumped back with a little shriek he'd never once heard come out of her. He moved, with half a thought to protect her from whatever was inside, but the scene in the chest had him recoiling as well.

Dolls. A lot of them. Mutilated and smeared in what Jack could only assume had been blood.

Chapter Eight

Chloe should not have been surprised. She certainly shouldn't have shrieked. Another joke gift. She should have known—she *had* known, but she'd wanted to live in hope that somewhere along the line, the name Brink hadn't been garbage. As long as this chest had remained closed, she could pretend there were nice family heirlooms inside. Artifacts of a family line that wasn't just waste.

She should have sucked it up, been a realist and dealt with this a million years ago. Because *now* she had to deal with it in front of Jack. Served her right, she guessed.

"It was a dumb thought," she managed to say, though her voice was rough. She moved forward, tried to keep her arms from shaking and failed as she flipped the lid closed. "No one's after this. Just his usual stunts. Probably laughed himself all the way to jail on this one."

Jack took her by the arm, started steering her out of the garage. Away from the chest, thank God. What was she going to do now? She needed to haul it out of here. She needed...

"You go on inside," Jack said. His voice was gentle, but *cop* gentle. Devoid of real emotion. Just getting the job done. "I'm going to call in Bent County. I'll put on gloves and look through it while we wait for Hart or Delaney-Carson to get here."

Panic spurted through her. No one needed to see this. No one needed to start sorting through all the gross, messed-up pointlessness of a childhood with Mark Brink as a father.

Worse than that, the idea of Jack sorting through all those horrible, gruesome dolls when she knew something worse might be lurking.

Dear old Dad had made sure to be clear that it could always, *always* be worse.

She didn't pull out of Jack's grasp, but she did move in front of him and plant her feet so he couldn't keep ushering her out. "Don't do that, Jack. Not alone. Not…" She couldn't articulate how little she wanted Jack wading through this. "He did this kind of thing. It's not—"

"Someone was sneaking around your place, willing to shoot at an officer. There are dead bodies buried on a ranch with your name on the deed. A mutilated snake was purposefully left on your porch. All in the span of forty-eight hours. We need to look into everything. No matter how off the wall it feels. No matter how little you want to."

"You think he did it. Murdered your parents. Buried them on his ranch. You think this is a clue, but—"

"*You* think he did it, Chloe," Jack said gently, and the grasp on her arm softened, his palm sliding down to her hand. He covered it with his, squeezed. "I don't know what to think. So we'll take it a step at a time. I don't want you seeing this. I'll go through it. You go inside."

She swallowed the lump in her throat that just kept growing. "There could be worse in there. I don't want *you* going through it. What if there's something…"

"Something?"

"He's an abusive, violet criminal. Those dolls could be

just a scare tactic he thought was funny, or they could be hiding something worse."

Jack studied her face, something grim and…looking a lot like fury seeming to darken his gaze. Emotionless cop gone, just like that. "Were the joke gifts he gave you when you were a kid *usually* hiding something worse?"

She held herself very still, purposefully blocking out old memories she didn't want to show on her face. Her father's had never stuck around long. She liked to pretend he hadn't been there at all.

But he'd done damage in what little spaces he'd had. It didn't take a *lot* of bad experiences to know he was capable of awful things. Only one, and the threat of a repeat.

She did not want Jack knowing that, but she couldn't seem to come up with a lie to get that protective look off his face. Like he could go back in time and make it all right.

"It doesn't matter," she managed.

"Chl—"

"I said, it doesn't matter, and it doesn't. This isn't about… It was a mistake to think this is connected. It's a mistake to start digging into…" But she couldn't finish that sentence because if her father was responsible for the dead bodies on the Brink Ranch—and God knew that was looking more and more likely—everything he'd done back then would be examined under a microscope to determine motive, means and opportunity.

She wanted to throw up.

"What happened to you when you were a kid isn't—"

She couldn't take his pity. She wouldn't. "I've had therapy, Jack. I've dealt with my garbage bin of a childhood. I don't need you and your perfect one psychoanalyzing me."

She sucked in a breath, immediately regretting everything she'd just said. She could have punched herself for how insensitive it was. Sure, he'd had a great childhood—but then, he'd also spent every second of his adulthood stepping into his missing parents' shoes. "I'm sorry."

He shook his head like it didn't matter. But it did. This all mattered, and she *hated* it.

She moved her hand so she was grasping his instead of the other way around. She looked into those dark, fathomless eyes, and she didn't care if she was begging. She just needed this to not explode on her. "Please. I wouldn't ask this of you if it didn't matter. Please. Don't." She wouldn't cry. "Let the detectives handle it. With the right gear, the right warning." She *wouldn't* cry. Not in front of Jack—her *boss*. Because that's what he was right now.

Not the guy who'd kissed her this morning like she was special. It didn't do any good to think about that completely separate moment.

"Okay." His free arm came around her, pulled her close. Even though they both wore their uniforms. Their gun belts. Their radios. He shouldn't do this. She shouldn't let him.

But she didn't pull away, because she was shaking, and if he held her, maybe she could find some anchor in the midst of all this mess.

JACK COULDN'T CONVINCE Chloe to go inside, but he did get her to sit down on the stoop of her cabin porch—where he'd just cleaned up snake remains yesterday.

Only forty-eight hours. No, he didn't like this, or that it pointed to something more *current* happening around a very old potential murder.

He glanced back at her. She'd been startled by the snake, but it hadn't really affected her. This? It had shaken her. He'd never seen her quite so affected by *anything*, not that he couldn't blame her for it. The dolls were creepy enough on their own—add the fact that it was clearly and purpose-fully done to mess with her by her own father...

Jack supposed it was a good thing Mark Brink was in prison over a thousand miles away, because the way all this information settled inside him was testing his usually impeccable control.

As it was, he focused on the present. He didn't sit next to her on the stoop. It seemed to agitate her more. So he stood just out of reach, waiting for Bent County to arrive.

When they did, Jack handled everything. He wasn't sure that was what she wanted, and he knew he could be over-bearing—his siblings made sure he knew. He didn't mind it when it came to them, but it bothered him with Chloe.

She had a say too, but this was... Like anything else, he couldn't protect her from *everything*. But he would protect her from what he could.

Besides, he was the sheriff.

So he instructed the deputies to take the chest away and search it with the utmost caution and keep everything as potential evidence for the time being. When the detectives arrived, Jack explained the situation, and they did what they were supposed to do.

Hart separated Jack from Chloe and asked *him* questions about what had happened while Laurel no doubt did the same with Chloe. Jack didn't like it, but he understood they were doing their job. A job complicated by the fact that the people involved were also cops.

Jack could see Laurel and Chloe on the porch, but Hart had pulled him out by his cruiser close to the street, so he had no idea what Laurel was asking or how Chloe was answering. But he had to focus on the questioning *he* was part of.

He explained what had led them to look at the chest, what

he'd seen, what Chloe had said about it. Hart noted down his answers, and once he was satisfied, he switched gears to all their other issues.

"Since Mark Brink would have lived on the land at the time of your parents' disappearance, we've already been looking into him," Hart explained, "in regards to the remains. Just to get an idea of the players if the ID is positive. We called the correctional facility in Texas, and they got back to us this morning."

Jack could tell by the way Hart said it that the news wasn't going to be good.

"He got out on parole last week."

Jack swore.

"So far he's cooperated with his parole officer. It'd be quite the feat for him to get up here, wait around until the cabin was empty, do all that with the mutilated snake and then get back for his check-in."

"A feat, but not impossible."

"No, not impossible," Hart agreed. "We're arranging to have an interview with him. It might be another day or two. Lots of red tape to wade through."

"Isn't there always," Jack muttered. He really had no idea what to do with this information. It was such a strange thing, to have all these answers visible but out of reach. There was still the off chance those remains weren't even his parents'—though he didn't hold out any hope for that.

Maybe he hadn't given up on hope, on answers, but he hadn't thought they'd land on his doorstep one random day with Chloe in tow. Surrounded by all these seemingly disparate events.

"Speaking of red tape," Hart continued. "Zeke got us hooked up with a forensic anthropologist. She got here this morning. We've got to get through some paperwork to make sure everything goes smoothly from a legal standpoint, but she should be able to get to work tomorrow. Once she can examine the remains, she'll have an ETA on identification. We'll keep moving forward with the investigation, but it's going to take time to narrow down time frames."

Jack nodded stiffly.

"We're sorry we don't have more clear-cut answers for you just yet, but we're working on it."

"Luckily, I know how it all works."

"Not sure how lucky that is."

Jack tried to force a smile but knew he didn't manage. He glanced back at the porch, where Laurel and Chloe were still talking. Chloe had definitely put her cop mask back on. She didn't look upset or rattled.

But it was lurking underneath. How could it not?

"Look, I know Brink is one of your deputies," Hart said, lowering his voice to almost a whisper even though Chloe wouldn't be able to hear them from this distance. "But this is bound to get messy. It might be better if you kept some distance. I'm not sure her and Ry Brink being in the Hudson Ranch-Hudson Sibling Solutions circle is the best move here."

Jack let Hart have his say, and he didn't bother to argue or defend himself. He just said his response in the simplest terms there were. "It's the only move here."

Because he'd be damned if he was going to keep his distance from Chloe when she might be in some kind of danger. He walked away from Hart, not about to wait for the man's permission.

He was a sheriff. Head of the Hudson clan. And damn if he was going to be scared of *messy* when Chloe might have to pay the cost of that fear.

Laurel moved away from Chloe before Jack reached the

porch, and she nodded at him. "I'll keep you updated on what we find. We'll treat it like a joint Sunrise-Bent County venture for as long as that makes sense. Unless you want to be kept out of this part too?"

Jack shook his head. "I want to know everything about that chest."

Laurel didn't say anything, but she didn't hide the fact she was studying him either. Then she shrugged and walked over to Hart, and the two took their leave.

Chloe approached Jack, chin up, eyes fierce and a little bright. He could already tell there was a storm brewing deep underneath.

"Whatever you're about to say, don't," he said. His temper was already on edge due to a million things, and he didn't need whatever she was gearing herself up to say to send him over.

"Why not?" she replied.

"Because I can tell it's going to tick me off."

She shook her head. "It's better if we don't stay with you, Jack."

"Better for who?" he returned, just barely holding on to that thread of calm.

"Everyone involved," Chloe said, and her expression was set, her voice firm, but there was something hiding underneath that cop mask. "Certainly better for you guys getting the answers you deserve."

"Did Laurel put that in your head, or is it your own wrongheaded thinking?"

She scowled at him, but he wasn't about to relent.

"Jack—"

"You and Ry are guests of the Hudson Ranch until we have some answers on the threats against you. I don't care what anyone, including you, has to say about it. That's what's happening."

"There aren't any threats against me. That snake *could* have been for Ry. Whatever my dad was pulling with those dolls happened *six* years ago. I'm not in any danger."

"I'm glad you feel that way. I don't."

"And Jack Hudson's feelings trump all else?" she demanded, but the heat wasn't there. She was just trying to pick a fight.

He was feeling a bit like letting her, but he took a deep breath. Reminded himself that whatever that chest of dolls was or wasn't, it had hurt her. Deeply enough that he'd seen all her usual masks fall.

He didn't want to add to that hurt. He never wanted to be even a contributing factor to her hurt.

But he had been. Not like this. Not deep, childhood wounds. But the nature of everything they'd been for the past year had not always been easy, and he knew...no matter how careful he tried to be, that she'd been hurt by the secret nature of what they did together outside of work.

And he knew she still believed it was for all the reasons *she* saw when that wasn't it at all. Maybe he'd have liked her to have given him more credit, to admit to herself that wasn't *him*, but... That wasn't very fair of him. He saw it more and more clearly as time went on, as little things about the way she'd grown up came out.

How she trusted anyone or anything, saw the good in anyone, *laughed* with people was beyond him. He was in *awe* of her.

Even as she kept going, determined to have that fight he couldn't muster up the anger for.

"Did it ever occur to you that I can handle me? And I can

handle Ry? And I can handle *this*?" she demanded, working up to mad so she didn't have to be sad, scared, hurt. *Clearly.*

It killed him how easy it was to see through it, even as she kept on.

"Did it ever occur to you that I don't need this Jack Hudson, king of the world, 'I'll protect everyone and everything the sun touches just because I slept with you'?"

It was the strangest out-of-body thing. To watch her get mad as hell, to watch her gear it toward him, and not find himself being reactive at all. No, it was like all those walls he'd carefully erected for so long just crumbled to dust. Not even dramatically. Just slowly and silently to ash that flew away on the breeze.

"Well?" she demanded, her cheeks pink with anger, her hands on her hips and everything about her combative.

But he saw that little kernel of vulnerability she was trying so hard to protect, and for the first time in his life, he found himself handing over his own without even thinking about it.

"Did it ever occur to you that I'm in love with you?"

Chapter Nine

Chloe knew what he'd just said. She'd heard it. He'd sounded out that word, spoken it. Right here.

But she couldn't *understand* it. She couldn't put together the *knowledge* with the reality of Jack Hudson standing there saying...

No. *No.* He was...

No.

This was the weirdest time to tell someone they...

No, he was just trying to trick her. To get what he wanted. Which was protecting everyone and everything. And yeah, it wasn't like he *hated* her, but it was... It was...?

Why was her heart doing this terrible, hopeful dance in her chest? She knew better. She knew so much better. Chloe didn't trust love. How could she?

"Jack..." She tried to say more, but her throat was so tight, she couldn't seem to get words out. And he was standing in her yard, looking so good and strong and perfect.

God knew she wasn't meant for *that*.

"I think somewhere deep down, you have to know that. You know me, Chloe. Why else would I break any rule?"

She couldn't come up with an answer for that, and she tried. She tried so hard.

"So yeah, I have some issues when it comes to protecting people. I wonder why," he said, so dryly she might have laughed in another context.

But he'd said he *loved* her, and there was absolutely nothing funny about this horror show.

It had to be horror coursing through her. What else could it be?

"I'm overbearing. I think I'm right pretty much all the time." He took a few steps forward, and she had no choice but to scramble back. Away. Until he stopped moving toward her.

He couldn't touch her right now. She'd…she'd crumble.

"But I don't cross lines," he continued. "I don't break rules. I don't do *gray area*. Except when it comes to you. And if that was about fun or sex or whatever, I would have resisted. I would have put a stop to it. I would not have engaged in this whole thing for a *year*."

"Secretly," Chloe whispered, because it was the only thing she had to hold on to right now. The last line of defense against whatever he was doing to her.

"Yes, secretly. Because no matter how or when this comes out, I know how it shakes down, Chloe. I know how people will treat you. How they'll treat me. There will be whispers for sure, at a minimum."

She couldn't breathe. He'd *thought* about an "after everyone found out"? He'd considered the *consequences*? When all she'd ever done was…be sure he wouldn't want them without thinking what they might be.

"I can take it. At worst, I suffer a few comments and lose a few votes during my next sheriff election, but I still win. I won't be a party to having people question you, though. Your character or anything else. I know that most of our department won't have a problem with this, but there's a wider world, and I won't listen to people at Bent County pretend to know who you are or what you stand for because of your relationship with me. No number of speeches or interventions or *loving you* can change what people will say when I'm not there to stop it, and I never want you to have to deal with that."

She could only stare at him. All this time... All this *time*, and she'd been so sure she understood what they were doing. She'd known part of it was about work, about not breaking his precious rules, but she hadn't thought about...

And he had. What it would really look like if people knew about them. He'd thought it through. And he cared, deeply, that it would affect *her*.

She wanted so badly to protect her heart. Everyone who'd ever had it had bashed it into a million pieces.

But Jack laid out the reality of their situation, and she could see it. He laid it out and she *knew* him.

Of course the secrecy was about protecting *her*. *Of course* it wasn't superficial, about her family reputation—poor Jack didn't have an ounce of superficial in him.

Which only left one thing.

"Jack, I can't..."

"You don't have to do anything, Chloe. That's not why I said it. I said it so you'd understand. So you'd stop fighting me on this because you think... I don't know. That it doesn't matter to me? I need you to be careful. I need you to *care* that something dangerous is going on, one way or another."

This time when he moved for her, she let him. Let him take her hands in his. Let him look at her like...

Like he loved her. Because Jack Hudson, somehow and very inexplicably, was in love with her. And Jack didn't lie, except maybe sometimes to himself. But this wasn't that.

"I care that you are safe, Chloe. That you are...*happy* isn't the right word, but that you're okay. I have no feelings one way or another on your brother. I know you love him. I know how hard and complicated that is for you, and I respect it. And because I love *you*, I'm going to honor it. For as long as it takes, I need to protect you and Ry. And I need you to let me. That's all I need from you right now."

The fact that he was including Ry, that he understood just how complicated and frustrating her love for her brother was, made the tears she'd so desperately been battling all afternoon fall over.

I need you to let me. She'd give him so much—anything, really. He had to know it. "You're not playing fair," she managed to say, even as tears trailed down her cheeks.

He reached out and wiped them away. "I might play by the rules, but that doesn't mean I have to play fair."

She managed a watery laugh, but it died quickly because maybe she could believe he loved her. Maybe she would give him that thing he needed—the chance to protect her and Ry. But he was ignoring something very important.

"You have to look at the very real possibility that my father killed or had something to do with the murder of your parents. You can't just brush it away. Because when this is all figured out, it's going to matter. You have to really think about what that's going to be like."

Jack nodded. "I have."

"But—"

"No. No buts. I understand. If it's true, if we finally have the answers my family has wanted for seventeen years, it'll be a relief. But it won't bring them back, and it won't change anything. Not really."

"I'll be a reminder."

"No. You're not an extension of your father, Chloe. Any more than you're an extension of your mother or Ry. You're you, and I love you."

He said it so earnestly, holding her hands, looking at her tearstained face. Coming up with an answer for every one of her arguments. Taking away all the excuses she'd held herself up on for the past year.

It was scary—the scariest thing, really, because this had the potential to go so very wrong. But when he looked at her like that, she wanted to be someone else, just for a little bit. Someone who could just enjoy the fact that the man she'd been pining after for far too long had feelings for her too.

No, not just feelings. *Loved* her.

"You know, I've been in love with you for longer," she managed to say, not quite sounding like her usual self, but closer. More in charge.

His mouth quirked up at one side. "Is it a contest?"

She nodded emphatically. "Absolutely."

"Okay, how about this?" He pulled her close, brought his mouth next to hers. "I'll love you best," he murmured. Then sealed that promise with a kiss.

JACK HUDSON WAS a planner. He had emergency backup plans to the emergency backup plans. And yet it had never served him. He'd focused for the past seventeen years on wielding more and more control, and still…he'd never actually gotten it.

Grant had gone to war. Palmer and Anna had gone to the rodeo. Cash had gotten his high school girlfriend pregnant at sixteen. Not exactly a great parental track record to his way of thinking, certainly not if he compared himself to what his parents might have been able to do.

Then, over the past two years, Grant had been hurt on Dahlia's case; Palmer had been hurt and Louisa had been kidnapped; Anna had gotten pregnant, almost burned alive; and Mary had been kidnapped by a madman. And that didn't even get into everything that had happened with Cash when his ex-wife had tried to frame him for murder.

And every time something terrible had happened, Jack had tried to hold on tighter and tighter only to be reminded it never really mattered.

Bad things happened.

Loving Chloe wasn't a bad thing, but it was a complicated thing, and for all the ways he planned for twists and turns of fate—the inevitable *bad*—he had not ever once come up with a plan for what happened on the other side of *I'm in love with you.*

They drove to the station in silence, the weight of it sitting there between them. Because now they had to go into work.

Maybe next time he could plan love confessions around their work schedule.

"You should have let me drive my own cruiser," she muttered as he pulled up to the building that housed the Sunrise Sheriff's Department.

"Everyone will understand why I want you riding two-man right now. In fact, they'll probably be surprised I'm not making you take some leave."

She glared at him. "I'll take leave over *your* dead body."

"I know, that's why I'm not going to make you." He'd certainly considered it, but he wasn't about to tell her that.

She grunted and pushed out of the car, and he realized this wasn't so much her real frustration as it was her trying to build that wall back. So they could walk into their place of work and not have what they'd just laid out between each other broadcast to the world.

Jack had long ago given up on the world being fair. He never expected it. But it struck him in a way it hadn't in a long time what a bad hand they'd been dealt with this.

Still, he let Chloe blaze her way in first, and he took his

time following. When he walked into the office, Suzanne immediately got to her feet. "Sheriff, is it true?"

For a second, Jack was distracted enough to think she was talking about everything that had just happened with Chloe. Which was ridiculous. The look on Suzanne's face was clear. Anguish.

Suzanne Smithfield, Sunrise's administrative assistant, had known both his parents. Well, everyone in town had. People loved to tell him stories about how one of his parents had helped them out of a bad situation. But Suzanne had been close personal friends with them. She'd gone to school with his dad, and his mother had babysat Suzanne's kids sometimes.

He managed a reassuring smile for Suzanne. "We don't have ID confirmation yet. It's probably going to take a while. Don't let the gossip mill upset you."

Suzanne sighed heavily. "The news hasn't made its way through town yet, but it will. And soon enough."

Jack nodded. "That's all right. I'll handle it."

"You handle too much, Sheriff."

"So they say."

She leaned in close. "All this stuff with Chloe's cabin… Is it related?"

Most people asking that question would put his back up, but he knew Suzanne cared about each and every Sunrise deputy like one of her own kids. She was worried about Chloe, nothing else. "We don't know yet, but Deputy Brink and her brother are going to be staying out at the ranch until we get it sorted. I also want her riding two-man for the time being, so keep an eye out if she tries to dance around that."

Suzanne nodded. "Good. That's good." Then she nodded to his office. "Messages are on your desk."

Jack nodded, then focused on being Sheriff Jack Hudson

and nothing else. He returned messages, worked on some paperwork, did what needed to be done. And if he occasionally took a walk around the office to get more coffee than necessary to check on Chloe, well...

Who knew that was what he was doing besides himself?

But she had calls to respond to and work, too, so their paths didn't cross, and that was fine. Great, even. Best all the way around.

If it settled in him like frustration, he was just going to have to get used to that.

Toward the end of the day, he got a call from Bent County. When he heard Hart on the other end, Jack doubted they had good news coming.

"We haven't got a hold of Mark Brink yet, but we did get a report he was spotted in Denver. Morning after the remains were found."

Denver. Pretty much halfway between Texas and them. "Going to ask around and see if anyone saw him here?"

"Already got a deputy on it. Laurel's also going to head out to the ranch and question Ry again."

"Why?"

"That's a pretty quick turnaround, Jack. Being in Denver the morning after a middle-of-the-night discovery? If it's connected, he had warning."

Jack closed his eyes and tried not to groan. He wanted to argue with Hart, but how could he? If he was in charge of the investigation, he'd been drilling Ry for information too.

"Phone records?" Jack asked, though it squeezed his heart to do it. Chloe was a realist when it came to her brother, but that didn't mean she was going to be okay with any of this.

"Working on a search warrant, but Laurel's going to see if he'll hand it over of his own free will. Ry doesn't strike me as a hardened criminal despite his rap sheet, but I don't know what kind of relationship he has with his father."

Jack didn't, either, and Chloe clearly didn't think Ry had one. Which was maybe true. Maybe not. Either way, Chloe wasn't going to be too happy with this turn of events. She'd want to head over to the ranch right now, intervene.

"I also wanted to talk to Brink about what we found in the chest," Hart said. "Can you transfer me? She can call me back later if she's out on a call."

"Are you going to tell her about Mark?"

"No, Sheriff. I'm only even telling you as a courtesy. It's an active investigation into her father. The less she knows, the better off we'll be."

"She doesn't have a relationship with her father."

Hart was quiet for a few humming seconds. "Regardless. She'll be kept in the loop in what directly affects her."

It was a clear-enough warning. Jack wasn't supposed to tell her either. He didn't like how that settled in him like betrayal instead of just the nature of the job.

"It's almost shift change. She should be available. Stay on hold for a second." Jack got up and stepped out of his office and peeked into the main lobby, where his deputies met for shift change.

Chloe was at the front desk, smiling over something on Suzanne's phone—probably the insane pictures Suzanne took of her cats dressed up like old Hollywood stars.

He hated to wipe that smile off her face, but when both Suzanne and Chloe looked over at him, he saw any enjoyment melt away. Because she knew it wasn't good news.

"Chloe, Detective Hart's on line one for you."

Chapter Ten

Jack shouldn't have called her Chloe in front of Suzanne. It was a dead giveaway. Maybe not to *everyone*, but Suzanne was not everyone. She had a keen eye, an even keener ear and a nose for things other people didn't want to share.

Jack had never once slipped up in front of anyone in all this time, and dread swept through her because she had a terrible feeling that Jack had used her first name because something really bad was just about to fall in her lap. Courtesy of Detective Hart.

Chloe wanted to ignore the call, run in the other direction, ask Jack to handle it. A million things that she wouldn't do, because whatever this was, it was all hers. Just like always.

She moved stiffly into one of the offices the deputies all shared, closed the door and gave herself a second to breathe before she lifted the phone receiver. Whatever it was, she could weather it. She'd gotten this far, hadn't she? "This is Brink."

"Hey. Detective Hart here. I just wanted to give you an update on what we found in that chest of yours."

Chloe swallowed, found a spot on the wall to stare at and made sure she sounded strong and firm. "Go ahead."

"Mostly, it was just the dolls. We're going to run some tests on the smears—determine fake or real blood and go from there. Some weapons were hidden inside some of the dolls. We'll have to keep and run tests on those too. See if they were used in any of your father's known crimes."

"Great." She hoped she didn't sound *too* sarcastic.

"There was also an old scrapbook. Delaney-Carson and I both looked through it, and we don't see any reason for Bent County to keep it. It seems more family heirloom than anything else. Whenever you have a chance to stop by County, you can feel free to pick it up."

She didn't know whether she wanted to laugh or cry or just rage. All that—dolls and weapons—and her father hadn't even been fully lying. There *was* a family heirloom hidden in there.

She should tell Hart to throw it in the incinerator. "I'll be by tonight."

"Okay. It'll be up with Administration. You know the drill."

"Yeah, thanks." She returned the phone to its receiver. Then she just stood there, still staring at the same spot. She didn't have her cruiser here; that was at her cabin. Her personal car was at the Hudson Ranch. She did *not* want Jack driving her over there. She didn't know what kind of reaction she was going to have to this scrapbook, and she didn't want him witnessing it.

She didn't want anyone with her when she picked it up, when she inevitably went through it even knowing it was pointless. Whatever she wanted to find wasn't going to be in some old, dusty book that may or may not even actually be a Brink family scrapbook.

But regardless, she wanted to handle all that alone. Where she didn't have to worry about how her reactions might affect how anyone viewed her.

She blew out a breath, closed her eyes and tried to find

her lifelong inner toughness. That thing she'd been building up since she was a kid. She had known, always, that life was nothing more than a series of blows to dodge and absorb as needed. Any good, you carved out yourself with hard work and fierce grit.

Why was she having such a hard time with these blows?

A knock sounded at the door. Chloe didn't have to be psychic to know who it was. She twisted the knob and pulled it open.

Jack stepped in, closed the door behind him and studied her.

Here was the answer to the question. Where was her grit? Well, this man had somehow washed it away. By taking care. By *loving* her.

And what was it going to get her, this love? Ridicule? Pain? Guilt? And so much fear that it would all disappear, she didn't know how anyone lived with the weight of *love* you chose.

"Everything okay?" Jack asked carefully.

"Yeah." She realized that Jack had been the one to tell her Hart was on the phone, which meant he'd talked to Hart first. "I'm sure Hart filled you in on everything."

Jack shook his head. "No. Just that he wanted to talk to you about the contents of the chest."

She shrugged, still not ready to look at him. "Running tests. Found some weapons. Mostly called because they found some old family scrapbook, I guess. I can go pick it up sometime."

"I'll drive you."

She forced herself to look at him, to be *strong*. She had not gotten this far in life by being an emotional weakling or coward. She would *not* be cut down at the knees just because he loved her. "Look—"

But this was Jack. Did she think there'd be some way to get around that bullheaded need to control and protect?

I need you to let me. He'd said that to her like...like she had any say. Like he had wants or needs he couldn't expressly make happen in the Jack Hudson world of control and determination.

Like *she* had that kind of hold over him.

"Two-man until we have answers, Chloe," he said firmly. "And I don't just mean at work. If it's not me, you're going to have to ask Baker or Clinton to drive you over. Or we'll head back to the ranch, and you can take Ry with you later tonight. Or Mary."

She wanted to do just that—pick someone else—to prove to him she could. No. To prove to *herself* she could. To put some space between them when she had to do something she knew would be emotionally painful.

But he'd said he *loved* her.

She couldn't wrap her head around why that put her more on edge than when she'd believed the whole thing had been about sex and nothing else. When she had convinced herself he was *embarrassed* of her family connections. That had been easy because it had been anger, she supposed. Indignation. Hard feelings that kept her silly heart guarded.

Now it was just soft feelings and too much outside stuff poking at her to bear.

"I need space on this, Jack." She wasn't going to cry again. Once was enough, but she could feel emotion mounting. So she needed to set a boundary. Or five hundred.

"I can give you space," he said, nodding like he was agreeing with her even though she knew better. "You want to look through it alone? Your choice, Chloe. But *someone* is going to be with you at all times when you're off the ranch until we can rule out a threat to you."

I need you to let me. I need you to let me. It kept ringing in her head, over and over. Like it was something she could count on.

When she hadn't been able to count on anything aside from herself in her entire life.

"Let's just go get it over with," she managed to say, not crying but sounding raspy nonetheless.

He nodded again; then he reached out. Just a quick, friendly squeeze of the shoulder. "I need to grab a few things. I'll meet you at my truck."

She gave him a sharp nod, refusing to react to the hand on her shoulder, the softness in his gaze or anything else.

Just had to get through the day. She could fall apart—alone—tonight. Then maybe tomorrow she'd have answers for how to deal with everything life had thrown at her today.

She collected her own things, met Jack at his truck. They didn't speak. She didn't even look at him. She watched out the window as he drove away from Sunrise and toward...

She frowned and sat a little straighter. "This isn't the way to County," she said with a frown. She glanced over at him. He was gripping the wheel, scowling ahead.

"We're going to need to stop by the ranch first."

"Why?" she asked because he seemed so serious, so determined, and she didn't understand why.

His scowl deepened if that was possible. "Delaney-Carson is interviewing Ry again. I figured you'd want to be there."

"Why is she doing that?" Chloe leaned forward, nearly screeching out the demand.

"There are some concerns he has a relationship with your father." Jack let out a long breath. "Mark Brink was spotted in Denver the morning after the remains were found."

"He's in prison."

"He's on parole." Jack looked over at her then. "Hart made it very clear I wasn't supposed to share any of this with you, but I don't want you finding it out from anyone else."

Another rule broken, a line crossed for *her*, and Chloe couldn't handle that. Not right now. She had to handle the actual information. "So, he was in Denver? What does that…" But she was a cop. She understood how you built a case. If her father had been halfway between Texas and Wyoming the *morning* the remains had been found, they were thinking someone had warned him the remains were going to be found. *If* he was involved, *if* he'd been on his way to Wyoming.

Was it even an *if* anymore?

"Ry doesn't have any connection to our father." Her father had loved to play mind games with her, but he'd actually knocked Ry around some. Ry wouldn't…

But with drugs involved, there weren't a whole lot of things she could count on Ry *never* doing. Including this. He could have called their father before he'd called her. Her father could have told Ry to dig there, and Ry didn't mention it because he knew how she felt about Mark Brink.

There were a lot of *could*s. Too many.

When Jack pulled up to the ranch, she once again didn't want to face what awaited her, but she didn't have time to wish for different. The detective's car was parked out front. She was already inside, talking to Ry.

Chloe knew she should let her. Let Ry handle himself. But…

"Can you not come in with me? I don't want the detective to think we're like marching in as Sunrise Sheriff's Department, trying to take over—or worse, make a mess of her investigation. I just want to be there if Ry needs me.

I'm not stopping anything." She said that last bit more for herself than Jack.

Jack nodded. "I'll go around back."

She swallowed what was beginning to feel like a perpetual lump in her throat. "Thanks." But before she could push out of the truck, Jack took her hand, held it in his and pressed their joined hands against his chest until she met his gaze.

Serious. So damn serious. "I know Ry's your responsibility, but he's not under your control, Chloe. Trust me, as a man who has spent the past seventeen years trying to control Anna's mouth, sometimes you just have to be there to catch them when they fall, not try to stop it from happening."

She wanted to be angry that he was trying to tell her what to do, but she saw it too clearly for what it was. Commiseration. She managed a nod, then to get her hand free. She got out of the truck, didn't look back at Jack. Just marched onto the porch and to the door, which was unlocked, so Chloe let herself in. It felt a little weird, but worry over Ry superseded any awkwardness she felt. She followed the sound of voices—Ry's agitated one—and found them in the living room.

Ry was pacing the room like a caged animal while Detective Delaney-Carson sat relaxed as could be on the couch. When Ry heard her enter, his chin snapped up.

"Chloe, why won't they leave me alone?" He pointed at the detective. "Isn't this harassment? I didn't do anything *wrong.*"

"Okay," Chloe agreed, because there was no arguing with her brother when he was this agitated. She turned to the detective, tried to smile. "I thought you'd already questioned us, Detective."

She nodded. "Yes, but you know as well as I do when new

information comes to light, a second, third or even fourth questioning might be necessary."

"What new information?"

The detective's expression bordered on disdainful now. "Deputy Brink, I'm not going to share—"

"She said Dad's out on parole and is acting like I know something about it or, like I'm hiding him or I don't know. But I didn't do anything wrong!"

Chloe wanted to melt into a puddle of embarrassment, but she kept her placid expression on her face as she faced the detective. "Are you charging my brother with anything?"

"No, Deputy. We're just asking when the last time he had contact with Mark Brink was, and answers have not been forthcoming."

Chloe tried to ignore her stomach sinking. If he wasn't answering... But she turned to her brother. No blame, no embarrassment, no frustration on her face. Just blank. "Ry," she said calmly, "it's a simple question. Even if you don't know the exact date, you have an idea. How long has it been?"

"You know Dad. He's not consistent. In one day, out the next. I don't remember talking to him since he went to prison, and I don't know why that's anyone's business, what it's got to do with those bones. I'm only twenty-four! You think I was a kid burying skeletons?"

"I don't think anything, Mr. Brink," the detective said, her voice on the chilly side. "And at the moment, you're hardly a murder suspect. What I am trying to do is gather information to solve a case. It would help if you could be cooperative instead of combative."

"You're accusing me of doing something wrong! You don't think I know how you people think? All your female-cop bull—"

"Rylan Jonas Brink," Chloe said sharply. Sharp enough that he was surprised into clamping his mouth shut. "That's enough. Now, are you saying you haven't had any contact with Dad since he went to prison?"

"I don't remember talking to him *once*," Ry grumbled.

Chloe turned to the detective, so tense it was a miracle her bones didn't simply shatter from the force of it all. "Do you have any more questions, Detective?" She expected to see fury or affront on the detective's face.

What Chloe saw was worse: pity.

"No. Not right now. Thank you, Deputy Brink. If I have any more questions, I'll let you know." She stood, but as she passed Chloe on the way out, she said something quietly enough so Ry couldn't hear. "If he changes his story, or if you find out something you think might help this investigation, I'd really appreciate it if you let me know. We all want the same thing here. Answers."

Chloe nodded jerkily. Because it was true. They all needed answers.

She stood in silence, watching her brother pace. She had no words. She had *nothing*. So she just watched him until he stopped pacing. Until he looked at her, all sheepish and sullen.

He was good at being angry, at blaming everyone around him, but he always broke in the face of her anger. Well, if he was sober.

"I'm sorry, Chloe," he said, crossing the room to her. "I didn't mean it. She just got me so riled up, poking at me with the same questions."

This was the problem with Ry. She believed he *was* sorry. In the moment. She just also believed he'd do it again and again because he wasn't sorry enough to change, to grow, to learn. He was determined to stay stuck in this everyone-else-is-to-blame place.

And she couldn't fix him.

She'd spent so many years trying to accept that. She wondered if she ever fully would be able to.

"How was working with Cash and Carlyle?" she asked, because she needed to make sure he hadn't ruined anything else today before she went back to the subject at hand.

He gave her a jerky shrug that reminded her of the little boy he'd been. She'd tried so hard to save him from everything, and she'd failed. "They have like a hundred of them."

"Of what?"

"Dogs." His mouth curved ever so slightly. "They didn't give us that speech in high school when they were telling us we had to think about our futures. Maybe if someone had told me, 'Hey, dog training is a thing people do,' I would have tried harder."

She didn't say anything to that, even though *she* had told him. *She* had tried to find any way of getting him to *care*, to put forth an effort. Vet school. Owning his own kennel or working on someone else's ranch. *Anything*.

But Ry had to blame someone else for where his life was. Always.

Which brought them right back to the subject at hand. "Ry, have you had *any* contact with Dad in the past year?"

"You heard what I told the detective."

"I did. And now I want you to look me in the eye and tell me that for an entire year, you haven't had a phone call, an email, a certified letter, nothing."

"I didn't do anything wrong," he said. Which was the third or fourth time she'd heard that in the last ten minutes. And didn't answer the question.

"Then what *did* you do?"

He stood there. Then slowly, his dark eyes filled with tears. "I'm sorry, Chloe. I really am."

Chapter Eleven

"He lied."

Jack looked up from the computer screen that had been giving him a hell of a headache. With Steve out and Chloe needing to ride two-man, adjusting the Sunrise SD work schedule was a hell of a puzzle he hadn't fully figured out yet. Even with him stepping in to cover daily shifts. So he didn't quite follow Chloe's dramatic statement. He only knew she was standing in the doorway, looking like a storm ready to break. "Who lied about what?"

"Ry lied to the detective."

Jack tried not to swear, tried to maintain a detached kind of calm that she no doubt needed, but he wasn't perfect. "Lied how?"

"All she wanted to know, allegedly, was if he'd had contact with Dad lately. He told her he hadn't talked to Dad since he went to prison, but he refused to hand over his phone, of course. And he kept saying he hadn't done anything wrong, and that's always when I know he has."

She looked up at Jack then. Tears swam in her eyes, but they didn't fall. "He's had contact with Dad over the past year. Text messages and emails." She raked her hands through her hair, loosening more strands from the once-tight braid she'd had at the beginning of the day.

"He said it didn't have anything to do with anything. Just father-son stuff. I can't believe he…" She was pacing the tiny office room. There was no room to pace, but she clearly couldn't sit still. Anger and frustration pumped off her, but underneath all that was the impossible pull of wanting to do the right thing for her family and needing to do the right thing for the law.

"I should have handled it better. I should have found a way to get him to admit it to the detective. He always lies when he's backed into a corner, and if I had—"

"You're not blaming yourself, are you? Because I know you know you're not to blame for Ry lying."

She took a breath and finally stopped pacing. She looked at him with heartbreak in her eyes. Then shook her head. "Bad habit."

"I know. So, let's work through this. He told the detective he hasn't had contact with your dad?"

She shook her head. "Oh, no, of course not. He said *I haven't talked to him* since he went to prison, so he's convinced it wasn't a *lie* because he only communicated in texts and emails. God, I'd like to strangle him."

"And he says these conversations were just generic. Did he let you see any of them?"

She shook her head. "He claims he left his phone at my cabin, and he'll show them to me later. I know he didn't, and I know he won't."

"So he is hiding something." Jack sighed. It just didn't add up. What would Ry be hiding? He'd been too young to really be involved in any kind of murder or coverup. Besides, if Mark Brink killed those people…

"He's protecting our father, for whatever godforsaken reason," Chloe said, clearly trying so hard to be strong. For what, he didn't know. Neither her father nor her brother really deserved that kind of dedication.

But even if they didn't, their behavior connecting to cold case murders didn't make sense either. "If Mark knew about the remains *before* Ry dug, how did Ry warn him before he dug? And if Ry knew your father committed those murders and is trying to cover for him, why would he dig there or anywhere? It doesn't make sense."

"I'm not sure what my father or brother does always adds up."

"Sure, but… We're missing something here. The timing doesn't work out for them to be purposefully covering up something Mark did that Ry knew about."

Chloe sucked in a breath. "We should let the detectives handle it. I'll tell them… I'll tell them…" She couldn't seem to get out the words. He hated why, but he understood it all the same.

"You don't want to tell Laurel what you know."

She looked up at him, her eyes still shiny, but clearly she had determined she wasn't going to cry over this. "Ry needs to be maneuvered. You can't just get answers out of him. And if there are answers to be had, I'm the best chance we have of getting them. If I involve the detectives, I just don't think it'll give us answers. Not without someone getting hurt."

She shoved her hands in her pockets, looked at some place on the wall just behind him, as if it'd give him the illusion she was making eye contact.

"I know it's wrong. I know I shouldn't still want to protect him. But he's not a murderer. Maybe Dad's wrapped him up in this but only because he knows how to manipulate him. Not because Ry did anything wrong. I mean, he did. He lied. I just…" She seemed to run out of words, or maybe they were lodged in her throat. Because she just stood there, looking miserable.

So he moved over to her. He pulled her close, rubbed his hand up and down her spine until *some* of that tension in her loosened. "Take a breath, Chloe. We'll work through it. One step at a time."

"I've got to stop laying this stuff at your feet. You're the real victim here. You and your family."

"Sounds like we're all victims."

She shook her head against his chest, but she didn't pull away from him. She let him hold her.

He figured if anything made sense about the two of them, it was this. They both felt they had to do it all, hold it all together, and because they did, the other was the only person they knew how to lean on.

"You shouldn't be comforting me. You've got your own awful stuff to deal with."

"Yeah, but mine is old, and while it's not *dealt* with, you went with me on that drive the other night. You hate heights, and you sat next to me and listened to me talk. Things I can't seem to admit to anyone else." He held her closer.

"But—"

He pulled her back so he could look into her gaze. He hadn't fully realized until all this had gone down how much she'd hidden from him in the past year. Old childhood hurts, insecurities. Trauma.

He'd had his own trauma, but he'd had a foundation to deal with it on. She'd had nothing but herself.

"All this bad stuff? It's not math. There's not a chart. You get to be upset. I get to be upset. And we'll comfort each other however we can. Love isn't a contest or a transaction, Chloe. It doesn't work that way."

Her chin wobbled, but she firmed it on an exhale. "I don't know how love works."

"Well, I guess you'll figure it out as we go."

She rolled her eyes, but not disdainfully. And she didn't pull fully away. But the misery was still in every line of her face.

"We need to get to the bottom of this, Jack. I don't want to go to Laurel, but you need answers. We all need answers."

"So we'll find them. Together."

"How?"

Maybe he'd been avoiding it, but he'd known, since this morning, since Chloe's safety had come into question, he couldn't play hands-off anymore. Not and live with himself.

"By making this a Hudson Siblings Solutions case."

CHLOE HAD HELPED the Hudson clan with cold cases before, but mostly in a very supplementary way: getting them information they couldn't get themselves, responding to active threats connected to their cold cases. But she'd never been involved in a full-fledged Hudson Sibling Solutions meeting.

It wasn't all that different from a family dinner. Everyone shoved together in the living room instead of the dining room. The low buzz of conversations, bickering and the most recent addition of a baby occasionally fussing while everyone arrived and got settled.

Carlyle was missing because she'd made up an excuse to use Ry to do some evening chores with her and Izzy out at the dog barns. Jack had offered to let Ry be part of the meeting, but Chloe had nixed that idea.

She loved her brother, wanted to protect him with all she was, even to the point of risking things she shouldn't risk, but she couldn't trust him with *anything*. Especially this. She might want to protect him from the repercussions of what he'd potentially done, but she wouldn't do it at the expense of finding the truth.

She didn't really think Ry had done anything wrong when it came to the skeletal remains, but she could see how any involvement with their father could mean he was mixed up in *something* wrong.

"This meeting better be about what I think it's about," Anna said, with baby Caroline situated on her lap.

The fringe conversations began to die out, and all eyes turned to Jack. Chloe had always known he'd taken on too much here with his family, felt a responsibility that was maybe bigger than necessary.

But she'd never so clearly seen it in action—everyone he loved turning their attention to him, looking to *him* for answers. Since he'd been eighteen years old. Her heart ached for the young man he'd been.

"The case regarding the skeletal remains—that, I'll point out, have not been positively IDed yet—has changed on us, gotten more complicated, and now it includes a potentially current threat."

"No one is threatening me," Chloe muttered, because for all that was mixed up and wrong, some mutilated snake on her porch with absolutely no information didn't lend itself to her being worried. The dolls in the chest were an old "joke" from her father. She didn't have any actual *fear* of a threat, but she was *letting* Jack take care of her.

Or trying to anyway.

"I think a mutilated snake on your porch is threat enough, whether we know what it's threatening or not," Mary said primly.

"Maybe it doesn't connect. The snake. Mark Brink. The remains. But the timing feels like too much of a coincidence," Jack continued. "I still want us supporting Bent

County detectives in all facets we can, but things have changed enough, I think we should launch our own investigation."

Chloe expected there to be *some* reaction from the Hudson siblings. A grim kind of excitement or relief that Jack was okaying what he'd previously forbidden.

But there was silence. Dahlia snuck a look at Grant. Palmer suddenly found the ceiling *very* interesting. Anna studied Caroline's socks as if they had the answers to the mysteries of the world on them.

Jack sighed. "So go on and get everything you've been gathering in secret and against my wishes. We're looking into it now. As a team."

"Thank God," Anna muttered. She looked over at Hawk, who got up and left the room. One person from every couple did the same, slowly returning with arms full of things. One by one, they dropped files, notebooks and printouts onto the table in the center of the room in front of Jack. Chloe's eyes widened as it became a tower of papers that nearly toppled over. She snuck a glance at Jack.

He didn't look the least bit surprised. Resigned, a little disapproving, but maybe even just a *hint* of pride.

Chloe realized then that he'd known they were doing it. Behind his back. Even though he didn't want them to. And he wasn't angry about it.

Something about him knowing and just…letting them, even when he didn't want them to. It settled in her like warmth. Everyone painted him as so rigid, and he *could* be on the outside, but on the inside…

He was someone else entirely. And she loved him so much, it turned into *anxiety* inside her. Because love could so easily be taken away. Especially with a last name like hers.

"I haven't put it in my notes yet, but I *may* have eavesdropped when Detective Delaney-Carson interviewed Ry again," Anna said. She looked over at Chloe. "He's lying."

Chloe nodded. "I know." She swallowed. She didn't want to share with *all* of them what she'd found out, because she wasn't sure they would agree with Jack that they should *all* work together.

And she wanted to protect Ry, but in the audience of everyone whose parents might be buried on her family ranch, she felt the need to be honest. Even at Ry's expense.

"He admitted to me he's had written contact with our father. I haven't figured out what they talked about yet, but I'm going to." She took a deep breath. "And I'll make sure to share it with you as it pertains to the skeletal remains, but I also understand this is complicated. Well, that *I* make it complicated. Threats or no, we're looking at my father and a ranch my name is on. I understand if there's a thread of mistrust here, and I don't have to stay."

Jack gave her a sharp look, but it was nothing on Mary's.

"Chloe Brink, I have known you since we were in kindergarten. And not once, in all that time, all those different phases of our lives, have I ever thought you were *anything* like your father or your brother."

Before Chloe could respond to that, Palmer spoke. Because Chloe knew that for all Jack and Mary were on her side, it wasn't unanimous. Palmer had made it quite clear he had his doubts about her.

"It doesn't matter if she's like them if she's more worried about protecting them than getting to the truth," Palmer said. He didn't budge when both Jack and Mary glared at him. He sat where he was, looking right at Chloe. "I don't have anything against you as a person, Chloe, but your involvement is complicated."

"I agree. That's why I'm saying I don't have to be here."

Mary and Jack immediately began to argue with her. Anna looked to be on the fence, while Cash and Grant said nothing. The significant others didn't add anything at first, but eventually, when the arguing was clearly going nowhere, Louisa cut through all the chatter.

Chloe looked over at her. She was gripping Palmer's hand. Clearly they'd had a few discussions about this.

"The real question is this," Louisa said once everyone looked over at her. "If you found something implicating your brother, would you turn him in?"

Chloe turned her gaze from Louisa to Palmer. He looked so much like Jack, was *nothing* like his older brother. Except in this. That stoic, stern expression.

She could lie. She could be a good liar when she wanted to be. Hell, she lied to herself on a daily basis. But she shrugged. "I really don't know. It would depend on the situation."

Palmer leaned back in his seat, flung his arm over Louisa's shoulders. "Then my vote is that you stay."

Chloe had already started standing up to leave before the words penetrated. "Wait, what?"

"You were honest. That's all that really matters. We can't have secrets in an investigation, but siblings… I wouldn't believe you if you'd said yes. But an *I don't know*? That, I get. God knows I thought I'd have to cover up for Anna committing a crime at some point in our lives."

"You mean, you haven't?" Hawk murmured.

Anna put her hands over Caroline's ears. "Not in front of the *baby*," she said with mock seriousness. "She's going to grow up thinking her mother is a saint."

This elicited a laugh from just about everyone in the room. A laugh. While they were sitting around talking about their parents' disappearance and potential murder. Her family's involvement in such a tragedy.

But, Chloe realized, here in a room where all the Hudsons were gathered—but not just Hudsons. Significant others and offspring too. Seventeen years of unknowns while life marched on had meant probably figuring out…you couldn't live your life constantly mired in that old tragedy.

So maybe she should stop living mired in the reputation other people had given her last name.

Chapter Twelve

They went over it all. The old information the police had gathered when their parents had disappeared, what his siblings had gathered in the past few days. Nothing new, nothing groundbreaking, but it was good to talk it through.

Jack was trying to convince himself it was good. He knew it wasn't true, but he *felt* like the only one struggling with the weight of what they were discussing. Not just anyone's skeletal remains—his parents.

Not positively IDed yet, he reminded himself. Or tried to.

Though they'd all done some of their own investigating over the years, there wasn't anything really new so far. Anna and Palmer had both been looking into any connection Mark Brink might have had to their parents. Mary had been looking through old ranch records to see if something jumped out connecting anything Hudson to the Brink Ranch. Cash had been working with Zeke and Zeke's connections to see if he could get more information on the crime scene as it was right now.

"So, we did all this and we're still in the same exact spot?" Anna groused.

"It's not the same exact spot," Mary said, clearly trying to sound optimistic. "Just like any cold case. We don't know which corner might lead us to a new thread. So we keep going. I still have old ranch records to look through, and we don't know what the forensic anthropologist might have to say. It's a step."

"It's a foolish step," Anna muttered.

"I think that's a sign someone is tired," Hawk said, earning a scowl from his wife. "Mary's right. We've got next steps. Let's call this a night. Caroline's conked out anyway," he said, gesturing to the sleeping baby in Anna's arms.

She sighed and got to her feet, and everyone else began to disperse, couple by couple.

Chloe stood. "I better go check on Ry. Make sure Carlyle hasn't scarred him for life." She tried to smile. It faltered.

"Did you want to go get that scrapbook?" Jack asked.

She waved it off, already heading out of the room. "Tomorrow morning is soon enough," she muttered. Then she disappeared. Jack wanted to follow her, but Mary started tidying up, so both he and Grant stepped in to stop her.

"Go to bed, Mary. We can clean up."

She frowned at them both, hands on her hips, but Walker urged her out of the room so that it was just Jack and Grant collecting debris. Jack figured they'd work in quiet. Grant usually did.

"So, how long has your thing with Chloe been going on?"

If it had been anyone else standing there asking him that question, Jack would have had a quick answer. An easy lie. He expected things like that from just about everyone.

But never Grant.

Grant, who most people would never guess was *married* to his wife, because he and Dahlia were so private they almost never engaged in even *hand holding* in front of people. Grant, who'd taken *eons* to propose to Dahlia, if compared to Mary, Anna and Palmer's quick jumps into commitment.

Who'd had a wedding so small, it had only been immediate family because they hadn't wanted an audience.

"What?" was all Jack managed.

But Grant didn't relent. *Grant*. The man who'd returned from war and kept every last effect of that to himself. No matter how obvious they'd been.

"I can repeat myself if you really need me to, but I think you know what I asked." He calmly stacked papers together.

"Who are you, and what have you done with my brother?" Grant, who was closest in age to Jack, who'd been his kind of right-hand man in keeping everything together that first year. Because he'd been the only one old enough to also drive. He'd helped with school runs and sports practices. If it hadn't been for Grant, who'd been *sixteen*, Jack would have fumbled the whole thing.

Grant's mouth curved ever so slightly. "It's a simple question, Jack. I know a lot about all the things a person tells themself that doesn't serve them. We'd hate to think you have to keep yourself some isolated paragon for the rest of us."

Jack wanted to be touched that Grant was concerned about him, but… "'We'?"

Grant's expression went *almost* sheepish. "It's been a topic of conversation."

"With *who*?"

"Well, I think it started with Carlyle, then it kind of spread from there. Not everyone believed it at first. Dahlia was an early believer though, and it's hard to argue with her. She observes things. Cash and Walker weren't so easily swayed, but recently…" Grant shrugged. "I think the lone holdout on that score is Palmer. He's convinced you'd *never* cross a line at work."

Jack wasn't sure what was worse: all the people who thought it was true or the fact Palmer was wrong about him.

"So you guys have been sitting around debating whether or not I have a relationship with Chloe?"

"You do know your family, right? And Carlyle? She brings it up every chance she gets. She's determined to be right. She is, isn't she?"

"Are you going to take my answer back to the collective?" Jack returned, a little bitterly even to his own ears.

"I don't have to. I can keep a secret." He shrugged as if it was that simple. And Jack wasn't sure if it was just who Grant was or because they were the closest that Grant was probably the only one he'd believe that from.

"I just didn't want you laboring under the assumption you weren't allowed to have a life too. Taking care of everyone has been your life for so long. I'm sure it's hard to realize we're all grown up and let that go. But we are. And we're all here. We're all good."

"It isn't that," Jack managed, though it wasn't so fully off the mark, he realized. "Maybe it was a little in the beginning, but… Working together complicates things. For Chloe."

"Life is complicated. You can't protect everyone, Jack."

He was a little tired of that getting thrown in his face at every turn, but… "I can try."

Grant shook his head, but he didn't argue. "Look, asking you about Chloe isn't the only thing I wanted to talk to you alone about."

"You want to probe deeper into my sex life for the past decade?"

Grant pulled a face, as Jack had hoped. He hadn't learned *nothing* from being Anna's older brother.

"No," Grant said stoutly. "We're not really telling everyone yet, but I figured you should be the first to know."

"Know what?" Maybe he should have seen it coming. Grant wasn't the first, but Jack was really taken off guard by Grant's next words.

"Dahlia's pregnant."

It shouldn't be a shock. Kids were going to follow marriage more often than not, but maybe Jack thought Grant would feel a little like he did. Like he'd already raised a family.

But Grant's mouth was curved, as wide as Grant ever smiled. Happy. Grant Hudson, war hero, married and starting a family.

Jack really didn't know how to absorb it, but what he tried to do in these kinds of moments was think back to their father. What would he have done?

But in this case, Jack didn't know. Because his father had never had the chance to parent *adults*. The idea of being a grandfather had probably never been one he'd entertained for too long, too busy getting his six kids grown first.

So Jack just had to rely on himself. He reached out, gave Grant's shoulder a squeeze. "You'll make a hell of a father, Grant. You've had some hands-on practice."

He shrugged. "Had some good role models to follow too." He patted Jack on the shoulder, like *he* was one of them. "You don't have to pretend with Chloe around us. No one's going to cause a problem here. Seems to me you guys should have *somewhere* you don't have to pretend."

"I'll, uh, talk to Chloe about it. Not sure how comfortable she'd be."

"Sure. I'll keep my mouth shut."

"Even to Dahlia?"

"Well, maybe not that shut. But she won't tell anyone. You have my word."

And Grant's word was good as gold. Always had been.

Jack didn't think he'd had much to do with that, but maybe…maybe some. A tiny, little bit. And it made him feel pretty damn good that he had.

CHLOE FOUND RY laughing with the dogs. Carlyle was watching them with an eagle eye, but from a distance. Giving Ry the illusion of being in charge.

It made her heart twist that it looked like he was handling it just fine. Why hadn't *she* been able to keep him out of trouble?

Well, didn't do to think about now. She walked over to Carlyle first. "Hey. How's it going?"

"As long as the animals are around? He's fine. Not irritating at all. Might have wanted to pound him on the walk over while he was whining about his tough lot in life—please, buddy, I win. Still, I think we'll be able to keep him busy and out of trouble without a pounding."

"I can't tell you how much I—"

Carlyle held up a hand. "Don't thank me. It's rude."

"How is thanking you rude?"

"Because it is," Carlyle replied. Then she gave Chloe a kind of sideways look. "So, is this whole protect-you-on-the-Hudson-Ranch thing Jack Hudson's version of trying to get in your pants?"

Chloe choked on a sharp inhale. "What? No!"

"Is that because he's already in your pants?"

"Carlyle!"

"So *that's* a yes." Carlyle looked back at Ry, who was getting the dogs into the barn one by one. "I *knew* it."

Chloe knew if there was anyone she'd slipped up around

when it came to *maybe* hinting she had a thing for Jack, it was Carlyle and only Carlyle. But… "You did not."

"I totally knew it. I just couldn't figure out why all the secrecy about it."

Chloe could hedge, lie, make up a story, but she was tired and emotionally wrung out, and hell, Carlyle was her friend. "He didn't want to tell anyone because he didn't want to see me get needled at work over it."

"Aw. That's actually sweet. You know, at first I thought he was kind of a cold fish, but he's grown on me. He's just like all uptight goody-two-shoes because he's always trying to make everything right. It's annoying as all get out, but it's kind of sweet when it doesn't tick me off."

Chloe shrugged jerkily. Sure, it was. That's why it was so damn unnerving. "Well, anyway. We still work together, so—"

"Weren't you applying for that K-9 job at Bent County?"

Chloe pulled a face. She hadn't told anyone about that… except Carlyle after a few too many at the Lariat one night.

"I'm not going to apply for some job just to… Whatever."

"No, you were going to apply for it because you love dogs and were getting tired of the same old same old in Sunrise."

Chloe hadn't hit Submit on the application because as much as she wanted to try her hand at the K-9 unit in Bent County, she hadn't wanted Jack or anyone else to read into her switching jobs. One way or another. Because she'd needed to prove to herself she was strong enough not to go switch jobs in the hopes she'd have a future with *some guy*.

"No one will think that I'm moving jobs because I want a different job when my relationship with Jack gets out. They'll think I'm weak and lovesick," she muttered.

Carlyle looked at her like she'd grown a second head.

"What does it matter what anyone else thinks? You *do* want a different job. And you're about as weak as a boulder."

Yes, but that's not what this was about. It was… It was… something. Carlyle just didn't… "You don't understand what it's like to grow up in a small town."

"No, but I do understand what it's like to be a grown up, Chloe. What other people think only matters if you let it."

It frustrated her because she didn't know how to argue with it. And with everything else going on, she wasn't handling that as well as she should. "Well, thanks for that afterschool special, Car, but I've still got to drive over to Bent County and pick some of my confiscated belongings up." She didn't want to wait until morning now. She wanted to get out and away. From everyone. "I'll deliver Ry back to his room."

Carlyle shook her head. "Leave him. Cash is going to have him pick out a dog to keep him company inside once he's got Izzy to bed. We'll handle it."

"You don't need—"

"Chloe."

"What?"

"Scram."

"Carlyle, he's my brother and my—"

"Burden? Cool. We'll handle it for a while. And if you keep arguing with me, I'm literally going to fight you."

Chloe glared at Carlyle, but also wouldn't put it past the woman. And she was feeling so…so…twisted up, she couldn't find any words to get through to Carlyle. So she left. Left her brother as someone else's responsibility.

The Hudsons and their extended little network wanted to take over her life? Fine. They wanted to take care of her lying, unpredictable brother? Great. They wanted to watch her every move because of some nonsense threat that *Jack* perceived there to be? Let them.

She didn't know why it was getting harder and harder to breathe. Like there was a pressure in her chest, so heavy that she couldn't even fill up her lungs. It was all too much like impending doom.

Because they couldn't handle *everything* for her. *Something* was going to crash and burn, and then it'd be all up to her again—and then what?

She was going to leave. Right now. Just get in her car and go. Get the scrapbook and then head home. *Her* home. She didn't want to be protected. She didn't want to be helped. She wanted…

She started to change her route. Walk for the front, where her car was parked, instead of the side door that would lead her back into the house. To Jack.

Jack. Who *loved* her for some reason. Who'd asked her to let him take care of her. Because *he* needed that.

She swore and stopped walking, right there in the middle of the yard, starlight sparkling all around her. She couldn't be that woman who just took off. Oh, she wanted to be. *God*, she wanted to be. But it would hurt him if she went off by herself, and even if she didn't think she was in any danger, all it would take is for one little thing to go off course for her to feel like she'd been wrong.

She turned back toward the house, and then there he was. Stepping out of the side door, the porch light shining a little halo around his head.

She loved him so much, it made her want to run away. Because what he didn't understand was that for all the ways she presented herself, for all the ways she thought therapy had helped her deal with her childhood trauma, deep down she saw—clearly, for the first time—how scared she was that it all just made her as unlovable as she'd always been treated.

But she *had* gone to therapy. She *had* faced a garbage fest of a childhood and worked on healing from those wounds. Maybe she wasn't all the way there, but it was about progress. Not perfection.

She walked over to him, not sure what to say or even who to be. It was like Ry unearthing all those bodies hadn't just caused a major issue. It was like it had turned her life inside out and nothing made sense anymore.

Least of all the man on the porch. No, least of all *herself.*

"Were you going somewhere?" he asked. Not with accusation. Not with anger. He likely felt a little bit of those things, but he didn't use them on her. That wasn't him.

So she told him the truth. No lie would form. "Thought about taking off."

"What changed your mind?"

She took the stairs, got close enough to him that she could see the way he watched her. Maybe there was a little flare of irritation lurking in his dark eyes, but mostly the only thing on his face was worry.

She leaned forward against him, wrapped her arms around him. "You."

He ran a hand over her hair. A sweet, protective gesture as he pressed a kiss to her temple. "Good."

That simple response almost made her laugh. But this whole *day* also revealed a truth that she was going to have to accept.

Everything was going to feel off-kilter and wrong until they got to the bottom of this mystery that connected to both their pasts. "Let's go get that scrapbook. I think I need to not have it hanging over my head."

He nodded. "Keys in my pocket. Let's head out."

He drove out to Bent County. They didn't really talk, just listened to the low strains of the old-fashioned country music he preferred. It suited the mood. Sad, mournful, a little weird.

When he parked and turned off the engine, he got out with her. It wasn't a surprise, exactly, but she had to fight the knee-jerk desire to tell him to stay in his truck.

They walked in together, smiled at the administrative assistant behind the desk. Sunrise worked with Bent County enough for Chloe to know everyone here by name.

"Hey, Linda. I'm here to pick up the relinquished property Hart left for me."

Linda tilted her head. "I'm sorry, Deputy Brink. Hart hasn't told me about any relinquished property. I don't think he's here, but Laurel is. Let me call her down." She lifted a phone to her ear.

Something didn't set right with that. Chloe looked up at Jack. He was frowning. But they didn't say anything, just waited for Detective Delaney-Carson.

A few minutes later, she strode into the lobby area. She stopped short and looked at both of them like she was surprised to see them there. "What are you two doing here?"

"Picking up the scrapbook Hart called me about this afternoon."

The detective's eyebrows drew together. "He told me he was going to drive it out to you before he went home."

Chloe exchanged a look with Jack. "That's not what he told us. He said I could pick it up whenever."

She nodded. "That was our original plan, but when you didn't show up, he was going to drop it by the ranch."

"Maybe take a pass at questioning Ry if he got the opportunity?" Jack offered, *sounding* casual.

Laurel studied Jack as if deciding what to say. Then she gave a little nod. "Yeah. Did he?"

"He never came by. Scrapbook or no."

Laurel's expression went from a puzzled kind of professionalism to flat-out worry. "I'll call him."

She took the phone Linda handed her, dialed the number and then waited. Her expression went from worry to cool, cop professionalism. But Chloe knew that meant something was *wrong*.

"He's not answering."

Chapter Thirteen

"Linda, can you get Hart's location? I'll take my cruiser and see if he stopped at home." The detective spoke calmly, smiled at the woman behind the desk. She gave no outward signs of distress or worry, but Jack could read it on her all the same.

Because this was out of the norm, and he knew *he* didn't like it, and he wasn't even Hart's partner.

"What can we do?" he asked her.

"Go home, Sheriff," Laurel said sharply, but when she turned to walk back into the station, Jack followed and so did Chloe.

"You've got two Sunrise deputies right here. Let us help."

"Sheriff, you know as well as I do you're both too involved in whatever this is to help in a professional capacity."

"I actually don't know that," Jack replied.

"Besides, I'm sure there's a reasonable explanation for all this," she continued, clearly ignoring him. But she didn't stop them from following her out the back exit of the station into the parking lot, which had personal cars and cruisers littered throughout.

Laurel strode toward some point only she knew, but then she came to an abrupt halt. In the dark, under the parking lot lights, one cruiser sat with its driver's-side door wide open. For a strange moment, they all stood there in stunned silence, looking at it.

"One of you go inside and tell Linda to get security footage of the parking lot up," Laurel said, her voice dead calm though she'd gone a little pale.

Chloe immediately turned and jogged back inside. Jack stayed with Laurel.

"How long would that have been like that without anyone noticing? Not long, right?"

Laurel shook her head as she approached the car. "Hard to say. Hart told me he was leaving about an hour ago. There hasn't been a shift change, so it's possible no one's been out here, but it's also possible he didn't leave right after he told me."

Jack peered into the open door of the car. There didn't seem to be signs of a struggle, but it was shadowy and dark in the car. Jack pulled out his phone and switched on the flashlight mode at the same time Laurel did.

Nothing appeared amiss, really, aside from the wide-open door. "Maybe he just forgot something?" It seemed like a leap—but then again, so did immediately jumping to conclusions about an open car door.

"No reason to leave the door open and kill the battery. Unless it was some kind of emergency." Laurel did a slow turn, eyeing the entire parking lot illuminated only by a few light towers. "It was still light out when he told me he was leaving. He's not... Whatever this is, it's not like him. *Something* happened."

Jack did his own looking around the parking lot. Bent County was hardly a bustling metropolis. Even though there was a police station right there, it wouldn't be impossible for something to happen out here and no one would see. Even if it was light out.

"He didn't get taken out of the police station's parking lot in broad daylight without someone seeing," Laurel said disgustedly, clearly more to herself than to Jack. "Without some kind of struggle. I don't know what this is, but it's not that."

Jack could hear what she was really doing: trying to talk herself out of thinking the worst. All while the worst was sitting right there in front of them.

"The footage is going to give us the answers we need. Let's go watch it."

"I don't like this," she muttered. "I told him we should have kept that scrapbook. It's all part of the Brink case. Not that I should be telling you this. Why are you even here?"

"Chloe might be a deputy at my department, but—"

"Come on, Sheriff. She's a lot more than your deputy. Anyone with eyes can see that."

Before Jack could react to *that*, Laurel was striding inside. Chloe met them halfway down the hall. "Linda says they're getting the footage up on the second floor."

Laurel looked at Chloe, then at Jack, then sighed. "All right, follow me." She took them up a set of stairs and then into a larger room clearly used for meetings. A man Jack recognized, though couldn't quite come up with a name, sat at a laptop.

He eyed Chloe and Jack, then Laurel. "Want me to put it up on the screen?"

Laurel nodded. In a few seconds, security footage of the police station parking lot showed up on the screen.

"What time you want?" he asked Laurel.

"Let's start at six. That's a little before when he told me he was leaving."

The footage sped up, people coming and going in quick time. When the man hit Play, the parking lot was empty aside from cars. Then Hart appeared. He had a box tucked under his arm.

"That's the scrapbook," Laurel explained, pointing to the box.

Hart opened his cruiser door, leaned in and put the box down, presumably on the passenger seat, though that wasn't fully visible from the camera angle. Then, before he slid into the driver's seat, he stopped, straightened and looked off into the distance with a puzzled frown.

Everyone held their breath as he turned and immediately began to jog off to the right—and quickly off-screen.

"We need footage of that side of the building," Laurel instructed the man at the computer.

"That side's a dead zone, Detective. We've only got cameras at entrances and exits—there aren't any in that corner."

Laurel swore.

"Does he see something, or does someone call out to him?" Chloe said, pointing to the screen. "Because he was getting in, but something stopped him. So someone had to have seen him. Something had to have gotten his attention."

"It's got to be a noise, right?" Jack returned. "He's getting ready to get *in* the car. Head down, then he looks over."

"But he leaves the scrapbook," Laurel added. "Keep rolling the footage," she told the man. "Because that scrapbook isn't there anymore."

Which meant sometime between when Hart went out of the parking lot and Jack and Laurel went out to the car, someone took it.

They watched. No one suggested they fast-forward the footage. They'd all investigated too many cases to let impatience get in the way of good police work. Seconds seemed to drag by, and tension settled into the air like a lead weight, wrapping around each of them as *nothing* happened on the screen. Minutes of just the trees blowing in the breeze and the sun slowly setting.

And then, *finally*, something showed up on the screen. A small figure, shrouded in a dark hoodie, moved quietly and stealthily up to the car, scooped up the scrapbook, and walked off the opposite side of the screen.

Laurel swore again. "I knew we should have kept it." She glared at Chloe. "What's in it?"

"How the hell should I know? I didn't even know it was in that chest."

"It's been in her garage, undisturbed for years. Anyone who wanted it could have gotten it easily. For years."

"Not if the person who wanted it was in prison," Laurel returned.

"If my father wanted it, he knew where it was and how to get to it. He could have sent Ry, and I wouldn't have thought twice about my brother hanging around my place. Detective, you can look into my father for anything you want, but it doesn't make sense to bark up that tree right now."

Laurel was still scowling, but she didn't argue with Chloe. "Here's what's going to happen: you're going to go back home and let me do my job."

"Who else is briefed on the case besides you?" Jack demanded.

Laurel's expression was stern. "I'll catch them up."

"We're going to look for him, Detective. With or without your permission or cooperation."

"I could have you arrested for tampering with an ongoing investigation."

Jack didn't take offense to the threat. He understood all too well what it was like to have no answers and someone you cared about in the middle of confusing danger. But he didn't bend either. "Or you could just let us help."

THEY WERE GIVEN the grunt job. They had trailed after Laurel as she'd gone from department to department, barking out orders. Then, when she'd finally stopped and turned to them, she'd told them to go search Hart's house.

Which was the grunt job because clearly Hart wasn't likely to have been there since before his shift today. Still, it was a necessary job, and Chloe and Jack drove from the police station over to Bent proper.

She couldn't blame the detective for keeping her out of most of it. Someone was going to call that parole officer in Texas and see where her father was, and if he wasn't verifiably in Texas tonight, he would be a top suspect.

But it didn't add up. Not to Chloe. Her father was shady as all get out, but he could have gotten that scrapbook whenever he wanted.

"There's something off here, Jack," she said, scanning the quiet street where Thomas Hart lived. She didn't know much about Thomas Hart's personal life, but according to Laurel, he lived alone in the little house they pulled up to.

A neat yard with no frills. A well-kept house with a porch light on in the dark.

Jack stopped the truck, and they both got out and studied the house from the front in what little light the porch and streetlamp offered.

"There's a lot of things off here, I think," Jack replied. "You don't have your gun on you. I want you to—"

"Follow behind. I know," she muttered, following him up to the porch. They'd knock on the front, then check around back. But Chloe didn't think they'd find anything here.

"The only person who knew about that scrapbook, far as I know, is my father. Nothing happened to it when it was only my father knowing. So what happened? Who got wind of it being with the cops?"

"Maybe that was the problem," Jack replied, rapping on the door. "Your father didn't want it with the police."

"I *am* the police."

Jack just shook his head as they waited. Chloe peered in the sidelight while Jack studied the front window, looking for a glimpse of anything. No one answered the door, no flicker of light or movement of curtains. Just stillness and silence.

Jack jerked his head, and Chloe nodded. They'd move around the east side of the house now. The street was quiet, the night heavy. As they moved around the side of the house, Chloe's nerves began to hum. In the front, the quiet had seemed like a comfortable small-town evening, but things were darker around back. Chloe kept even closer to Jack.

There were no lights on back here, so the postage stamp backyards all ran together like one big shadow. Some houses had lights on inside, shining in little cracks around curtains, but not many.

Jack pulled out a flashlight he must have grabbed from his truck. The beam shone across the grass, to a nice patio equipped with a ridiculously complicated-looking grill and then to a sliding glass door on the back of the house. Another curtain pulled tight. No lights here either.

"He's not here," Chloe said in a whisper. Not because they really needed to whisper, but because the night seemed to call for it.

"No."

But before they could discuss it further, something beeped, and it was so incongruous to the quiet night around them that Chloe nearly screamed.

Funny how she could almost always put her cop hat on, put the fear of danger to the side, but something about this case involving her father in *any* way made her feel more like the little girl who'd been terrified of him and less like the woman she'd built herself into.

He wasn't even *here*.

Jack pulled his phone out of his pocket. Someone was *calling* him, because little pinging noises were hardly her father jumping out of the shadows to be her own personal bogeyman.

Jack answered, and Chloe could hear the faint hum of a female voice on the other line but not the actual words. And still, something about the way Jack held himself told her it was bad news.

"Thanks, Mary. Keep me updated."

He turned to her in the dark. She couldn't make out the expression on his face, but he touched her shoulder.

Bad, *bad* news.

"Ry's missing."

She didn't know what she'd been expecting. But not that. She *should* have expected it, but somehow it took the wind right out of her. "But…" No *but*s. That's what Ry did.

She always screwed it all up, no matter how hard she tried.

"I'm sorry, Chloe."

She shook her head, not that he could see it in the dark. Maybe it took her off guard in *this* moment, but she'd also been ready for this in the long run. "I can track his phone. Maybe." She pulled her own phone out of her pocket, ignoring the way her hand shook. "I wasn't about to leave it up to chance. It's something I used to do when he was in high school, and I was trying to keep him in school. I haven't done it for years, so I was hoping he wouldn't notice and turn it off." She clicked the screen on her phone, brought up the location tracker and hoped.

The map moved around, zooming into a spot. Chloe

would have felt immense relief, but he was in the middle of a campground by the mountains.

Not just any campground.

"That's where my parents were camping the night they disappeared," Jack said, his voice devoid of any and all emotion.

Chloe felt like her chest was caving in, but she didn't let it show. Couldn't. "If you don't want to go there, we can—"

"I'm going," Jack said sharply. But his voice softened on the next words. "This might connect, Chloe. Ry. The scrapbook. Hart missing. We can let someone else lead this. One of our guys. One of theirs. I can take you back to the ranch, but—"

Chloe shook her head. She had always protected her brother, would always want to, but now, in this moment, she realized if he was really involved in this… She wouldn't be able to stomach getting him out of it.

She took Jack's arm and pulled him back toward the truck. "Let's go."

Chapter Fourteen

Jack drove out to the campground he hadn't been at in a very long time. For the first few years after his parents' disappearance, he'd scoured every inch. Over and over again, with any free moment he had—which weren't many, when he'd essentially been raising five kids. But he'd found time.

He'd always found time. No doubt his siblings had as well. Always so sure there had to be an answer here. But that answer had never been found. Even now, knowing those skeletal remains were likely his parents, it didn't feel like answers were really within reach. Just farther and farther away.

It didn't bother him as much as he'd thought it would. He hadn't been fully cognizant of how the past few years had changed him. Even if now he could pinpoint it back to a moment.

Grant had finally left the military and come home for good a few years ago. That had been such a relief, not just for him but for the entire family. Tragedy hadn't struck again. Someone else in their family hadn't been here one day and gone the next.

Jack hadn't done more than glance at his parents' case since. He hadn't even driven down the road that led to the forest preserve. Maybe not consciously, but he'd avoided poking at that old wound in the same ways he'd been doing up to that point.

He didn't know if anyone else had felt that way. He wasn't even sure he'd fully realized it until this moment, driving into the forest preserve, realizing how much of his parents' case he'd put away.

Because somehow all the Hudson kids had made it into adulthood, not unscathed but alive. Building lives and families all their own. Digging into old tragedies felt like begging for trouble.

Yes, someone deserved to pay for what had happened to his parents. He still hoped someone *would*.

But what would be the cost?

It didn't matter. Answers or no. Trouble was here, in the shape of skeletal remains, missing detectives, the woman he loved and her runaway brother. So he had to see it through.

They didn't call Bent County. Jack knew they should. They were possibly going into something dangerous, and doing so without backup and without every local law enforcement agency having the information was risky. A risk neither of them should be taking. A risk he'd never take.

If it wasn't for her.

He drove, and neither of them suggested calling it in. Neither of them suggested anything. Chloe was as silent as he was. She was no doubt dealing with her own demons. Because Ry taking off *around* the same time Hart disappeared into presumably thin air felt ominous—connected, even if he couldn't see how. And there was no doubt in Jack's mind that Ry's disappearance was why neither of them were calling it in.

Bringing in other people would make it harder to protect Ry, no matter how little he deserved protecting.

When Chloe finally spoke, it was to give him directions

to follow different twists and turns in the dirt road to find Ry's location somewhere within the preserve. Not too deep in it, or they'd be losing reception, and they wouldn't be able to track Ry's location if he didn't have service either, so that was good.

"Maybe we should approach on foot," Jack suggested when Chloe said they were getting close. "Gives us the element of surprise to really figure out what's going on here before Ry or whoever knows someone is coming."

"Yeah," Chloe agreed. Jack pulled off the road on the dirt shoulder. He turned off the car. "Grab the flashlight. I've got the only gun, so I want—"

"Me to stay behind. I know, Jack."

She didn't snap it. She sounded so defeated, it was like a little stab to his heart. That so many people in her life had failed her and lead her to all *this* mess, and she'd held up so well to all of it, but when did it get to be too much?

Jack knew there was nothing he could say about Ry, about her father, about *her* that could make this better. He hated that he couldn't do something to make this okay.

But there was no way to fix it, so they got out of the truck. Quietly, she came around to his side. She had her phone on, and the screen illuminated her face. She didn't look *affected* by what was going on, but her usual cop face had an air of exhaustion to it.

She switched on the flashlight from his truck and moved the beam around in front of them. "I think if we follow this road, then take the first right we come across, it'll lead us to him."

She didn't mention the possibility it wasn't Ry himself. That they could stumble upon just his phone and nothing else. So Jack didn't either. Why verbalize what they both knew?

"Got it," he replied instead. He followed the beam of light

she held, making sure she stayed behind him enough that he felt reasonably sure he could stop anything unexpected from hurting her.

They moved in quiet precision. Jack was sure they were both trying to keep their minds blank, pretend like it was any Sunrise Sheriff Department case. Nothing that involved his parents or her brother.

When the flashlight beam illuminated a turn in the dirt road, Jack took it. They quickly found it wasn't actually a road, just a path to a parking area. Chloe came up next to him, sweeping her light around the dirt in front of them. Stopping when it landed on the lone car parked in the lot.

A car Jack recognized. Chloe's car.

Jack lifted his gun, looking around what little of the parking lot he could see in just the flashlight beam. It seemed to be deserted aside from the car. He glanced over at Chloe, who would be hurt by this. No matter what it was. Her brother had left the Hudson Ranch—likely hot-wired her car, since Jack doubted she'd left her keys behind—and was quite clearly up to no good.

Jack could tell she was looking straight ahead, staring hard at her car parked there. Jack couldn't make out her expression in just the glow of the flashlight, but he could feel the hurt radiating off her.

She audibly swallowed. "I'm calling Detective Delaney-Carson," she whispered, reaching for her pocket.

Jack put his hand over hers before she could grab her phone. "We can handle this, Chloe. You don't have to call it in if you don't want to."

She finally turned to look at him. He couldn't make out her features in the dark. She was just a shadow, but her voice was convincing enough. Firm and determined. "Yes. Yes, I do."

CHLOE'S HAND SHOOK as she held the phone to her ear, but she didn't think Jack saw the tremor. He was busy watching all around them, making sure they weren't sitting ducks.

For what, she didn't know. Whatever was going on... nothing added up or made any sense. But she could feel danger in the air like an impending storm.

There wasn't any movement from the car. No sounds but the rustles and chirps of an evening in the wilderness. Wherever Ry was, it wasn't right here. Chloe refused to let her mind bound ahead to worst-case scenarios. Most likely, he was out here scoring a hit from some drug dealer.

Funny how she *hoped* that was all it was.

The phone rang and when the detective answered, it was with a terse, "Yes."

"It's Deputy Brink. We haven't found any sign of Hart, but my brother took off from the Hudson Ranch. We've tracked him to a parking lot in the Franklin Forest. I don't know if it connects to Hart, to the scrapbook, but I think you should send someone over. We've found my car that he used, abandoned in a lot."

There was a pause. "I'm coming myself," she replied. "We got word from Texas. Mark Brink didn't show up for his last parole meeting. He's missing."

Chloe didn't swear. She couldn't even muster up surprise. Maybe she didn't think her father was behind stealing that scrapbook because it didn't make any sense, but maybe she was giving him too much credit to think he *had* to make sense.

"I'll send you our exact location," Chloe said.

"Good. I'll be there soon."

The call ended, and Chloe sent the location to Delaney-Carson. She took a deep breath, staring at her car. Parked. Ry's phone must be in the car, but Ry wasn't.

Unless…

She swallowed down a bubble of fear. If he was hurt, well, she'd deal with it. "Let's look at the car but not touch anything. I don't want anyone accusing us of tampering." Because if she stood here waiting for Laurel without doing anything, she'd think of a million terrible situations that involved Ry bloody and dead somewhere and she couldn't…

She was so angry at him, but she knew herself well enough to know she'd make a wrong choice if she let herself get too worked up about the possibilities of him being hurt. And she… She'd made too many bad choices when it came to her brother.

That ended now.

"Chloe—"

"If I say we should look at it, we should look at it. If you want to go first and keep me behind you, I'd start moving." She knew she was being a jerk when Jack was trying to be protective and sweet, in his way, but she was holding on by a thread.

She needed to do everything she could to treat this like a crime scene that had nothing to do with her. To treat Jack like a fellow cop, not the man she loved.

They moved forward in tandem, Chloe training the flashlight on the car. They were quiet, watching for movement, listening for sound. But there was nothing as they got close enough to the car to look inside.

Chloe swept the beam over the entire car and in each window, heart in her throat, *praying* it would be empty.

And it was. There was nothing amiss inside. It looked almost exactly like it had when she'd left it on the Hudson Ranch, with the one exception of Ry's phone lying in the console.

That made her nervous, of course, but at least it wasn't a body.

At this point, Ry had made bad choices. She could accept that. She had given him every opportunity to make different, better choices. He'd refused. She could mourn that, but she couldn't keep blaming herself for it.

But she could never stop hoping he was alive. Hoping he'd find some way to get himself out of all the choices he'd made. Maybe it hurt her heart, but that was the bottom line now.

Meanwhile, Jack Hudson stood beside her, offering *not* to call the authorities they needed to call, wanting to protect her—and if that meant bending his very strict moral code, apparently he was willing to do it.

Chloe couldn't let him. It would just about kill her.

"I want to know who he talked to, but we better wait for Bent County to open the door with gloves. There might be prints that give us a hint as to what's going on. If he was here with someone else." She looked out into the darkness around them. "Meeting someone? I don't know. But it's going to be Bent County's job to figure it out."

Jack nodded. "Okay, but if he drove your car here, left it here, we should be able to pick up his trail for a little while." Jack reached for the flashlight. He didn't take it from her but pushed it down a little so the light illuminated their footprints. Nothing super clear, but enough of an indentation to tell that someone had been walking across the makeshift lot. "Or we can stay here and wait."

It was up to her. A lump formed in her throat. Funny how she wouldn't mind him sweeping in and making the decisions for her right now. But that was because these were the kind of decisions she had to make for herself, even if she didn't want to.

Chloe used the beam, searching out footprints that weren't hers or Jack's. Eventually she zeroed in on a pair that was either Ry's or some other random person's. Jack walked ahead, gun drawn and at the ready, as her beam led them away from the parking lot and into the low grasses that made up the field in front of them. There was a path, it looked like, though it was hard to tell in only the beam of the flashlight if it was just from animals trampling through or an actual marked hiking trail in the forest.

She didn't want to follow his footsteps too far with Bent County coming, but it was hard to hold herself back knowing Ry could be out there. Doing who knew what.

"Chloe."

Jack had that tone in his voice. Like something bad was coming, but she didn't see what it could be. She looked around, she listened, but nothing.

Then his hand came over her wrist, he pulled her a little forward and he moved the light beam to something on the ground.

It was just a small little circle, but Chloe had been a cop too long not to know what blood dropped onto dirt looked like.

Her hand shook for a second, but only a second. The light trembling was enough for her to ground herself. To remind herself she was strong, capable. A *cop*, not a big sister who'd failed.

She moved the beam up the trail. Not much farther up, there was another spot, about the same size as the first.

She took a few steps forward, and Jack never released her hand, but he didn't stop her. He moved with her.

The third circle was bigger. Noticeably so. She inhaled, knowing it was shaky. Knowing she couldn't quite make herself immune to this.

Someone was bleeding, and the chances it *wasn't* Ry felt really, really low.

"What do you want to do?" Jack asked her quietly. "Wait or follow?"

They should wait. That would be the safe thing to do. But as much as she was ready for her brother to face the consequences of his actions, she wasn't ready for him to be hurt. Or worse, dead.

"Follow."

Chapter Fifteen

Jack walked in front of Chloe, following the lead of the flashlight she held. Every few steps, there was a splotch of blood. Sometimes they got smaller, but then they'd get bigger again.

Jack gripped his gun. He occasionally looked out into the dark around them but never caught sight of anything, never heard anything that seemed out of place. Even though he was on edge, there wasn't that feeling of impending danger to him and Chloe.

But there had been danger here, that was for sure. The blood splotches along the trail no longer got smaller, only bigger, until they became almost a continuous trickle of blood.

Every so often, Jack glanced back at Chloe holding the flashlight. He could feel the tension pouring off her. She was worried it was Ry doing the bleeding, and so was Jack. The other option wasn't much better—that Ry had been the person to cause the bleeding in someone else. Both were going to be hard pills to swallow for Chloe. But there was no pill to swallow until they figured out what was going on here.

Jack wondered how long they could walk before they found something, before Bent County arrived at the parking lot and wondered where they were. He wondered a lot of things on this slow, nerve-racking walk that never seemed to end.

The trail narrowed, and the trickle of blood seemed to disappear. Though, more likely, whatever had been bleeding was now bleeding in the grass rather than the dirt.

Jack paused, not sure whether to press on or study the grassy sides of the trail for the blood. No doubt it didn't just miraculously stop bleeding.

"Jack." Her voice trembled on just the single syllable of his name.

He heard it then. The rustle and clicking sounds. Not a human threat, but animal. Still, he wasn't sure why that would scare Chloe, who'd grown up around wildlife and the potential threat and danger of them just as much as he had.

Until he turned to where the beam was pointed. Two pairs of eyes glowed back at them. But it wasn't the animals—coyotes—that had caused that reaction in Chloe. It was what they were standing next to.

A human body.

Jack moved without fully thinking. Just placed himself between her and the body. Just made sure his body stopped the beam of light from reaching that far. He hadn't seen the details, just the body—the very still body—being studied and perhaps other things by the coyotes.

"It's Ry, isn't it? It's… He… Someone…"

Jack moved forward and pulled her into him. "We don't know that, Chloe."

Her breathing hitched on a little sob. "It's *someone*."

He wanted to give her his gun and tell her to follow the trail back to the parking lot. Wait for the cops. He wanted her to let him handle whatever this was. But it would leave him with only his phone for a light and with no other form of protection. He didn't think the coyotes would be much of a problem if he didn't approach, but he'd have to approach to identify the body.

Chloe needed to know. For sure. So he couldn't send her back yet. He had to...

"Stay here. Put your phone flashlight on, and give me this one." He pried the flashlight from her fingers. He didn't think she was holding it so tight because she didn't want to relinquish control, but because she was in shock.

"Chloe," he said sharply. She jerked her gaze to him. "Pull out your phone. I'm going to get closer and see if I can get an ID."

She shook her head. "Jack, they'll... You can't approach wild animals feeding."

"I'll be careful. You stand right here."

"Jack."

But he ignored her protests and moved forward. Luckily, she stayed put, or he would have had to stop. He didn't want her seeing whatever this was, but he knew she needed answers.

He'd get her those answers.

He pointed the beam back at the animals. They didn't move, but they watched him approach. Then they started to move a little nervously. Low growls began to emanate from where they stood.

Jack made a few ridiculous noises, loud and sudden, hoping to scare the coyotes off as he approached. They were clearly reluctant to leave the body, and reluctant to deal with Jack. They backed off a *little*, though not as far away as Jack would have preferred.

He moved the beam from the coyotes to the body. An arm was bloody and mangled, no doubt some from the coyotes, but perhaps some from whatever injury had caused the trail of blood, because most of the body looked to be intact.

Jack circled, hoping to get closer to the head and face. As he did, he saw hair, and immediately knew it wasn't Ry because the brown was too long and peppered with gray.

"Chloe, it's not Ry," he called out to her, still trying to creep close enough to get a glimpse of the face without upsetting the coyotes too much. He kept making noises and flashing the beam of the flashlight at the animals, hoping to keep them back.

They did keep inching away, but they didn't stop their warning growls or take off like he might have preferred. Still, he got to a better angle, slightly closer, and was able to point the light at the face of the body.

Not Ry. Familiar, but Jack wasn't sure... Until it dawned on him just who it was.

He let out a slow breath, then began to back away from the body, from the coyotes, back toward Chloe.

When he reached her, he realized she was shaking. She hadn't turned the light on her phone on, but she held it in her hands.

"Chloe."

"It's Ry, isn't it? It has to be. It's the only thing that makes sense." She was crying. Panicking, clearly.

He had his hands full and wasn't quite sure whether to put down the light or the gun. In the end, he placed the flashlight on the ground and gripped her arm with his free one. "Chloe, listen to me, sweetheart. It's not Ry."

She nodded, like him touching her finally got it through to her. When she finally spoke, her words were choked. "Then who is it, Jack?"

He took a deep breath. He didn't want to draw it out, and still... It was hard to say. "It's your father."

CHLOE DIDN'T BREAK DOWN. Or at least, she didn't lose it over the fact her father was dead. That information kind of helped her pull herself together. Breathe again, wipe her cheeks. In those first few moments, she couldn't have cared less about her dead father. She had just been so damn relieved her brother hadn't ended up that way.

So far.

Then the chaos had started, which was kind of a nice distraction. It was this strange, buzzing foundation to whatever was going on inside her. Jack took her back to the parking lot, where Detective Delaney-Carson had arrived and was investigating the car.

Jack told the detective everything—or at least, Chloe thought he had. The panic that it had been Ry lying in a bloody, dead heap had been hard to fully come out of. And the fact of the matter was, even knowing it *wasn't* Ry didn't ease her worry. Because Ry was still out there somewhere since this was her car in the parking lot.

Maybe Ry was the aggressor, but more likely to Chloe's way of thinking, he was another victim to whatever their father had dragged him into.

Detective Delaney-Carson called in more backup, and pretty soon there were cops everywhere. Dealing with the coyotes and the body, and determining what their next steps were going to be.

Jack had tried to convince Chloe to go back to the Hudson Ranch multiple times, and even the detective had suggested it, but Chloe couldn't budge. Not until they found Ry.

She kept expecting to feel something when they brought her father's body out of that field in a body bag. Some sort of…not grief, obviously, when he'd been nothing to her, really, besides a tormenter. But she'd expected to feel *something*.

Instead, there was nothing but an odd sort of numbness

when it came to her father's death. Murder. Whatever it was. The only feeling she really recognized was worry over Ry, over whatever was going on with Hart missing, about what this all meant for Jack's family. Really, about what this all *meant*.

Because as much as she'd felt her father didn't have anything to do with stealing that scrapbook, there were no leads here. No answers. Just a dead man. So it was more questions and no leads.

"Deputy Brink, I'd like to ask you a few questions."

"I think any questions can wait," Jack said, stepping in between the detective and Chloe herself.

It was funny how she could appreciate the gesture but not want it all the same. "No, I'd like to answer all the questions I can right now. I want my brother found. No matter what."

Jack moved to the side, still standing beside her but no longer blocking the detective, and it was the combination of sticking up for her and being able to stand aside that gave her the ability to lean on him, when she usually didn't want to lean on anyone.

"Do you have any reason to believe your brother could have killed your father?" the detective asked.

Chloe let that question settle over her. It was the natural one to ask, and it was one she'd been asking herself since Jack had broken the news to her. "My father was a cruel man. He was verbally, emotionally and physically abusive toward Ry. But in the way of abusers, Ry might have spoken badly about him, he might have even hated him, but he did what my father told him to do. Is it *possible* Ry had a moment of snapping? Of finally refusing and that resulted in some kind of altercation that left my father dead? Sure, it's possible. Is it plausible? No. Because he's still an immature boy seeking the wrong people's approval."

And he was out there. Somewhere. Probably in this forest preserve. And maybe her brother was capable of murder.
Maybe that was in him, and she was blind to it. Maybe her
father had pushed and pushed, threatened, started it. Maybe
Ry had finished it and panicked. Possible. So possible.

And yet she just couldn't visualize it. She couldn't buy
into it. Not with Hart and that scrapbook missing. There
was some thread they were missing. Eventually, the detectives would find it, and normally she would step back and
let them.

But she couldn't do that with Ry missing.

"Deputy Brink, I'm going to ask you to go home," the
detective said. "Or to the Hudson Ranch. I'm going to ask
you to leave this up to Bent County to investigate."

"Are you going to expect me to listen?"

There was a pause. The detective looked at the scene
around them. Flashlights and cops and a vast wilderness
that could hide so many answers. Then her gaze returned
to Chloe, and she shook her head. "No, I'm not."

"Good."

"Just try to stay out of my guys' way. And keep me in the
loop. I think the timing is too coincidental. I don't know how
it doesn't connect, but if Hart and that scrapbook have nothing to do with your brother and father, that means we've got
two cases to solve instead of one. I need your cooperation."

Before, Chloe might have hesitated, being worried about
Ry and trouble. But they were in the same position, really.
The detective's partner was missing, someone she probably
cared about from years of working together. Someone she
was responsible for due to the nature of their jobs. Chloe's
brother was missing, and she loved the little rat bastard.

Connected or not, they were problems that needed solving

no matter what. So they'd have to work together. "You've got it."

Someone hailed the detective, and she excused herself. Chloe turned to Jack and took a deep breath. She met his gaze—not cop-blank but worried. About her.

"I'm going to ask you to go home, Jack."

"Chloe—"

"Hear me out. This is… This place has meaning to you. Bad meaning. You shouldn't have to scour it and be reminded. You can send Baker or Clinton out to help me. I can ask Carlyle to come out—she's got the skills to help me look for Ry. Or even Zeke would probably help. It doesn't have to be you *here*."

"It doesn't have to be, no. But it's going to be."

She'd known that was going to be his answer. She'd known she wouldn't be able to talk him into leaving. And still, she'd needed to hear him say it. To get that stern, irritable look from him at her even suggesting he left her to this.

"I love you, Jack." And who the hell cared if there were cops all around them. She loved him, and no matter what horrible things were happening, they were going to make this one thing work.

She was determined.

Chapter Sixteen

Jack didn't bother to try to convince Chloe to go home and rest and eat first, though he wanted to. It would be the smart thing to do. He knew this rationally.

But he'd also been in her position before. He knew too well what it felt like to have a family member in danger. There'd be no rest, no taking care of herself, until they'd exhausted every resource in finding Ry.

Because it was one thing for Ry to be missing, running off on his own volition, but to be missing with one body already found was something else. Something urgent.

But where to begin? The cops were crawling all over the parking lot and crime scene, gathering clues, compiling evidence. Of course, their focus was on a dead Mark Brink and a missing detective, not Ry. Not yet. Not when they had one of their own missing.

"What if we follow that trail past where my father was found?" Chloe suggested. "Ry didn't come back to the car, and I'm not sure I buy that he and my father were out here if they weren't together. Especially with *my* car. Ry had to go somewhere. Somewhere in the preserve."

Jack didn't want to burst her bubble, but they had to analyze all the facts. "Your father might have had a vehicle. Ry could have taken that." Or been taken *in* that, though

Jack didn't point it out. Maybe they didn't need to analyze *every* possibility. "Whoever killed your father could have had a vehicle."

"Did you see evidence of anyone else?" Chloe returned.

He hadn't, though, in fairness, it was hard to determine what was wind mark and what was made by car and human in the dirt of the parking area. It wasn't an often-visited area since the campground was on the other side of the preserve. You'd have to be a pretty intrepid hiker to be on this side. So a lack of evidence of other people *could* point to something.

He supposed it was just as possible Ry was still in the preserve as not. But it was a *vast* preserve. "I'm not sure even with Laurel's okay they're going to let us walk down that trail again."

"Let's go around and meet it up a ways after." Chloe looked down at her phone screen and the map of the forest preserve she'd pulled up. "If we walk back to the road, then take it a while, we can cut over. Should be light by then, and we'll have an easier time of meeting up with the trail from the road."

Jack wasn't sure it was the best idea, but he knew Chloe needed to feel like she had a handle on something. Besides, even if it was the wrong avenue to go down, the entire Bent County Sheriff's Department was also looking into this whole thing. They could stumble into finding Ry as well.

Hopefully alive. Hopefully not a murderer.

But first, he had to be found, so Jack nodded at Chloe, and they started walking back out to the road. There was a hint of a sunrise to the east. She was right: it wouldn't take long for the light to catch up with them.

That would be good. That would help. Jack told himself this over and over again. That he was the sheriff, that this was his *job*. Not a painful tightrope walk with the woman he loved, trying to unearth secrets that would hurt them both.

"Losing service," Chloe muttered, holding her phone up to the sky as if that might help. "I don't think we should cross over to the trail just yet. We need to go at least another half mile." She lifted her hand, poked at something on one of those high-tech watches Jack couldn't begin to understand.

"You know, you should get one, Jack," she said, as if she'd read his mind.

"I don't even like my cell phone. Why would I want it on my wrist?"

She shook her head, her mouth curving ever so slightly. The old, familiar argument was something like a comfort in the middle of all this unfamiliar.

"Do you know where it was?" she asked, not looking at him as they walked.

He didn't have to be a mind reader to understand what she was asking. "The campground on the north side was the last place anyone saw them. I've been up and down every inch of it, and this preserve. We're pretty far away."

She nodded. "Ry was too young to have been involved in that, but... Maybe we should head that way after we follow the trail for a bit. I don't think any of these things make sense enough to connect, except for the timing. I want to ignore the timing, I really do, because it feels so circumstantial. But..."

"Timing is part of it. I agree. We'll head out that way if the trail doesn't offer anything."

This time, she did look over at him. "Another thing you don't have to be here for."

"I'll be here," he said, and realized she had said the same exact thing, at the same exact time, mimicking his deep voice while she did it.

He frowned at her, but there was no heat behind it. In truth, he was glad she could still make fun of him in the midst of this mess.

Still, he wanted to make sure she understood. "Not leaving your side, Chloe."

She reached out with her free hand, laced her fingers with his. "Thanks."

They walked, hand in hand, in silence for the rest of the way until her watch beeped, signaling they'd walked far enough to cut through the low-level brush and find the trail.

The world was all alight now, still pearly and dim, but they wouldn't be risking twisting an ankle or stepping on something that didn't want to be stepped on by heading off-road to cut toward the trail.

They'd taken only a step or two off the road when they both paused. Jack thought he'd heard something from behind them. Likely from the parking lot, where even now a couple of Bent County deputies were working; though that wasn't the direction the sound had *seemed* to come from.

But in their stillness, Jack heard it again. A noise. A human noise. From the opposite direction of the parking lot. It had to have been.

Because it was someone's voice. And whatever they'd said sounded a lot like *help*. The cops certainly wouldn't be yelling for help.

"Is that someone calling for help?" Chloe asked, her hand squeezing tight in his. Too hopeful, too desperate for it to be Ry.

So he held her still to keep her from immediately running toward it and hated having to be the voice of reason. "Sounds like it—but we need to be careful, Chloe. We don't know what we're dealing with. Calls for help are just as likely tricks to—"

"I know, Jack," she said, but she was already moving toward the noise. Though she didn't pull out of his grasp, just pulled him along with her. Back onto the road and farther up.

He could have stopped her, but he didn't have the heart. They'd approach carefully. Together. They'd protect each other.

Jack realized they were close to the edge of the preserve that backed up to the highway. It could have been a trick of noise carrying. It could have been...

But as they walked around a curve in the road, they both spotted someone. Jack put his free hand on the butt of his weapon as he scanned the area. One solitary figure. Stumbling.

Too tall to be Ry, but there didn't appear to be a weapon, a threat. Still, Jack didn't take his hand off his gun until...

Both he and Chloe seemed to recognize the man at the same time, because they said his name and moved forward at a jog in unison.

When they reached Hart, he stumbled a little when he lifted his head to look at them. It was clear he'd been hurt. Blood crusted over the side of his face. But he was alive, and that was better than Mark Brink.

It wasn't Ry, and that was a shame for Chloe, but maybe it was a lead. If all these disparate things connected.

"Hart, what the hell happened?" Jack asked, dropping his hand off his gun and offering an arm for the man to lean against him. The fact that Hart did gave way to just how hurt he was.

"It was a woman," he rasped. Jack couldn't make sense of the words right away.

"A woman?" Chloe repeated gently. She stood on the other side of him, ready to take any other needed weight.

"I was getting into my car at the sheriff's department, and I heard a woman scream for help," Hart said, clearly trying to find the strength to stand on his own two feet as he recounted what had happened. "I looked over and I saw her. So I jogged over. I think I did…? I don't know. It's a little fuzzy. The next thing I really remember is waking up. Which I did, because I fell." He gestured with one arm, hissed out a breath, clearly in pain. "Not sure where I was. I think I might have been dumped out of the back of a truck. Once I could, I got up and started walking, hoping to find someone."

That would make sense, as they were close to the highway out here. Jack surveyed the distance between where they were and the parking lot where the other Bent County deputies were. Too far.

"We'll call you an ambulance," Jack said.

"Call Laurel. She'll get it sorted and know I'm okay all in one fell swoop, and she can pass it around to my family."

Chloe nodded and pulled her phone out of her pocket, taking a few steps away—in search of service, no doubt.

"I don't know what the hell's going on, Sheriff," Hart said in a quiet tone Chloe wouldn't be able to hear. "But I do know whatever it is ties to the Brink family. There's just no way it doesn't."

CHLOE JOGGED AWAY in search of service. Jack and Hart followed at a slower pace, and when she finally had a bar, she lifted her phone to her ear and called Detective Delaney-Carson.

She tried to feel relief as they moved through the next steps. A sense of happiness that even though Hart was hurt, he hadn't ended up like her father.

But Ry was somewhere out there, and she wasn't sure

she'd feel anything good until she knew where. Until she knew he was okay.

With the phone call made, Chloe fell back into step with Jack and Hart. Chloe wondered if they should have him sit and rest, but if he'd suffered any kind of concussion, he probably needed to stay alert.

"What did this woman who called for help look like?" Jack asked Hart.

Hart licked cracked lips. He needed water. Probably some stitches for that gash on his head. They should really let him take it easy, but Chloe wanted answers, so she didn't stop Jack's questions.

"I don't really remember. It happened so fast. I heard it more than anything. 'Help.' Someone needed help." He said it as if trying to convince himself when it was clear that it had been a ploy. A ploy to get him away from the scrapbook, and that had to have been perpetrated by more than one person.

And none of those people could have been her dead father. He hadn't had the scrapbook on his corpse.

Ry also couldn't be involved in that. Because Hart had disappeared *before* Ry had taken off from the ranch. So he wasn't involved. She tried to comfort herself with that knowledge.

But she was too much of a cop not to accept that while he hadn't been part of the ploy to distract or hurt Hart, that still didn't mean he couldn't be involved in other things that connected.

Some comfort.

"I didn't have my full belt on me, but I did have my gun. They took it," Hart said with disgust. He stumbled a little, even with Jack holding him up, so they stopped their progress.

Chloe knew she shouldn't keep poking at him. He was hurt. But… "They also took the scrapbook. Out of your car. From the security footage, it seems like that's what they were after. Them letting you go seems to add credence to that theory."

Hart scowled. His gaze lifted briefly to Chloe, but then he looked back at Jack. He didn't say anything to that, so Chloe continued.

"You guys looked through the scrapbook when you had it. Right? You looked through it and couldn't find any evidence of note. But Delaney-Carson said she thought you should keep it, and you were the one who wanted to give it back."

"She wanted your take on it," Hart confirmed.

"So, what was in it?" Jack asked.

"It was black-and-white pictures. Old people. Ranches. Homesteader stuff with plat maps. Boring. Pointless." He glanced at Chloe again. And even though she could see suspicion in his gaze, she couldn't get mad at a man with a bloody face who couldn't even walk without help right now.

"I figured if it connected to what's going on, you'd lead us to whatever connection once you had it."

Then she realized what Hart's plan had *really* been. "You were going to follow me." It shouldn't make her angry. It was decent enough police work.

But it was barking up the wrong tree, so she couldn't quite ignore the feelings of frustration bubbling up inside her.

"I was going to investigate," Hart said coolly.

By following me. But she supposed she didn't need to argue with an injured man. It didn't change anything. He'd been hurt, the scrapbook had been taken and she didn't have the first clue as to *why*.

"Did you ever see the woman who called for help? Stranger? Maybe someone familiar?" Jack pressed.

Hart took some time to think about it. "I'm not really sure. I think… There had to have been two of them, right? If I went to help the woman, someone had to jump me from behind." He gestured at the bloody portion of his head.

True. And either one could have been the person in the hoodie who'd come back and taken the scrapbook. But there also could have been a third. Too many people involved now. What kind of sense did that make?

The ambulance finally came and so did Detective Delaney-Carson, relief etched in every line of her face. She explained that she'd called his family, asked him a few questions and then instructed the ambulance to take him away.

Laurel watched the ambulance go, then turned to face them both. Her expression was grim, her words all warning.

"We're dealing with two attackers—that we know of, there could have been more. These could be our murderers, or there could be more. I'm going to go to the hospital in a bit so I can ask him some more questions once he's been fully checked out. I know you guys want answers just as much as I do, but I wouldn't recommend heading out into this isolated place just the two of you. That's begging for trouble."

When neither Jack nor Chloe said anything, she sighed. Then she opened the bag she was carrying. She pulled out a couple of granola bars and two water bottles.

"This won't do much, and I'd recommend a full meal and some sleep, but you're not going to listen, so…" she said as they took the offered sustenance. "I have to focus on my investigation, my guys. Understand the risks before you go wading into it."

Chloe nodded and glanced at Jack, who was doing the same.

"I'll leave you to it then. Watch your backs. I'll try to

contact you when we get some answers, but if you go out there, it'll be hard to reach you."

Again, silence seemed to be the best response, so Chloe kept her mouth shut and so did Jack.

Laurel shook her head. "It's a bad idea, guys."

But she turned and left them to it without any further warnings.

Chloe wasn't sure what their next move was going to be, but she'd search every inch of this forest preserve to find Ry. And she couldn't possibly go home and rest or eat before she did.

"She's right," Jack said once Laurel was gone.

Chloe turned to face him, her stomach sinking. Because she couldn't go back to the ranch and just wait. She *couldn't*. She knew he wouldn't leave her to handle this alone, but she couldn't possibly let him bulldoze her into going back to the ranch. "Jack—"

"Just the two of us *is* begging for trouble," he said firmly. Then his gaze moved from the horizon to meet hers. "So let's call in reinforcements."

Chapter Seventeen

A little over an hour later, they had a group of Hudsons and Daniels huddled together in the morning sun at the center of the forest preserve. Zeke, Carlyle, Grant, Hawk, Anna and Palmer had all come out. Louisa would join them later, after she was done working at her parents' orchard, if it took that long.

Because this was what family did. Jack had spent a lot of years considering himself the solitary, lone leader. The person who had to keep it all together without leaning too hard on anyone else for help. He'd spent a lot of time and energy trying to protect his siblings from pain, danger, risk.

Of course, he'd always had help, particularly from Mary and Grant in those early years, but he'd also made sure most of the responsibility lay on his shoulders. Or tried to.

If there was anything the past few years had taught him, it was that he didn't need to do that anymore. It had been hard to let go of all the responsibility he felt had defined him, but he thought he was finally really getting there. His siblings' lives the past few years certainly hadn't given him much choice.

Still, he hated asking for help. But for Chloe? He'd ask anyone. Because she was part of it too. She'd given him some hope for a future, even if he worried how well he'd be able to give her what she deserved.

But for right now, they had to find her brother.

He explained the entire situation to everyone who'd come, and Carlyle and Anna flanked Chloe like two sentries ready and willing to fight for her.

Because she wasn't alone, and she wasn't going to be. None of them would let her be. He hoped she was beginning to understand she didn't have to take it all on her shoulders herself too.

Grant had had the presence of mind to bring a paper map they could spread out and all look at to determine how they'd approach the search.

"Chloe and I will take the campground," Jack said, pointing to it on the map. He met Chloe's gaze because she'd opened her mouth to argue, but one sharp look from him and she closed it. He wasn't going to repeat himself about being by her side. It was a done deal.

"We'll approach from the south end. Zeke and Carlyle, I'd like you guys to come at it from the north." Because Zeke and Carlyle hadn't come into the Hudson orbit until long after their parents were gone, so they shouldn't have any emotional connection to the campsite. He'd send his siblings off into other corners and hope that it wasn't a mistake.

"Can I beat him up if I find him first?" Carlyle asked darkly, holding a grudge against Ry for sneaking away on her watch.

"With my permission," Chloe returned vehemently.

Jack could see she was trying to hold on to a kind of tough outer demeanor, and maybe it would have been better for Chloe if he'd paired her up with Carlyle. Maybe it was selfish to want to keep her in his sight, by his side.

Well, so be it.

As for his siblings, he paired them up and gave them their assignments. Anna argued with him about a few minor details, because of course she did, but when Chloe took his side, Anna backed off.

"Most of us won't have cell service as we move deeper into the preserve, but everybody has a flare, right?" Everyone nodded. Palmer had brought packs that would keep them going for a while, provided everyone with water and a weapon as well as a flare. They could feasibly spend the rest of daylight hours out here searching.

Jack hoped it wouldn't come to that.

"No matter what, everyone meets back here at four. No exceptions."

Everyone murmured their assent, then began to pair off into vehicles that would lead them to their different corners. They'd go to their assigned areas, canvass on foot for a few hours, then meet back here in the middle of the preserve.

Hopefully, with a safe-and-sound Ry Brink in tow.

Jack climbed into the driver's seat of his truck, waited for Chloe to get into the passenger side. They said nothing. Jack just drove through the twists and turns of paved roads, then gravel ones, until they approached the campground.

Tension seeped into him. If those skeletal remains on the Brink Ranch were his parents, there was nothing about this place that should make him tense, that should make dread and grief settle deep in his gut. Because if they'd been buried elsewhere, there was likely no remnants of what had happened to them *here*.

And yet no matter what he *thought*, what he knew, the feelings were twisting around inside him as they got out of the truck at the entrance to the campground. He shouldered the pack Palmer had brought for him and tried to shake away his unease as he scanned the area.

On this side of the preserve, spruce trees towered and reached for a bright blue sky. It dappled the campground in dark shadows in direct contrast to the sunny day. At the front of the truck, Chloe reached out and took his hand.

None of his inner scolding had settled the anxiety he felt, but her hand in his did. It didn't take it all away, but it soothed some of those jagged feelings. They were in this together, whatever the answers might be.

They moved forward in unison, not quite sure what they were looking for. Signs of life. Signs of Ry. *Signs*.

The campground had some tents and some campers. Definitely not as deserted as other areas of the park. So he and Chloe walked down the little campground road, eyeing each campsite for anything that might stand out.

There was an older couple huddled around a campfire, putting together some kind of lunch. Jack didn't realize he'd stopped walking until Chloe gently tugged at his hand. He looked away from the couple and toward the road. He couldn't bear to look at Chloe and see sympathy on her face.

It didn't do him any good to think that his parents might be doing just that if they'd lived. They hadn't, and he had to focus on the living. But Chloe let go of his hand, tucked her arm around his waist so they were walking hip to hip.

He managed a slow, big breath that loosened the tightness in his chest. Focus on the living, on the future. On the task at hand. Which all centered on her.

They reached the end of the campsite road. Carlyle and Zeke would be catching up to them soon unless something had happened. Both Jack and Chloe looked around. Then Chloe pointed at a little outhouse. "There's a trail there. Are there more campsites that way?"

"Usually not when the campgrounds have empty sites closer to the facilities, but let's go check."

They moved past the outhouse, onto a trail that led to overflow campsites. Jack didn't see any tents set up along the trail, but as he and Chloe began to move, he heard someone. Just the whisper of a word, like a curse under someone's breath. And then the heavy, pounding footsteps of someone running.

Away.

Jack swore himself, turning to see someone's quickly retreating form.

Not just *someone*. Ry.

So Jack took off after him.

CHLOE WANTED TO cry with relief, and at the very same time, she wanted to beat her brother up. Tears threatened, but luckily, running as hard as she could through the forest helped keep them from leaking out.

If Ry was running, it was bad in that he was probably mixed up in a hell of a lot of trouble. Because he had to have seen it was them, so he wasn't in the kind of trouble he wanted help with.

But he was *running*. So he was alive and whole, and no matter how angry she was at him, relief lightened all her harsher emotions.

She was going to *figuratively* kill the little bastard. Right after she hugged him so tight, she was sure he was okay.

Jack had longer legs and could move faster for short-term distances, but Chloe had a better stride for longer distances and, because of her smaller size, was able to dodge trees with more agility, so after a bit of running, she bypassed Jack and was quickly gaining on her brother.

"Rylan Jonas Brink, stop running right now!"

He didn't listen, though he looked back over his shoulder. Tactical mistake, because after a couple more steps, he tripped and then went sprawling. Giving Chloe just enough time to catch up to him and pounce.

He struggled under her tackle, trying to buck her off. "I didn't do anything!"

She got her knee in his back, managed to wrench one arm behind him even as her breath sawed in and out. "Then why are you running?" She resisted punching him though she itched to, even as she was desperate to hug him and hold him tight. Alive, *alive*.

And in so much damn trouble.

"Let me," Jack said beside her. She realized he was holding handcuffs, and she sighed. She adjusted her hold so Jack could do the honors.

Though she wouldn't have minded cuffing her brother herself in this moment.

Jack secured Ry's hands behind his back and dragged him back a few feet so that he was in a sitting position and could lean against a tree trunk.

Ry's gaze moved back and forth, from Jack to Chloe, then beyond them as if he was looking for someone to come rescue him. Or maybe take him away.

"What are you guys doing here?" Ry demanded, falling back on being surly and accusatory. Because why wouldn't he, cuffed and outnumbered?

She really hoped whatever he'd gotten himself mixed up with, whatever punishments ended up being doled out, would get through his thick skull and make him realize he could be so much more than he allowed himself to be.

"What are *we* doing here?" Chloe said, barely resisting a sneer. "You snuck away from the Hudsons. You *stole* my car. What the hell do you think we're doing here?"

"I'm just borrowing it! Why do you always have to over-react?"

Chloe had often wondered if her brother would give her an aneurysm, but this really took the cake. She took a deep breath, trying to resist the urge to scream at him.

"Why did you take my car to that parking lot, leave your phone in it and end up all the way over here?" Jack asked, his voice low and calm. Clearly trying to de-escalate the situation.

Chloe didn't know if that was possible. "And how?" she added darkly.

"I don't—"

"Don't lie to me." She pointed her finger at him, narrowly resisted poking him. Hard. "Do you know what kind of trouble you're in right now? Tell the damn truth, Ry."

Ry rolled his eyes, and she would have reached out and punched him, probably, but Jack put a hand on her arm. She swallowed down the suddenly swirling anger. Or tried to.

She didn't know how to get through Ry's thick head, and he was making it impossible to feel any kind of sorry for him.

"You'll just get ticked off, but there's nothing to get mad about," Ry said, in his usual defiant, oh-so-victimized way. "Dad wanted to meet up. He's on parole, so it'd have to be quick so he could get back to Texas. I knew it'd get back to you if I did it anywhere where people could see, so we agreed to meet here. I drove over and I waited for him, and he didn't show. I knew you'd start looking for me, so I figured I'd just walk around for a bit."

It was a lie—or at least, partly a lie. She doubted very much Ry had walked all the way from the parking lot to this campground. Maybe it was *possible* in the hours that had passed, but he didn't look like he'd done any major walking or hiking.

Granted, it didn't look like he'd killed anyone, either, but she didn't know what to think about his ability to do that anymore. So she told him. Flat out.

She knelt next to him, looked him straight in the eye.

Not because she wanted to soften the blow, whatever blow it would be, but because she wanted to watch every last inch of his reaction. "Dad's dead, Ry."

She watched as Ry's expression drooped and his entire face blanched. There was no shifty discomfort, no guilt, just straight-up shock. "Dead? He shouldn't be…" Ry swallowed. "You saw him? Dead? You're sure he's dead?"

"Yes."

"But…" Ry shook his head. He looked up at Jack, then back at Chloe right in front of him. Some little war played out over his expression, but she had seen Ry guilty enough times to know none of it was guilt. She'd seen him lie enough times to know what he was working through wasn't a lie.

"Chloe, you have to get out of here." He said it seriously, urgently, leaning forward. "I've got it handled, okay? But you've got to go. She'll…"

She? It made Chloe think of what Hart had said: a woman had called for help. A woman was involved. Did this connect to Hart more than their father? But Ry didn't say anything, just trailed off.

So she leaned forward too, got in his face. "Who, Ry?"

He shook his head vehemently, his eyes wide and worried. "I can't tell you, Chlo. Please. *Please.* Save yourself. Just let me go. There's no way it works out if you don't get out of here. Fast." He was so earnest, and yes, Ry was a good liar when he wanted to be, but she saw something like genuine fear in his gaze.

Like he actually was trying to protect her. She leaned back a little, his fear sparking her own. Ry trying to be noble felt more worrisome than anything else that had happened today.

She reached out, gripped his shoulder tightly. Hoping some kind of connection would get through all…whatever this was. There was always this wall between them, and she needed to scale it. His attitude, his refusals. Hurdles he refused to acknowledge. But she had to get through to him somehow. "You need to be straight with me. For once. Damn it, Ry. For once, tell me what the hell is going on."

He leaned forward, so close that their noses were almost touching while she held on to his shoulder. When he spoke, he enunciated each word clearly, his eyes a maze of fear and determination she'd never seen in him before.

"I can't tell you, Chloe."

"Good boy," a female voice said, and Chloe dropped Ry's shoulder, whirling as best she could on her knees. Jack had also turned and had his gun out and pointed at the voice— but there was more than one woman standing around them. And they all had their own guns, trained at each of them.

Chloe stared at the trio in utter disbelief. It had been so long since she'd seen the woman with a gun pointed at Jack, she only recognized her because she saw so much of her own face in the woman.

Her mother.

The one with a gun trained on Chloe herself was also familiar. She'd had an off-again, on-again relationship with her father when Chloe was a teen. Sarah, if Chloe remembered correctly. It had been a volatile enough relationship that Chloe had once had to mop up the woman's bloody nose. She'd been fifteen at the time, maybe? The third woman, with a gun pointed square at Ry, looked vaguely familiar, but Chloe couldn't place her. Maybe another one of her father's girlfriend's? She was on the young side, so maybe one of Ry's?

Either way, Chloe didn't know what on earth to make of any of it. She looked at Jack. He had his sheriff's face on and was unreadable, gun held calmly and relaxed, pointed at Chloe's mother. But it was three guns to one.

"I'd put the gun down, Deputy," Jen Rogers said, smirking at Jack. "Or it's going to get real bloody, real quick."

"It's *Sheriff* these days, Jen." Because of course Jack had had dealings with her mother when he'd been a deputy for the county years ago. Why wouldn't he have?

"Well, *Sheriff*, put the gun down, or I start shooting."

Chapter Eighteen

Jack didn't immediately drop the weapon. If any of the women really wanted to shoot, they could have done it before drawing anyone's attention. They could have killed them all, then and there, because he and Chloe had been so intent on Ry.

A mistake. His own. But he couldn't worry about how he'd failed just yet. He had to get them out of this first.

"Sarah?" Jen—Chloe's mother—said, her gaze never leaving Jack's. "If he doesn't put the gun on the ground by the time I count to three, shoot her," she said, clearly referring to Chloe. "To kill."

Jack knew it wasn't a bluff. Part experience, part the look in Jen's eyes. He held his hands up in mock surrender, or maybe *temporary surrender* was a better term. Slowly, he crouched and gently laid the gun in front of him.

Just as slowly, he straightened.

"Courtney? Collect his gun."

The third gunman—someone Jack felt like he vaguely recognized, probably from run-ins with the law—scurried over and picked up his gun. Jack could have stopped her, but he was afraid it would prompt Jen or Sarah to start shooting.

Maybe they didn't want to take them all out, but he wouldn't put it past Jen.

Jen's attention turned from Jack to Chloe. "Didn't I always tell you to listen to your brother?"

"Yes, because you shared all his worst impulses," Chloe returned, her voice cool, calm and collected even as fury shone in her eyes.

But Jack was relieved she looked more mad than emotionally hurt, more determined than scared. They could get out of this if they kept their wits about them.

Or so he'd keep telling himself.

"Mom, make them let me go," Ry groused from where he sat on the ground, still handcuffed. "This hurts."

Jen looked at Ry sitting on the ground, eyes narrowed. "Do you think I'm *brainless*?"

Ry didn't meet his mother's gaze. He looked down at the ground. "No, ma'am."

"Get up, then. Your feet aren't cuffed, and your legs aren't broken. And stop whining."

Ry struggled to get up on his own. Jack didn't feel the need to help him, though Chloe was clearly fighting the impulse.

Jack considered the interaction between Ry and his mother. What Ry had said before Jen had shown up made him rethink…everything. Ry had clearly been working with these women, not with Mark Brink. But what did that mean for the murder? For the scrapbook that connected to the *Brink* family, not Jen Rogers? Why would she have hurt Hart, taken the scrapbook? Was it really all disparate parts that didn't connect? Or was there something bigger he couldn't fathom?

Jack wasn't sure which would be worse.

"Why'd you try to kidnap a cop, Mom?" Chloe asked, sounding bored.

"I didn't *try*. I succeeded," Jen snapped.

Jack wasn't sure it was smart to rile Jen up, considering she was clearly a violent criminal, but Chloe probably had a good sense of her own mother no matter how little they'd communicated recently. So he followed Chloe's lead.

"Why didn't you kill him, then?" he asked, keeping his voice and demeanor conversational. "Because we found him, and he'll survive. Probably ID you pretty quick, and then what?"

Jen barked out a laugh. "They'd have to *find* me. What do I care if they ID me? I could have killed him. Don't for a second think I couldn't have—or that I won't kill you." She waved the firearm in the air like she was swatting at an irritating gnat. "We didn't need a missing cop. That always makes your kind crawl out of your holes. Can't have one of your own disappearing, can you? Honestly, we would have left him bleeding in the parking lot, but we needed a little bit more time to create confusion."

She sighed heavily, surveying Jack and Chloe. "Cops. Always causing problems." She shook her head, then looked at the two women she was with. "We'll have to do this one special, girls."

The two women with her nodded like they knew what that meant. Jack did not think *special* was going to be good.

"What about him?" Courtney asked, gesturing her gun at Ry.

"Good question. Not sure yet. Let's get everyone home and go from there. Courtney, you take the lead. You three will follow. Sarah and I will handle the rear."

"Where are we going?" Chloe asked.

"On a fun little hike, sweetie. You just used to *love* those, didn't you? Anything to escape me, right?" Jen demanded, bitterness and something akin to hysteria tinging her tone.

Courtney started off down where Ry had initially run.

There was no clear trail, but it was easy enough to follow the woman. Chloe walked stiffly at Jack's side, and Ry stumbled behind them. Unnecessarily, in Jack's estimation.

But Ry was in handcuffs. Chloe and he were free. They didn't have their weapons anymore, but they had training. Jack still had his pack on. Play their cards right, they could take down all three women without anyone getting too hurt, set off a flare, and end this here and now.

But the guns made it riskier than he liked. He'd have to bide his time.

Jack considered it his good fortune that he'd been over every last yard of the forest preserve, especially this area around the campground. Wherever the women took them, he'd have a general idea of where they were and where they'd need to go to get out.

He thought about the flare in his pack. The women hadn't searched it yet—clearly not quite the thorough criminals they fancied themselves. Not that he could currently use the flare, so maybe he shouldn't pat himself on the back just yet.

"Have they found him yet?" Jen asked. When the question was met with silence, she reached forward and tugged Chloe's ponytail. Hard.

Before he thought the move through, Jack reached forward and grabbed Jen's wrist to stop her from hurting Chloe. Which earned him a gun shoved into his chest.

He dropped Jen's wrist immediately, then held up his arms slowly. "Let's everyone keep their hands to themselves."

"Yeah, *let's.*" She studied him through narrowed eyes, then Chloe.

"Have they found who?" Chloe asked, her voice devoid of any emotion. But when Jack slid a glance at her, her hands were curled into fists. Fury flickered in the depths of her dark eyes. And she was purposefully drawing her mother's attention away from *him*.

And it worked. "Your father, of course." Then Jen's mouth spread into a wide smile.

Jack was stunned silent. He hadn't known what to expect, but this was...

"You killed Dad?" Chloe said, sounding as shocked as he felt.

Jen laughed. "Of *course* I killed him. That's what this is about. That's what it's *always* been about."

There was something about the way she said *always* that settled in Jack all wrong. *Always.* Here in this campground. Where his parents had last been seen.

Always. Like *all* the way back. Like skeletal remains on a ranch Jen might not have owned but would have had access to at the time. Would have known where to bury bodies without them being found. "You killed my parents."

Jen flashed a grin at him. Mean and with a frantic kind of glee in her eyes. "You're finally catching on, *Sheriff.* Good for you."

CHLOE THOUGHT SHE was going to be sick. Of all the things she was prepared for, all the worst-case scenarios she'd considered, her mother's involvement in any of this had never once crossed her mind.

And it should have. Dad and Ry had always had a contentious relationship. Abusive, yes. Ry had been somewhat submissive to Dad on occasion. But they'd *fought*.

It was their mother who had true control over Ry. Always had. Chloe had just been under the impression Mom had taken off and was as no-contact with Ry as she was with Chloe.

Chloe tried to wrap her mind around it all. Years of...her mother being a cold-blooded killer from way back? Even if she couldn't put murder past her volatile mother, her killing Jack's parents just didn't make any sense that she could come up with.

So she asked the simplest, most concise question she couldn't swallow down. *"Why?"*

"You should learn a lesson, Chloe, from his bitch of a mother." She jerked her chin at Jack. "Sticking your nose where it doesn't belong is always going to come back to bite you in the ass."

She heard Jack's intake of breath, but she couldn't look at him just yet. She would crumble if she did. And if she reached out for him, comforted him in any way, her mother would see. And pounce on it like it was a weakness.

Chloe wouldn't be a weakness. She wouldn't risk Jack. Not now. They had to save each other. And she couldn't think about what this revelation meant to him if she was going to accomplish that.

"Move along now. Not much farther." Jen gestured with her gun, so Chloe felt she had no choice but to swallow and follow Courtney once more. Courtney led them through thick trees, over a tiny trickle of a creek and to the craggy rock face of a mountain.

Jen and Sarah came around to the front of them, stopping at a small crevice in the rock. Jen pointed at it. "In you go."

"Mom, you can't make me go in there with them!" Ry said, sounding like a petulant teenager. When he was a *grown* man. Would he ever get over himself? After this, if they survived, Chloe was finally going to have to accept the answer was no.

Jen stepped forward, up to Ry. Chloe recognized the expression on her face. It *looked* sympathetic, but that was how you knew something awful was coming.

Before Chloe could step in front of Ry—because old impulses die hard—their mother whipped her gun back and slammed it across Ry's face so he fell backward and onto his butt. Chloe tried to catch him, but she hadn't been fast enough.

"Get in the cave. Now," Jen said.

Chloe grabbed Ry by the elbow, and Jack grabbed his other. Pulling him toward the crevice, still cuffed. All while Ry moaned and sniveled.

Chloe hesitated at the opening of the crevice. All dark. All black. A small, little opening. Chloe wasn't even sure Jack would be able to fit through if he tried. She tried to swallow an old panic fluttering around in her stomach. She didn't like heights and she didn't like enclosed spaces.

She had learned to keep her fear of heights hidden from her parents, but only because her fear of enclosed spaces had been something she hadn't known she should hide until her parents had used it against her when she was a little girl. Mom especially. She'd loved to lock her in the little closet in their apartment in town.

Chloe had to focus very hard on not remembering, on not going back to those old feelings of being a helpless little girl. She was an adult. She was a cop. She could handle this. She could survive it—just like she had then.

"Go on, Chloe. Get in there," Mom said in a little singsongy voice, clearly reading her panic and enjoying it.

Chloe took a deep, steadying breath. She wouldn't give her mother the satisfaction of panic. Not when she had to somehow protect Ry and Jack from whatever this turned out to be.

Because if she'd confessed to essentially three murders, Jen had no plans to let them go. Maybe she wasn't ready to kill them yet for some unknown reason, but that had to be the plan.

"I'll go first," Jack murmured as they approached the rock. "Push Ry in after me, and I'll pull. Then you." He looked at her, right in the eye. "Got it?"

He was trying to be her anchor, and she appreciated it. Because she needed one, and if anyone could be one, it was him. Jack Hudson.

Who is in this mess because of you. Whose parents are gone because of yours.

And who loved her anyway, she reminded herself. Because he did. She saw it in his eyes, in his move to protect her *and* Ry. So she would be strong for him as much as for herself.

Jack flattened himself against one side of the rock and shuffled in through the crevice, just barely making it. Chloe couldn't see him, but she pictured his dark, steady gaze and helped Ry maneuver himself inside as well.

She glanced back at the trio of women with guns. She knew she shouldn't do it, shouldn't give her mother a chance to see her fear. But it was her mother she studied now.

"What are you doing, Mom?"

Mom's mouth curved into a vicious smile. "Ruining as many lives as I can. Just like how your father and high-and-mighty Laura Hudson tried to ruin mine."

It made no sense. It had never made any sense. Her mother's unending well of anger, of blame, of needing to hurt anyone and everyone she could reach.

"Get inside, Chloe. Or I start shooting."

Chloe nodded and then pushed herself through the crevice. Inside, it was so dark. Damp and cold and dark and—
A hand clasped around her forearm and gently pulled her inside.

Jack.

She wanted to lean into him, but she was afraid to allow

herself the weakness. Afraid of what her mother might see and use against her.

So she held herself upright and tried to allow her eyes to adjust to the dark. But not long after they'd all gotten inside, a light clicked on. A lantern, some battery-powered thing hanging from a hook dug into the rock face. The cave was much bigger than the crevice had let on and was full of things. Makeshift beds, a table, a whole little outdoor-kitchen setup. Like people lived here.

Mom had said *home*. Was this… Was *this* where she'd been living all these years? It didn't make any sense, except that it explained why no one had been able to find her. A cave in a remote forest preserve.

But…why?

Chloe watched as Sarah settled herself in a chair at the entrance of the cave, gun pointed in their direction. Had the three of them been together all this time? She understood them conspiring to kill her father. And they'd clearly spent years planning it, as Mark had been in prison for six years now.

But Jack's parents… So many years ago. It just made no sense.

"Make yourselves comfortable," Sarah said with a mean smile.

Mom entered, standing next to Sarah, scowling. "For the love of God, shut him up," she said, referring to Ry.

Chloe looked down at her brother. His mouth was bleeding, and he was making little whimpering noises. Chloe felt a mix of worry and sympathy and bone-deep anger that he'd been part of this at all. "Come on, Ry, buck up," she told him. Just like she had when they were kids and she had to be the strong one. The one to protect them both.

He glared up at her, anger in his gaze. Anger when he

was half the reason they were here. For so many years, she'd given him a pass. Because their childhood had been rough. She'd blamed herself for not being strong enough, smart enough, *good* enough to save him from all the trouble *he* caused.

But she'd had no one, and she'd turned out okay. Better than okay. She'd cobbled together a damn good life for herself, and Ry had complained and blamed and worn his victimhood like a second skin.

Chloe just wished she'd realized all this sooner.

"I thought you didn't want the hassle of cops trying to find other cops," Jack said, sounding so calm and in control. He couldn't be, though. Not knowing the woman standing in front of him had killed his parents. He was holding on to their training. He was dealing with the crisis at hand.

Chloe felt like everything she'd ever learned about being a cop, about de-escalating a situation, about self-preservation, had deserted her. Her entire world twisted inside out.

Except Jack.

Jen smirked at him. "Sure, it's a hassle when you don't have time to do it right. When there's too many witnesses. Now I have all the time in the world to make sure you all end up just like your parents, Sheriff. Because that's what happens to people who butt their noses in where they don't belong. They *disappear* without a trace."

Chapter Nineteen

Without a trace. Those words landed like blows because it was true. His parents had disappeared without a trace. Jen had committed a crime that she'd escaped for seventeen years, and Jack still wasn't sure what had prompted Ry to find those remains—accident, on purpose, it didn't matter.

Jen Rogers knew how to get away with murder, and he had to put that knowledge away. Set it aside so they could figure out how not to be her next victims.

Jack wondered if Jen knew they had a group of people already on-site. People who, come four o'clock, would start looking for them. And knew exactly where they'd been. Had she been watching them all this time, or had she stumbled upon them in the campground simply because of Ry?

He considered bringing it up to see if it would prompt Jen to panic, to make a mistake. That's all he needed. One little mistake.

"Now, I want both your cell phones," Jen said, holding out her free hand.

"What are you going to do with those? We don't have service in a cave. Can't ping us in here."

"It's called *distraction*, Sheriff. Now, hand them over."

Jack reached into his pocket. He considered "accidentally" dropping the phone. Destroying it rather than have it be used against him. But Chloe was taking hers out. She looked back at him and held her hand out like she'd take his too. So he tried to give it to her.

But she didn't take it. She put hers in *his* hand and gave him a look. A meaningful look.

Then he realized what she was trying to tell him. She had that damn smartwatch on her wrist. No one would be able to track them in this *cave*, but it was something. A potential lifeline. Without reacting, he took the two phones and walked them over to Jen. He handed them out to her.

She took them. Then she smiled at him. "You look like your dad."

Even knowing it was meant to hurt, meant to elicit a reaction, he couldn't stop it from landing. He *did* look like a carbon copy of Dean Hudson. He was reminded every time he looked in the mirror of the father he lost all too soon.

"Your mother could have survived, you know."

Jack held Jen's mean gaze. Inside, he was a riot of pain, but he kept his expression bland. And he said nothing.

"It could have just been your worthless father. Trying to tell me how to parent my children. Trying to get me into trouble with all those nosy family-service agents." Jen's self-satisfied smirk faded into an angry scowl, like she was reliving it. "I would have settled for just taking him out. She could have escaped. But she had to try and save your father."

"It's what people with souls do, Jen," Jack returned, ignoring how rough his voice sounded. "Help each other. Save each other. Love each other."

"No one's ever done that for me!" she shouted, stomping her foot like a child. And Jack could see where Ry had gotten some of his self-victimization. It stemmed from right here. He could almost feel bad for the guy. Almost.

Jen kept on shrieking. "No one did anything for me, ever!"

Jack shrugged. "Sounds like you deserved it."

Even in the orangish glow of the lantern light, he could see her face mottled red with rage. Her hands had curled into fists. Sarah murmured something softly to her, and Jen inhaled sharply, then let it out slowly. Calming herself, minute by minute, until she aimed one of her nasty smiles at him again.

"I want you to know, they died begging for mercy."

He should let it go—God knew, he should let it go. But when it came to his parents, their memory, he couldn't let her have the last word. "Sounds like they died fighting for it."

She let out a cry of rage then, guttural and furious. She wrenched back her arm. Jack went with instinct and blocked the blow by grabbing her arm before she could slam the gun across his face like she'd done to Ry.

It was a mistake—he knew that the minute his hand had come into contact with her arm. But it was just instinct, self-preservation.

It was pure stubbornness and anger that kept his grip on her arm. Until she lifted her left hand, and there was a gun in that one too. Pointed right at his head. *Then* he thought better of his fury and hurt.

"No!" It was, shockingly, Sarah's voice. She leaped off the chair, grabbed Jen's left arm. Jack still hadn't let go of her right. So she was now being held—on one side by her partner and on one side by her victim.

"You can't shoot him," Sarah said, seeming afraid. Desperate. "It's not the plan. You said it yourself. We can't deviate from the plan. We've already messed up once. We can't mess up again. It all goes to hell. You *know* that."

Jack was so surprised by the unexpected save that when Jen ripped her arm out of his grasp, he didn't even try to hold on. He stepped back, giving the women the space for their argument, and hopefully the distraction was enough so that Jen's anger was pointed to the woman she worked with.

Maybe that was a weakness that would allow them to escape.

"They're *my* plans," Jen said, her entire body turning toward Sarah. Her back to Jack and Chloe and Ry behind them. Like none of them even mattered. Like they couldn't be a threat.

Could he tackle her now, Jack considered? Would Chloe be able to get to Sarah's gun in time to take her out before retaliation? But that still left Courtney, who was presumably outside the cave.

But what if she wasn't? Was it worth the risk? Jack kept himself ready, watching, waiting for just the right moment— and he knew Chloe beside him was doing the same exact thing. Poised and ready to lunge.

He wanted it to be now, but it wasn't. But they would know when it was. They'd be ready. He believed that.

He had to.

"Any mistakes today have been *your* fault. I think you know that," Jen was yelling at Sarah.

Sarah's eyes widened, a mix of fear and offense. Panic, maybe. But she stood up to Jen. "I do *not* know that! It was your plan that was faulty. We did everything you said! Courtney got Ry to lure Mark here. *I* took the first shot and didn't kill him. *Just* like you said. I—"

"You hesitated! You know you hesitated! If you'd taken that shot when you were supposed to, I could trust you. But now? I can't. So I think we need to retool our plan."

Sarah was shaking her head. "We have to stick to the plan, or we'll get caught! I'm not getting caught!" She pointed her finger in Jen's face, panic mounting. "I'll tell the cops *everything*. I'll tell them it was your idea, your plan. Lure Mark here. Get Chloe away from the scrapbook. I'll tell them—"

The sound of a bullet exploding out of a gun erupted around them. Instinct had Jack jumping back toward Chloe, who'd hit the deck with her hands over her ears.

When he looked up, he saw Jen holding a gun in each hand while Sarah lay on the ground, still and lifeless. A pool of blood slowly growing bigger around her.

"You won't be able to tell them anything now, will you?" Jen said to Sarah's lifeless form. She blew out a breath, shrugged her shoulders a few times like she was shrugging away tension. "Man, I feel better." She turned to face them, evil smile back in place. "Now. It's time for a new plan."

THE GUNSHOT WAS still echoing in Chloe's ears. She didn't let herself look at the dead woman on the ground. She looked up from the defensive position she'd fallen into and focused on the woman who might kill them all.

Chloe couldn't remember ever loving her mother. Even when she was a little girl, too young to understand her childhood was a dangerous disaster, she'd wondered why her mother had bothered to have one child, let alone two.

And still, this was all such a shock. Bits and pieces she could make sense of, but the whole of what was happening, what had happened, was just too bizarre to fully fathom.

Clearly Mom's plan had been to kill Mark and get away with it. She was teaming up with Mark's other victims to do it. She'd killed Jack's parents because they'd called family services on her.

But what did it have to do with the scrapbook?

There were no answers to that yet. No answers could come if they didn't survive.

So she focused on the one most important thing to her.

She would find a way to get Jack out of this. She certainly wasn't about to let her mother make another Hudson a victim of her sociopathic ways. No matter what. Chloe would do anything and everything to get him out.

"Now you have more bodies to clean up," Chloe pointed out. Her voice was steady, her tone cool. She kept her expression blank when her mother turned to sneer at her.

"It's not about the bodies. That's easy." She gestured at the cave. Like...there were bodies back there, deeper in the cavern. A shudder chased down Chloe's spine, though she ignored it.

"And some bodies, like your father's, don't matter. No one will care that Mark Brink was murdered in cold blood. They'll do some cursory due diligence, then mark it down to his past." Her lips curled back even farther. "*Hudsons* and *cops* are different, though. We've got to make sure there's no trace. It's not about *bodies*, it's about trails."

"Forensic investigations have come a long way in seventeen years. You'd be surprised how easy it is to pin you to Mark Brink's murder," Jack said blandly.

Every time she poked at her mother, he did too. He took her lead and ran with it. It gave her hope that somehow they could outsmart her mother. They were good cops, a good team. They could do it. They just needed a chance.

Jen took a threatening step toward Jack, those guns in her hands making Chloe have to fight the need to step between Jack and her mother. To protect him.

It would be a death sentence for him. Chloe knew that.

"Even if they could pin it on me, even if they bothered, they couldn't find me. Do you know how long I've been here? Right here. Living, loving and laughing my ass off while no one could find *anything* about your do-gooder parents."

The whole time. Ever since Mom had just not come home one day and Chloe had spent the next few years struggling to keep Ry on the straight and narrow, trying to keep Dad from ruining their lives. Mom hadn't been running away, chasing a score or a guy or whatever.

She'd been living in a *cave*? "But why hide if no one knew you'd murdered the Hudsons?"

"Your *father* was meant to stumble over those remains and get himself into a heap of trouble. Your *father* was supposed to take the fall. But he never did listen, did he? He never followed through or did what he should. So I had to adjust my plans. You see, Chloe, one thing you never could understand was the beauty of *patience*. Always had to be going, moving, doing. Sometimes sitting and waiting is the best thing in the world. Because no one will ever know. And Mark Brink is dead. Finally."

Chloe didn't see how sitting and waiting had been best for her mother. Jen had always been mean, cruel, narcissistic and rotten to the core. But she had never been quite this unhinged, or so it had seemed to Chloe at the time. Chloe supposed she should be grateful because *unhinged* left room for error. One little mistake and Chloe or Jack would take advantage of it and get out of this.

Chloe was sure of it.

Courtney stepped through the cave entrance. She nearly stumbled when she saw the body on the floor, but aside from a wide-eyed expression, she didn't voice any surprise. She blinked once, then turned toward Jen.

"A couple saw them running after Ry and called the police." Her voice betrayed her a little. It shook.

"Damn interfering busybodies," Jen said grimly. "They'll be crawling all over now."

"I don't think we should do it here," Courtney said, eyeing Chloe, Jack and Ry before turning her attention back to Jen. "We need to move."

Chloe didn't know what *do it here* meant for sure, but she had a bad feeling it meant *kill them*.

Jen shook her head. "Moving is too dangerous with cops crawling around. We need a distraction. Time and a distraction." She turned to face them. "Ry, get over here."

Chloe looked over her shoulder and watched as her brother struggled to his feet, keeping his eyes downcast and refusing to meet her gaze as he shuffled over to their mother.

"You're going to go out to that campground. You're going to let a cop find you—don't you go searching them out, just let them find you. You're going to hedge, lie a little bit, take your time, but eventually you'll confess you saw your sister and the sheriff, and you told them where the scrapbook is."

"They'll arrest me if they think I had anything to do with the scrapbook!"

Jen laughed. Low and mean. "Yeah, so what? A lot worse happens if you don't." She jerked her gaze to Jack. "Uncuff him. And give him that backpack you've got on. That'll prove he saw you guys."

Jack didn't respond right away. He looked at Chloe. She couldn't think of a way to get out of this—and as much as it pained her to be thinking about Ry's well-being after all this, Ry would be safer in jail than he was here. So she gave Jack a little nod.

He pulled the key out of his pocket and tossed it toward Jen. She didn't catch it, but she did scowl at him. "I can't *wait* to make your death slow and painful."

"I've never known a drawn-out murder to work out for the murderer," Jack replied.

Jen's smile was pure *evil*. "Remind me to give you a step-by-step of how I took my sweet time with your parents." She picked up the key he'd thrown. "But first things first." Roughly, she jammed the key into the cuffs and released Ry.

"You tell them you sent them off to find the scrapbook. You tell them Mark told you he left it in a hotel room in Hardy. You don't know the specifics, but that's what he told you, so that's what you told them. Do you understand?"

Ry nodded.

"If you don't do exactly as I say, what happens?"

"The pit," he said, sounding like the little boy Chloe remembered all too well. Not always sweet, but always trusting.

Chloe didn't know what *the pit* was—no doubt some kind of torture. Mom was always good at that.

"You didn't like your last stint in the pit, did you?"

Ry shook his head vehemently.

"What's better, Rylan? The pit or getting arrested?"

"Arrested," Ry muttered.

"That's right. Go get the backpack off him," she said, pointing to Jack.

Ry trudged over. He didn't meet Chloe's gaze or Jack's, just kept his eyes on the ground and held out his hand. When Jack didn't immediately hand it over, Ry slowly looked up.

Even slower, Jack shrugged the backpack off. With careful, precise movements, he held it out to Ry. When he spoke, it was low and quiet. Maybe Jen heard over by the entrance, maybe she didn't, but Chloe figured it didn't matter. It was only the truth.

"She deserved better, Ry."

Ry didn't say anything, didn't even give her a glance. He just took the bag and scurried back over to their mother.

"Not one wrong move, Rylan. Not *one*," Jen said menacingly.

He gave a little nod. He took a step toward the cave entrance but then looked back at her and Jack. "Sorry, Chlo," he said, before Jen pushed him out the crevice of the entrance.

It was funny. She almost believed he was.

But what she didn't believe was that he'd help.

Chapter Twenty

Jack knew better than to count on Ry going against his mother's wishes and helping them out of this mess, but he hoped for Chloe's sake Ry might mess up his assignment somehow. If he ran into Zeke or Carlyle back at that campground, they'd surely see through him. They'd retrace his steps.

Or, if he had even an ounce of intelligence, he'd use the flare in the pack and really help them.

But Jack wouldn't depend on Ry to fix this for them. He and Chloe would have to devise a plan. One that took into account that his family was out there and would start looking for them. All they had to do was stay alive past four o'clock.

"Do you think he's actually going to listen?" Courtney asked Jen in a low voice, but in the cave, it carried over to him and Chloe.

"He knows what happens to him if he doesn't," Jen replied darkly.

"What if—"

"That boy is a *coward*. Always has been. Always will be. Besides, we have secret weapons. So *many* secrets. Let's go show them one." She turned her attention from Courtney to Jack and Chloe. "You're going to turn around. You're going to start walking. And you're not going to stop until I tell you to."

Jack shared a look with Chloe. It was two against two now, and going deeper in the cave was only asking for trouble when it was clear Jen's plan was to kill them. Why keep giving her easier and easier ways to get away with it?

"I don't think we will, Jen."

Chloe inhaled sharply, but she nodded. She moved so that they stood shoulder to shoulder, facing Jen and Courtney and eyeing the cave exit behind them. All they had to do was get past them without getting shot.

Without getting *fatally* shot, really. He knew Chloe wouldn't appreciate it, but if *he* drew both their gunfire, she could get past them. Get out. Maybe there'd be a chance. Oh, she wouldn't thank him for that. She'd end up beating herself up for it, especially if he did get fatally wounded.

But she'd be alive.

"You will because if you recall, *I've* got the upper hand. *All* of the upper hands. You do what I say."

"So we can die the way you want us to?" Chloe shook her head. "Pass."

"Pass?" Jen replied, then she laughed. High-pitched and out of control. "*Pass*, she says. Oh, Chloe, you did not inherit *any* of the Rogers family smarts, did you?"

"I hope to God not."

Jen was aiming her gun at Chloe now, and Jack knew he needed to do something. Intervene before she ended up dead here in this dark damn cave. Not on his watch.

"It seems to me this only works out for you if we follow what you say. I don't think we have much interest in this working out for you, so I guess we're at an impasse. I guess you'll have to shoot us." He tried to angle his body so he was in front of Chloe, but she was doing the same thing to him.

He wanted to tell her to quit it, wanted to shove her out of the way, which distracted him enough that he wasn't giving Jen the attention he should have been.

"As you wish," Jen replied with a shrug. Then he didn't have a chance to so much as blink. Jen must have pulled the trigger as she lifted the gun. The pain that blasted through his shoulder was more shock than the sound of the gun going off.

CHLOE FORGOT EVERYTHING in that moment. Every minute of training, every potential threat around them. She only saw Jack stumble back and blood bloom on his shoulder, and she leaped for him.

She looked around wildly for something to stop the bleeding and came up with nothing. *Nothing.*

"I'm okay. It's okay," he said, but he did not sound like himself. He was in pain. He had been *shot*.

"It's not okay," she returned, pulling the hem of her shirt into as much of a ball as she could and pressing it to his shoulder.

His hissed out a pained breath. "Trying to convince myself here, Chloe." He swore once, twice. He didn't sit still, moving around as if trying to find some comfortable position, even though a *bullet* had passed through his shoulder.

"Stop moving. I have to put pressure on it. I have to—" The yank at her hair took her by surprise because she'd let panic and worry and *love* blind her to the imminent threat. She fell back as Jen stepped forward.

"Am I clear now? You can either fight and die right here or you can get on your feet and move."

Chloe held Jack's pained gaze. She couldn't let him die here. She couldn't. But they couldn't go deeper into this cave. Not with his wound, not with her mother's plans clear.

Jen wanted it too much, when it would be so easy to just shoot them right now.

Clearly she had something deeper in the cave where she thought she could kill them and get away with it. Chloe would die before she gave her mother that.

It had to end right now. "Sounds like it's easier for you if we move. So maybe we choose to die right here."

"Do you think I won't shoot you both?"

Chloe knew she would. Knew this wasn't looking good. But if they walked any farther, it would be over. And maybe no one would ever find them. Another Hudson mystery.

No. She wouldn't let that happen. "If you're going to kill us, I'd much prefer you get caught."

Fury stamped all over her mother's features. It reminded Chloe too much of a childhood she'd spent a lot of time blocking out. Her therapist had told her not remembering a lot was a *bad sign*, and now Chloe fully understood what she meant by that. She'd blocked out *this*. That violence. That total lack of empathy for another human being.

Chloe didn't want to leave Jack's side, but she forced herself to stand. To face her mother. "And if you're going to kill us anyway, I might as well *fight*." She took a few steps forward, bracing herself for pain, for a gunshot wound to stop her in her tracks.

But instead, there was a voice.

"Drop your weapons."

Chloe whirled around, and nearly wept right then. Carlyle stood next to her brother, Zeke, both with guns trained on Jen and Courtney.

But Chloe also knew her mother. So she dove immediately into her mother's legs, hoping to knock her off her feet so she wouldn't have a chance to shoot *anyone*. It worked.

Jen tumbled down on top of Chloe, but not before another gunshot went off.

Hopefully Carlyle's or Zeke's. *Please, God.* She scrambled out from her mother's weight. Jen kicked, clawed, pulled, but Chloe could fight too. She managed to get the gun from her mother, to wrestle her into submission.

Zeke came over to her and knelt on the other side of Jen, pulling out a zip-tie and using it to bind her hands together. Chloe looked over at Courtney. She was in the same position as Jen now, so Zeke must have gotten her first.

Chloe pushed to her feet. They needed to get Jack to the hospital. A gunshot wound to his shoulder wasn't good, but if they could get him...

He was lying completely prone on the floor now. More blood. Not just on his shoulder, but lower. Carlyle had something pressed to his abdomen. He'd been shot again. *No, no, no.*

She scrambled over to him. Repeating his name. Maybe crying. She didn't know. But he was pale, and he wasn't moving or responding to her in any way and *oh God.*

"He's breathing, Chloe," Carlyle said sharply. "So put something on that shoulder."

Chloe looked around for something, even as tears clouded her vision. But then chaos erupted around them. Just absolute chaos. Screaming. Yelling. Pounding footsteps. But she just concentrated on Jack's breathing. Because he was breathing. She felt like as long as she stayed here, her hand on his chest, his heart, she could *will* him to keep breathing. As long as he was breathing...

Someone pulled her off, and she fought them. If they pulled her away... If...

"Let the medics help," Zeke said, firm and authoritative

in her ear as he banded her arms at her sides to stop her from fighting him.

Carlyle stepped in front of her, blocking her view of Jack. Jack. Who'd been shot twice. *Twice.* Because of her.

"They're going to take him to the hospital. He's going to be okay," Carlyle said.

"How do you know?" Chloe demanded.

And Carlyle didn't answer. Because the truth was, he might not be. And she would always have to live with that.

Zeke's grip on her loosened. She would have crumpled then and there, but Carlyle held her up by an arm. Medics were working to find a way to get Jack out of the small crevice of the entrance.

A couple of cops had Jen and Courtney cuffed, face down on the cave ground. They screamed and argued and fought, but they weren't going to be a problem anymore. They were going to go to prison. For murder. Multiple murders.

It should have been a relief, but nothing would feel like relief until she knew Jack would be okay.

They had to stand in this awful cave while the medics got Jack out, while the police got Jen and Courtney out. Chloe would have hyperventilated if not for Carlyle rubbing a supportive hand up and down her back.

When they were finally given the go-ahead to leave, Chloe knew there'd be questions. So many questions. But she wouldn't be able to answer any of them until Jack was okay.

When she emerged from the cave, she saw her brother. He was cuffed, sitting on the ground, a deputy talking down at him.

She could only stare. He'd betrayed her. He was part of *all* this. When he looked up and saw her glaring at him, his eyes got big and shiny.

"I know I messed up, Chlo, but I fixed it. Didn't I?" he called across the distance between them. Cops looked at her; Hudsons looked at her.

She stared at her brother.

"He found Zeke and I," Carlyle said quietly, standing next to her. But Chloe could hear the disgust in Carlyle's voice. "We were pretty close, but we hadn't found the entrance to the cave. He is why we found you in the nick of time, and we didn't have to shake it out of him."

She wanted to feel good. She wanted to feel relief. Her brother wasn't all bad. He'd helped. Even with Mom threatening him the way she had, he had asked Carlyle and Zeke for help. He'd done the right thing.

She wanted to believe that, but she saw him sitting there and knew he'd just done the *easiest* thing. Because he always did. So she just felt *angry*. Because Jack was hurt. And sometimes doing the right thing was too little, too late.

She walked over to him. He wanted reassurance. He wanted to know he'd done okay. After being such a huge part of how this had all gone so badly. Years ago, she would have reassured him. Forgiven him.

Today, she had nothing left. "If he dies, I'll never, ever speak to you again," she said. "I will never lay eyes on you again. I will never, ever have anything to do with you. Ever."

Ry's eyes widened, and the hope in them died. "You're choosing him over me?"

"No, Ry. I'm choosing *me* over you. I will always love you, but I can't be part of your life anymore. Not until you can take some responsibility for it. Maybe jail will teach you that. Maybe it won't. I won't know because I won't be in contact. I won't be helping. I'm done." She should have said all those things years ago. Now, just like him, it was too little, too late.

But she'd done it.

"That isn't fair!" he yelled. After all he'd done, he thought anything should be *fair*.

She shook her head and walked away from her brother. She hoped someday he'd find some better version of himself. But until he did…she was done.

Chapter Twenty-One

Jack thought he heard a baby crying. Where had a baby come from? It was nighttime. Somewhere. Where was he?

Cave. Cave? The cave and— *Chloe*. He tried to say her name, but nothing came out of his mouth except a raspy kind of noise. He couldn't seem to open his eyes. Heavy, too heavy. After the spurt of panic, he told himself to breathe, to count, to settle. He couldn't protect anyone if he couldn't open his eyes.

He started to become aware of things. The beep of machines, the feel of something on his arm. The sound of people shuffling. He managed to open his eyes to bright, blinding white. Hospital.

Well, he was here, so he had to be alive, he supposed. But then he caught sight of a woman. A woman with dark hair and soft eyes. Maybe he was dead after all. "Mom?"

But it only took a second or two to realize it wasn't his mother. It was Mary. "Sorry," he rasped.

Her smile was a little strange, definitely teary. He tried to get his brain to engage as he looked at her standing there next to his hospital bed. She looked different. She had a little bundle in her arms. Even with his brain fuzzy, that all made sense to him. "Mary."

"Sorry Walker couldn't help you guys. We were a little busy."

"You had the baby." A baby. He'd been fighting for his life, and she'd been giving birth. What a strange, strange life.

Both his sisters had *babies*. He remembered *them* being babies, and now they were mothers. His brain was too fuzzy to fully comprehend all this. He wanted to sit up. He wanted to ask a million questions.

"You're going to have to hurry up and get better so you can hold him," she said. She didn't cry, but he could hear the pain and fear in her voice.

"I'm okay." Of course, he had no idea if that was true. He'd been shot. Twice, if he remembered correctly. He tried to move, but he couldn't quite manage and the pain was starting to flutter above the fuzzy feeling.

"You will be. We'll all baby you till you are."

"I can't sit up. Let me see him, huh?"

She tilted the bundle until he could see the scrunched up little face of a sleeping newborn with a shock of dark hair.

"The problem is, I married a man whose last name is Daniels."

Jack didn't quite follow. "Why is that a problem?"

"I could hardly name my son Jack Daniels," Mary replied, looking lovingly down at the newborn in her arms.

"Why would…" He wanted to shift uncomfortably. "You don't have to name anyone after me."

Her eyes were full of tears. "Of course I don't have to. But I wanted to—Walker and I wanted to name our son after the best men we knew. You're at the top of that list, for both of us. I want that legacy for my son. I wanted him to have someone he knew, someone he'd spend his life looking up to. So he always knew what was right. Because his name-sake would be right there, showing him."

Jack was completely and utterly speechless. "Well." But he remembered Chloe talking about legacies, and ghosts and how being sad is not all that bad. It felt like a million years ago.

"So, we did the best we could, all things considered," Mary said with a little sniff. She used her shoulder to wipe a tear off her cheek. "This is Jackson Dean Daniels. If we end up shortening it, he can go by JD. But it's after you, it's because of you. His name. Who we all are." She started crying again, tears rolling down her cheeks. "I'm so glad you're okay."

Okay. That cave. Today. This whole thing. "Chloe? Ry? I... I don't remember exactly..." Chloe had been okay. She had been. Had to be.

"They're both fine. Carlyle and Zeke got to you guys just in time. Jen Rogers and her two accomplices have been charged with the murder of Mark Brink and our parents. I knew you'd want the details, and they're still wading through them all. But everything with the bones, with the snake and Detective Hart, it was all part of planning to murder Mark without Chloe getting any wind of it."

Jack closed his eyes. His mind was whirling in too many directions. He wanted to see Chloe. Wanted to see for himself she was okay, but she wasn't here. Mary was and...

And after sixteen years, they finally knew. "We've got answers now, Mary. Who killed Mom and Dad. Why... If you can call it a why. Everything we tried to find all these years."

"It's so strange," she said, her voice a creaky whisper. "I just don't care."

He managed to open his eyes, and she was gazing down

at her son, those tears still on her cheeks. She kept talking. "You're okay, and I have him. We all have…so much. It's a tragedy to have lost them. It'll always be a tragedy. But answers didn't change anything. Us all living our lives on the foundations they gave us. That's the only thing that matters."

It was such a strange thing, to agree. After years of thinking having answers would change something in his life, he now had those answers and nothing changed. Not really.

"Mary, where's Chloe?"

"She's fine."

"That isn't what I asked."

"She… We aren't sure where she went. She got checked out by doctors, answered all the police's questions, but we kind of lost her in the fray. It's okay. Carlyle and Anna are out trying to track her down, but we know she's okay."

He tried to sit up, but he couldn't. He cursed his own weaknesses. Cursed everything. "She's going to blame herself. She can't seem to help it. I just—"

"Don't worry, Jack. We'll find her, and we're all going to make sure she knows just where she belongs."

Here. She belonged right *here.*

CHLOE KNEW SHE couldn't just sit in the hospital parking lot forever. She had to act. She had to… She didn't want to see him, and she didn't think she'd ever be able to breathe again if she didn't see with her own two eyes that he was okay.

He wouldn't blame her. He'd be irritated she blamed herself. She understood all these things rationally, but she could not seem to move past all the swirling things she knew about Jack and who he was and the horrible things she felt about herself.

Hey, this is why we go to therapy. Well, she'd have a doozy of a session at her next appointment.

"What the hell are you doing here?"

Chloe looked up to see Carlyle stalking up to her, Anna not far behind.

"We've been looking all over for you," Anna said.

Chloe shook her head. "You should be with Jack. You should—"

"And who do you think Jack wants to see?" Anna returned. "Come on. Get up. Let's go."

They stood on either side of her, taking her by the arms and hauling her to her feet. But she didn't let them pull her to the door.

"I can't go in. I wanted to. I just…"

They didn't let her go, but they did stop trying to pull her.

"Chloe, you've had a day," Anna said, as gently as Chloe had ever heard her say anything. "But neither you nor Jack are going to rest until you see each other. Trust me. I know." Because her husband had been shot last year, and she'd been hurt too. So maybe she was right, but…

"My mother killed your parents, Anna."

"Yeah. Hell of a thing."

Like it was that simple. "My brother made it worse. Everything…it all connects to *me*."

"Self-centered much?" Carlyle said under her breath, making Anna snort out a laugh.

"I just want to curl up and die." Which was not something she would have ever admitted to out loud if she wasn't having a *day*, she supposed. And she didn't really want to die. She just wanted…

"Wow, that's super melodramatic," Carlyle said, and she was gently tugging her forward.

"I'm impressed. I didn't think you had it in you," Anna added, also applying pressure to move her forward.

"You guys…"

"Chloe, we know you. All of us. I get it, better than most, how having a parent with that kind of evil in them can mess you up, but you're too well loved to let what other people have chosen ruin your life."

Too well loved. Ouch.

"*And* Jack loves you. He needs to see you. And since you love him, you're going to get over yourself and go see him." Anna gave her yet another tug.

Chloe didn't know how to argue with that, so she was somehow being pulled down hospital corridors and to a hospital-room door. Anna shoved it open. "Go on, now." Then Anna and Carlyle stood shoulder to shoulder like they were blocking any potential exit.

So Chloe *had* to step in. Had to look.

Jack was in a hospital bed. Hooked up to all sorts of awful things. But his eyes were open, and he was talking to Mary.

Chloe must have made a noise, because Mary turned, and Jack looked over at her. She would have kept looking at Jack, but Mary was holding something. She was... "Mary... You... You had the baby."

In the middle of all this *awful*, a baby had been born.

Mary smiled at her and took a few steps closer, holding the baby so Chloe could see his face. "Meet Jackson Dean Daniels."

Chloe looked at the little newborn. She'd never been around babies much. The little bundle seemed like an alien lifeform to her. And still...

"He's perfect." She couldn't help but smile down at the baby, especially when he blinked open his deep blue eyes and seemed to be squinting at her in suspicion. "Perfect." *Jackson.* After Jack, no doubt.

It made her want to cry all over again.

"I think so," Mary agreed. Then she looked at the doorway. Chloe looked over her shoulder to see Walker standing there.

"Good to see you both in one piece," he offered, presumably to Chloe and Jack. But he didn't tear his gaze away from Mary or the bundle in her arms. "Time's up, honey. You need to rest."

Mary nodded, but as she passed Chloe, she leaned close. "Stay with him until someone else comes, okay? I don't want him alone."

Chloe wanted to argue. She wanted to run away. But that was just childish and probably her exhaustion talking. She nodded at Mary, then hesitantly moved closer to Jack in the bed.

He looked too big for it. Too vital. He'd been shot twice. Gone through surgery. And still he seemed just like himself. When she felt like a bag of broken, rusty, disparate parts.

"Hi," she offered.

"Hi," he returned. And said nothing else. Just kept that steady gaze on hers.

Everything inside her felt bruised. He didn't say anything, just looked at her with dark eyes. But she had seen that expression on his face for a while now. In every smile, in every secret goodbye in the dark, in the way he protected her. In the way he let her in when he let no one else in.

And still, all the ways today connected to her felt like a wall she couldn't cross. So she fell back on what she usually used as a shield. That cop persona she'd developed.

"The police arrested everyone, including Ry. They're all turning on each other, so sentencing should be straightforward once they get that far. There are still some questions. The scrapbook is missing, and no one will spill on why it's so important. So there's work to be done. Bent County will handle it, though."

He gave a little nod but still didn't speak.

"Jack, I—"

"I need you to do me a favor," he said, cutting her off, even though his voice was weak and raspy.

And because it was, she immediately swallowed the apology. She'd do anything for him. Always. "Okay."

"I need you to never, ever, for the rest of our lives, say you're sorry to me about this."

She should have known. "Jack—"

"Listen to me. It hurts. It hurts to watch you blame yourself when you dug your way out of all that trauma, all that awful, and made yourself into a smart, *honorable*, wonderful person. I don't look at you and see them. Never did. Never will. And I know you can't magically wipe away any feelings you have on the matter. I get that they're complicated and messy, but I love you no matter what. So I can't take any apologies when *you* have nothing to apologize for. Okay?"

She *knew* he was right, but she hadn't felt it. Until he said it. Then it was like... God, she could breathe again, even as tears filled her eyes. She took the rest of the steps so she stood next to the bed now. She wiped at her eyes with the backs of her hands. She wanted to touch him, hold him, but... "I don't want to hurt you."

"Then stop crying, Chloe." He held out his hand at kind of an awkward angle, she supposed because that was the only way he could manage it. She took his hand, and he squeezed.

Him, lying in a hospital bed, trying to make *her* feel better. She grabbed the chair that was situated a ways away from the bed and drew it closer so she could sit next to him. So she could press her forehead to his hand. She couldn't quite stop crying, but she tried.

"I'm not sure I would have... I'm glad you're okay. I'm..."

She looked up. Met his gaze. Pain was in his expression. Physical. Emotional. The whole gamut. "How about we leave it at, I love you and I'm glad you're here."

He smiled a little, but he didn't say anything at first. Just kept looking at her in a way that made her want to fidget.

"What do you say we get married?"

Her mouth dropped open because *what*? "What?"

"We've been together for about a year now. Why not?"

"Because a million reasons. And we have *not* been together. Sneaking around to have sex is *not* being together. What kind of meds are you on?"

"Okay." He yawned, winced a little. "We can wait."

She didn't know why that made her feel deflated. She clearly just needed sleep. But he just lay there in the bed, holding her hand, starting to look sleepy and…

"I put in an application to Bent County." She hadn't been going to tell him. Not until she got the job—*if* she got the job. But it just seemed right, somehow.

It was his turn to be surprised. "What?"

"They're starting a K-9 unit, and I wanted to be a part of it."

"I thought the applications on that closed a few months back?"

"They did, but one of the people fell through, so they've got one position. I… I didn't do it originally because I didn't want anyone to think I was doing it for you. To have you." She swallowed, looked down at their entwined hands. "I didn't want *you* to think that, or maybe I was afraid that… I don't know. Afraid. Period. Always. I just… The past few days have been a mess, but it was a mess you were there through. No matter what. You didn't leave my side. Even when it hurt. Even when it got you shot. You were there and…"

She looked up at him.

"Chloe, marry me. Please. Because no matter what, I'm always going to be there."

She wanted to laugh. And cry. And…agree. Most of all, agree. Not try to think it through, not try to worry it out. She just wanted him. "Okay," she managed.

"What changed your mind?"

"Seemed wrong to say no twice to a guy who was shot twice by my own mother," she said, sniffling as tears kept falling over her cheeks.

"Yeah, that is a bit much."

But it wasn't the truth. There were so many truths, but the main one had hit her over the head when she'd first come in. "You look at me the way Walker looks at Mary."

"I believe that's called *lovesick*."

"I'll take it. Because I've never had… No one's ever cared. Not the way you do. And you're not perfect. I want to punch you half the time, but you are the best man I know, Jack Hudson."

"That's mighty handy, because I happen to believe you deserve some best, Chloe Brink. And I plan on giving it to you."

And Jack Hudson always came through on plans.

* * * * *

COMING SOON!

We really hope you enjoyed reading this book.
If you're looking for more romance
be sure to head to the shops when
new books are available on

Thursday 27th February

To see which titles are coming soon, please visit
millsandboon.co.uk/nextmonth

MILLS & BOON

LET'S TALK

Romance

For exclusive extracts, competitions
and special offers, find us online:

f MillsandBoon

X @MillsandBoon

◎ @MillsandBoonUK

♪ @MillsandBoonUK

Get in touch on 01413 063 232